P9-BBV-279

PATHFINDER

PATHFINDER

ORSON SCOTT CARD

Simon Pulse
NEW YORK   LONDON   TORONTO   SYDNEY

SIMON PULSE
An imprint of Simon & Schuster Children's Publishing Division
1230 Avenue of the Americas, New York, NY 10020
First Simon Pulse hardcover edition November 2010
Copyright © 2010 by Orson Scott Card
All rights reserved, including the right of reproduction in whole or in part in any form.
SIMON PULSE and colophon are registered trademarks
of Simon & Schuster, Inc.
For information about special discounts for bulk purchases,
please contact Simon & Schuster Special Sales at 1-866-506-1949
or business@simonandschuster.com.
The Simon & Schuster Speakers Bureau can bring authors to your live event.
For more information or to book an event contact the Simon & Schuster Speakers
Bureau at 1-866-248-3049 or visit our website at www.simonspeakers.com.
Designed by Mike Rosamilia
The text of this book was set in Cochin.
Manufactured in the United States of America
2 4 6 8 10 9 7 5 3 1
Library of Congress Cataloging-in-Publication Data
Card, Orson Scott.
Pathfinder / Orson Scott Card. — 1st Simon Pulse hardcover ed.
p. cm.
Summary: Thirteen-year-old Rigg has a secret ability to see the paths of others' pasts,
but revelations after his father's death set him on a dangerous quest that brings new
threats from those who would either control his destiny or kill him.
ISBN 978-1-4169-9176-2
[1. Science fiction. 2. Identity—Fiction. 3. Psychic ability—Fiction. 4. Time travel—
Fiction. 5. Interplanetary voyages—Fiction. 6. Space colonies—Fiction.] I. Title.
PZ7.C1897Pat 2010   [Fic]—dc22   2010023243
ISBN 978-1-4424-1427-3 (eBook)

To Barbara Bova
whose boldness made everything possible:
I miss you every day.

CONTENTS

CHAPTER 1
If a Tree Falls

Saving the human race is a frantic business. Or a tedious one. It all depends on what stage of the process you're taking part in.

· · ·

Rigg and Father usually set the traps together, because it was Rigg who had the knack of seeing the paths that the animals they wanted were still using.

Father was blind to it—he could never see the thin shimmering trails in the air that marked the passage of living creatures through the world. But to Rigg it was, and always had been, part of what his eyes could see, without any effort at all. The newer the path, the bluer the shimmer; older ones were green, yellow; the truly ancient ones tended toward red.

As a toddler, Rigg had quickly learned what the shimmering

meant, because he could see everyone leaving trails behind them as they went. Besides the color, there was a sort of signature to each one, and over the years Rigg became adept at recognizing them. He could tell at a glance the difference between a human and an animal, or between the different species, and if he looked closely, he could sort out the tracks so clearly that he could follow the path of a single person or an individual beast.

Once, when Father first started taking him out trapping, Rigg had made the mistake of following a greenish trail. When they reached the end of it, there were only a few old bones scattered where animals had torn the carcass many months ago.

Father had not been angry. In fact, he seemed amused. "We need to find animals with their skins still fresh," said Father. "And a little meat on them for us to eat. But if I had a bone collection, these would do nicely. Don't worry, Rigg."

Father never criticized Rigg when it came to his knack for pathfinding. He simply accepted what Rigg could do, and encouraged him to hone his skill. But whenever Rigg started to tell someone about what he could do, or even speak carelessly, so they might be able to figure out that he had some unusual ability, Father was merciless, silencing him at once.

"It's your life," said Father. "There are those who would kill you for this. And others who would take you away from me and make you live in a terrible place and make you follow paths for them, and it would lead to them killing the ones you found." And, to make sure Rigg understood how serious this was, he added, "And they would not be beasts, Rigg. You would be helping them murder people."

Maybe Father shouldn't have told him that, because it haunted Rigg's thoughts for months afterward—and not just by giving him nightmares. It made Rigg feel very powerful, to think that his ability might help men find criminals and outlaws.

But all that was when Rigg was still little—seven or eight years old. Now he was thirteen and his voice was finally changing, and Father kept telling him little things about how to deal with women. They like this, they hate that, they'll never marry a boy who does this or doesn't do that. "Washing is the most important thing," Father said—often. "So you don't stink. Girls don't like it when boys stink."

"But it's cold," said Rigg. "I'll wash later, just before we get back home."

"You'll wash every day," said Father. "I don't like your stink either."

Rigg didn't really believe that. The pelts they took from the trapped animals stank a lot worse than Rigg ever could. In fact, the stink of the animal skins *was* Rigg's main odor; it clung to his clothing and hair like burrs. But Rigg didn't argue. There was no point in arguing.

For instance, this morning, before they separated, they were talking as they walked through the woods. Father encouraged talking. "We're not hunters, we're trappers," he said. "It doesn't matter if the animals run from us right now, because we'll catch them later, when they can't see us or hear us or even smell us."

Thus Father used their endless walks for teaching. "You have a severe case of ignorance, boy," he often said. "I have to do my best to cure that sickness, but it seems like the more I teach you, the more things you don't know."

"I know everything I need to know already," Rigg always said. "You teach me all kinds of strange things that have nothing to do with the way we live. Why do I need to know about astronomy or banking or all these languages you make me speak? I find the paths of animals, we trap them, we sell the furs, and I know how to do every bit of it."

To which Father always replied, "See how ignorant you are? You don't even know why you need to know the things you don't know yet."

"So tell me," said Rigg.

"I would, but you're too ignorant to understand the reasons why your ignorance is a fatal disease. I have to educate you before you'll understand why it was worth the bother trying to tan your brain." That's what he called their schooling sessions: tanning Rigg's brain.

Today they were following the trail of an elusive pench, whose pelt was worth ten otters, because penchfur was so thick and the colors so vibrant. During a brief lull in Father's endless teaching, during which he was presumably trying to come up with another problem for Rigg to work out in his head ("If a board fence is nine hands high and a hundred and twenty yards long, how many feet of four-inch slat will you need to buy from the lumbermill, knowing that the slats come in twenty- and fourteen-hand lengths?" Answer: "What good is a nine-hand-high slat fence? Any animal worth keeping inside it can climb it or jump over it or knock it down." Then a knuckle on the back of his head and he had to come up with the real answer), Rigg started talking about nothing at all.

"I love autumn," said Rigg. "I know it means winter is coming, but winter is the reason why people need our furs so I can't feel bad about *that*. It's the colors of the leaves before they fall, and the crunching of the fallen leaves underfoot. The whole world is different."

"The whole world?" asked Father. "Don't you know that on the southern half of the world, it isn't even autumn?"

"Yes, I know that," said Rigg.

"And even in our hemisphere, near the tropics it's never autumn and leaves don't fall, except high in the mountains, like here. And in the far north there are no trees, just tundra and ice, so leaves don't fall. The whole world! You mean the tiny little wedge of the world that you've seen with your own ignorant eyes."

"That's all the world I've seen," said Rigg. "If I'm ignorant of the rest, that's your fault."

"You *aren't* ignorant of the rest, you just haven't seen it. I've certainly *told* you about it."

"Oh, yes, Father, I have all kinds of memorized lists in my head, but here's my question: How do you know all these things about parts of the world we can never ever see because they're outside the Wall?"

Father shrugged. "I know everything."

"A certain teacher once told me that the only truly stupid man is the one who doesn't know he's ignorant." Rigg loved this game, partly because Father eventually got impatient with it and told him to shut up, which would mean Rigg had won.

"I know that I know everything because there are no questions to which I don't know the answer."

"Excellent," said Rigg. "So answer this question: Do you know the answers to the questions you haven't thought of yet?"

"I've thought of all the questions," said Father.

"That only means you've stopped trying to think of new ones."

"There *are* no new questions."

"Father, what will I ask you next?"

Father huffed. "All questions about the future are moot. I know all the answers that are knowable."

"That's what I thought. Your claim to know everything was empty brag."

"Careful how you speak to your father and teacher."

"I chose my words with the utmost precision," said Rigg, echoing a phrase that Father often used. "Information only matters if it helps us make correct guesses about the future." Rigg ran into a low-hanging branch. This happened rather often. He had to keep his gaze upward, because the pench had moved from branch to branch. "The pench crossed the stream," he said. Then he clambered down the bank.

Vaulting over a stream did not interrupt the conversation. "Since you can't know which information you'll need in the future, you need to know everything about the past. Which I do," said Father.

"You know all the kinds of weather you've seen," said Rigg, "but it doesn't mean you know what weather we'll have next week, or if there'll be a kind of weather you never saw before. I think you're very nearly as ignorant as I am."

"Shut up," said Father.

I win, said Rigg silently.

A few minutes later, the trail of the pench went up into the air and kept going out of sight. "An eagle got him," Rigg said sadly. "It happened before we even started following his path. It was in the past, so no doubt you knew it all along."

Father didn't bother to answer, but let Rigg lead them back up the bank and through the woods to where Rigg first spotted the pench's trail. "You know how to lay the traps almost as well as I do," said Father. "So you go do it, and then come find me."

"I can't find you," said Rigg. "You know I can't."

"I don't know any such thing, because no one can *know* a false thing, one can only believe it with certainty until it is contradicted."

"I can't see your path," said Rigg, "because you're my father."

"It's true that I'm your father, and it's true you can't see my path, but why do you assume that there's a causal connection between them?"

"Well, it can't go the other way—you can't be my father *because* I can't see your path."

"Do you have any other fathers?"

"No."

"Do you know of any other pathfinder like you?"

"No."

"Therefore you can't test to see if you can't see the paths of your other fathers, because you don't have any. And you can't ask other pathfinders whether they can find their fathers' paths, because you don't know any. So you have no evidence one way or another about what causes you not to be able to see my path."

"Can I go to bed now?" asked Rigg. "I'm already too tired to go on."

"Poor feeble brain," said Father. "But how it could wear out I don't know, considering you don't use it. How will you find me? By following my path with your *eyes* and your *brain* instead of this extraordinary ability of yours. You'll see where I leave footprints, where I break branches."

"But you don't leave footprints if you don't want to, and you never break branches unless you want to," said Rigg.

"Ah," said Father. "You're more observant than I thought. But since I told you to find me after the traps are set, doesn't it stand to reason that I will make it possible for you to do it, by leaving footprints and breaking branches?"

"Make sure you fart frequently, too," Rigg suggested. "Then I can track you with my nose."

"Bring me a nice switch to beat you with when you come," said Father. "Now go and do your work before the day gets too warm."

"What will you be doing?"

"The thing that I need to do," said Father. "When you need to know what that is, I'll tell you."

And they parted.

Rigg set the traps carefully, because he knew this was a test. Everything was a test. Or a lesson. Or a punishment from which he was supposed to learn a lesson, on which he would be tested later, and punished if he hadn't learned it.

I wish I could have a day, just a single day, without tests or lessons or punishments. A day to be myself, instead of being Father's project to make me into a great man. I don't want to be great. I just want to be Rigg.

Even taking great care with the traps, leaving them in each beast's most common path, it didn't take *that* long to set them all. Rigg stopped to drink, and then to empty his bladder and bowel and wipe his butt with leaves—another reason to be grateful for the autumn. Then Rigg backtracked his own trail to the place where he and Father parted.

There wasn't a sign of where Father went. Rigg knew his starting direction because he had seen him go. But when he walked that way, Father had left no broken branches, no footprints, nothing to mark his passing.

Of course, thought Rigg. This is a test.

So he stood there and thought. Father might mean me to continue in the direction I saw him go when we parted, and only after a long time will he leave a mark. That would be a lesson in patience and trust.

Or Father might have doubled back as soon as I was out of sight, and left in another direction entirely, blazing a trail for my eyes to see, but only after I had walked blindly for a while in each random direction.

Rigg spent an hour doubling back again and again, so he could search for Father's signs of passing in every direction. No luck, of course. That would have been far too easy a challenge.

Again he stood and thought. Father listed the signs he could leave; therefore he isn't going to leave any of those signs. He'll leave different signs and my job is to be creative and think of what they might be.

Rigg remembered his own snotty remark about farts and sniffed the air, but he had only the ordinary human sense of smell and he couldn't detect a thing that way, so that couldn't be Father's game.

Sight and smell haven't worked. Taste seemed ludicrous. Could Father leave a clue using sound?

Rigg gave it a try. He stood in absolute stillness so that he could truly hear the sounds of the forest. It was more than holding his body still. He had to calm himself and concentrate, so that he could separate sounds in his mind. His own breathing—he had to be aware of it, then move past it so he could hear the other sounds around him. Then the near sounds—a scurry of a mouse, the scamper of a squirrel, the jarring notes of a bird's song, the burrowing of a mole.

And then he heard it. Very distant. A voice. A human voice. Impossible to know what words it was saying, if any; impossible to know if it was Father. But he could tell what general direction it was coming from, and so he moved that way, trotting along a path used by many deer so he could make good time. There was a low rise on the left that might block sound—he wanted to get past that; he knew there was a stream to the right, and if he got too close to that the babble of the water might drown out the voice.

Then he stopped and went into stillness again. This time he was reasonably sure the voice was Father's. And he was more certain of the direction.

It took two more stops before he could hear the voice clearly enough to run continuously till he reached Father. He was saving up some choice criticisms of this tracking method when he finally reached the spot where the voice was coming from, a clearing where a large tree had recently fallen. In fact, the path of the falling tree was still sparkling blue. There was little occasion to follow plants, since they moved so little, except a bit of waving and bending in the breeze, but this tree must have fallen only a few hours ago, and the movement of its fall had marked a bright path through the air.

Rigg couldn't see Father at all.

"Where are you?" he asked.

He expected some remark with a barbed lesson in it, but instead Father said, "You've come far enough, Rigg. You've found me."

"No, I haven't, Father."

"You've come as close as I want you to. Listen carefully. Do not come any closer to me."

"Since I don't know where you are —"

"Shut up," said Father.

Rigg fell silent and listened.

"I'm pinned under the tree," said Father.

Rigg cried out and took a step toward the tree.

"Stop!" cried Father.

Rigg stopped.

"You see the size of the tree," said Father. "You cannot lift it. You cannot move it."

"With a lever, Father, I could —"

"You cannot move it because I have been pierced by two branches, completely through my belly."

Rigg cried out, imagining the pain of it, feeling his own fear at Father's injury. Father was never hurt. Father never even got sick.

"Any further movement of the tree will kill me, Rigg. I have used all my strength calling to you. Listen now and don't waste what life I have left on any kind of argument."

"I won't argue," Rigg said.

"First, you must make your most solemn promise that you will not come look at me, now while I'm alive or later after I'm dead. I don't want you to have this terrible image in your memory."

It couldn't possibly be worse than what I'm imagining, Rigg said silently. Then he silently gave himself Father's own answer: You can't possibly know whether what you imagine is worse than the reality. I can see the reality, you can't, so . . . shut up.

"I can't believe you didn't argue with me right then," said Father.

"I did," said Rigg. "You just didn't hear me."

"All right then," said Father. "Your oath."

"I promise."

"Say it all. Say the words."

It took all Rigg's concentration to obey. "I promise solemnly that I will not come look at you, either now while you're alive or later after you're dead."

"And you will keep this promise, even to a dead man?" asked Father.

"I recognize your purpose and I agree with it," said Rigg. "Whatever I imagine might be awful, but I will know that I don't know that it's true. Whereas even if the reality is not as bad as what I imagine, I will know it is real, and therefore it will be a memory and not my imagination, and that will be far more terrible."

"So because you agree with my purpose," said Father, "following your own inclination will lead you to obey me and to keep your oath."

"This subject has been adequately covered," said Rigg, echoing Father's own way of saying, We have achieved understanding, so let's move on.

"Go back to where we parted," said Father. "Wait there till morning and harvest from the traps. Do all the work that needs doing, collect all the traps so you don't lose any of them, and then carry the pelts to our cache. Take all the pelts from there and carry them back to the village. The burden will be heavy, but you can carry it, though you don't have your manheight yet, if you take frequent rests. There is no hurry."

"I understand," said Rigg.

"Did I ask you whether you understand? Of course you understand. Don't waste my time."

Silently Rigg said, My two words didn't waste as much time as your three sentences.

"Take what you can get for the pelts before you tell anyone I'm dead—they'll cheat you less if they expect me to return for an accounting."

Rigg said nothing, but he was thinking: I know what to do, Father. You taught me how to bargain, and I'm good at it.

"Then you must go and find your sister," said Father.

"My sister!" blurted Rigg.

"She lives with your mother," said Father.

"My mother's alive? What is her name? Where does she live?"

"Nox will tell you."

Nox? The woman who kept the rooming house they sometimes stayed in? When Rigg was very young he had thought Nox might be his mother, but he long since gave up that notion. Now it seems she was in Father's confidence and Rigg was not. "*You* tell me! Why did you make me think my mother was dead? And a sister—why was this a secret? Why haven't I ever seen my mother?"

There was no answer.

"I'm sorry. I know I said I wouldn't argue, but you never told me, I was shocked, I couldn't help it. I'm sorry. Tell me what else you think I should know."

There was no answer.

"Oh, Father!" cried Rigg. "Speak to me one more time! Don't punish me like this! Talk to me!"

There was no answer.

Rigg thought things through the way he knew Father would expect him to. Finally he said what he knew Father would want him to say.

"I don't know if you're punishing me with silence or if you're already dead. I made a vow not to look and I'll keep it. So I'm going to leave and obey your instructions. If you're not dead, and you have anything else to say to me, say it now, speak now, please speak now." He had to stop because if Father wasn't dead he didn't want him to hear that Rigg was crying.

Please, he said silently as he wept.

"I love you, Father," said Rigg. "I will miss you forever. I *know* I will."

If that didn't provoke Father into speech, nothing ever would.

There was no answer.

Rigg turned resolutely and walked back, retracing his own bright path among the trees and underbrush, along the deer path, back to the last spot where he had seen his father alive.

CHAPTER 2

Upsheer

Ram Odin was raised to be a starship pilot. It was his father who adopted the Norse god of the sky as their surname, and it was his father who made sure Ram was absolutely prepared to go into astronaut training two years before the normal time.

Every bit of surplus wealth on Earth had been used to build humanity's first interstellar colony ships; it took forty years. Under the shadow of moondust that still blocked out more than a third of the sun's rays from the surface of Earth, the sense of urgency flagged very little, despite the human ability to get used to anything.

Everyone understood how close the human race had come to extinction when the comet swept past Earth and gouged its way into the near face of the moon. Even now, there was no certainty that the Moon's orbit would restabilize; astronomers were almost evenly divided among those who thought it would sooner or later collide with Earth, and those who thought a new equilibrium would be achieved.

So all who had survived the first terrible years of worldwide cold and famine dedicated themselves to building two identical ships. One would crawl out into space at ten percent of lightspeed, with generation after generation of future colonists living, growing old, and dying inside its closed ecosystem.

The other ship, Ram's ship, would travel seven years away from the solar system and then make a daring leap into theoretical physics.

Either spacetime could be made to fold, skipping ninety light-years and putting the colony ship only seven years away from the earthlike planet that was its destination, or the ship would obliterate itself in the attempt . . . or nothing would happen at all, and it would crawl on for nine hundred more years before reaching its new world.

The colonists on Ram's ship slept their way toward the fold-point. If all went well, they would remain asleep through the fold and not be wakened until they neared their destination. If nothing happened at all, they would be wakened to begin farming the vast interior, starting the thirty-five generations that the colony must survive until arrival.

Ram alone would remain awake the entire time.

Seven years with only the expendables for company. Once engineered to do work that might kill an irreplaceable human being, the expendables had now been so vastly improved that they could outlive and outwork any human. They also cost far more to make than it cost to train a human to do even a small part of their work.

Still, they were not human. They could not be allowed to make life-and-death decisions while all the humans were asleep. Yet they were such a good simulation of human life that Ram would never be lonely.

•   •   •

For as long as Rigg could remember, Father had been his only home. He could hardly count the rooming house in the village of Fall Ford. The mistress of the house, Nox, didn't even keep a permanent room for them. If there were travelers filling all the rooms, Father and Rigg slept out in the stable.

Oh, there had been a time when Rigg wondered if perhaps Nox was his mother, and Father had merely neglected to marry her. After all, Father and Nox had spent hours alone together, Father giving Rigg jobs to do so he wouldn't interrupt them. What were they doing, if not the thing that the village children whispered about, and the older boys laughed about, and the older girls spoke about in hushed voices?

But when Rigg asked Father outright, he had smiled and then took him inside the house and made him ask Nox to her face. So Rigg stammered and said, "Are you my mother?"

For a moment it looked as if she would laugh, but she caught herself at once and instead she ruffled his hair. "If I had ever had a child, I'd have been glad if he'd been one like you. But I'm as barren as a brick, as my husband found to his sorrow before he died, poor man, in the winter of Year Zero, when everyone thought the world would end."

Yet Nox was *something* to Father, or they would not have

come back to her almost every year, and Father would not have spent those hours alone with her.

Nox knew who Rigg's mother and sister were. Father had told *her*, but not Rigg himself. How many other secrets did she know?

Father and Rigg had been trapping in the high country, far upriver from Stashi Falls. Rigg came down the path that ran on the left side of the river, skirting the lake, then coming along the ridge toward the falls. The ridge was like a dam containing the lake, broken only by the gap of the falls. On the one side of the ridge, the land sloped gently down to the icy waters of the lake; on the other side, the land dropped off in a cliff, the Upsheer, that fell three hundred fathoms to the great Forest of Downwater. The cliff ran unbroken thirty leagues to the east and forty leagues to the west of the river; the only practical way to get a burden or a person down the Upsheer was on the right bank of the falls.

Which meant that Rigg, like everyone else lunatic enough to make a living bringing things down from the high country, would have to cross the river by jumping the ragged assortment of rocks just above the falls.

Once there had been a bridge here. In fact, there were ruins of several bridges, and Father had once used them as a test of Rigg's reasoning. "See how the oldest bridge is far forward of the water, and much higher on the cliff wall? Then the bracing of a newer bridge is lower and closer, and the most recent bridge is only three fathoms beyond the falls? Why do you think they were built where they were?"

That question had taken Rigg four days to figure out, as they tramped through the mountainous land above the lake, laying traps. Rigg had been nine years old at the time, and Father had not yet taught him any serious landlore—in fact, this was the beginning of it. So Rigg was still proud that he had come up with the right answer.

"The lake used to be higher," he finally guessed, "and the falls was also higher and farther out toward the face of Upsheer Cliff."

"Why would you imagine such a thing as that?" asked Father. "The falls are many fathoms back from the cliff face; what makes you think that a waterfall can move from place to place?"

"The water eats away at the rock and sweeps it off the cliff," said Rigg.

"Water that eats rock," said Father. But now Rigg knew that he had got it right—Father was using his mock-puzzled voice.

"And when the lip of the cliff is eaten away," Rigg went on, "then all the lake above where the new lip is, drains away."

"That would be a lot of water each time," said Father.

"A flood," said Rigg. "But that's why we don't have a mountain of rocks at the base of the falls—each flood sweeps the boulders downstream."

"Don't forget that in falling from the cliff, the boulders shatter so the pieces are much smaller," said Father.

"And the rocks we use for crossing at the top of the falls— they're like that because the water is already eating down *between* the rocks, leaving them high and dry. But someday the water will undermine those rocks, too, and they'll tip forward and tumble down the falls and break and get swept away, and there'll be a *new* level for the falls, farther back and lower down."

That was when Father started teaching him about the way land changes with the climate and weather and growth of plants and all the other things that can shape it.

When Rigg was eleven, he had thought of a question of his own. "If wind and rain and water and ice and the growth of plants can chew up rock, why is Upsheer still so steep? It should have weathered down like all the other mountains."

"Why do you think?" asked Father—a typical non-answer.

But this time Rigg had already half-formed his own theory. "Because Upsheer Cliff is much newer than any of the other mountains or hills."

"Interesting thought. How new do you think it is? How long ago was this cliff formed?"

And then, for no reason at all that Rigg could think of, he made a connection and said, "Eleven thousand, one hundred ninety-one years."

Father roared with laughter. "The calendar! You think that our calendar was dated from the formation of Upsheer Cliff?"

"Why not?" said Rigg. "Why else would we keep a memory that our calendar began in the year eleven-one-ninety-one?"

"But think, Rigg," said Father. "If the calendar began with the cataclysm that could raise a cliff, then why wasn't it simply numbered from then? Why did we give it a number like 11,191 and then count *down*?"

"I don't know," said Rigg. "Why?"

"Why do you think?"

"Because when the cliffs formed"—Rigg was not going to give up on his idea—"they knew that something else was going to happen 11,191 years later?"

"Well, we reached Year Zero when you were three. Did anything happen?"

"Lots of things happened," said Rigg. "A whole year's worth of things."

"But anything worth remembering? Anything worth building your whole calendar around?"

"That doesn't prove anything, Father, except that the people who invented the calendar were wrong about how long it would take to get to the thing they thought would happen in Year Zero. People are wrong all the time. It doesn't prove that the calendar didn't *begin* with the formation of Upsheer."

"Good thinking," said Father, "but, of course, wrong. And why are you wrong?"

"Because I don't have enough information," said Rigg. It was always because he didn't have enough information.

"There's never enough information," said Father. "That's the great tragedy of human knowledge. No matter how much we think we know, we can never predict the future."

Yet there had been something in Father's tone that Rigg didn't trust. Or maybe he simply didn't trust Father's answer, and imagined he heard it in his tone.

"I think you know something," said Rigg.

"I should hope so, as old as I am!"

"I think you know what was supposed to happen in Year Zero."

22

"Calamity! Plague! The end of the world!"

"No," said Rigg. "I mean the thing the calendar-makers were thinking of when they started in eleven-one-ninety-one."

"And how would I know that?"

"I think you know what it was," said Rigg, "and I think it actually happened, right on schedule."

"And it was so big and important that nobody noticed it except me," said Father.

"I think it was something scientific. Something astronomical. Something that scientists back then knew would happen, like planets lining up or some star in the sky blowing up or two stars crashing or something like that, only people who don't know astronomy would never notice it."

"Rigg," said Father, "you're so smart and so dumb at the same time that it almost takes my breath away."

And that had been the end of that. Rigg knew Father knew something, and he also knew Father had no intention of telling him.

Maybe Nox would know what happened in Year Zero. Maybe Father told her *all* his secrets.

But to get to Nox, Rigg had to get down Upsheer to the village of Fall Ford. And to get down Upsheer, he had to reach Cliff Road, which was on the other side of the falls, and so he had to cross over the very place where the water ran fastest, the current strongest, and where he knew the boulders were being undermined and eaten away and it was quite possible that his step on one of the rocks would be the tipping point, and it would tumble over the falls and carry him down to his death.

And his consolation, all the way down, until the water or the rocks or just the force of landing pulverized him, would be that at least there'd be a big flood of water gushing out of the lake, so he wouldn't die alone, the whole village of Fall Ford would be swept away in moments.

He remembered that this had been one of Father's test questions. "Why would people build a village in a place where they *know* eventually there'll be a terrible flood with no hope of survival and no warning in time to get away?"

"Because people forget," Rigg answered Father.

"That's right, Rigg. People forget. But you and I, Rigg—we don't forget, do we?"

But Rigg knew that it wasn't true. He couldn't remember a lot of things.

He remembered the route across the rocks. But he didn't trust that memory. He always checked it again when he got to the starting place, just above the surface of the lake.

It seemed so calm, but Rigg knew that if he dropped a stone it wouldn't sink into the water, it would immediately be pushed toward the falls, moving as rapidly as if someone under the water had thrown it. If he dropped himself into the water, he, too, would be over the cliff in about two seconds—having been bashed into six or seven big rocks along the way, so that whatever fell down the waterfall would be a bloody bashed-up version of Rigg, probably in several pieces.

He stood and looked out over the water, seeing—feeling—the paths of countless travelers.

It wasn't like a main road, which was so thick with paths that

Rigg could only pick out an individual with great difficulty, and even then he would lose the path almost at once.

Here, there were only hundreds, not thousands or millions of paths.

And a disturbing number of them did not make it all the way across. They got to this spot or that, and then suddenly lurched toward the cliff face; they had to have been swept away by the water.

Then, of course, there were the ancient paths. This is why Rigg had been able to figure out about the erosion of the rock, the way the falls moved back and lower over time. Because Rigg could see paths that walked through the air, higher than the falls and fathoms outward. These paths jogged and lurched the way the current paths did, for the people who made those paths had been crossing on another set of rocks that penned in a higher, deeper lake.

And where the bridges used to be, thousands of ancient, fading paths sweeping smoothly through midair.

Of course the land had moved, the water had lowered. Someone who could see what Rigg could see was bound to figure out that the falls kept moving.

But today, here is where they were, and these rocks were the rocks that Rigg would have to cross.

He always chose a route that almost everyone had crossed safely; he always tried for a route that was well back from the edge.

Rigg remembered—or remembered Father telling him about it, which was as close to memory as didn't matter—how Father had first discovered Rigg's ability to find old paths, right here at the footcrossing of the water. Father had been about to leap, carrying little Rigg, from one stone to another, and Rigg shouted, "No!" He made Father take a different path because, as Father told him, "You said, 'Nobody fell into the water this other way.'"

Rigg saw now the thing he saw then: Paths from stone to stone, different people, days or years or decades apart. He saw which of the paths of fallers were old and which were new. He chose a route that looked dry, that had been used most recently.

He saw his own past paths, of course.

And, of course, he saw no path at all belonging to Father.

What an odd thing for a son to be blind about—to see every person in the world, or at least to see the way they went, except his own father.

This time Rigg had to make doubly sure of his calculations, because he had to make the crossing with many pounds of bulky, unwieldy furs and hides bound on his back. A crossing he could make easily, carrying only a canteen and traps and a bit of food, would now require him to jump onto too small a rock; he would overbalance and fall in.

He was three leaps out, on a dry platform of rock a full two fathoms wide, when he caught a glimpse of movement and saw, on the far side of the water, a boy of about ten. He thought perhaps he knew him, but since Rigg only came to Fall Ford a few times a year, more or less, and didn't always see everybody, it might be the younger brother of the boy he thought it was; or it might be a boy from another family entirely, or a complete stranger.

Rigg waved a greeting and the boy waved back.

Rigg made his next leap, and now he was on a much smaller rock, so there'd be no room to make a run. This was the trickiest place in his crossing, where he was most at risk of dying, and he thought that perhaps he should have let down his burden on the big rock he had just left, and crossed with only a third of the furs, and then gone back for the rest. He had never made this leap with such a burden — Father always carried more than half.

It wasn't too late to go back to the big platform and divide his burden.

But then he saw that the boy had moved out onto a rock. It was much too close to the lip of the falls — Rigg knew that it was the beginning of a path that had the most deaths of any.

Rigg waved and gave a sign with both hands, as if he were pushing the boy back. "Go back!" he yelled. "Too dangerous!"

But the boy just waved, and made the push-back sign in return, which told Rigg that the boy hadn't understood him. Obviously Rigg could not be heard above the roaring of the water as it swept among the rocks.

The boy leapt to the next rock, and now he was on a path that was pure peril. It would be hard for him to get back now, even if he tried. And the boy was apparently so stupid he was determined to go on.

Rigg had only a moment to decide. If he went back the way he had come, he could set down his burden and then take a dangerous path that would get him nearer to the boy, perhaps near enough to be heard, near enough to stop him. But it would take time to get the furs off his back, and he'd be farther from the boy while he did it.

So instead he simply made the leap he was already planning. He did it exactly right, and a moment later he was ready to leap for a slightly bigger rock. He made that leap, too.

He was only two stones from the boy.

The boy jumped one more time, and almost made it. But the water caught just a part of one foot and swept his leg toward the lip, and it threw the boy off balance and he whirled around and both his feet went into the water, and the water pulled savagely at him.

The boy wasn't quite stupid after all. He knew he was doomed to lose the rock he was on, so he tried to catch at a smaller rock that was right at the lip of the falls.

He caught it, but the water whirled him around so that he hung by his fingers from the outward, dry edge of the rock and his body dangled over the vast drop to the river below.

"Hold on!" cried Rigg.

A whole winter's trapping, and he was about to discard it in order to have a slim chance of saving the life of a boy so stupid that surely he deserved to die.

It took Rigg only a moment to get the thongs untied, so he could shrug the load of furs from his back into the water.

He was so close to the lip now that the huge bundle caromed only once against the rocks as it hurtled toward the lip of the falls and then flew out into empty air and fell.

Meanwhile, Rigg dived for the rock that the boy had not quite made; Rigg made it, even though the boy had splashed water onto the surface and made it wet. "Hold on!" Rigg cried again. All he could see of the boy now was his fingers on the rock.

There wasn't room on the rock for Rigg to jump for it; though it was very close, it was too likely that he would kick the boy's fingers in the process of stepping there. So instead, Rigg knelt on his rock and then let himself topple forward, planning to catch the boy's rock with his hands, making a bridge of his body.

Only something strange happened. Time nearly stopped.

Rigg had been in tense situations before. He knew what it was like when your perceptions became suddenly keener, when every second was more fully experienced. It *felt* at such times as though time held still. But it did not really happen that way. As Father explained it, there were glands in the human body that secreted a substance that gave greater strength and speed at times of stress.

This was not the same thing at all. As Rigg let himself fall forward, an operation that should have taken a second or less, it was suddenly as if he were sinking slowly into something very thick. He had time to notice everything, and while he could not turn his eyes any faster than he could move any other part of his body, his *attention* could shift as rapidly as he wanted it to, so that anything within his field of vision, even at the edges, could be seen.

Then his attention was engaged by something far stranger. As time slowed down, so did the paths he saw in the air. They thickened. They became more solid.

They became people.

Every person who had tried to cross these rocks at this place became, first a blur of motion, then solid individuals, walking at their real pace. Whoever he concentrated on, he could see walking, jumping, leaping his or her course across the rocks. As soon as he focused his attention on someone else, the other people all became a streak of movement again.

So in mid-fall, he became aware of, *concentrated* on, a bare-legged man who was standing right in the middle of the rock to which the young boy was clinging. The man's back was to him; but because Rigg was falling so slowly, he had plenty of time to register that the man was dressed in a costume rather like those on the old fallen statues and crumbled friezes of the ruined buildings where the newer of the two old bridges had once rooted into the cliff.

Rigg realized that he was going to fall right into the man. But he couldn't be solid, could he? This was just part of Rigg's gift, weirdly changed in this moment of fear, and the paths were never tangible.

Yet this man looked so real—the hairs and pores on his calves, a raw place where something had scraped against his ankle, the frayed and half-opened hem of his kilt, the drooping band of embroidery only half-attached to it. Once the man had dressed in finery; now the finery had become rags.

Whatever ill-fortune had come upon the man, the fact remained that at this moment he was in Rigg's way. Rigg thought: The people I'm not paying attention to become blurs of motion. If I turn my thoughts away from him, he, too, will become insubstantial.

So Rigg tried to focus on a woman who had tried to make the leap to this same rock, but had slipped and fallen immediately into the current and been swept over. He did this—and saw the horror on her face, flashing almost immediately to the death look of an animal that knows there is no escape. But then she was gone, and his attention returned at once to the man in front of him. If he *had* become insubstantial for a moment, he was solid enough now.

Rigg's forehead smacked into the man's calf; he felt the force of it, yet he was moving so slowly he could feel the texture of the man's skin on his forehead and then, as Rigg's head was compelled to turn, the abrasion of the hairs of his leg on Rigg's face.

Just as Rigg's face was forced to turn in order to slide down the man's leg, so also the weight of Rigg's head and shoulder striking the man caused his leg to buckle, and the man twisted, started to topple forward.

I came to save a boy and now I'm killing a man.

But this man was a soldier or athlete; he whipped around in mid-fall and reached out and clutched the rock, so that when he fell he dangled from both hands.

His left hand completely covered the right hand of the boy.

Apparently two solid objects *could* occupy the same space at the same time. Or, technically, not at the same *time*, because the man was actually here hundreds of years ago, but to Rigg it was the same moment. The man's hand was solid. Rigg could feel it as his own hand, flung out by reflex to support himself after the collision with the man's leg, slid across the rock and rammed into the fingers of the man's right hand.

The result was that Rigg stopped sliding forward barely in time to keep his knees from sliding off the previous rock and into the water. Rigg's body now made the bridge between rocks that he had planned to make. The man had, without meaning to, saved Rigg's life.

But Rigg had not returned the favor. First he knocked him off his perch and toppled him over the side; and then Rigg's hand, sliding across the rock, had jammed into the man's fingers and shoved his right hand from the lip of the stone.

Now the man held on only by his left hand—the hand that completely covered the right hand of the dangling boy Rigg was here to save.

The man's hand was not transparent in any way. It was real, thick, muscular, tanned, hairy, callused, spotted with freckles and ridged with veins. Yet at exactly the same time, Rigg could also see the taut, slender, nut-brown fingers of the boy, starting to slip just a little. Rigg knew he could help the boy, could hold him if he could only reach past his fingers and get ahold of his wrist. The boy was smaller than Rigg, and Rigg was very strong; if he could lock that wrist between his own fingers he could hang on to him long enough to get his other hand out for the boy to grab.

He could imagine it, plan it, and he could have *done* it except that he could not get past the thick wrist and forearm of the man.

You're already dead, for decades and centuries you're dead, so get out of the way and let me save this child!

But when Rigg's hand clutched at the man's forearm, trying to get through him to the forearm of the boy, the man felt him and seized the opportunity. His right hand came up and caught Rigg by the wrist with a grip as much stronger and thicker than Rigg as Rigg's grip would have been stronger and thicker than the boy's wrist.

And the weight of the man began to drag Rigg forward.

Rigg's right knee dipped into the current, and if the man

had not had such a tight hold on him, he might have been swept away; at it was, it spun his body so he lay on his side. But that took his knee back out of the water, so once again his body was a bridge between stones.

Still the man's weight dragged at him. Rigg momentarily lost all thought of the boy—he couldn't save anybody if he himself was dragged off the cliff.

Rigg clutched at the man's fingers with his other hand and pried his little finger up and bent it backward, backward. All of this took forever, it seemed—he thought of the movement, and then, slowly, his hand obeyed, reached out, clutched, pried, pushed.

The man let go. With agonizing slowness his right hand slipped away from Rigg, his fingers sliding over Rigg's skin. Just as slowly, Rigg righted himself so that he could once again try to reach out for the boy; but still the man's left hand covered the boy's right.

Just as Rigg's hand once again settled over the man's left wrist, trying to get past him or through him or under him to reach the boy, Rigg saw the boy's fingers lose their grip and slide away from the rock, slowly, slowly . . . and then they were gone.

In fury and frustration and grief at his failure, Rigg raised his hand to strike downward at the man's hand. It did not enter his mind that he was preparing to do murder. In Rigg's time the man was already long since dead, no matter what the outcome here; all Rigg knew was that because that man had suddenly become visible and tangible, Rigg had not been able to save the boy—a boy he almost certainly knew in the village, if he could only place him.

But Rigg never got the chance to complete the action of striking the man. Instead time sped up again, became normal, the man simply disappeared without Rigg seeing whether he fell or somehow managed to clamber back up onto the rock, and Rigg's fist struck only stone.

A moment later, Rigg heard a scream. It couldn't be the boy—he would already have been so far down before the scream began that he could not have been heard where Rigg was, and the scream went on much too long. Yet it was not a man's scream—the voice was too high.

So there was someone else on the shore, someone else who had seen the boy die. Someone who might help Rigg get himself back off this rock.

But of course no one could help him. It would be insane for anyone to try. It had been insane for Rigg to try to save the boy. For here he was, his body bridging two stones, barely out of the water himself, and if he even bent his knees he would be carried away by the torrent.

He inched backward, trying to get his knees back onto the rock where his toes were. Already his arms and shoulders were aching with the strain of holding himself like a bridge. And now, when he might have used the slowing of time to help him pay attention to even the slightest move he made, his fear gave him no more than the normal degree of heightened concentration.

Yet after a while his knees were on the hind rock, and he was able to rise up on his hands till he was as high as he could get above the water, and his fingers still had enough strength in them that he could shove himself up and back, and . . .

He shoved, rose up, and then teetered for a moment that felt like forever, unsure whether he had pushed too lightly and would fall forward again, or pushed too hard and would tumble off the back of the rock.

But he found his balance. He stood up.

A rock hit him in the shoulder just as he was standing up. For a moment he lost his balance, could have fallen, but he recovered and turned to see a boy of perhaps his own age, maybe older, standing on the first rock from the shore, where the dead boy had started his fatal journey, and he was preparing to hurl an even bigger rock.

It was not as if Rigg had anywhere to hide.

So he had no choice but to try to slap the rock away with his bare hands. Rigg quickly discovered that his own slapping motion caused him to lose his balance as surely as if the rock had hit him. Somehow, though, he managed to twist himself and turn his fall into a lunge that got him, barely, onto the next rock back from the falls.

"Stop it!" cried Rigg.

But the rock-throwing boy couldn't hear him. Only the boy's scream had been loud enough to be audible over the roaring of the water.

Now Rigg recognized him—*this* was Umbo, a village boy, son of the cobbler, who had been his best friend when they were both much younger, and Father had kept him longer in Fall Ford than in recent years.

Now Rigg realized why he had known the boy who fell—it was Umbo's little brother, Kyokay, a daredevil of a boy who was always getting into trouble and always taking insane chances. The boy's arm had been in splints, healing from a break, during the time Rigg and Umbo had been friends, but even then he would climb impossible trees and leap from high places onto rough ground, so that Umbo constantly had to go and stop him or rescue him or scream at him.

If I could have saved Kyokay, it would have been a gift to my friend Umbo. A continuation of the many times I helped Umbo save the boy back when he was even smaller.

So why is Umbo trying to kill me by throwing stones? Does he think I *made* Kyokay fall? I was trying to save him, you fool! If you were there on the bank, why did you let him go out on the rocks? No matter what you saw, why didn't you try to find out what really happened before you passed a death sentence on me?

"People are never fair, even when they try to be," Father said more than once, "and few are the ones who try."

Rigg made it back to the rock where he had been when he first saw Kyokay. If I had just stayed here, he thought, and let the boy take his chances and, of course, die, Kyokay would be no *more* dead than he is now, and I would have been so far from him that no one could possibly have blamed me for his death.

And I'd still have my furs, and therefore I'd be able to take money with me on my journey to wherever in the world my mother and sister might be.

Umbo was still throwing rocks, but few of them came close now, and with so much rock to stand on, Rigg could dodge those easily. Umbo was weeping now in his fury, but still Rigg could not hear his words, nor hope to be heard himself if he tried to answer. Rigg could think of no gesture that would say, "I did nothing wrong, I tried to save him." To an angry, grieving boy like Umbo, a shrug would look like unconcern, not helplessness; a bow would look like sarcasm instead of respect for the dead.

So all Rigg could do was stand there, waiting until Umbo gave up. Finally he did, running from the water's edge back into the woods.

Either he's heading down Cliff Road to the village, where he'll no doubt tell everybody whatever he believes happened here, or he's lying in wait till I come closer.

Rigg hoped Umbo was waiting to ambush him. He was not afraid of fighting Umbo—Rigg was strong and agile from his life in the forest, and besides, Father had trained him to fight in ways that a cobbler's son would never have learned to counter. Though if it came to driving tiny nails through thick leather, Umbo would no doubt prevail. Rigg only wanted to get close enough to explain what happened, even if they were fighting while he talked.

When Rigg got to the other side, Umbo was gone—Rigg could see his path, bright and clear and fresh in the air, heading right down the difficult part of Cliff Road.

Rigg would like to have taken a different way, in case Umbo set some trap for him, but there *was* no other way down the cliff, except of course the ever-present option of falling. That was half the reason for Fall Ford's existence as a town, this road up the cliff. At the bottom it *was* a road, an ancient one, high-curbed and paved with large stones, switching back and forth up the steep slopes at the base of Upsheer.

But then the switchbacks got narrower, the ramping road

gave way to a high-stepped path, and paving stones gave way to carved and weathered rock, with makeshift repairs or detours where some ancient calamity had torn away the original path. Still, it was just possible for someone to carry a burden in both hands up the road, and for a boy like Umbo, bounding down, energized with grief and rage, it would take very little time to reach the bottom.

If Rigg still had his huge bundle of pelts and skins, that would be a problem. Umbo would have plenty of time to get to the village and back again, no doubt with men who would believe his story and who, in their rage, might not listen to Rigg's version of events.

As it was, if Rigg hurried, he would be at the bottom of Cliff Road and away before Umbo could get back. And unless he or someone else in the village had an ability like Rigg's, there would be no tracking him. An expert tracker was hard to track, Father had told him, since he knew what signs a fugitive shouldn't make in the first place.

Father! Rigg felt another pang of grief, as fresh as the first, and tears came into his eyes. How can I live without you? Why couldn't you hear the groaning of the wood and get out of the way before the tree fell on you? Always so quick, always so perceptive—it's almost unbelievable that you could ever be so careless.

And I still need you. Who will explain to me what caused time to slow, caused all those people from the past to appear, caused that man to block my way so the boy died?

Tear-filled eyes don't find a good path. So Rigg stemmed his grief, cleared his eyes, and continued through the woods, looking for the back way to get to Nox's rooming house.

CHAPTER 3
Nox's Wall

What training could they have given Ram Odin that would help him when the seven years of tedium ended and it was time for his decision?

The ship's computer already knew the entire procedure for the fold. The process was far too complicated for a mere pilot to be able to take part in it. Ram's job was to read and hear the reports of the computers, and then decide whether to go ahead.

But the decision was not an easy or an empty one. As the ship began its strangely twisted acceleration into the fold, data would be generated on a vast scale. The computers would begin their reduplicated analyses and fuzzy predictions of what was happening, what might happen, what would happen during the fold itself.

At any point, Ram could abort the procedure, based on what the computers told him. The computers would generate odds and likelihoods, but Ram was quite aware that the odds were all fiction. It was possible that none of the predictions would resemble the outcome.

And no matter how many times the computers repeated any one prediction, that did not make it the most likely outcome. It might mean nothing more than this: The computers and the software all contained the identical set of false assumptions or built-in flaws that made all prediction worthless.

Ram was an expert pilot, a deep-thinking astronomer and mathematician, his creative faculties well-practiced. Everything that training could do had been done. But it still came down to this: Who was Ram Odin? Would he bet his life and the lives of all the colonists on the unknown leap into a fold in spacetime?

Or would he, in the moment, decide that it was better to use known technology, generate the scoopfield, start harvesting interstellar hydrogen, and drive forward through ninety lightyears of ordinary spacetime?

Ram knew, or thought he knew, what his decision would be. He had said so, many times, during the testing and screening of potential pilots for the mission: Unless there is information from the computers that makes the jump seem recklessly dangerous, I will proceed. Even failure will be enormously valuable—you will see what happens to the ship, you will harvest the monitors that will be trailing behind us, you will know.

But now, seeing the reports, talking to the expendable that sat in the copilot position beside him, Ram realized that there was no such thing as "enough" information, and no way to set aside fear. Oh, his own fear he had mastered. What caused him problems was the vicarious fear for all the people sleeping in their berths; the fear that they would jump into the fold but never come out, or come out in a strange place that was much too far from any planet to make colonization possible.

How did I become the one to make this decision for everyone?

•   •   •

In settled country, even the wildest wood is wound about with paths. Children playing, couples trysting, vagabonds seeking a place to sleep undisturbed. Not to mention the countless practical needs for going into the forest. Mushrooms, snails, nuts, berries—all will bring people across the fields and into the trees.

Running steadily, lungweary, Rigg could still see the most recent paths. He knew which woods should be empty of people, and those were the paths he chose. Several times he had to abandon wild country and strike out across fields or through orchards, but always he knew from the paths which houses were empty, which roads safe to cross.

He came at last to the back approaches to Nox's rooming house. She kept a large vegetable garden with rows of pole beans, where Rigg crouched to scan the house.

A crowd had already gathered in front of the house. They weren't a mob—not yet—but Rigg heard their shouted demand that Nox let them search for "that child-murderer." Because Rigg had taken a roundabout way, Umbo's version of events had had plenty of time to spread through the village. And it was well known that here was where Father and Rigg always stayed.

Of course Nox let them in. Since Rigg really wasn't inside,

what reason would she have for refusing them, which would invite them to burn the place down?

Rigg couldn't see the men who searched the house — they were behind walls — yet somehow, in a way that blended into vision but wasn't actual sight, he could still track the men's paths through the house. All he could sense was the pace at which new paths appeared, and their position relative to each other and the outside wall of the house.

Yet this was enough for him to know that they were almost frantic in their search. They seemed to run up and down the stairs, and walk all around each room. There was bending, crawling, stretching upward. For all he knew they were slashing open the beds and dumping out trunks.

But of course they found nothing, since their quarry was outside in the bean patch.

And if they widened their search and found him here, they would assume Nox knew he was there. It might go very badly for her.

So as the paths converged again on the front porch, Rigg scampered for the back door and slipped inside the pantry. He dared not go upstairs or to any public room, because the regular residents were there.

From the pantry, Rigg could sense the movement of members of the crowd. They set two men to watch in front and two in back. Several men did indeed search through the garden.

I shouldn't have come here, thought Rigg. Or I should go back out into the wild and wait for a year and then come back. Maybe I'll be able to grow some kind of beard by then. Maybe

I'll be taller. Maybe I'll never come back at all—and never know who my mother is, or find my sister . . .

Why couldn't Father have simply *told* him instead of making him come here? But a dying man has the privilege of deciding his own last words, and when to stop talking.

Rigg tried to imagine what it would be like for Nox, when at last she came to the pantry. If he was standing up and looking at her, she was likely to scream; that would draw attention, certainly of the residents, and perhaps of the guards outside. He needed to be sure she remained silent, which meant she should feel neither shocked nor threatened.

So he sat down in a corner and hid his face in his hands. She wouldn't be startled by seeing his eyes, nor face an unexpected stranger looming over her as she opened the door to the room. It was the best he could do.

It took two hours before Nox was able to calm down the guests, who were, of course, frightened or angry about the intrusion and search. Two of them packed up their things and left. The rest stayed, and finally it was time—past time—for Nox to start preparing dinner.

"Too late for soup, no time for anything that takes any time to cook," Nox was grumbling as she opened the pantry door.

Rigg was not looking up, so he couldn't be exactly sure she even noticed him, as she unsealed the flour and sugar bins to draw out the ingredients for quickbread. She had to have seen him, but gave no sign. Only when he lifted his head very slightly, enough to see her, did she whisper, "Stay here till after dinner," though Rigg knew well that the noon meal there hardly deserved the lofty title of *dinner*. Then Nox was out of the pantry, closing the door behind her.

Dinner was served, during which the two guests who had left came back—there were no other rooms in town, and after all, the murderer had *not* been found in the house, so surely that made this the safest rooming house in Fall Ford, since this one had been found most definitely killer-free.

Finally, when Rigg sensed that all the guests had gone out again, Nox opened the pantry, came inside, and closed the door behind her. Her voice was the tiniest of whispers.

"How did you keep them from finding you when they searched the house? You haven't learned how to make yourself invisible, have you?"

"I came in after they searched."

"Well, thanks for dropping by. It's made everybody's day."

"I didn't kill that boy."

"No one in their right mind thinks you did."

"He was hanging from the lip of a stone and I even dropped all my furs so I could try to save him, but Umbo thinks what he thinks."

"People always do. Where's your father?"

"Dead."

That left her silent for a long while.

Then, finally, "I honestly didn't think he knew how to die."

"A tree fell on him."

"And you came back here alone?"

"He told me to. He told me to come to you."

"Nothing about killing an odd child or two on the way?"

44

For a moment, Rigg thought of telling her about the man from centuries ago that he might or might not have killed as well. But that would mean telling her about his pathfinding, and things were complicated enough already. She'd probably think he was insane and therefore cease believing that he had not killed Kyokay. So Rigg ignored her provocation. "He told me you'd tell me where my sister and mother are."

"He couldn't tell you himself?"

"You say that as if you think he might have explained himself to me."

"Of course he didn't." She sighed. "Trust him to leave the hard jobs to me."

"You've known my mother was still alive my whole life long, and you never bothered to mention it to me?"

"I've known only since he was about to lead you out on this last jaunt," she said. "He took me aside and made me memorize some names and an address. He said I'd know when to tell somebody."

"It's now," said Rigg.

"Fat lot of good it'll do you," said Nox, "with men watching my house."

"I'd rather die knowing."

"First tell me how that boy died."

So Rigg told her what had happened, except that he left out any mention of the man from another time whose hand had covered Kyokay's. He was sure she could sense that he wasn't telling the complete story, but it still seemed better not to tell her about his abilities.

Nox seemed to take it all in stride. "Trust that idiot Umbo to accuse you before trying to find out the truth. And you lost all your furs?"

"I didn't really lose them, since I know where they are," said Rigg. "They're somewhere downriver, hung up on rocks or branches."

"Oh, you can be funny? I'm *so* glad to hear it."

"It's laugh or cry," said Rigg.

"Cry, then. Give the old man his due."

For a moment, Rigg thought she meant the ancient man at the top of the falls. But of course she meant Father. "He wasn't all that old."

"How can anyone tell? He was coming to this house when I was a child, and he looked no younger then."

"Will you tell me now where I need to go?"

"I'll tell you—so you'll know what address it was you never made it to. Nobody's letting you out of town today."

"Names," Rigg insisted.

"Are you hungry?"

"I'll be eating the flesh of warmed-over rooming house owner if you don't tell me now."

"Threats. Tut tut. Naughty boy. Raised without manners."

"Exactly," said Rigg. "But I do have a lot of experience with killing animals larger than myself."

"I get it," said Nox. "You're so clever. Your mother was—is—Hagia Sessamin. She lives in Aressa Sessamo."

"The ancient capital of the Sessamoto Empire?"

"That very city," said Nox.

46

"And what is her address?" asked Rigg.

Nox chuckled. "Not a very good listener. Your father always said, 'If I could only get him to pay attention.'"

Rigg was not going to be put off. "Address?"

"I told you, she's *Hagia Sessamin*."

"And that means she doesn't need an address?"

"Ah," she said. "Apparently your father omitted any explanations about Sessamoto politics. Which makes sense, come to think of it. If you get out of Fall Ford alive, get to Aressa Sessamo and ask for the house of 'the Sessamin.' Ask anyone at all."

"I'm some kind of royalty?"

"You're a male," said Nox. "That means you could fart royal blood out of your ears and it wouldn't matter. It was an empire ruled by women, which was a very good plan while it lasted. Not that most cities and nations and empires aren't ruled by women, one way or another." She stopped and studied his face. "I'm trying to figure out what you're not saying to me."

Rigg said the first thing that came to mind. "I have no money for the journey. The furs were all I had."

"And you come begging an old housekeeper for a few coins from her stash?"

"No," said Rigg. "Nothing, if you can't spare it. If you have a little, I'll borrow it, though I don't know when or if ever it's going to be possible for me to repay you."

"Well, I'm not going to advance you anything, or lend it, or even give it. Though I might ask *you* for a loan."

"A loan? When I have nothing?"

"Your father left you a little something."

"When were you going to tell me?"

"I just told you." She pushed a stepladder into place against one of the sets of rough shelves and started to climb. Then she stopped.

"If you try to look up my skirt, I'll poke needles into your eyes right through your eyelids while you're asleep."

"I'm looking for help, you give me nightmares, thank you so much."

She was on the top step now, reaching up for a bin marked DRY BEANS. Rigg looked up her skirt mostly because she told him not to, and saw nothing at all of interest. He could never understand why Nox and other women, too, were always so sure men wanted to see whatever it is they concealed under their clothes.

She came down with a small bag. "Wasn't this nice of your father? To leave this behind for you?"

She opened the little bag and poured its contents into her palm. Nineteen jewels, large ones, of more colors than Rigg had imagined jewels could have, and no two alike.

"What am I supposed to do with these?"

"Sell them," she said. "They're worth a fortune."

"I'm thirteen," Rigg reminded her. "Everyone will assume I stole these from my mommy. Or a stranger. Nobody will imagine that I have them by right."

Out of the bag Nox took a folded sheet of paper. Rigg took it, looked at it. "It's addressed to a banker in Aressa Sessamo."

"Yes," she said. "I can read."

Rigg scanned it. "Father taught me about letters of credit."

"I'm glad to hear that, since he never taught *me* any such thing."

"It says my name is Rigg Sessamekesh."

"Then I suppose that's what your name is," said Nox.

"This is worthless until I get to Aressa Sessamo," said Rigg.

"So live off the land, the way you and your father always do."

"That works in the forest. But long before I get to Aressa Sessamo, it'll all be towns and farms and fields. I hear they whip you for stealing."

"Or put you in jail, or sell you into slavery, or kill you, depending on the town and what mood they're in."

"So I'll need money."

"If you make it out of Fall Ford."

Rigg said nothing. What could he say? She didn't owe him anything. But she was the closest thing to a friend he had, even if she wasn't his mother.

Nox sighed. "I told your father not to count on my giving you money."

"He didn't. He saw to it I had a good-sized bundle of furs— all I could carry."

"Yes, yes, so I *will* give you something, but it won't be enough for you to ride a carriage. It won't be enough for you to ride *anything*. And you'd be wise to keep off the roads for a good long way. I have a feeling that nobody's going to get new shoes or shoes repaired in Fall Ford until a certain cobbler gives up on finding you and gutting you like a fish."

Rigg heard something outside the pantry. "When did we decide to stop whispering?" he asked.

Nox whirled around and flipped open the pantry door. There was nobody there. "We're fine," she said.

Then there came a pounding on the front and back doors of the house, both at once. "We know you have him in there, Nox! Don't make us burn down the house!"

Rigg shuddered with panic, but otherwise he couldn't move, he couldn't even think.

Nox pinched the bridge of her nose. "I'm getting a headache. A big fat throbbing one, relentless as a moth."

She spoke as if it were a mere annoyance that they had realized where Rigg was hiding. Her calmness dispelled most of his fear. "Do you think we can talk them out of this? Or will you try to keep them busy while I climb out on the roof?"

"Quiet," she said. "I'm building a wall."

Since her hands were doing nothing at all, Rigg assumed her wall must be metaphorical. A wall between herself and her fear?

As if he had asked aloud, she whispered an explanation. "A wall around the house. I'm filling it with a will to turn away."

He should have known that Father would have become her teacher because she had some kind of interesting talent. "They're already at the door."

"But nobody will want to come any farther. For as long as I can sustain it."

"How long is that? Minutes? Hours?"

"It depends on how many wills are attacking it, and how strongly determined they are," she answered.

She took her fingers from the bridge of her nose and walked to the back door, then spoke through it to the guards in back.

"I'm opening the front door in a moment, so you might as well go around."

"Do you think I'm fooled?" asked a male voice from the other side. "As soon as I leave, you'll come out the back."

"Suit yourself," said Nox. Then, to Rigg, she said softly, "That's how you get people to outsmart themselves. If they think they've found your plan, they'll stop looking for it."

"I heard that," said the man on the other side of the door. "I can do that spell myself."

"We weren't doing a spell," said Nox. "We were just talking."

As they walked to the front door, Nox added, for Rigg's ears alone, "Don't go through the door when I open it."

She opened the door. Standing right there were two burly men. One was the blacksmith, and one a farmer from an outlying homestead. Just behind them, but off the porch, stood the cobbler Tegay, father of the dead boy Kyokay. His face was streaked with tears and Umbo was clinging to his arm, half-hidden behind his father's bulk.

Rigg wanted to run to Umbo and tell him what had happened—tell him everything, the magic and all, so that Umbo would understand that Rigg was only trying to save Kyokay, and had risked his own life to do it. Umbo would believe him, if they only had a chance to talk.

The two men at the door made as if to come inside—to burst in, from their posture—but after a shifting of weight they remained outside after all.

"He was not here when you searched," said Nox. "I did *not* know he was coming."

51

"You say," said the farmer.

"I say," said Nox, "and you know my word is good."

"How do we know that?" asked the blacksmith.

"Because I pay my bills promptly," answered Nox, "even when my tenants haven't paid *me*." Then she called more loudly. "Tegay!"

"You don't have to shout," said the cobbler softly, from behind them. They moved aside a little, so Nox and Tegay could see each other.

"Why do you accuse this boy of killing your son?"

"Because my boy Umbo watched him throw Kyokay over the falls."

"He did not," said Nox.

"I did too!" cried Umbo, taking a step closer to the porch.

"I'm not calling you a liar," said Nox. "I'm saying that you are telling, not what you saw, but what you concluded from what you saw."

"Same thing," said the blacksmith.

"Umbo," said Nox. "Come here."

Umbo stepped back and stood close to his father again.

The cobbler said, "I'm not letting him into that house, not while that child-killer is there!"

"Umbo," said Nox, "what did you actually *see*? Don't lie, now. Tell us what your eyes actually witnessed."

Rigg knew that Umbo would tell the truth—he was no liar. Then he'd realize for himself that Rigg hadn't thrown or pushed, but had only reached out to try to save.

Umbo looked wildly from Rigg to Nox and then up at his father. "It happened like I said."

It surprised Rigg that Umbo would persist in his mistake. But perhaps Umbo was afraid to change his story now. Everyone knew how Tegay beat him when he was angry.

"I see," said Nox. "You were supposed to be watching Kyokay, weren't you? Keeping him out of danger. But he ran away, didn't he? Ran ahead of you, and when you got to the top of Cliff Road, he was already out on the rocks."

Tegay's face changed. "Is that true?" he asked his son.

"Kyokay didn't obey me, but I still saw what I saw," Umbo insisted.

"And that's my question," said Nox. "Scrambling up that road, you were out of breath. You had to watch your handholds and footholds so you wouldn't fall. There are moments you can glimpse the falls and see what's happening. But you wouldn't have stopped to look, would you?"

"I saw Rigg throw Kyokay into the water."

"While you were still coming up the road?" prompted Nox.

"Yes."

"And when you got to the top, what did you see?" asked Nox.

"Kyokay was hanging from the lip of a stone, dangling over the falls. And Rigg was stretched out across two stones trying to slap and pry at Kyokay's hands! And then he fell." On that last sentence, a sob burst from him at the memory.

"And then what did you do?" asked Nox.

"I went back to the shore and picked up stones and threw them at Rigg."

"You thought you could avenge your brother with *stones*?"

"Rigg was having trouble getting back onto his feet. I thought I could make him lose his balance and fall in."

Hearing Umbo admit to having tried to kill him was infuriating. "And you nearly did, too," said Rigg.

Nox hushed him with a gesture. "Umbo, you saw your brother die a terrifying death, falling from the top of Stashi Falls. You thought you understood what happened from the glimpses that you saw. But let me tell you what really happened."

"You weren't there," growled the farmer.

"Neither were you, so keep your mouth shut," said Nox calmly. "Rigg just came back from two months of trapping. On his back he was carrying all the furs that he and his father had gathered. Did you see that bundle of furs?"

Umbo shook his head.

"Yes, you did," said Nox. "That's what Rigg was throwing into the water when you caught a glimpse of him as you scrambled up Cliff Road. That's what got swept over the falls, not your brother. Your brother was already dangling from the rock. Rigg got rid of his burden so he could go and try to save him."

"No," said Umbo. But he did not sound very certain.

"Think," said Nox. "Rigg must have done *something* with his furs. Where were they? Would he have left them on the other side? What do Rigg and his father *always* do with the furs they bring to town?"

Umbo shook his head.

"And then you say Rigg stretched himself across two rocks. Why? To slap at Kyokay's fingers and push him from his perch? Why would he need to do that? How long could Kyokay have held on anyway? Did he have the strength to climb back up onto the rock? Was the rock even big enough?"

"I don't know," said Umbo.

"The only story that makes sense is the true one," said Nox. "Rigg was crossing where he and his father always crossed—far back from the falls. Only a foolish daredevil of a little boy would try to cross on the stones near the edge of the falls."

A few of the men in the crowd murmured their assent. And Rigg's respect for Nox grew. Even better than Father, she knew how to speak patiently, clearly, in a way that created trust, that built up the right story in the minds of these men.

"We all know how reckless Kyokay was," said Nox. "How many of us have seen him walking along roofs and climbing high trees and showing off in a dozen different ways? That's why your father told you to watch him, to keep him from . . ."

"From getting himself killed," said Tegay softly.

"Rigg was where *you* were supposed to be, doing what *you* were supposed to do, Umbo," said Nox. "Looking after Kyokay. He sacrificed two months of labor, all the goods he had in the world, so he could try to save your brother. He risked his life, stretched out between two rocks, to try to get to your brother's hand and pull him up. But then your brother lost his grip and fell. And there was Rigg, balanced over the rushing water. If he dipped even a knee into that stream, he'd be swept over the falls. And while he's trying to get back from the edge alive, what happens? You throw rocks at him."

"I thought he . . . I thought . . ."

"You were angry. Someone was guilty of something terrible.

Someone had done something wrong and needed to be punished," said Nox. "Someone. But it wasn't Rigg, was it?"

Umbo burst into tears. His father held him close.

"It wasn't Umbo either," said Tegay. "It was Kyokay. He never believed in danger. He wouldn't obey. I don't blame Umbo. I don't blame Rigg, either." He turned to the other men gathered there. "Let no man lay a hand on Rigg for Kyokay's sake," he said.

"Why do you believe her?" asked a man from farther back in the crowd.

"She's a spellcaster," said another. "She's ensorceled you."

"She wasn't there. She talks like she knows but she wasn't there."

Nox pointed a finger at the man who spoke last. "Why do you want to believe the worst? Why are you hungry to do a killing here today? What kind of man are you?"

"He killed a child!" the man cried. Rigg had seen him around the village, but didn't know him. He wasn't anyone very important, until now—now he seemed to be the leader of the angriest men in the mob. "I say Rigg's father had the furs and it all happened the way Umbo said!"

"That would be a very clever guess," said Rigg, "except my father is dead."

Silence fell on the crowd.

"That's why I was carrying all the furs," Rigg continued. "I was coming back alone."

"How did your father die?" asked Tegay, with a gruff sort of sympathy.

"A tree fell on him," said Rigg.

"A likely story!" shouted a man in the crowd.

"Enough!" shouted Nox. "You searched through my house, causing all kinds of damage, and I bore it for the sake of Kyokay and his grieving family. But Umbo admits he saw only a glimpse here and a glimpse there. Rigg had no reason to kill Kyokay — there has been nothing but friendship among these boys. Instead Rigg sacrificed his furs and risked his life trying to save him. It's the only story that makes any sense at all. Now go away from my rooming house. If you want blood, go home and kill a chicken or a goat and have a nice feast in memory of Kyokay. But you'll shed no blood here today. Go!"

Even as the crowd began to break up and wander away, the angriest man muttered loudly enough for Rigg to hear: "Murdered his father in the woods and came home to murder our children in their beds."

"I'm sorry your father's dead," Tegay said to Rigg. "Thank you for trying to save my little boy." Then the cobbler burst into tears and the blacksmith and farmer led him away.

Umbo stood alone for a moment, looking up at Rigg. "I'm sorry I threw stones at you. I'm sorry I blamed you."

"You saw it how you saw it," said Rigg. "I don't blame you."

He would have said more to Umbo, but Nox closed the door.

"How did you know all the things you said?" asked Rigg. "I didn't tell you all of those things."

"I know the place," said Nox. "And I already heard Umbo's story when he told it before, during the search."

"The wall you made just now — what does it do?"

"It weakens everyone's will but mine, so they begin to want a little less of what they want, and a little more of what I want. And just now I wanted peace and calm and forgiveness. And I wanted them to stay out of my house."

"But it didn't seem to affect some of the men," said Rigg.

"My wall had no effect on the men far out in the crowd. Only on the ones who were close to me. It's not really that much of a talent, as the good teacher was fond of telling me, but it worked well enough today. Though it wore me out. If Tegay had really wanted your murder, he could have outlasted me. But he didn't. He knew Kyokay was a foolish boy. Everyone said the child was doomed to kill himself doing some foolish jape, and then he did. Tegay knew that."

"But then magic is real," said Rigg. "You have magic."

"Think," said Nox. "Is the thing *you* do magic? Seeing the paths of every creature? Thousands of years ago they passed, and you can still see the path? Is that magic?"

So Father had told Nox all about his pathfinding, after commanding Rigg never to trust anyone with the secret. When Father said to tell no one, he apparently meant to be careful and tell only those you could trust. It made a lot more sense than an ironclad rule. "It's a thing I can do," said Rigg.

"But it's not a spell, you didn't learn it, you can't teach someone else to do it, it's not magic, it's a sense you have that others happen to lack, and if we understood it better we'd see that it's just as natural as—"

"Breathing," said Rigg. He knew how to finish the sentence because it was one that Father had said many times. "Father taught you to understand your talent, too."

"He tried to teach me many more things than I actually learned," said Nox. "We didn't tramp together through the woods for hours and days and weeks and months at a time, the way you did. So he didn't have time to teach me the way he taught you."

"I didn't know Father was so old. To teach you when you were young."

"How old do you think *I* am?" asked Nox.

"Older than me."

"I was sixteen and your father—the man I knew as Good Teacher—had been teaching me for three years before he left Fall Ford. He said he had to go get something. I was seventeen when he came back with you in his arms."

"So Father went to the city and fell in love and got married and they had a baby and then he *left* her and it only took a year?"

"A year and a half," said Nox, "and who said anything about falling in love? Or getting married? He got a child, and it was you, and he brought you back here, and now you have a fortune in jewels and a letter of credit and you'll have most of my meager savings to take with you. You're going to leave on your journey now, today, before it's dark, and you're going to get as far as you can before you rest."

"Why?"

"Because there were men in that crowd who still believed Umbo's first story—violent men—and I don't have the strength to build my wall again today."

They went to the kitchen and he helped her make quickbread and then she packed some of it along with cheese and salt pork in a knapsack. Meanwhile, he sewed her little bag of silver and bronze coins to the tail of his shirt, which he then tucked inside his trousers. He tried to give her one of the jewels in exchange, but she refused it. "What would I do with it here? And each one of these is worth a hundred times more than all the coins I gave you. A thousand times more."

While they worked, Rigg thought of his father and how, in all his teaching, he had left out so many things, yet had told them to Nox. It left a bitter feeling in his heart, to know how little Father had trusted him; yet it also made him feel closer to Nox, since she had held so many secrets without ever telling them. Well, now she could certainly tell them to Rigg, couldn't she? "Why do you call him Good Teacher instead of using his name?"

"It was the only name I had for him."

"But his parents wouldn't have given him a name like that," said Rigg.

"I've had guests stay here who had names stranger than that—given to them by their parents. I had a man whose first name was Captain, and one whose first name was Doctor, and a woman whose first name was Princess. But if you want a different name for your father, try the one he used in that paper—Wandering Man. That's the name he went by in this place, before I started calling him Good Teacher. Or Wallwatcher, or Golden Man."

"Those are names from legends," said Rigg.

"I've heard people call your father by such names. *They* took it seriously enough, even if he laughed. Names come and go. They get attached to you, and then you lose them, and they get attached to someone else. Now let me concentrate on making this bread. If I don't pay attention to it, it goes ill."

It wasn't much, but she had just told him more information about Father than he had ever heard from the man himself.

It was still three hours before sundown when he set off.

"Thank you," he said, taking leave of her at the back door.

"For what?" she said dismissively.

"For lending me money you couldn't afford," said Rigg. "For making bread for me. For saving my life from the mob."

She sighed. "Your father knew I would do all that," she said. "Just as he knew you'd have the brains to find a way here without getting yourself caught and killed."

"Father didn't know I was going to try to save a stupid boy on Stashi Falls."

"Are you sure of that?" asked Nox. "Your father knew a lot of things he shouldn't have been able to know."

"If he knew the future," said Rigg, "he could have dodged the damn tree." And after that, Rigg couldn't think of anything else to say, and Nox seemed eager to get back inside the kitchen, because she had a whole supper to prepare for her guests, so he turned and left.

CHAPTER 4

Shrine of the Wandering Saint

"How did I ever become the one to make this decision for everyone?" Ram asked aloud.

"You spent six years winning your way through the testing process," said the expendable.

"What I meant was, Why is this choice being left up to one human being, who cannot possibly have enough information to decide?"

"You can always leave it up to me," said the expendable.

That was the failsafe: If Ram died, or froze up, or had a crippling injury, or refused to decide, any of the expendables was prepared to take over and make the decision.

"If it were your decision," asked Ram, "what would *you* decide?"

"You know I'm not allowed to answer that, Ram," said the expendable. "Either you make the decision or you turn it over to me. But you must not ask me what I would decide. That would add an irrelevant and complicating factor to your decision. Will you choose the opposite in order to assert the difference between humans and expendables? Or follow me blindly, and then blame the expendables, on which you have no choice but to rely, if anything goes wrong?"

"I know," said Ram.

"I know you know," said the expendable, "and you know that I know that you know. It spirals on from there, so let's just assume the dot dot dot."

Ram chuckled. The expendables had learned that Ram enjoyed a little sarcasm now and then, so as part of their responsibility to maintain his mental health, they all used the same degree of sarcasm in their conversations with him.

"How long do I have before I have to make the decision?"

"You can decide any time, Ram," said the expendable.

"But there has to be a point of no return. When I either miss the fold or plunge into it."

"Wouldn't that be convenient," said the expendable. "If you just wait long enough, the decision gets taken out of your hands. You will not be informed of any default decision or point of no return, because that might influence your decision."

"The data are so ambivalent," said Ram.

"The data have no valents, take no sides, lean in no direction, Ram," said the expendable. "The computers do their calculations and report their findings."

"But what do I make of the fact that all nineteen computers have such different predictions?"

"You celebrate the fact that reality is even more fuzzy than the logic algorithms in the software."

"Whoop-de-do," said Ram.

"What?"

"I'm celebrating."

"Was that irony or loss of mental function?" asked the expendable.

"Was that a rhetorical question, a bit of humor, or a sign that you are losing confidence in me?"

"I have no confidence in you, Ram," said the expendable.

"Well, thanks."

"You're welcome."

Ram wasn't quite sure he had made the decision even as he reached over and poked his finger into the yes-option box on the computer's display. Then it was done, and he was sure.

"So that's it?" asked the expendable.

"Final decision," said Ram. "And it's the right one."

"Why do you think so?"

"Because live or die, we'll learn something important from jumping into the fold. Thousands of future travelers will either follow us or not. But if we don't make the jump, we'll learn nothing, have no new options."

"A lovely speech. It has been sent back to Earth. It will inspire millions."

"Shut up," said Ram.

The expendable laughed. That laugh—it was one of the reasons why the expendables made such good company. Even knowing that it was programmed into the expendable to laugh at just such a moment, and for just this long, tapering off in just such a way, did not keep Ram from feeling the warmth of acceptance that laughter of this kind brought to primates of the genus *homo*.

. . .

Rigg scanned for recent paths as he walked briskly through fields and woods. No one could hide from him. If someone had moved within the last day or two his path would be intense, and if in the last hour or so, it would be downright vivid. So if someone had set up an ambush for him, he would see by what route they had approached their hiding place, and he could avoid them.

So within a few hundred yards of Nox's rooming house, Rigg went between a couple of buildings and stepped into the road. The whole course of the ancient highway from Upsheer to the old imperial capital at Aressa Sessamo was packed with hundreds of thousand of paths, but most of them were old and faded, left over from ancient times when there was a great city atop Upsheer, and Fall Ford had been a sprawling metropolis at its foot. These days the paths were in the hundreds per year instead of thousands.

Rigg's heart was full of Father's death now, and the death of the boy at the falls just this morning, and the strange man from the past. Rigg could not keep his mind on any one of them. Instead, with a kind of franticness his thoughts would skip from one to another. Father! — but the horror of seeing the boy's hand, knowing it would slip away — and the man clutching at him, dragging Rigg toward the edge.

Father wouldn't let me see him, dying with a tree pressing on him, so I wouldn't have to live with the memory. Now I've seen something nearly as awful to haunt my dreams.

He was rounding a bend when he saw it — a very recent path

of someone crossing the road, scrambling up an embankment, and then lying down in thick bushes.

He did not even slow down—but he drifted to the far side of the road. And as he got closer, he was able to recognize the path. It was the same one he had followed down Cliff Road, and had seen again behind the boy who faced Nox in the doorway of her house.

"Umbo!" called Rigg. "If you plan to kill me, then come ahead and try. But don't wait for me in ambush. That's a coward's way, an assassin's path. I didn't mean to let your brother die, I truly meant to save him."

Umbo rose up among the bushes. "I'm not here to kill you," he said.

"You seem to be alone," said Rigg, "so I believe you."

"My father banished me," said Umbo.

"Why?"

"I was supposed to keep Kyokay out of trouble." There was a world of misery and shame in the words.

"Kyokay was too big for you to control," said Rigg. "Your father should know that. Why didn't *he* watch him?"

"If I said that to my father . . ." Umbo shuddered.

"Come down out of the bushes," said Rigg. "I don't have much time to stay and talk. I have to get as far as I can before dark." He didn't bother to explain that he could find his path as easily by night as by day.

Umbo half slid, half stepped down the slope. He fetched up on the road at a jog, and came to a stop right in front of Rigg. They were about of a size, though that would probably change— Father had been very tall, and Umbo's father was no giant.

"I'm going with you, if you'll let me," said Umbo.

Umbo had tried to get Rigg killed with his accusations back at Nox's house. And now he wanted to be Rigg's traveling companion? "I don't think that's a good idea."

"You know how to live and travel on your own," said Umbo. "I don't."

"You're not going as far as I am," said Rigg.

"Yes I am," said Umbo. "Because I have nowhere at all to go."

"Your father will relent in a day or two. Just linger at the fringes of town until he comes looking for you to apologize." Rigg remembered the time when, drunk, Tegay the cobbler had threatened to kill Umbo the next time he saw him. Umbo and Rigg had both believed him—they were about five years old—and so they fled into the woods on the west bank of the river. It wasn't six hours before Tegay came out of his house and hollered, then pleaded for his son to come home.

"Not this time," said Umbo, no doubt remembering the same event. "You didn't hear him. You didn't see his face when he said it. I'm dead, he said. His son Umbo died at the falls along with the brother he was supposed to take care of. 'Because *my* son would have done all he could to save his brother, not watched another boy try to do it and then accuse him falsely of murder.'"

"So you're saying it's somehow *my* fault that your father threw you out?"

"Even if he changes his mind," said Umbo, "I can't stay here. I spent my whole life worrying about Kyokay, watching out for him, protecting him, hiding him, catching him, nursing him. I was more father to him than Father ever was. More mother to him than Mother was, too. But now he's gone. I don't even know why I'm alive, if I don't have him to keep watch over. His constant chatter—I never thought I'd miss it." And he began to cry. He cried like a man, his shoulders heaving, and sobs almost howls, his cheeks flowing with tears and making no effort to hide them. "By the Wandering Saint," Umbo finally said. "I'll be a true friend to you, Rigg, though I was false to you this very day. I'll stand by you always, in everything."

Rigg had no idea what to do. He had seen mothers and fathers comfort crying children—but those had been little kids, crying eye-rubbing baby tears with little hiccupy sobs. A man's tears needed a man's comfort, and as Rigg thought back to any experience that might show him what to do, Umbo came out of it himself.

"Sorry for letting go like that," said Umbo. "I didn't know that was going to happen. Thanks for not trying to comfort me."

What a relief, thought Rigg. Doing nothing happened to be exactly the thing to do.

"Let me come with you," said Umbo. "You're the only friend I have."

And it occurred to Rigg that with Father dead and Nox left behind, Rigg had no other friend than Umbo. If he truly was Rigg's friend.

"I travel alone," said Rigg.

"Now that's just stupid," said Umbo. "You've never traveled alone, you were always with your father."

"I travel alone *now*."

"If you can't have your father, you won't have *any* companion?"

Then, as Father had trained him, Rigg thought past his

feelings. Yes, he was hurt and angry and grieving and filled with spite and bitter at the irony of Umbo now asking him for help, after nearly getting him killed. But that had nothing to do with deciding the wisest course.

Will Umbo be trustworthy? He always has been in the past, and he seems truly sorry for accusing me falsely.

Does Umbo have the stamina for the road I travel? He doesn't have to. I have money enough to stay at inns if the weather turns bad.

Will he be useful? Two strong young striplings would be much safer on the road than one boy alone. If there came a time they needed to keep watch at night, there'd be the two of them to divide the task.

"Can you cook anything?" asked Rigg. "I can always catch some animal we can eat, but . . . meat begs for seasoning."

"You'll have to do it," said Umbo. "I've never cooked meat."

Rigg nodded. "What *can* you do?"

"Put a new sole on your shoes, when you wear a hole in them or the stitching comes out. If you provide me with the leather and a heavy needle."

Rigg couldn't help but laugh. "Who brings a cobbler along on a journey?"

"You do," said Umbo. "For the sake of the old days, when I kept the other boys from throwing rocks at you for being a wild boy from the woods."

It was true that Umbo had looked out for him when they were much smaller, and Rigg was seen as a stranger among the village children.

"No promises," said Rigg, "but you can start the journey with me and we'll talk about how well or badly it's working at the end of each day."

"Yes," said Umbo. "Yes."

Rigg strode boldly into the great stream of ancient paths that flowed up and down the road like a river going both ways at once. Rigg thought of what he had seen at the top of Stashi Falls—how everything had slowed down and the paths had become people rushing by. Now he understood that all these paths still contained a vision of the real person passing, a vision that could become real. Now he was plunging into that flow of people up and down the road, swept onward with half the current and yet at the same time fighting his way upstream against the other half.

"Are you in a rush?" Umbo asked when he caught up and began to jog alongside Rigg. "Or have you changed your mind and you're deliberately leaving me behind?"

Rigg slowed down. He had merely been walking as fast as he and Father always did on every journey, but few adult men and no boys Umbo's size could match the pace without real exertion. Umbo was strong and healthy, only a little smaller than Rigg, but he was a cobbler's son, a village boy. His legs had never tried to cover distance this way before, taking long strides every hour, day after day.

Rigg almost answered as heartlessly as Father always had: "Keep up if you can, and don't if you can't." But why should he speak like Father? Rigg had always resented his utter unwillingness to make any concessions to Rigg's age and size.

So instead of giving a snippy, cold answer, Rigg simply slowed down and walked at Umbo's version of a brisk pace.

They said very little for the two hours until dusk obscured the path. The silence felt wrong—and when Rigg realized it was because in times past Kyokay had always been with them, keeping up a stream of chatter, it felt even more wrong.

At last, though, it was dark enough that while Rigg could still find his way among the paths, Umbo could not.

"It's dark," said Rigg. "Let's get some sleep."

"Where?" asked Umbo. "I can't sleep while I'm walking, and I don't see an inn or even a barn."

"You *can* sleep while walking," said Rigg, thinking back to all-night pursuits of fleeing animals. "Or something like sleep, and something like walking. You just aren't tired enough yet to fall asleep on your feet."

"And you've done that?"

"Yes," said Rigg. "Though it isn't very efficient, since you can't see your way and you fall down a lot."

"Which has nearly happened to me three times in the last five minutes."

"So we'll go off the road a few yards—far enough that anyone on the road will fail to see us."

Umbo nodded and then, because it was dark, added, "Good plan. Except the part about leaving the road and walking in the dark among the brambles."

"We're coming to a side road," said Rigg. He knew it was there because he could see the paths of quite a few recent travelers take a turn from the highway. Wherever they had gone, they all came back the same way and rejoined the road. He couldn't explain how he knew any of this without telling Umbo about his pathseeing, and so he made no explanation at all. Umbo must have thought Rigg was familiar with this area, since he didn't ask how Rigg knew they were coming to a path.

They walked only a dozen yards into the woods beside the road and found themselves standing before a very small temple — or a very substantial shrine. It had stone walls and a heavy flat wooden roof topped with living grass to keep it cool.

None of the paths that came here was much more than two hundred years old. This was a fairly recent shrine.

"The Wandering Saint," said Umbo.

"The what?" asked Rigg.

"We used to play the game — you'd be the Wandering Saint, or I would, or Kyokay, and the others would try to push him off the cliff, over the falls. You know."

But Rigg did not know what Umbo was talking about. It can't have been very important or surely Rigg would remember. And what a horrible game, anyway — to play at falling off the cliff! If that's how Umbo and Kyokay played when Rigg wasn't there, no wonder Kyokay thought it was all right to dance around on the edge of the falls.

Umbo stared intently at Rigg's face. "Are you insane?" asked Umbo. "It's our local saint."

"What's a saint?" asked Rigg. "You swore by one before — the same one? This wandering one?"

"A holy man," said Umbo impatiently. "A man some god has favored. Or at least some demon has been merciful to."

Gods and demons Rigg had heard about, but Father had no patience with such ideas. "There are some gods and some demons whose stories are based on real things that happened to real men," Father had taught him. "And some that are completely made up—to frighten children, or get them to obey, or to make people feel better when something goes terribly wrong in their lives."

Now a new category had been added: *saint*.

"So this saint isn't a god, he just has a friend who is."

"Or a demon who favors him. Like a pet. They go out hunting or whatever. Ordinary people just stay away from the gods and demons as best they can. It's the saints we talk to, since they're so thick with the powerful ones. But you know this, Rigg. You went to Hemopheron's lessons same as me."

Rigg knew Hemopheron, the schoolteacher for the boys whose parents could afford the tuition. Rigg had gone with Umbo now and then, but Father had ridiculed him for it, pointing out that if Hemopheron knew anything, he wouldn't be teaching in Fall Ford. "I'll teach you everything you need to know," Father had said. But he hadn't, after all. He had held back some of the most important bits. In fact, Rigg wondered if Father had mostly taught him things he *didn't* need.

"Come inside," said Umbo. "We can stay here—it's a sanctuary for travelers, all the shrines of the Wandering Saint are. The only curse on it comes if we desecrate the place."

"Desecrate?" asked Rigg.

"Poo or pee," said Umbo. "Inside it, I mean."

They were standing there in nearly complete darkness, just

a bit of starlight seeping in through the door. There were walls. There was a floor.

"Well," said Rigg, "I'd better go back out before I lie down on this very hard stone floor to sleep. In fact, since it isn't raining, I think I'll sleep outside."

"But . . ." Umbo began.

"You'll be fine inside, if that's where you want to be," said Rigg. "And I'm used to sleeping outside."

"You're rejecting the hospitality of the saint?"

"On the contrary," said Rigg. "I'm preserving the holiness. Of this place. Because I intend to poo and pee all night."

Umbo stayed inside when Rigg came out and found a place to empty his bladder. He didn't really need to do anything else, so he walked a quarter of the way around the shrine and found a place where, using his fingers, he could rake together a reasonably soft bed of soil and leaves.

But he couldn't get to sleep because this was all too strange. He had never come to this place, but since they rarely traveled on the North Road that was no surprise. This business of saints and gods and demons—Rigg did not remember ever playing such games as Umbo described. And gods and demons were things that people invoked without actually seeming to believe much in them. I mean, when you curse "by Silbom's left testicle" you can't be terribly worried that the god might take offense and come and punish you—and that had always been the favorite oath of the blacksmith.

Yet Umbo seemed absolutely certain that he and Rigg *had* played these games, and that everyone—including Rigg—knew about saints. How could such a thing be? How could two people who had played together quite a lot as children have such completely different memories, but in just one area?

Rigg heard Umbo come out of the shrine. "Rigg?" he called out.

"I'm over here," said Rigg. "You're welcome to sleep outside near me—it's a lot softer and it's not a cold night."

"No," said Umbo. "Where did you pee and all?"

"You don't have to use the same place."

"I want to *avoid* the place," said Umbo. "I don't want to step in anything."

"Oh—go away from the door to the left and you won't be anywhere near my personal mud."

Umbo gave a little hoot of laughter. "Personal mud."

"That's what . . ." but then Rigg didn't finish the sentence. That's what Father always called it. What would Umbo know—or care—about that?

Thinking about Father made Rigg sad all over again, and to keep himself from crying he shut his eyes and started working through some of the problems in topology that Father had been training him in. Visualizing a fractal landscape was always a surefire sleep inducer, Rigg had found—no matter how much you explored it, going in deeper or coming out to a wider view, there were always new forms to discover.

He woke up at the first light of dawn. He was a little stiff from the chill of the morning—it was cold, he could see his breath—but he had shaken out the kinks by the time he got back to his spot from the night before and added to the mud. Then he went across the clearing to the other side, where there was a burbling stream with clear water. He filled three smallish water bags—another habit he had learned from traveling with Father. "You never know when you might break a bone and have to go a long time before someone finds you."

"You'll find me, Father," Rigg had replied, but Father would not find him now. And the water would be for two travelers, not one.

Umbo hadn't stirred yet when Rigg got back to the shrine. Rigg got his little pack open and pulled out the food Nox had given him. Having accepted Umbo as a traveling companion, by the custom of the road the food belonged half to him. From his own half, then, Rigg ate only a little. He didn't want to have to stop and hunt very much, this close to Fall Ford; he'd let the food linger as long as he could before he worked the setting of traps into the nightly routine.

It was full light before Umbo came out of the shrine, groaning and walking like a cripple.

"Stone floor," said Rigg. "It'll do it every time."

"But it has walls," said Umbo.

"And a door that doesn't close."

"It doesn't have to close," said Umbo, "with the saint's protection."

"So what happens if robbers come and decide to kill everyone and take what they have? This withering saint appears and stands in the doorway and withers at them?"

"*Wand*ering Saint," said Umbo, looking pained.

"I know, I was joking," said Rigg.

"You shouldn't joke about sacred things," said Umbo.

"What's *happened* to you?" asked Rigg.

"I need to make mud — is that what you call it? That's what's about to happen to me."

Umbo went off for a while and then came back and said, "You have any food?"

"You didn't bring any?" asked Rigg, assuming that he hadn't.

"Just this sausage," said Umbo. "My sister hid it in my hat — she rushed after me and gave me my hat. I think Father hit her for the hat — for giving me anything at all. But he might have killed her for the sausage. Well, not killed, but you know."

"Share the sausage. Here's what Nox gave *me*. Halves on everything."

"I know the traveler rules," said Umbo.

"This is your half."

Umbo looked from half to half.

"It was even when I divided it," said Rigg.

"It's *still* even as far as I can tell. Haven't you eaten?"

"I've eaten as much as I want. I want this food to last."

"What good is it to make the food last? So the animals who find your starved corpse will have something delicious to eat and leave your flesh alone?"

"I had what I need," said Rigg. "We often go for a few days on short rations, just for practice. You get so you kind of like the feeling of being hungry."

"That is the sickest thing I've ever heard," said Umbo.

And then, once again, Umbo was caught up in sobs. Only for a moment — just four great heaves of his chest, a brief storm of tears. "By the Wandering Saint," said Umbo. "I just think of

Kyokay and there it is." He made some pretense at laughing. "It's going to be really embarrassing if I ever do this in front of somebody."

"What am I? A stump?" asked Rigg.

"I meant somebody who wouldn't understand. Somebody who wasn't there."

By that system of thought, Umbo could mourn for his brother all he wanted, but Rigg had better not shed tears for Father, since nobody else was there. But Rigg wasn't in the mood for a quarrel. They had a long way to walk today, and Umbo wasn't used to walking, and the last thing they needed was to be snippy with each other from the start.

"Eat," said Rigg. "Or smear the food into your hair, or whatever you intend to do, but let's get it done. The sun's up now, so we've already lost a half hour of traveling at least, and there'll be other people on the road before long."

"Oh, are we avoiding them?" asked Umbo.

"*I* am," said Rigg. "If they come from Fall Ford, anyway. Looking for me. Or you, for that matter. And strangers coming the other way—what are they going to think of boys traveling without adults with them? We have to be ready to dodge into the woods whenever anybody's coming. I don't want a lot of conversations with strangers out here."

"A lot of travelers come through Fall Ford," said Umbo. "They never harm anybody."

"In Fall Ford they're outnumbered. They might act very differently when they outnumber *us*."

"What are you scared of?"

"Well, let's see. Death first—that's a big one. And pain. And having somebody take away what pathetic few things I own." He didn't see any reason for Umbo to know about the jewels and the letter of credit. Travelers' law of sharing didn't extend to money or trade goods or other valuables.

"I've never even thought about that until . . ."

Rigg thought Umbo was going to cry again, but he didn't after all.

"Well, Umbo," said Rigg, "you've spent your whole life in a village. It's a lot safer there, unless somebody accuses you of murder and they work up a mob to come and kill you."

Umbo looked away—ashamed? angry?—so Rigg dropped the subject. Not a good topic for humor yet. Father would have understood that joking about the worst things is how you get them tame and under control.

"Look," said Rigg. "I've spent my life traveling. But in the wild, not on populated roads. Father and I always stepped out of the road when we were carrying pelts on our backs, because we don't have the agility to fight or even to run away, unless we drop the pelts, and then they can be stolen. So it's a habit, for safety. And I figured I don't know what kind of danger we're going to face on *this* road, but it can't hurt to stick to the same habit. If you want to travel with me, you're going to need to comply with that. All right?"

"You can hide, I'll stay in the road."

"That's what I said," Rigg said, letting himself sound a little annoyed. "If you stay in the road, and something bad happens to you, then if we're traveling together I'm honor bound to defend you. And the whole point of my leaving the road is to *avoid* having to defend anybody. So if you don't want to leave the road whenever I say, and hide as long as I say, then we aren't traveling together. We're each on our own. Is that how you want it?"

"Sure, no," said Umbo quickly. "I wasn't trying to cause trouble. I just ache all over and the idea of constantly getting off the road and hiding in the woods just doesn't sound very good to me. Besides, you move like a senoose, so quiet you could surprise a snake. I crash around like a drunken cow."

"I've never seen a drunken cow," said Rigg.

"Then you've never laughed," said Umbo. "Of course, if somebody catches you giving ale to a cow, they'll turn *you* into shoe leather."

"So you're done eating? We can go?"

"Yes," said Umbo. He picked up his few possessions and headed, not down the path toward the road, but straight toward the shrine entrance.

"Where are you going?"

"We're not going to set out on a journey without paying our respects to the Wandering Saint, are we? I thought that's why you picked this place to stay last night—for the sanctuary and for the blessing."

It wasn't worth arguing. Rigg followed Umbo inside.

A smoke hole had been left in the middle of the roof, and it allowed in enough daylight that now Rigg could see that the walls were painted. Not just decorations, like the ones the women wove into their cloth in Fall Ford, but actual figures of people.

He couldn't see all that clearly, but well enough to see that the same man—or at least a manlike thing with the same clothing—kept showing up in every wall section.

"It's the life of the Wandering Saint," said Umbo. "Since you seem never to have seen it or even heard of him before."

Rigg walked around, beholding the legends of the W.S., for Rigg was already thinking of him that way. He always made initials and acronyms out of phrases that he thought were getting too repetitive. "Personal mud" had long since become "p.m." in his mind.

Here the W.S. brought two lost children back to their joyful mother. On the next panel, he fought off a bear that was about to devour a poor family's milk ewe. All sorts of brave and good deeds.

When we were growing up, thought Rigg, we called these Hero Stories and *that's* what we acted out when we played. Kyokay always wanted to be the bear or the ruffian or the enemy troop, he never wanted to be the one that got rescued, even though he was the smallest. The gods didn't even come into it.

But he didn't want to talk about it with Umbo. It was too disturbing that their memories had grown so different.

"Come on," said Rigg. "What is it we have to do before we can leave?"

"Just this," said Umbo. "Look at the stories and remember the Wandering Saint."

"Then I'm done."

"Except that you started with the second panel," said Umbo. "You missed the whole beginning, which is when the Wandering

Saint first encountered his demon and gained the power to make it disappear. That's how he's able to do all these good things — he can command demons to disappear."

"Can?" asked Rigg. "He's still alive?"

Umbo laughed. "No, I don't think so. I mean, not in the body. Did you know that there are people who said your dad was the Wandering Saint?"

"No," said Rigg. "Nox said they called him 'Wandering Man,' sometimes, and *she* called him 'Good Teacher,' but nobody ever said 'Saint.'"

"They used to whisper it all the time," said Umbo. "Among other things. I guess they never talked like that in front of you."

"Nobody ever mentioned the . . ." He let his voice trail off before he could say something annoying, like "Nobody ever mentioned the stupid Whimpering Saint at all."

Instead of picking a quarrel, Rigg dutifully went to the first panel and saw at once that it was a depiction of the top of Stashi Falls, seen as if you were hovering in the air about three rods away from the face of the falls. A man was dangling from a single stone right at the lip of the falls, water spraying down (or so it seemed the painter wished to suggest) on both sides of him, while a fierce demon squatted on the stone and pried up on his fingers.

Then, still on the same picture of the falls but a little over to the right, there was the same man (by the costume anyway) dangling from the same rock, only instead of a demon there was a wad of something nondescript and the man now had two hands on the stone and was raising himself up.

"That was the miracle, see?" said Umbo. "You've really never heard of him? If you're just lying to make me tell this story I'll fart in your food, I swear it."

"What miracle?"

"The demon knocked him off the falls and the Wandering Saint barely caught himself by one hand on a dry rock. Then the demon smashed at his hand, and when the Saint grabbed onto the demon's arm, the demon pried up his fingers. A lot of people draw the Wandering Saint with two fingers of his right hand permanently bent up and away from the others, but that's just grotesque," said Umbo.

Rigg didn't really care about the fingers. Couldn't Umbo see that this was a picture of what happened yesterday on the cliff? But of course he couldn't. Umbo had seen only his brother Kyokay. He had never seen the man that Rigg fought with to try to get *through* him so he could reach Kyokay's hand to save him.

This is the man I fought. He was real—but he was from the past, and stayed in the past. He didn't die after I lost sight of him. When time sped back up and I stopped prying his fingers, he must have thought a miracle happened. And when he climbed up onto the stone—he must have been so strong!—there would have been no sign of me.

Except there was *something* on the rock. "What's this?" asked Rigg.

"Oh, that's not supposed to be there. That's really in the second story, but they just put it there to remind us of it so they could use the other panels for other tales. It's a fur."

"A fur?"

"When the Wandering Saint came down the Upsheer, he was cold and frightened, and he went to the great pool in the river where the cascade makes a mist, and caught among stones he found a fur, completely dressed out and ready for him to use it. It was from the demon, of course—the demon now recognized the Wandering Saint as a man of power, and so he gave him the fur as a tribute."

I dropped my furs in *this* time, not in that man's time, thought Rigg. But . . . maybe a fur got hung up on rocks for a brief while at the top of the falls, and maybe, just as time slowed down so I got shifted into the past where this man was, the last of my furs got swept right past the stone and . . .

He wanted to blurt out the truth to Umbo, but felt the long habit of silence about his abilities hold back his words. Father had forbidden him to tell anyone.

But Father had told Nox, hadn't he? Because he trusted her.

Well, I trust Umbo. Or at least I want to. And if I'm traveling with him, how can I hide what I do with paths? Do I have to pretend that I don't know where roads lead, or when someone is approaching, or where someone has laid an ambush? Maybe Umbo isn't trustworthy. But if he is, this journey will be a lot better for not having to hide what I can do.

"Umbo," said Rigg. "I'm the demon."

Umbo looked at him with a little anger showing. "That's not even close to being funny."

"Come on, didn't you say we used to *play* at being the W.S.?"

"The what?"

"The Wandering Saint."

"How are we going to get the blessing if you ridicule this place, and him, and all he did for travelers?"

Now Rigg began to see why Father had warned him never to come up against a man's religion. "Nothing makes people angrier than finding out somebody thinks they're wrong about how the universe works." It had been a mistake to try to tell Umbo anything. "Sorry," said Rigg.

"No you're not," said Umbo. "You weren't even joking. Do you really think that you're a demon?"

"I'm thirteen years old, and I'm just ordinary." Then Rigg walked out of the shrine, to show that he thought the discussion was over. If Umbo refused to drop the matter, then this idea of traveling together wasn't going to work.

Umbo stayed inside the shrine for a while, then came out, acting a little huffish as he gathered up his few things. Clearly he was ready to go, and was marking time until he could say what he needed to say.

Rigg was about to tell him that it was all right, Umbo could go back home and Rigg would continue his journey alone. But Umbo spoke first. "You're not ordinary."

"Is that good or bad?" asked Rigg.

"I'm sorry I got so angry. I've just never—nobody ever says a bad thing about the Wandering Saint. And nobody calls him the 'W.S.'"

Rigg wasn't going to play this game—the apology that was really just a continuation of the argument.

"Believe what you want," said Rigg.

"I was thinking I should leave you. Go back home before you bring down a curse on us."

Oh, so the W.S. has the evil eye now, thought Rigg. But he didn't say anything.

"I don't know if it's safe to travel with you if you're going to mock him like that," said Umbo, and he sounded afraid as well as angry. "But then I remembered how your father talked about saints and demons, back when he was teaching me . . . things. So you were only talking like your dad."

Rigg remembered now that Father *had* taken Umbo out on walks in the woods or through the fields. Not recently, but when they were both about eight or nine. And Father was *teaching* him?

"For what it's worth, I wasn't mocking," said Rigg, "I was *realizing* something."

"That you're a demon?" said Umbo scornfully. "I know you're not."

"No, I realized that the demon in the Wandering Saint story wasn't a demon at all," said Rigg. "So I'm not a demon, but I'm the person who did the things that the demon in the story supposedly did—and before you start getting mad at me again, *you* watched me do it."

"The Wandering Saint was hundreds of years ago," said Umbo. He was barely containing his impatience.

"I'm not lying, and I'm not joking," said Rigg. "When I was trying to save your brother, the reason I couldn't do it was because this *man* appeared. I was jumping to try to get to your brother, and suddenly there he was." There was no reason to complicate things by trying to explain about the paths and how for the first time ever they turned into people. "I fell into him and it knocked him into the water."

"I didn't see anything like that."

"I know you didn't," said Rigg. "I'm not saying you saw *him—he* was in the past. I'm saying you saw *me* do the things the demon does in that story."

"So he's there hundreds of years ago, and you're there a couple of days ago, and you bump into him and knock him into the water?"

"Exactly," said Rigg, ignoring the tone of mockery in Umbo's voice. "The water swept him over the edge, but he caught himself on the very same rock where Kyokay was hanging on. Kyokay in the present, and him in the past, and they overlapped. His hand was completely covering Kyokay's hand."

Umbo rolled his eyes and jammed his hat on his head, sausage and all.

"Why not wait to make up your mind until you hear me out?" said Rigg. "Even if you don't believe me, *I* know it happened, and if you believe in saints and demons and curses, which I think are impossible, why not *consider* the possibility that I saw and touched a man from the past at the same time I was trying to get past the man so I could grab your brother's arm?"

"'Consider the possibility,'" Umbo echoed. "You really do sound like your father."

"And was my father stupid or a liar, so that you have to reject anybody who sounds like him?"

Umbo's face suddenly changed. "No," he said. "Your father wasn't stupid. Or a liar." He looked thoughtful.

"So I had to get past this man's hand so I could save Kyokay. I pounded on his hand. Then he grabs my other arm and I can see he's going to pull me over—I mean, he outweighed me by about twice, it's not like he could have held on to *me* and dragged himself up on the rock. So I pried up his fingers. Two fingers. So he'd let go of me."

"I knew I saw you trying to pry up Kyokay's hand!" said Umbo, angry again.

"You did not!" cried Rigg. "You saw me making a prying motion but you never saw me holding on to Kyokay's fingers because I never touched him. I couldn't! The W.S. was in the way! It was his fingers I was prying—fingers that you couldn't see because he was still trapped back there in the past."

"You just don't know when to stop, do you," said Umbo.

"I'm telling the truth," said Rigg. "Believe what you want to."

"The W.S.—the *Wandering Saint* was three hundred years ago!" Umbo shouted at him.

"Father warned me not to tell anybody anything about what I do," said Rigg. "And now I see why. Go home. I'm done with you."

"No!" shouted Umbo. "Don't do this!"

Rigg forced himself to calm down. "I'm not doing anything," he said. "I told you a true story, you think I'm lying, and I don't see how we can travel together after that."

"What you said about your father," said Umbo. "Warning you not to tell people about what you *do*."

"Right, well, I don't *do* anything."

"Yes you do, and you have to tell me."

"I don't tell things to people who believe I'm a liar," said Rigg. "It's a waste of breath."

"I'll listen, I swear I will," said Umbo.

Rigg couldn't understand why Umbo had suddenly changed— why he was now so eager to hear. But Umbo seemed sincere. Almost pleading.

He could almost hear Father saying, "You don't have to answer someone just because he asks you a question." And so Rigg replied as Father had taught him to—with another question. "Why do you want me to tell you?"

"Because maybe you're not the only one with a secret your father said never to tell anybody," said Umbo softly.

"So are you going to tell me yours?" asked Rigg.

"Yes," said Umbo.

Rigg waited.

"You first," said Umbo, even more softly. Like he was suddenly very shy. Like Rigg was dangerous and Umbo didn't want to offend him.

But Father had known a secret of Umbo's, one that he had never told to Rigg. So maybe that meant Father would approve of Rigg trusting Umbo.

"I see paths," said Rigg. "I see them wherever any person or animal has ever gone. And that's not really it, either. I don't *see* them, not with my eyes, I just know where they are. They can be on the other side of a bunch of trees or behind a hill or inside the walls of a house, and I can close my eyes and the paths are still there."

"Like . . . a map?"

"No. Like . . . streams of dust, strings of dust, cobwebs in the air. Some of them are new, and some old. Human paths are different from animal paths, and there are colors, or something like colors, depending on how old they are. But it means that I can see the whole history of a place, every path that a person has ever walked. I know it sounds crazy, or like magic, but Father said it had a perfectly rational explanation, only he would never tell me what such an explanation might be."

Umbo's eyes were wide, but he said nothing. No mockery now, no accusations.

"Up there at the top of Stashi falls, just as I was trying to get to your brother, everything changed. All of a sudden it was like the paths *slowed down*. I hadn't ever realized they were moving, but when they slowed down I could see that the paths were not something the people left behind as they passed—they *were* the people, and I was seeing into the past. Only everything had always moved so fast that I didn't realize it."

"Everything slowed down," said Umbo.

"Or my mind sped up," said Rigg. "Either way, the paths became people doing the same motions, over and over. Except when I looked at one of them, concentrated on him—then he did it just the once. I figured he wasn't real. Just a vision of the past, like the paths I see. I walk right through them all the time. So I lunged at the stone—and I hit him and knocked him off. He wasn't a dream after all, he was solid and real. Solid enough that I could knock him down, pound his hand, pry up his fingers. I didn't know how to get rid of him. And Kyokay died while I was trying."

Umbo sank to the ground. "Do you know why time slowed down? Why the paths turned into people? Into the Wandering Saint?"

Rigg shook his head, but even though he didn't have an explanation, Umbo seemed to believe him now.

"I did it," Umbo said. "You might have saved Kyokay, except time slowed down and that's why the Wandering Saint appeared." His face twisted with anguish. "I couldn't see him. How could I know that I was making him appear?"

Now Rigg understood why Umbo had started to believe him. Umbo's secret, the one that Father had told him never to tell, was a strange gift of his own. "You had something to do with that slowing down of time."

"Your father noticed me doing it," said Umbo. "When I was little. That's why he came to the shop so often. He talked to me about what I could do. It used to be I could only slow down time around myself—you know, when I wanted to keep playing for a while longer. I guess what I was really doing was slowing down time for everybody else, or speeding it up for me, but I was little, and what I saw was that everybody else started moving really slowly and I had time to do whatever I wanted to do. It could only last a few minutes, but your father knew what I was doing somehow, and he gave me exercises to do so I could learn how to control it. So I could slow time down exactly where I wanted it to slow, and nowhere else. When I was running up Cliff Road and I was out of breath and exhausted and I caught a glimpse of Kyokay falling, I . . . slowed him down. I mean, I practically stopped him."

"Father never said anything about you," said Rigg. "I mean, about you having a . . . thing like that."

"He was a man who could keep a secret, wasn't he?"

Like never mentioning that Rigg's mother wasn't even dead—yes, he could keep a secret all right.

"But this explains it," said Rigg. "Why I don't remember anything about this W.S. I mean, I don't understand it, but it at least makes some kind of weird sense. I was the one who was *in* the story. Until you slowed time and I knocked the man off the rock, he probably never fell at all. But once it happened, then the past changed for everybody else. Now everybody knew the stories of the W.S.—except me. Because I was the one who was there with him, and I *did* it. So my past wasn't changed. I don't remember it, because to me it didn't happen until yesterday."

"Excuse me while I stab myself in the eye with a stick," said Umbo. "None of this makes any sense. I mean, I was there, too."

"But you didn't slow down time for yourself," said Rigg. "You didn't touch the man, and I did. Why else does this shrine exist to honor a man I never heard of, only you say everybody knows about the Wandering Saint *and his story*. But *I* remember *doing* everything the demon supposedly did. So because I was the one who made the change, I can still remember how it *used* to be, and everyone else remembers how it *is now*."

"Rigg," said Umbo, "I don't know why I decided to ask you to let me travel with you. Talk about this all you want, but I did not need to find out that I caused Kyokay's death by stopping time. Do you get that? That's the *only* change I care about!"

"I know," said Rigg. "Me too." But as soon as he said it, he knew it wasn't true. Somehow the combination of their gifts had changed the world. Because they were ignorant of what was going on, it had prevented him from saving Kyokay. But the solution to ignorance was obvious. They had to do it again so they could figure out how it worked.

Rigg took Umbo by the arm and started leading him — no, almost dragging him — toward the road.

"By the Wanderi—" Umbo began. "What are you doing?"

"We're going to the road. The Great North Road. The place is thick with paths. Every one of them is a person. It isn't just a few like right there at the edge of the cliff. It's hundreds of them, thousands if we go back far enough. I want you to slow down time so I can see them. I'm going to prove to you that I'm not making any of this up."

"What are you going to do?"

"See whether we can do this thing on purpose." When they got to the highway, Rigg walked out into the middle of the road. "Do you see anybody?"

"Just a crazy guy named Rigg."

"Slow down time. Do it — for me, right here. Slow it down."

"Are you insane?" asked Umbo. "I mean, I know you're insane, one way or another. Because if people become solid when I slow down time, you're going to get trampled to death by ten thousand travelers."

"I think the only one who gets solid is the one I'm concentrating on," said Rigg. "Slow me down."

"So you turn people solid just by concentrating on them?"

"While you're slowing them down, yes," said Rigg. "Or at

least I think that's how it worked. Here, I'll leave the food by the side of the road, so if I do get trampled, you can have all of it."

"Wow, thanks," said Umbo. "Dead friend, free lunch."

"Are we still friends?" asked Rigg. "Even though we remember the past so differently? I never played Wandering Saint with you—we played hero games, that's what I remember. But at least we both remember playing *something* together, right? That means we're still friends."

"Yes," said Umbo. "That's why I'm here with you, fungushead, because I'm your friend and you're my friend and by the way, I have very *clear* memories of your playing Wandering Saint with me and Kyokay because you did all these death scenes of the bear and the wolf and everybody the Wandering Saint defeated. That happened. So there is some version of your life where you lived in a world where the Wandering Saint was respected by everybody."

"You're right, this is complicated," said Rigg. "It's like there are two versions of me, only I'm the wrong one—I'm here in the world with a W.S., even though I never lived in it, and the me who *did* live in it, he's gone."

"Like the *me*," said Umbo, "who lived in the world with your hero games, whatever they are."

"Slow down time for me," said Rigg. "Let's just do it and see."

"Kyokay got killed by doing crazy stuff on an impulse. Think this through, Rigg. Don't stand in the middle of the road. Come to the edge. There have to be fewer people here at the edge."

"Right," said Rigg. "That's good, that's right." He walked out of the middle of the road and then looked back at Umbo. "Now."

"Not while you're looking at me," said Umbo.

"Why not? What happens, your pants fall down?"

"You weren't looking at me when I did it up on the cliff," said Umbo. "And shouldn't you be watching the road so that nobody bumps into you?"

"Umbo, I can't look both ways at once. No matter where I look, somebody's going to be coming up behind me and walking right through me."

"You're going to die."

"Maybe," said Rigg. "And maybe my body will just disappear in our time here and I'll show up as a mysterious corpse in the past. Maybe I'll be the Magical Dead Kid and they'll build a little temple for me."

"I really hate you," said Umbo. "I always have."

"Slow down time for me," said Rigg.

And, just like that, with Umbo glaring at him, it started to happen. Umbo hadn't waved his hands or muttered something like the magicians did when traveling players came to town.

Rigg deliberately kept his eyes out of focus—it was pretty easy, considering what came into view when time slowed. The middle of the road was so full of blur that Rigg was grateful he had moved to the edge. Because here the blurs became more individual, he could see people's faces. Just glimpses as they blurred past, but he finally picked one man and watched how he hurried, looking neither left nor right. He seemed to be a man of authority by his attitude, and he was dressed opulently, but in an outlandish costume whose like Rigg had never seen before.

At his hip, his belt held a scabbard with a sword in it. On

the other side, the side nearer to Rigg, a sheathed knife had been thrust into his belt.

Rigg fell into step beside him, reached down, snatched the knife and drew it out. The man saw him, reached out immediately to grab him or take back the knife—but Rigg merely looked away and focused on somebody else, a woman, and at the same time he called out to Umbo, "Bring me back!"

Just like that, all the blur people became mere paths of light, and Rigg and Umbo were alone on the road.

Rigg was still holding the knife.

Now he could see that it was quite a lavish thing. Fine workmanship in the metal of the hilt, with jewels set in it that seemed the equal in quality of any of those Father had left for him, though they were smaller. And the thing was sharp-looking; it felt wicked and well-balanced in his hand.

It had been in the past, and Rigg had brought it into the present.

"That knife," said Umbo, staring at it with awe. "It just—you just reached out and suddenly it was there."

"Yes, and when the owner of it tried to take it back, to him it must have seemed that suddenly I was *not* there. Just like the demon."

Umbo sat down in the grass beside the road. "The Wandering Saint story—it really happened—but it wasn't a demon."

And then Rigg had a sudden thought, and just like that, *he* burst into tears, nearly the way Umbo had. "By Silbom's right ear," he said, when he could speak. "If I had just been able to take my mind off him, the W.S. would have disappeared and I could have saved Kyokay."

They wept together then, sitting by the side of the road, realizing that if either one had understood at all what their gifts were doing, Kyokay might still be alive.

Or, just as likely, Kyokay would have fallen anyway, dragging Rigg with him. Who knew whether Rigg could really have drawn him up onto the rock? Who knew whether they both could have hopped from rock to rock and made it to safety even if Rigg had dragged the younger boy back up?

The weeping stopped. They sat in silence for a while. Then Umbo said a really foul word and picked up a rock and threw it out into the road. "There was no demon. There was just us. You and me, our powers working together. We were the demon."

"Maybe that's all the demons ever are. People like us, doing things without even knowing what we're doing."

"That temple back there," said Umbo. "It's a temple to *us*. The Wandering Saint was just an ordinary guy like the one you took the knife from."

"He was actually pretty extraordinary."

"Shut up, Rigg. Do we always have to have a joke?"

"Well, *I* do," said Rigg.

"So let's fix it," said Umbo. "Let's go back to before your father got killed, and stop him and tell him what happened and then he won't have a tree fall on him and you won't be out on the rocks upstream from the falls just when Kyokay—"

"Two reasons why that's a really bad idea," said Rigg. "First, if I'm not there, Kyokay falls. Second, you can't watch him more closely because *I'm* the one who experiences the time change, not you, so you won't know anything about what's going to happen, you'll just keep doing the same thing. Third, we can't go back and talk to Father. Or shove him out of his path. Ever."

"Why not?"

"Because Father doesn't have a path. He's the only person— he's the only *living thing*—that I've ever known that didn't have a path of any kind."

"Are you sure?"

"After ten years of seeing and watching and studying paths, you think I might be wrong when I say that the one person I was close to all the time had no path?"

"Why didn't he?"

"I don't know," said Rigg. "But I think you and I can both agree that Father was a really unusual man."

"Why do we have these abilities if we can't go back and save Kyokay?" demanded Umbo.

"Are you asking an invisible saint or a god or something? Because I don't know. Maybe we *can* save him—that time. But how do we know he doesn't just get himself killed the next day doing some other stupid thing?"

"Because I'd watch him," said Umbo.

"You already watched him," said Rigg. "He couldn't be controlled. And meanwhile, we might change a thousand other things that we don't want to change."

"So our gifts are completely useless," said Umbo.

"We have this knife," said Rigg.

"*You* have a knife," said Umbo.

"At least you're not suddenly remembering a whole bunch

of stories about men who appear out of nowhere and steal fancy knives and then disappear," said Rigg.

"If Kyokay stays dead, then all of this is useless."

"All of *this*," said Rigg, "us being together, talking, finding out what we can do together—all of this happened because Kyokay went up on the falls and I tried to save him, and failed. So if we save Kyokay, does that make it so none of this happens? Then how would we go back to save Kyokay?"

"You already proved that you can change the past!" said Umbo.

"But I never did anything that mattered," said Rigg. "Or at least I wasn't able to accomplish anything I *wanted* to."

Umbo reached out his hand for the knife. Rigg handed it to him at once. Umbo pulled it out of the sheath and pressed the point of it against a spot on the heel of his hand. It punched in almost at once, and blood welled up around the blade.

Rigg snatched the knife back. Umbo stared at his palm, making no effort to stanch the bleeding. Rigg wiped the blood off the blade with a handful of dewy grass, but he didn't say anything to Umbo. Whatever crazy thing Umbo was doing, he'd explain it when he felt like it.

"Now the past is real," said Umbo softly. "I've been wounded by it." Then he, too, tore up a wad of damp grass and pressed it to the wound in his palm. "That stings like a hornet," he said.

"I guess now you know why your mother taught you never to poke yourself with a knife."

"She's a smart one, my mom," said Umbo. "Even if she did marry some angry idiot of a cobbler."

"I hate the way you make a joke out of everything," said Rigg.

"At least mine wasn't funny," said Umbo.

They picked up their things. Rigg dried off the clean blade on his shirt, and slid it into the sheath. Then he tucked the knife he had stolen about two thousand years ago into his belt, and they set off down the Great North Road toward Aressa Sessamo.

CHAPTER 5

Riverside Tavern

"Has anything happened yet because I made the decision to go ahead with the fold?" asked Ram.

"Yes," said the expendable. "You remained in command of the ship."

Ram was a little irritated to learn that the decision had been a test of him rather than a real decision. "So you were going ahead no matter what I decided?"

"Yes," said the expendable. "It's in our mission program. You never had a choice about that."

"Then what am I here for?" asked Ram.

"To make all the decisions after the fold. Nothing is known about what happens after we jump. If you had proven yourself timid before the jump, you would be regarded as unfit to make decisions afterward."

"So if I was too timid, I would have been replaced. By you?"

"By the next crew member we awakened and tested. Or the one after that."

"So when does the real jump happen?"

"In a week or so. If we don't blow up before then. Spacetime is being very naughty right now."

"And nothing I might do can stop it?"

"That's right, Ram."

"And what if none of the crew turned out to be capable of making a decision that would satisfy your criteria?"

"Then we would command ourselves until we got to the target planet."

"'We' . . . meaning the expendables?"

"We the ship. All the computers together."

"But the ship's computers don't agree on anything."

"That's one of the many reasons we were all hoping you'd do the right thing."

Ram hadn't missed the one bit of information the expendable had given him. There was zero chance that it had been an inadvertent slip. "What do you mean, spacetime is being naughty?"

"We keep generating fields and forces, and things change. They just don't change the way anyone predicted."

"And when was I going to be told that?"

"When you asked."

"What else should I ask in order to find out what's going on?"

"Whatever you're curious about."

"I want to know what spacetime is doing."

"It's stuttering, Ram."

"What does *that* mean?" asked Ram.

"There seems to be a quantum system of timeflow that has never been seen or suspected before."

"Meaning that instead of a continuous slide into the fold, we're finding that spacetime reforms itself in a series of discrete steps?"

"It's going to be a bumpy ride, Ram."

.   .   .

After three weeks on the road, Rigg and Umbo had long since exhausted the food they brought with them, and hunting for small game was taking more and more of their days. Just because Rigg could see the paths of the animals didn't mean that setting traps would catch them. In this part of the world, the animals were far more wary of humans than they had been up in the wild highlands of the south.

So they were hungry as Rigg led the way to the public house that filled the five or six rods of land between the river and the road.

"This doesn't look like much of a place," said Umbo doubtfully.

"It's all we can afford," said Rigg. "If we can afford it."

"It isn't much of a town, either," Umbo added.

Rigg looked around him. The buildings were all fairly new, and had the look of shabby construction. A thrown-together kind of town. But from the paths weaving through the area, Rigg could tell that it already had a lot of people. "You could drop Fall Ford into the middle of it and nobody could tell."

"Well, my standard of a good-sized town has changed a little over the past three weeks."

"And my standard of a good-sized *meal* has changed, too," said Rigg. "If I set traps we might have some squirrel or rabbit by morning, or we might not. They've got food in there right now."

By now they stood outside the door of the tavern. A couple of burly rivermen brushed them aside as they went in. "Out of the way, privicks." Rigg had heard that term more than once, as they passed through towns they couldn't avoid. At first the word had been whispered, but lately it was openly used to insult or diminish them. It might have been more effective if Rigg had had the slightest idea what it meant.

"So let's go in and see if we can afford the food at this public house," said Umbo. "Or stomach it."

A riverman came lurching out of the tavern, cursing over his shoulder at someone inside. He took a swipe at Rigg, who was inadvertently blocking his way. Rigg dodged aside, but fell, and several men standing not far off laughed at him.

"Privick's got himself covered in mud!"

"Trying to plant himself to see if he'll grow."

"Hey, privick, better go wash yourself!"

"Privicks don't know about washing."

"Then let's duck him in the river and show him how it's done!"

Umbo helped Rigg rebound to his feet, and they dodged inside the door. Rigg had no idea whether the rivermen really meant to do anything to him, but he didn't want to stay and see. They were all big men. Even the shortest of them had massive arms and barrel chests from poling and rowing up the river. Rigg knew how to defend himself, even without weapons—Father had seen to that—but only one at a time, and he knew that if they took it into their minds to hurt him, he couldn't stop them. That knowledge put a cold knot of fear in his belly, and it didn't go away just because a door closed between them.

The tavern was dark inside—the shutters were nearly closed against the cold outside, but no lanterns had yet been lighted. A dozen men looked up at them, while two dozen more kept their eyes on their mugs, their bowls, or their cards and dice.

Rigg walked to the bar, where the taverner—who looked to be at least as large as the largest of his customers—was setting out a half dozen bowls of a thick stew that made Rigg almost faint with hunger, though it had only been two days since he last ate. But the hunger didn't drown out the fear that had begun outside and got worse in here.

"We serve men here, not boys," said the taverner, sounding more bored than hostile.

"We've been walking three weeks down the road from the south," Rigg began.

The taverner chortled. "You have 'upriver' writ all over you, no need to tell a soul."

"We need a meal," said Rigg. "If you won't serve us here, then maybe you could tell us where we could buy bread and cheese for the road."

"Boys *nor* beggars," said the taverner. "I don't get up in the morning wishing to see much of either."

"We're not beggars. We've got enough coin, if your price is fair."

"I'm surprised privicks even know what money is," said the taverner, "let alone what 'enough' might be."

Umbo usually kept still when they had to talk to people, since Rigg could put on a higher dialect than the one they spoke here, and nobody had to ask Rigg to repeat himself. But Umbo spoke up now, sounding a little annoyed. "What's this 'privick' they call us?"

"It's just an old word," said the taverner. "It means 'upriver folk.'"

Umbo sniffed. "That's all? Because it sounds like an insult."

"Well," said the taverner, "privicks aren't too famous for being smart or talking well or dressing like decent folks, so there might be a bit of contempt in it sometimes."

"We're decent enough not to pee in the river for downstream folk to drink," said Umbo, "and we don't have no insult for travelers from the north."

"Why would you?" said the taverner. "Now, are you going to show me your money or am I going to throw you out?"

Again, the knowledge that this man could force Rigg to do whatever he wanted filled him with dread. Instead of feeling in his purse for a single jackface, Rigg filled his hand with all the coins from the moneypurse tucked into the waistband of his trousers, meaning to look through them quickly to find the one he wanted. The taverner reached out at the moment Rigg was opening his fist to show the money, and their hands collided. All the coins were jostled out of Rigg's hand and hit the counter. They sounded so loud in the quiet room. There were too many of them.

The taverner's eyes grew narrow and he looked out into the room. Rigg didn't turn around. He already knew that all eyes were on him, that everyone in the room had mentally counted the money. If only he had not let fear make him hurry; if only he had taken the time to feel for the single coin with the money still in his purse. Now he felt panic surge through him, knowing he had already done something stupid, and chance had made it worse.

Rigg could hear his father's voice saying, "Don't let the other man control what you do." And, "Show little, say less." Well, he hoped he was keeping his fear well-hidden. But he couldn't think of anything to do, not before the taverner flung out his hand, scooped the coins to the edge of the bar, and dropped them into his other hand. Then he walked to the end of the bar, where he opened a door.

"Follow me," said the taverner.

Rigg wasn't sure whether he meant for them to clamber over the bar and go through the same door, or find another way. Before he could decide, a door on their side of the bar opened and the taverner beckoned. He led them to a tiny room with nothing but a table and two chairs in it, and some books and papers on the table.

The taverner poured their coins out of his hand onto the table. "You bring whole new worlds of meaning to the word 'stupid,'" he said wearily.

"It was you knocking into my hand that spilled the coins," said Rigg.

The taverner dismissed his words with a wave of his hand. "Who did you rob and why do you think I won't turn you in?"

Don't let the other fellow control what you do—it might be too late, but he could obey it now. So instead of defending himself against the charge of thievery, Rigg moved the conversation back to his real business here. "So it's enough money to buy a meal and lodgings."

"Of course it is, are you mad?"

"Seven rivers have joined the Stashik since we left Fall Ford," said Rigg. "It's so wide now we can hardly see the other side sometimes, and it seems like the price of everything gets bigger right along with the river. Last town where we ate, a baker charged us a jackface for a small loaf of stale bread, and he wanted two kingfaces for a night's lodging."

The taverner shook his head. "You were cheated, that's all. And who wants to stay in some tiny fleabitten room in a baker's house? You pay me *one* fen and you can stay two nights, or stay one night and I give you five shebs in change."

Rigg touched the coins in turn. "You call this a 'fen'? And this is a 'sheb'?" Rigg knew the names of all the coins—including denominations so large that Father said they never actually minted the coins—but it had never occurred to him that the same money might be called by different names just because he had walked a few weeks on the Great North Highway.

"Why, what do *you* call them?" asked the taverner.

"'Kingface' and 'queenface,' but we stopped calling them anything when people laughed at us."

"I'm surprised you're still alive to tell the tale," said the taverner, "the way you spread that money out for all to see."

"You knocked it out of my hand," said Rigg. "I thought you did it on purpose."

The taverner covered his eyes. "It never occurred to me you'd bring up more than one coin out of your purse." He put his hand atop Rigg's head and turned his face so they were eye to eye. "Listen, boy, maybe nobody killed you back south, but you're

108

right aside the river here, and this is a river tavern, and these are rough men who wouldn't think nothing of tipping you into the river to take a pair of shebs out of your pocket, never mind a fen. And they'd do it for a ping if you riled them somehow. Now every man in that room knows you have a lot of money and very little brain."

"None of them could see," said Umbo stubbornly.

"You think they're deaf? Every man of them could name all the coins you dropped by the sound alone."

Rigg understood now, well enough. Rules were different here. In Fall Ford a man's money was safe in his pocket or in his palm, because no one would think to take it. But that was because everybody already knew how much money everybody else was likely to have, and if somebody popped up with more of it after somebody else got robbed, it wouldn't take much of a guess to solve the crime. Here, though, in towns like this, the citizens couldn't know but a tiny number of their fellows, and the rivermen came and went so that nobody knew anybody. Not known means not caught, if they weren't taken in the moment of the crime, because the rivermen could be many leagues away by morning—or merely asleep on their boat, and their fellows reluctant to admit it or let a stranger go on board to search.

Father had warned Rigg how the rules changed when you traveled far, and he always warned that the bigger the city, the lower the level of civilization, which had seemed to make no sense to Rigg until now. Because the rules of civilization might be obeyed by however so many people you choose, it only took a few who despised those rules and you'd be in danger. "The worst of predators is man," Father had said, "because he kills what he does not need."

"Like us," Rigg had said. "We leave the meat behind, most of the time."

"The meat feeds the forest scavengers," Father had answered, "and we need the pelts."

"I'm just agreeing with you. We kill like men," Rigg had said, and Father had replied in a surly voice, "Speak for yourself, boy."

Now Rigg was seeing it for himself. "Seems to me," said Rigg, "the baker who cheated us harmed us more than anyone here."

"That's because you haven't left my tavern yet. They wouldn't dare attack you in here, but I can promise you'll have many companions joining up with you the moment you leave the place, and you'll be lucky if they only turn you upside down to shake out the coins and leave you with your skin and bones unbroken."

"How does anyone get through here alive?" murmured Umbo.

The taverner turned sharply, his hand flashed out, and this time his hand was not so gentle resting on a boy's head. "To get through here safe, two boys wouldn't be traveling alone—they'd have adults with them. They wouldn't be barefoot, and dressed in oafish privick homespun. They wouldn't come any nearer the river than the road out there, and that in daylight only. They'd never enter a riverside tavern. They'd never spread coins across the bar or take out more than was needful. And if they break all these rules, they *still* survive if they happen to run into me on a day when I feel particularly magnanimous. Now, the supper rush is about to begin, and then it's a night of drinking and whoring for rough men whose money I mean to have, with a minimum of breakage. You're going to stay in this room."

"In here?" asked Rigg. "What do we do in here?"

"One of you lies on the table, the other underneath it, and you sleep if you can, but you don't sing, you don't talk loudly, you don't show your face at the window, and you don't—"

"What window?" asked Umbo.

"If you can't find the window, I guess you can't show your face at it, so you'll actually obey me," said the taverner. "The last thing is, when I lock the door from the outside, you don't panic, you don't start thinking I'm making you my prisoner, you don't scream for help, and you don't try to escape."

"Isn't that exactly what you'd say if you *were* holding us for ransom?"

"Yes," said the taverner. "But who'd pay?" He walked to the door, closed it behind him, and they heard the chunk of the lock as he turned the key.

Immediately Rigg was on his feet, scanning high along the walls.

"Looking for the window?" asked Umbo.

"Found it," said Rigg. He pointed up, high on the wall above the door. It might be facing toward the inside of the tavern, but what was coming through the slats of an old shutterblind was daylight.

"How did you know it wasn't on the outside wall?" asked Umbo.

"I can see the paths of the builders. Few others have climbed that high on the walls, but now and then someone does, and that's where they went."

"It occurs to me," said Umbo, "that your little talent with pathfinding only works to see what people *did*, not to help us with what they're about to *do*."

"True enough," said Rigg. "But what's your little talent good for, either, when it comes to defending ourselves?"

"I slow down time," said Umbo.

"I wish," said Rigg. "*That* would be useful."

"I think I know what I do!" said Umbo.

"I've been thinking about it," said Rigg. "You weren't slowing down time for me—I walked at the same speed as the man I saw."

"And picked his pocket—"

"Do you want me to find him and put it back?"

"If I don't slow down time, what is it I'm doing when I make it so you can see paths turn into people?"

"You speed up my mind."

Umbo threw his hands in the air and sat down. "Speed you up, slow down time, it's the same thing. I already said so from the start."

"You've lived with it all your life, Umbo, you decided what you thought it was when you were little, and you've never had a need to change your mind. But think about it. When you slowed me down, and I walked along with other people, what did it look like to you? You could still see me, couldn't you?"

"Yes."

"Did I walk slower? Or faster?"

Umbo shrugged off the proof. "Then what *am* I doing? Because I'm sure doing something if you can see people that you never ever saw before I did it."

"You're speeding up my *brain*. The speed at which I see things, and notice them, and think about them. All those people who left those paths behind them, they're always there, but only when my *brain* starts seeing and thinking faster can I actually see them. And only when I really concentrate on one person can I *touch* him and take things from him and pry up his miserable fingers to try to get to Kyokay." Saying that, Rigg felt the grief of it rise inside him again, and he stopped talking.

Umbo closed his eyes and thought for a while. Finally: "So I make you smarter?"

"I wish," said Rigg. "But I can see things that I couldn't see before, and touch things I couldn't touch."

Umbo nodded. "I always thought of it as slowing down time, because when I first started doing it around other people, they'd say things like, 'Everything slowed down' or 'the whole world started going slower.' They didn't know I was doing it, they thought it was something that just . . . happened. And that's how it seemed to *me*, too. And then your father heard my mother talking about a time like that, and he looked at me and somehow he knew that I had done it. That's when he took me aside and started helping me learn how to control it. To be able to affect only one person. Myself or somebody else. Whoever I chose."

"At the falls, you were aiming at Kyokay, and you got me, too, by accident."

"I didn't say I got to be *perfect* at it. You and Kyokay were kind of far, and I was climbing up the cliff, and I couldn't even see you most of the time." Umbo leaned his elbows on the table and hid his face in his hands. "But what good is it, anyway, whatever it is we do. If you can only see the past and I can only make other people think faster, then what can we even do with it?"

"I got a knife."

"A nice sharp one," said Umbo, holding up the palm he had cut with it, now mostly healed, though the scar was red. "Can you fight one of these rivermen with it? What about three of them?"

"If you really *could* speed me up," said Rigg, "I could run around so fast they wouldn't see me, and I could kill six of them before they knew what was happening."

"Wouldn't that be nice," said Umbo. "Meanwhile, they're beating *me* up because I'm just sitting there, so as soon as one of them hits me, I stop speeding you up, so then they catch *you*."

"Well, it's a good thing we *can't* do it, then, isn't it?"

Through the walls Rigg could hear the noise from the common room of the tavern. Nothing angry-sounding, but lots of talking. Shouting, really. When he could make out words, they were cheerful enough. Even horrible curses sounded like joking between friends.

"Wouldn't it be nice if he brought us food?" said Umbo.

"Suppose somebody beats us up. But doesn't kill us," said Rigg.

"Let's hope for that."

"But then later, we go back to the place and I find the path they took to get to us. You slow down time —"

"I thought you said that wasn't what I—"

"That's what I'm used to calling it," said Rigg impatiently. "You do that thing, and I've got a sledgehammer and as they're stepping toward us, ready to beat us up, then one by one I smash them in the knees. Every single one who takes a step toward me."

Umbo was smiling. "I bet after a couple of them fall over screaming with their knees all bent the wrong way, the rest hop away like ebbecks."

"And we don't get beaten up after all," said Rigg. "So actually we're perfectly fine."

Umbo laughed. "It's better than revenge, because we stop them before they do it in the first place!"

"The only thing I don't get is how it could possibly work," said Rigg. "The only reason we'd be doing it is because they beat us up. But then afterward, we can't remember why we attacked these guys, because we don't have a bruise and they never laid a hand on us."

Umbo thought about that for a while. "I don't mind that," he said. "Who cares if we remember? We'll just trust ourselves that we wouldn't do that kind of thing unless we had a good reason."

"But if all we remember is smacking people with sledgehammers, and never the reason why . . ."

"Well, don't worry about it," said Umbo. "With any luck they'll kill us, so we won't be able to go back in time and stop them, and so we won't remember anything cause we'll be dead."

"That eases my mind," said Rigg.

Then something dawned on Umbo. "You remembered growing up without any stories of the Wandering Saint, right? So you still remembered the way things were before you changed things in the past."

"And you didn't."

"I think that's convenient," said Umbo. "One of us will remember how it was before we changed things, and the other one will remember the way it went *after* we changed it."

Something still bothered Rigg about Umbo's analysis, if he could only figure out what it was. "So let's say we get beaten up, like I said. I don't forget the part about getting beaten up. So I remember all the things we did after getting beaten—how we hid, how somebody nursed us back to strength, and then how we went back to the place and got even. But you *don't* remember. All you remember is the *new* way, where they almost beat us up but some of them fall over with their knees broken and the rest run away. So . . . *you* didn't go anywhere to recover from your injuries, because *you* never *were* hurt. So in this new story, where you didn't have to recover from injuries, what did you do instead? And why did you end up coming back with me to prevent something from happening, when you don't remember it happening at all? It's just impossible."

"Here it is," said Umbo. "We both do both things. Only right at the moment where you break their knees, you lose one memory and I lose the other."

"It still doesn't work," said Rigg, "because if we both see the bad guys fall over and we walk away, then we have to somehow do the things we did before so we end up at the place at the right time to break their knees. How will we know when that is?"

Umbo leaned over and started beating his forehead softly against the table. "I'm so hungry I can't think."

"And it's too cold in here to sleep," said Rigg.

"And we've still got the ability to change the past together, only whatever we do, we just figured out that it can't be done."

"And yet we do it," said Rigg.

"We're like the most useless saints ever. We can do miracles, only they're pretty worthless."

"We can do what we can do," said Rigg. "I won't complain about it."

"Remind me why we didn't go back in time and rob enough people in the past that we could afford passage on a downriver boat?"

Rigg lay down on the floor. "Ack! It *is* cold."

"So get back up on the chair where it's warm."

"We're going to die in this room," said Rigg.

"That solves all our problems."

The door opened. A woman almost as large as the taverner came in carrying two bowls with spoons in them.

"Speaking of saints," said Umbo, "here's one with the miracle of food."

"I'm no saint," said the woman. "Loaf will tell you that."

"Loaf?" asked Rigg, smelling the stew and staring at the bowls. She set them down on the little table and Rigg and Umbo instantly sat down.

"Loaf is my husband," she said. "The one who locked you in here instead of throwing you and your money out into the street the way I would have."

"His name is Loaf?" asked Umbo, his mouth already full.

"And my name is Leaky. You think those names are funny?"

117

"No," said Rigg, stopping himself from laughing. "But I do wonder how you got them."

She leaned against the wall, watching them shovel in the food. "We came from a village out in the western desert. Our people name their babies before the next sundown, and they pick the name because of what we do or look like or remind somebody of, or from a dream or a joke or any damn thing. And we have to *keep* that name until we earn a hero name, which almost nobody ever manages to do. So Loaf looked like a big loaf of bread, somebody said, and I drooled and puked and peed in a continuous dribble of *something* so my father started calling me Leaky and he wouldn't let my mother change it on my naming day, and I've beaten about a hundred people into the ground for laughing at my name. Do you think I can't handle you?"

"I have a deep abiding faith that you can," said Rigg, "and I'll do my best not to earn a beating. But I have to wonder, when you came here why didn't you change your name? Nobody in these parts knew you, did they?"

"You think we're the kind of folks to start out in a new place by *lying* to everybody?"

"But it wouldn't be a lie if you changed your name. Then you just say, 'My name *is* Glorious Lady,' and since that now *is* your name, it isn't a lie."

"Anybody calling me Glorious Lady is a liar, even if it's my own self," she said. "And you're getting closer to that beating every time you open your mouth. Next time just put food in it."

Rigg had food in his mouth the whole time he was talking, chewing and swallowing in the pauses, but he knew what she meant.

"You're sleeping in here tonight," Leaky announced. "I'm going to bring you some blankets."

"A lot of blankets, I hope," said Umbo.

"Plenty, compared to sleeping outdoors on a night like this. Isn't that what you've been doing for the past few weeks?"

"But we don't like it," said Umbo.

"I don't mind," said Rigg.

"And I don't care what you like or don't like," said Leaky.

"I like this soup," said Umbo.

"It's stew," said Leaky. "Trust a privick not to know the difference." As she left, she relocked the door behind her. They buckled down to the serious business of eating every scrap of food they could see.

As they neared the bottoms of their bowls, they slowed down enough to talk a little.

"I'm still hungry," said Umbo, "but my stomach is packed solid and I can't fit anything in."

"That's how you get fat," said Rigg. "Eating even after you're full."

"I guess I just *remember* being hungry so clearly that being full doesn't wipe out the hunger."

"If the people of Fall Ford named babies the way Loaf's and Leaky's village did, I wonder what your name would have been," said Rigg. "'Turdmaker'!"

"Yours would be 'Crazy Baby.'"

"The craziness didn't show up till later," said Rigg. "Mostly since knowing you."

True to her word, Leaky returned quite soon and seemed

surprised that they had already finished eating. She held up their bowls and made a show of looking for some trace of the stew. "If you barf because you ate so fast, make sure you keep it all on the blanket or I'll have you scrubbing the puke off the floor till it smells like fresh-cut lumber in here."

"It smelled a lot worse than puke when we got here," said Umbo. "We'd be improving it."

"It's the only reason I'd ever be glad you came here. Strip off those filthy traveling clothes before you get into these blankets. And I mean *all* of them." With that she left again. Again they heard the door lock — but only just barely, as it was so noisy out in the common room.

"She likes us," said Umbo.

"I know, I could feel it too," said Rigg. "She's really glad to have us here. I think she loves us like her own children."

"Whom she murdered and cut up into the stew."

"They were delicious."

Rigg stripped off his clothes and even though he really was cold now, he had the promise of the blankets to encourage him. There was such a great pile of them that he wouldn't have to curl up with Umbo to stay warm. That would make a nice change, because out in the woods, Umbo had moved around a lot in his sleep, leaving them both to wake up freezing cold five times a night.

The door opened.

"Hey, we're naked in here!" protested Rigg. Umbo just dragged a blanket up to cover himself.

As Leaky set down a chamber pot, she said, "Don't splash when you use this, and for the sake of Saint Spider, keep the lid on tight when you're done or I'll never get the stink out of this room." She set a basket of large leaves beside the pot. "These go *inside* the pot when you've used them."

"We're from Fall Ford," said Umbo. "That far upriver, sheeshee don't stink."

"You just don't notice, sleeping with the pigs like privicks do." She closed the door and locked it again.

They took turns using the chamber pot and when they were done they both agreed that a tight-closed lid was an excellent idea.

"I liked those leaves," said Umbo. "Way more comfortable than any we used in the woods."

"I'll make it a point to find out what tree they come from and pull one along behind us in a big pot on wheels."

Rigg spread out his blanket, folded it double thick, and then covered himself with two more while Umbo did the same. The light of the Ring came through the high window, which had apparently been angled for just that purpose. There were no branches above them to block it out.

"The leaves outside made for softer sleeping," said Rigg.

"But there are no stones jabbing me," said Umbo. "And no bugs or snakes or other vermin crawling all over me."

"So far," said Rigg.

He waited for Umbo's retort—something like "If I don't see them, I don't care"—but Umbo said nothing at all.

Can you believe it? thought Rigg. Umbo's already asleep. And in that moment, so was Rigg.

CHAPTER 6
Leaky and Loaf

It was still two days before the jump into the fold when Ram suddenly found himself strapped into his chair. The expendable was kneeling in front of him, looking up into his eyes.

"Was I asleep?" asked Ram.

"We jumped the fold, Ram," said the expendable.

"On schedule and I simply don't remember the past two days? Or early?"

"We generated the seventh cross-grain field," said the expendable, "and the fold came into existence four steps earlier than predicted."

"Was it *the* fold or merely *a* fold?" asked Ram.

"It was the fold we wanted. We're exactly where we were supposed to be."

"What a convenient error," said Ram. "We inadvertently trigger fold creation four steps early, and yet it still takes us to our destination."

"All the folds, all the cross-graining of fields, everything we did was polarized, so to speak: It always pointed us exactly where we wanted to go."

"So spacetime, naughty as it was, suddenly got the idea and leapt ahead of us?"

"We got ourselves caught in the midst of a stutter," said the expendable. "We were trying to avoid that because we didn't know what would happen to us in a stutter—most of the computers predicted the ship would be sectioned or obliterated."

Ram had been scanning all the reports from every part of the ship. "But neither happened. We're still intact."

"More than intact," said the expendable.

"How can you be *more* than intact?" asked Ram.

• • •

The floor was hard and the room was cold, but Rigg awoke feeling more comfortable than he had in many days, and he burrowed down into the blankets to see if he could sleep a little longer.

"They took our clothes," said Umbo.

Rigg opened one eye. Umbo, wrapped in a blanket, was sitting on a chair looking glum in the dim light eking its way down through the shutterblind.

"Probably having somebody wash them," said Rigg.

Then he realized that if their clothes were gone, it meant someone had come into the room without waking them. They could have taken anything. Rigg bounded up from his blankets and searched for his pack. It was right where he had left it, and the money was where he had tucked it when he undressed.

"Not thieves," he said.

"Well, we knew *that*," said Umbo.

The key sounded noisily in the lock. Was it that loud last night? Not with the noise from the common room to drown it out. But when someone came and took their clothes?

Leaky came in, not bringing breakfast, not carrying clean clothes. She merely stood there looking coldly at them. "Wrap yourselves in something and come with me. Right now."

Rigg didn't know what to make of her attitude. She seemed furious, and yet also much more respectful than she had been last night. She averted her gaze as they rearranged their blankets to cover themselves a bit more securely, then stood aside for them to pass through the door.

The common room was empty except for Loaf, who stood behind the counter, propping himself on it with straight arms. In front of him a white cloth was spread. At the end of the counter was a pile of rags that Rigg immediately identified as his own and Umbo's unwashed clothing.

As he came nearer, Rigg saw something on the cloth sparkle in the light from the half-shuttered windows. Large gemstones, of different colors. Eighteen of them.

"Where's the light blue one shaped like a teardrop?" asked Rigg.

Leaky walked beyond him to the pile of clothes and slid it toward the middle of the bar. "Find it yourself, saints know we didn't take it." Rigg began at once examining the waistband of the trousers—which had been neatly sewn closed again in each spot where a stone had been.

Loaf's voice was a low growl when he spoke. "What do you mean, having such wealth on you, and talking poor as you did?" Like his wife, Loaf was angry—and yet he was also deferential.

"Asking for our charity," added Leaky, "when all the time you had *that*."

"We didn't ask for your charity," said Rigg, "we offered you money—too much money, if I recall."

"And acted like you were afraid of running out of it," said Leaky sullenly, "which you couldn't do if you live to a hundred."

Rigg worked his fingers along the waistband of the trousers on the counter. He found where the light blue gem had been sewn, and there it was indeed, though harder to feel because it was also involved with a vertical side seam, which thickened the cloth over it. He pulled it out and laid it on the cloth. There was no reason to hide it now. If Loaf and Leaky were thieves, they wouldn't be laying out the stones, they'd be pretending they knew nothing about them. If they had even allowed Rigg to wake up alive.

"It's my inheritance from my father," said Rigg. "He said I should take it to Aressa Sessamo and show the stones to a banker there."

"Inheritance?" asked Loaf, looking wary. "If your father had wealth like this, why do you dress so poor?"

Rigg understood the question. Loaf was asking if the jewels were stolen; but even if they weren't, the man wanted to make sense of the contradiction.

"We lived our lives in the forest," said Rigg. "We trapped furs

125

for a living. I'm dressed in the clothing that was useful to me — we never needed any better. There *is* no better for the work we did. And as for being wealthy, the first I knew of these jewels was after my father died, and the woman who had them in safekeeping gave them to me."

"That was a very trustworthy woman," said Leaky.

"And you are no less trustworthy," said Rigg, "or I would not be seeing these laid out on the bar."

Loaf snorted. "For coins such as you had," he said, "someone might kill you and toss you in the river. But a boy who owned such jewels as these, someone would come looking for him. A man might hang. And if I turned up with such as these, who would believe that I got them honestly?"

"Who would believe *me*?" asked Rigg. "Part of Father's inheritance was the letter to the banker."

"Then would you mind if we saw the letter?" asked Loaf. His words were polite, but his tone was firm, as if to say, it's time *now* to dispel all doubt.

For a moment Rigg hesitated. Do they think that with the letter they might steal the jewels and prove a right to them? But he set aside his suspicion at once. If they meant him harm, he could not stop them. So why not suppose they meant well? Or at least well enough?

"I'll get it," said Rigg. "It's in my pack."

"No, send the other boy," said Loaf. "I don't want you to let these jewels out of your sight."

Umbo glared at Loaf and then at Rigg. "You might have told *me*," he said.

"I shared all my coin with you," said Rigg, "and my food and all. But these couldn't be spent anywhere we've been or anywhere we're going. What was to tell?"

Umbo turned his back and went for the pack. He was back in only a few steps and thrust the pack into Rigg's arms.

Rigg set the pack on a stool and pulled out the letter. He laid it on the bar.

Loaf squinted over it. Leaky reached out and snatched it away. "For saints' sake, Loaf, we all know you read as fast as a toadstool turns into a tree." She scanned the document, moving her lips a little and humming a note now and then. "It's an obvious fake," she said.

Loaf stood up straight and looked down his nose at Rigg.

But Rigg knew the letter was genuine, and if it wasn't, Leaky would have no way of knowing. "If it's a fake, I didn't fake it," Rigg said. "The woman I got it from said my father wrote it. He never showed it to me while he was alive, but it looks like his handwriting." Rigg looked at Leaky. "Have you ever seen his handwriting?"

"I don't have to," said Leaky. "It's signed by the Wandering Saint. That's like having it signed, 'The Ring.'"

"That would be a really stupid thing to do, but he didn't do it," said Rigg. "Read that signature again."

She scowled and read it again, moving her lips even more pronouncedly. "Ah," she said. "'Wandering Man' instead of 'Wandering Saint.' But it's still not even a name."

"It's one of the names his father went by," said Umbo.

"What's his real name, then?"

"All his names were real," said Umbo. "He answered to them."

They looked at Rigg, who said, "I never called him anything but 'Father.'"

"Why do you think you can judge this paper?" asked Umbo. "It isn't written to you. It's written to a banker in Aressa Sessamo. So we'll take it to *him*. Give it back."

It was bold of Umbo to demand "back" something that he had never held. But Leaky put it in his hand all the same. Umbo scanned it, reading quickly—for the village schoolteacher in Fall Ford did his job—and then passed it on to Rigg.

"So your father made up names for himself and signed them on legal documents," said Leaky. "You already know what I think of people who use false names."

"Doesn't matter what you think of this boy's dead father," said Loaf curtly, earning a glare from his wife. "I believe the boy and the letter, and whether the father came by the money honestly or not, the son surely did."

"What are you going to do, then?" Leaky demanded. "Adopt him? He certainly lied to *us*."

"I never said a word to you that wasn't true," said Rigg.

"You said those coins were all your money!"

"Do those jewels look like money to you?" said Umbo.

"Why did you take my clothes in the first place?" asked Rigg. "I'm the one whose belongings were taken by stealth in the night."

Flustered, Leaky said, "I was going to wash them."

"They don't look any cleaner to me," said Rigg.

"Because I picked up your trousers and I could feel something in the waistband."

"And you had to rip open the seam and take it out?"

"My wife's no thief," said Loaf, glowering.

"I know she's not," said Rigg. "But she's been spitting out accusations and suspicions, and I wanted her to see that those can go both ways. I have more cause of complaint here than she does—but I'm not complaining, and it's time she stopped being suspicious of me for giving far less grounds."

"The boy's a lawyer," said Loaf to his wife.

"Honest men don't need lawyers," she said huffily.

"Honest men are the ones who need them most," murmured her husband, and when she made as if to argue with him, without even looking at her he raised his hand as if to smack her backhand across the face. He didn't hit her and obviously never meant to, but she rolled her eyes and fell silent. So it seemed that a hand raised for a smack was the downriver equivalent of putting a finger to your lips.

"If you give me back my clothes," said Rigg, "I can sew these jewels back into the waistband and we can leave."

"No," said Loaf. "In Aressa Sessamo, that letter will do you good. Here it does none, and you need to turn one of those jewels into money."

"I thought we had a lot of money," said Rigg. "Too much of it."

"I said you had enough money that rivermen would kill you for it," said Loaf. "But prices get a lot higher the farther down the river you go. You'll be out of money long before you get to Aressa Sessamo, no matter how carefully you eke it out."

"Is there a bank in *this* town?"

"Not yet," said Loaf. "But I can accompany you downriver

to the first city that has one. It's a place where I'm known well enough, and I can vouch for you. I can also keep you safe along the way."

"Why would you do that for us?" asked Rigg.

"For money, you dunderheaded boy. I'm an honest man but not a rich one. We'll get to the bank—the banker's name is Cooper—and when he gives you the money, he'll give a fee to me. And don't fear I'll cheat you—we'll let the banker set the price. Fair value for my protecting you and leading you there."

"The banker is your friend, not ours," said Umbo.

"But you're the one with the jewels," said Loaf. "So that'll make him your friend, not mine." Then he pointed at Rigg. "Or rather, *his* friend, not either of ourn."

"What kind of banker is named 'Cooper'?" asked Umbo. "Are the coopers around there all named 'Banks'?"

"The city where he lives has a law that family names are passed along father to son, husband to wife, regardless of whether the name itself still fits. He once had a distant ancestor who was a cooper, that's all it means."

"It's a very dull way of naming people," said Leaky.

Loaf turned to Rigg again. "I'll make money from taking you, but it's money fairly earned, since without me you're so likely to be dead before you get out of Leaky's Landing."

"Is that the name of this tavern?" asked Rigg, wondering why it wasn't named for Loaf, since at least his name suggested something edible, while Leaky's name seemed a recommendation against staying there on a rainy night.

"It's the name of the whole town," said Leaky.

"They named it for you?" asked Umbo.

"Maybe they did, maybe they didn't," said Leaky.

"This termite-supper town?" said Loaf. "They called it six-teen different things till we got here and told them that they had to settle on a name or we wouldn't build the tavern here. I suggested they name it for me, and so they named it for her just to prove that they don't have to do what they're told, even though it was the best advice they've ever had. Population's tripled in the fifteen years since they named it."

"What does having a name matter?" asked Umbo.

Loaf rolled his eyes. "I can hear the land speculator saying, 'Come and buy land here and build a house in a town so saint-forsaken that we don't even know its name!' or a traveler saying, 'Let's stop for the night at that inn in that town, you know the one, the town with no name?'"

"They get the point," said Leaky.

Rigg wanted to know what the plan was. "So are we leaving for . . . the town with the banker named Cooper —"

"Does *that* town have a name?" asked Umbo. "Or are they waiting for you to move there and name it for them?"

"Leaky's Landing is new," said Loaf. "That *city* has had people there for twice five thousand years. It's as old as the world. Nobody even knows the language it was first named in."

"It's called 'O,'" said Leaky.

"And it has the Tower of O in it," said Loaf, as if they should know all about it.

"There must not have been many cities in the world when

131

they named it," said Rigg. "Are there other old cities named for vowels?"

Loaf looked at his wife, rolled his eyes, and said, "It's going to be a long trip." Then he turned back to Rigg. "To answer the question you should have asked, I'll say that before we set out for O, we're going to buy you some clothes that won't attract notice. Not too rich, not too poor, definitely not of woodsy leather, and equally *not* the latest fashions from upriver. You," he said, pointing to Umbo, "will pass for my son, dressed like me."

"I'm excited," murmured Umbo.

"And like a son, you'll get cuffed in the head when your mouth gets smart like that," said Loaf.

"No he won't," said Rigg, moving closer to Umbo.

"If I wanted to get hit," said Umbo, "I could have stayed at home. My father did it plenty. For free."

Leaky laughed. "He was joking, you fools. This is a rough town with a lot of hitting, but Loaf never lays a hand on any, except when he throws troublemakers out."

"I had my fill of hurting people when I was in the army," said Loaf. "I won't lay a hand on you."

Umbo relaxed, and so did Rigg.

"Umbo is my son," Loaf went on, "and Rigg will be my wife's brother's boy, your cousin, and his family have a bit more money than us. He was visiting us and we're taking him to meet his father's men in O."

"Why all the lying?" asked Rigg.

"To explain why your clothes will be nicer than ours. When we meet Cooper, he has to believe you are what you say. The letter means something but not as much as you'd like, since it wasn't addressed to him. *He* doesn't know Wandering Man any more than I do. So he has to look at you and see a boy who might come from a family with money."

"If the banker catches us lying about anything," said Rigg, "then he won't believe the jewels are mine."

"We'll tell *him* as much of the truth as he needs to hear. The lies are for nosy people along the way, to explain why you're dressed different from us. And why you talk so much better than your friend."

"He does not!" said Umbo, outraged.

"Are you deaf, boy?" asked Leaky. "This Rigg here sounds like he's been to school. The way he pronounces his words so clear."

"I've been to school!" said Umbo.

"I mean a *downriver* school," said Leaky. "We get travelers like that now and then. You really can't hear the difference in the way he talks?"

"He talks like his father," said Umbo. "What do you expect?"

"That's my point," said Loaf. "You talk like a privick, and he talks like a snooty boy from the schools. He talks like *money*."

"Well, I only know how to sound like who I really am," said Umbo.

"And that's why I'm calling you my son," said Loaf, "and him my rich nephew, so why are we having this argument? Besides, I'm going to do the talking anyway. Don't answer if anybody asks you a question, just look at me. Got it?"

"Yes," said Rigg.

"This is so stupid," said Umbo.

"You say that because it's not your money," said Leaky.

"Not yours either," Umbo insisted.

"This boy never backs down," Loaf growled.

"That's what makes him a good friend," said Rigg.

"*Some* of the money's ours," Leaky said to Umbo. "In exchange for the clothes we're going to buy you two and the passages we're going to pay for and the days Loaf spends away from here and the bouncers I'll have to hire when he's not here to keep the peace. If we don't make a fair profit on this great and noble service we're providing you, then he's a stingy lad and you're no better."

"I'll pay fairly," said Rigg. "And just so you know, Umbo speaks like an educated boy from Fall Ford, but Father taught me to talk in several different accents and a few completely different languages, too. At home I talk just like Umbo, but for the last week I've been talking the way Father said they talk in Aressa Sessamo, cause people understood me better and laughed less."

"Of course they did," said Loaf. "That's the imperial city. And your father sounds like a man who meant you to travel."

Rigg remembered telling Father that he already knew everything he'd ever need to know—but Father knew all along that Rigg would not be spending his whole life trapping animals in the mountains. Father might not have told Rigg anything about his plans for Rigg's future, but he'd certainly prepared him to speak wherever he went. Maybe someday Rigg would even have a use for all the astronomy and physics Father taught him. Maybe it would matter that Rigg knew that the Ring was made of dust and tiny stones circling the world, shining in the night because of reflected sunlight. Now *that* would be a journey!

They went to buy clothes right away that morning; the tailor measured and by evening the clothes were delivered—two of everything for each of them, in different fabrics. "Why do I need two?" asked Umbo.

"So you can wear one while you clean the other," said Leaky. "Though it's no surprise you don't know about washing."

Rigg interrupted before they could bandy words yet again. "So should I open up a seam and put the jewels back in my clothes? And if I do, which pair of trousers? I tell you I don't ever want to be caught wearing the wrong pair if a thief steals the other, or if I have to run from somebody."

"The jewels aren't very big," said Umbo. "Can't you just keep them in a little bag in your pocket?"

Loaf wouldn't have that. "Pickpockets take whatever they find. Never put in your pocket anything you mean to own for long."

"I'll make you a ribbon to put around your waist and tie right tightly," said Leaky. "And you hang a little bag from the ribbon, inside your trousers, right in front. No one will see it, or if they do, they'll think it's your boy parts."

"Your family jewels," said Umbo, chortling.

But at that moment, Rigg caught something in Umbo's eyes, some emotion he couldn't identify, something that made his eyes shine a little. And he thought: He hasn't completely forgiven me for letting Kyokay die. It was one thing before, when he didn't know about the jewels. He could forgive me then, and share blame. But now that he sees me as rich, and knows I hid it from him, it changes everything. He thinks he has reason not to trust me. Does that mean I have reason not to trust him?

It took four days to make the downriver passage to O. First thing the boat's captain said when they booked passage was, "Pilgrims?" and later Loaf explained that thousands of people a year go to visit the Tower of O. To the captain, though, he told the story that they had agreed on, and Rigg realized that the most important part of the tale was the part about meeting his "father's men." It told the captain they were looked for, and by a man of power. They'd be safe enough aboard this boat.

At first it was a delight to travel by boat. The river did all the work—even the rivermen aboard the boat had little enough to do. They were there for the return voyage, when they'd have to pole and row to get upstream against the swift current. For now the rivermen lolled about the deck; and on the cabin roof, where passengers were required to stay, Loaf and Rigg and Umbo did the same.

Until Rigg's legs began to feel twitchy for lack of use. Father had never let him spend a single whole day abed—not even when he was sick, which wasn't often. Umbo seemed content enough, and Loaf was positively in heaven, dozing day and night, whenever he could.

It was one of those times when Loaf was sleeping and Rigg was walking around and around the corral—for so it seemed, this small platform edged with a fence—that Umbo came up to him. "Why can't you hold still?"

"I never got much practice at it," said Rigg. "It requires a talent for laziness."

"So what do you see? Paths on the river, too? The people aren't actually walking, except the insane ones, they just sit there. So do they leave a path even though they're holding still?"

"Yes," said Rigg. "They're moving through space so they leave a path."

"All right, then that brings another question. I learned in school that the world is a planet moving through space, and the sun moves through space, too. So when the world moves, why don't all our paths get left out in space? If the world's like a boat, then even if we're standing still, we should be leaving paths behind us in space because the world is moving us, the way this boat moves us even while we're sitting here."

Rigg closed his eyes, picturing it—all the paths leading out into space.

"It *should* do what you said," Rigg finally answered. "But it doesn't. That's all I know. All the paths stay where people passed by, on the land or in boats. So I guess there's something that holds the paths to the exact place on Garden that the people moved through, no matter how long ago. Maybe gravity holds the paths in place. I don't know."

Umbo held his silence for a while, and Rigg thought the conversation was over. But Umbo was just coming up with new questions. "Can we do something here on the boat?" asked Umbo. "I mean, you know, practicing that thing we do?"

"I don't see how," said Rigg. "The crew would see me walking around and wonder what I was doing. And like I said, there are no paths on this boat, the paths are all hovering above the water, where other boats dragged people through the air. Our own paths are behind us, floating exactly this high above the water. I can see yours right up the river."

"But that's all the better. You just wait till some path comes right across this platform, and then you do something."

"What would I do? Give some poor guy a shove so he falls in the water, five hundred years ago? That would be murder, if he can't swim."

Umbo sighed. "I'm just so bored."

"I have a better idea. Let's try to teach each other how to do the other one's thing."

"Nobody taught us to do what we do already," said Umbo.

"That's not even true. Father worked with you, didn't he? Helped you sharpen it and focus it."

"Yes, well, that's right, but I could already *do* it, he just trained me."

"So maybe instead of having *none* of each other's ability, we only have a very very little so we never noticed it," said Rigg. "So you try to explain it to me while you're doing it, and I'll try to point out the paths as we pass through them."

"There's not a chance it will work," said Umbo.

"Then let's find *that* out. Come on, we're both bored, this is something to do."

"Sh," said Umbo. "I think Loaf is waking up."

"Unless he's been awake the whole time, listening."

Umbo grimaced. "It would be just like him."

But Loaf seemed not to have heard anything. He was per-

fectly normal toward them when he woke up—surly and deferent and helpful all at once.

Rigg asked him, "You worked the river yourself, didn't you?"

"Never," said Loaf.

"But you're as muscular as these men."

"No I'm not," said Loaf. "I'm much more so."

Rigg looked at him carefully. "I can see that you're different
from them, but not how."

"Look at my right shoulder and then at my left. Then look at
the rivermen."

Rigg and Umbo both looked. Umbo saw it first, and chuckled.
"They favor one side."

Now Rigg could see it. They were each stronger on one side
of their body than the other, from years of working the same side
of the boat.

"On military boats they're not allowed to do that," said Loaf.
"They make them change sides in regular shifts so they stay even."

"So were you a military boatman?"

"Military, but not on a boat," said Loaf. "Before I met Leaky
and married her and built the tavern, I was in the army. Got to be
a sergeant, a good squad of tough men."

"Did you fight in any wars?" asked Umbo.

"We haven't had a war in my lifetime," said Loaf. "Even the
People's Revolution was back when I was a baby. But there's
always fighting and always killing, because there are always
people who won't do the will of the People's Revolutionary
Council, and always wild people at the edges of civilization who
won't respect the boundary or any other law. Barbarians."

"So are you a bowman?" asked Umbo eagerly. "A swords-man? Or do you work the pike or the staff? Will you show us?"

"The boy is in love with the idea of soldiering," said Loaf. "Because you've never seen a man holding all his guts in his lap, begging for water because he's so thirsty, but has no stomach left for the water to go into."

Umbo gulped. "I know people die," he said. "They die at home, too, and sometimes in pretty terrible ways."

Rigg thought of Father under the tree and Kyokay slipping from the rim of Stashi Falls. At least he hadn't actually seen what the tree did to Father's body, or what happened to Kyokay when he hit the turbulent, rock-filled water.

"Nothing is more terrible than the way men die in war," said Loaf. "One slip and your enemy has the best of you. Or you're walking along and suddenly, pfffft, there's an arrow in your throat or your ear or your eye or your back and if you aren't killed outright, you know it's over for you, it saps the strength from you."

"But you had an equal chance," said Rigg. "Or maybe not equal, but you were trained for it. Killing and therefore dying. It can't be a surprise to a soldier when he dies."

"Take it from me, boy, death is always a surprise even if you stand there staring it in the face. When it comes, you think, 'What, *me*?'"

"How do *you* know," said Umbo. "You've never died."

In answer, Loaf lifted up his overshirt and revealed his chest and belly. The man was so huge that Rigg had assumed he was fat, but no, his whole body followed the bulges and creases of his musculature, and veins stood at the surface everywhere instead of hiding in layers of fat.

And running right up his belly, just a little off center to the right, there was a savage scar, still partly red, and it hadn't been stitched up right, so the skin puckered on one side or the other all the way up and down it. "I'm the man who held my guts in my hand," he said. "I counted myself as dead. I refused to let my men waste any time trying to take me off the battlefield. I named another man as their new sergeant and ordered them to retreat with the rest of our men. Later they went ahead and won, but they never came back to the battlefield. They knew there'd be nothing left of anyone."

"Why not?" asked Umbo.

"It doesn't sound very loyal," said Rigg.

"Scavengers, my boys," said Loaf. "The battlefield was empty no more than a minute before these women and old men and boys were among the fallen, killing the wounded and taking their clothes and weapons and whatever else could be found. War brings 'em, like crows to carrion. So there I lie, expecting to die—hoping it doesn't take long because it hurts in waves like the sea, each one pounding through me and I'm thinking, this is the one that carries me off into death, but it didn't. I hear footsteps, I look up, and there's this huge woman standing over me."

"Leaky," said Umbo.

"Of course it's Leaky, you daft boy, but I'm telling the story and I decide when to say things out loud."

"Sorry."

"So I look up and she's looking down and she says, 'You're

a big one,' and I didn't say anything because it was a fool thing to say, what does it matter how big a dead man is? Then she says, 'You've stopped bleeding,' and I says, "I guess I'm empty.' It comes out as a whisper but she heard me and she laughs and says, 'If you can talk and you can joke you aren't going to die.' Then she pulls away my armor—which the other fellow's sword had sliced through like butter, that's what happens when your armor is built by somebody's cousin and he makes the steel out of tin-plated dirt. Anyway, she stitches me up—and a right lousy job she did of it, I'd say, but the light was failing and I was going to die anyway, so who cares? She says to me, 'The skin's all cut but the stomach and bowel look to be unhurt, which is why you didn't die. A knuckle deeper and you'd already be dead of it.' So she hoists me up on her shoulder—me! heavy enough even without my blood—and takes me home and says that by scavenger law I'm her slave. Only when I got better, we were in love like a pair of heroes and we got married and I went home and tossed my old wife and sold the house and land and took my vast fortune and built the tavern in a scabby little mushroom village and turned it into a town and a regular stop for the river traffic. So her not killing me and taking my stuff, but taking me instead— that changed the world, my lads."

"Hard on your first wife," said Rigg.

"I was away eight solid years the last time, and when I got home she had three children under five that looked like three different men had done me the service of a substitute. You telling me I did wrong?"

"At least she waited a couple of years faithful," said Umbo.

"And at least I didn't kill her, which was my right. I only tossed her out instead of killing her, because Leaky says, 'Let's not start with blood,' and also because I vaguely remembered we were in love once. And besides, I never fathered a child on her, no more than I have on Leaky, so I reckon a woman has a right to her babies, don't she? Wherever she has to go to get them."

"A tolerant philosophy. But she'd kept the farm for eight years and you took it right away from her."

"The servants worked it," said Loaf, "and it was *my* farm, just like she was my woman, and those *weren't* my children. I didn't lay a hand on her, but even a saint would sell the farm and take the money from it. She could go for shelter to the dad of one of her little ones, if he'd take her."

"You're soft, then," said Rigg, but he smiled so that Loaf would know he was teasing.

"Yes, boy, jest all you like, mock me hollow, but I *am* soft. That's what Leaky did to me. That and the one that gave me this scar. They took the war right out of me. But I still train for it. When I'm on land, that is. Train every day, an hour or two, using all the weapons. I can still put an arrow where I want to, within twenty rods. If I hadn't slipped in horseflop on the battlefield he'd never have put his sword in me, that's how good I was. And I still am, barring the changes that fifteen years of not having an opponent better than a drunken riverman makes in an old veteran."

It was good to know that Leaky was the one who talked him out of killing his old wife. She could brag about how *she* would have thrown Rigg and Umbo in the river, or tossed them out on the mercy of the rivermen that first night—but Rigg understood now that Leaky and Loaf were kind people, and only had to look and talk tough because of their clientele.

"Does Leaky train with you?" asked Umbo.

Rigg expected him to get cuffed for his impertinence, but Loaf only laughed. "Who else?" he said. "No, she's no fighter, not like me, but she puts on the pads and helps me through my steps and stings. Nobody else I know can match my reach, except her. I'm right big, you know. So we're out at dawn, practicing an hour in full light. And it's not a bad thing if rivermen see us at it, them as aren't nursing hangovers. So they know that even when I'm not there, she holds her own."

In the early afternoon of the fourth day, they saw it: the Tower of O, rising above the trees that lined the river. It was almost invisible against the lead-grey wintry sky, but they could all see it, a steel cylinder rising up and rounding off in a dome at the top.

"So we're there," said Umbo, and he and Rigg headed for the ladder down to the main deck.

"Wait," said Loaf. "We won't reach O till tomorrow noon, or later."

"But it's right there!" said Umbo.

"Look how hazy it is. This is clear air, and if it was as close as you think it is, it wouldn't look that way."

If the tower was still a day's journey away, Rigg wondered, how could it rise so high above the trees? "How tall *is* it?" he asked.

"Taller than you imagine. Do you think people would make

pilgrimages to see it, if it was just *tall*? Besides, the river takes a wide bend that way, and we'll lose sight of it for hours, and then we come back at it from another direction before we get to see how big it really is. It's a wonder of the world, to think any nation or city had the brains and the power to build such a thing. And yet it's completely useless. They say it takes a day to climb to the top, but I don't know how anybody would know that, the whole thing's sealed off, and not because the Council of O made some law—no, it's sealed off inside so you can't get deep enough inside to figure out even what they built it for."

Rigg watched the Tower of O until the light gave out so completely that it was invisible. He wondered what his father might have known about the Tower of O. He knew everything, or so it seemed. But he'd never thought to give Rigg a lesson about this place.

CHAPTER 7

O

"Was it *the* fold or merely *a* fold?" asked Ram.

"The fold was there," said the expendable. "All nineteen of the ship's computers report that the fold . . . was jumped."

Expendables made no careless decisions about sentence structure. Nor did they hesitate, unless the hesitation meant something. "'Was jumped,' you said, but you didn't specify that it was jumped by *us*," said Ram.

"Because apparently we did not do the jumping," said the expendable. "We emerged in exactly the position we were in at the beginning of the jump."

"And were we still moving?" said Ram.

"Yes."

"So what position are we in now?" asked Ram.

"We are two days' journey closer to Earth. The physical position we were in two days ago."

"So we came out of the fold reversed," said Ram. "Heading the other way."

"No, Ram," said the expendable. "We came out facing away from Earth, just as we were when we went into the fold."

"We don't have a reverse gear," said Ram. "We can only move in the direction we're facing."

"All the computers report that we are proceeding forward at precisely the same velocity as before. They also report that our position keeps progressing backward toward Earth."

"So we're moving forward and backward at the same time," said Ram.

"Our propulsion is forward. Our motion is backward."

"I hope you will not remove me from command if I admit to being confused."

"I would only question your sanity if you were *not* confused, Ram."

"Do you have any hypotheses that might explain this situation?" asked Ram.

"We are not hypothesizers," said the expendable. "We are programmed instruments and, as I pointed out to you before, decisions about what to do after the jump are entirely up to our resourceful, creative, highly tested and trained human pilot."

Ram thought about it.

• • •

As they started seeing the buildings of O, Rigg was amazed at how different they were. During the weeks he and Umbo had walked along the North Road, changes had been gradual. Farms had become more frequent, villages larger, buildings a bit more grand. Thatch gave way to shingle and tile, oilcloth to shutters and occasional panes of glass. Leaky's Landing had an air of newness about it, but the town was of the same wooden construction, the same roof angles, the same alternation of cobble, gravel, and corduroy on the streets, depending on the whim of the owners of the buildings abutting them.

But the trees lining the river had concealed any such gradual changes, and the current moved them much faster, so that as they approached the docks of O it was like entering another world.

Everything seemed to be made of stone—and not the grey-brown rocks of the mountains, either, but a pale rock, almost white with streaks of warm colors in it. No moss had been allowed to grow on any of it, except down near the water—it gleamed warmly in the noonday sun.

By contrast, the Tower of O shone with the glaring coldness of a steel blade. And since it was larger by far than any other structure, and many times higher than the tallest trees, the whole city gave the impression of the pale hand of a very white woman, holding a fierce dagger upward toward the sky.

As the boat drew nearer the docks, however, that impression faded. The docks were as dirty and cluttered and busy as docks anywhere. Not all the buildings were stone after all; in fact most buildings were wooden structures, though with roofs only of tile or, to Rigg's amazement, tin. So much metal as to cover a roof! Rigg could see that the impression that all was stone came from a few dozen large buildings that rose much higher than the jumble of wooden warehouses, taverns, and shops selling mementoes of the Tower of O. From a distance, all he had seen were the white-stone walls of those buildings; close up, he could hardly catch a glimpse of them from the narrow streets, where each story of every building jutted out beyond the one below, until at the third or fourth story houses across the street from each other were so close that, as Loaf said, "A man could take a mistress across the street and neither of them leave their house."

Rigg expected that they would first secure lodging, but Loaf grimaced and said no.

"So we're going to carry our packs and goods to the banker?" asked Rigg.

Loaf drew them over away from the crowded street to the open space near one of the large stone buildings. "Listen," he said, "the boat passage and the cost of food and of your clothes have me close to broke. The places I could afford right now would be of such a low nature that we wouldn't dare to leave our belongings in them anyhow. I'm a taverner, my boys, and I know what the dockyard inns of O are like. Everything depends on getting Mr. Cooper to convert one of these . . . items . . . to money at full value, without anyone else getting a glimpse of them. Then we can afford to stay in a respectable place without hardly making a dent in your fortune, young Rigg. That's why we're stopping nowhere, but finding Mr. Cooper's bank."

Loaf seemed to know his way through the maze of streets and only had to backtrack twice. To Rigg this seemed like a miracle, since there were few street signs high up on the buildings, and even then they weren't always right.

"Oh, that's the old name," said Loaf when Umbo noticed one of them. "Then they made a boulevard and put the name on that. This is now . . . something else that I can't remember. It doesn't matter. You don't learn by names here, you learn by landmarks and turnings."

"How can they have landmarks here?" said Umbo. "Every street looks just like every other."

"If you lived here, you'd see the differences plain enough," said Loaf. "I could ask anyone here and get directions to Cooper's bank because he faced his building in grey stone—not to show too much pride, you see, so grey not white—and then he set a clock high on the wall. You ask anybody, 'Where's the banker's clock?' and if they don't know, they must be a tower pilgrim because no one as lives here wouldn't know the place."

They passed many a food vendor, and when Umbo suggested stopping at one, Loaf just pulled him away and kept them on the road. "So you eat some greasy slab of meat and go in to see Mr. Cooper with fat dripped all over your hands and sleeves and the front of you. Then he throws us *out* as being the kind of people who have no house to eat in or table to sit at or napkin to drape with."

"But we *don't* have any of those," said Umbo.

"Exactly, and we mean to have them, so we'll be hungry and thirsty in the bank, but we won't look like poor privicks."

"We *are* poor privicks," muttered Umbo. Loaf ignored him.

But Rigg thought about it. Umbo *is* a poor privick, though in Fall Ford his father did as well as anyone else, and his family was never hungry, nor was anyone else's. During lean times they shared about, knowing that every man and woman worked as hard as any other, if they could, and they all watched out to make sure no old widows or spinsters starved or froze in the winter. But of food sold by vendors on the street no one got a taste, because there were no such. Only Nox cooked food for strangers, and you had to come at mealtime for a bite; she never brought the food out into the road, she never called out the name of the dish.

Strange how, just by being in a different place, a boy who always had enough and never wanted for anything could now be poor, and had to go hungry for fear that someone will notice his poverty.

And Loaf, too. In Leaky's Landing he was prosperous, and mocked the privicks as merrily as anyone. But here in O, so far downstream, *he* was a privick, too, though better at disguising it, since he had traveled the world a good bit more.

I'm the only one who isn't a poor man here, or at least might not end up so. Even though I'm the most upriver of all, having lived above the falls most days of my life, wandering with just my father in the deepest forest with few paths of men among the beasts and trees. But because of nineteen jewels in a bag hanging from a ribbon at my waist, I may soon be rich compared to them.

And yet they are my friends on this journey, the only friends I have. And if I prosper, they will prosper. The money may be mine, but the benefit will be for all of us. Loaf will go home with a fine profit for his kind service. Umbo can stay with me or go back upriver if he wants, this time in fine clothes and with the passage money for as far upstream as oars and poles can go. Let him go home and be the richest young man in Fall Ford, and then see whether his father shuns him. No, Tegay the cobbler will usher him into his house and offer his son his old place at the table.

People talk of magic and miracles wrought by the saints — and if they saw what Rigg and Umbo had done together, conjuring out of thin air a fine bejeweled knife, they'd be accounted saints or mages themselves — but none of these miracles is as potent or useful as a sudden flow of money into a man's pocket. Then the transformation is like changing rainy to sunny weather, which no evil mage or generous saint can do except in the silliest old stories.

They arrived at the greystone building just as the large clock set high in the wall began chiming so loudly Rigg was surprised he hadn't heard it clear down at the docks, though none of the locals seemed to be startled by it. At the door, a man dressed all in grey, wearing a short sword and holding a quarterstaff, stopped them and looked them up and down.

Loaf had already warned them many times to stay silent and say nothing, so Rigg merely looked at the guard with candid interest, showing no apprehension or any other thing if he could help it. Just wide-open eyes, regarding him. Whether the man could read the dread and the hope behind his eyes, Rigg could not guess. But at least Rigg wasn't blurting things out, or showing the gems around, the way he had spilled his money on Loaf's bar.

The man stared especially long at Rigg, trying perhaps to break the steadiness of his gaze. But Rigg had done this exercise with Father, so the more the man tried to stare him down, the calmer Rigg became, the steadier his gaze. Until the man looked away.

Then Loaf spoke to him. "I see that you can recognize quality, however weary the traveler," said Loaf. "This boy and I"—he indicated Umbo—"have kept company with young master here, to ensure his safe arrival here at Mr. Cooper's bank. But Mr. Cooper has had dealings with me before. I'm Loaf of Leaky's Landing now, but once a sergeant major in the People's Army, and I have accounts here, credit and debit both."

"Then the boys stay outside," said the guard.

"I'm not here on my own business, but on young master's, and we go inside all three."

"Then you go inside none. What do your accounts matter, if the business isn't your own? And this boy"—he gestured with the head of the quarterstaff toward Rigg—"he's no customer of Mr. Cooper's."

"And yet Mr. Cooper would be sorry to lose his custom," said Loaf without a hint of temper. "Mr. Cooper has trusted me with loans before, and I have trusted him with my deposits. Let him say for himself if he trusts me now when I say this boy is worth a thousand times the trade that Mr. Cooper's bank has had with me. Mr. Cooper knows I lie not, and pay my debts, and that is honor enough to win us entrance, I think you'll find."

"Mr. Cooper wants no visitors right now," said the guard.

"And yet I say he *will* want us," said Loaf, still as pleasant as could be. Rigg thought: It must be a skill a taverner has to have, if he's to succeed—to stay calm and friendly in tone and look, regardless of the provocation. And it was quite possible the guard was showing so much resistance precisely because it was obvious that Loaf could pick the man up and break him against the stone walls if he was so inclined. The guard had to prove he was both brave and manly, by making Loaf stand begging at the door. Though in fact, now that Rigg thought about it, Loaf had not begged, but rather demanded, however cheerfully, nothing less than exactly what he wanted.

Which is what Father taught *me* to do, if I can only over-master my fear.

Rigg forced himself to become calm, slowing his breath and relaxing his muscles. If Rigg was to be a worthy son of his father and claim his inheritance, he would have to stay clearheaded and confident, putting fear aside. He could not afford to wait until he was as old as Loaf to have that kind of sureness.

When the guard turned around and went inside—leaving the doorway unattended, Rigg noticed—it had not been more than a minute or two that he'd delayed them at the door. And his return was even swifter, and his manner completely changed, for when the door reopened, the grey guard bowed deeply and solemnly, and ushered Rigg inside first, taking him at Loaf's valuation. Rigg, for his part, carried himself in a relaxed manner, as if being treated with deference were the most normal thing in the world to him.

The moment they were inside, a sharp-faced old woman led them up a wide flight of stairs while the guard returned to duty at the door.

"Why are these stairs so wide?" asked Umbo. "Do so many people have to go up and down them at the same time?"

"No," said Loaf, patient-sounding as if talking to a favored son.

And that was right, Rigg thought—as right as Rigg remaining silent, as if he had no curiosity about the place.

"It's important for a banker to impress those who are not yet his customers with how prosperous he is. A rich banker will not be tempted to steal from his customers, and his wealth shows that he knows how to use money wisely."

Umbo opened his mouth to speak, but Rigg put up a finger that the old woman could not see, twitching it to warn Umbo to keep silence. For Rigg knew exactly what Umbo was going to say, since he had thought of it himself: A banker who looked rich might have gotten that way precisely by stealing from his customers. But now was not the time to bandy words that they would not want repeated to Mr. Cooper.

So they walked in silence up yet another flight, which ended in a spacious landing with a huge double door paned with glass at the far end of it. Other, more modest doors led off on either side.

The old woman brought them to a halt a few steps short of the great doors, and though there was no one to be seen, she said, not particularly loudly, "Loaf of Leaky's Landing, former master sergeant of the People's Army, and two boys, one of whom he vouches for as being of quality, sir."

Without any hand touching them, the doors opened, but not by swinging in or out. Instead they slid aside to left and right, and in front of them was a large, bright room, with many tall windows in the walls and a table larger than the one in Nox's dining room. Bookshelves filled the gaps between the windows, and they were jammed with books, not a space left over.

Mr. Cooper himself stood at the largest window, directly behind the table, silhouetted by the bright light coming through it. He faced outward, as if there were something important to examine on the wall of the building opposite.

"Come in and be seated," said Mr. Cooper, his voice like a whisper of someone speaking directly into their ears.

As they walked through the doorway, Loaf stopped them long enough to show them a finger pressed to his lips, to remind them that only Loaf was to do any talking. At first, Rigg decided to comply, letting Loaf take care of everything. He'd handled things well so far.

Yet Rigg knew that it was only his fear and self-doubt that made him imagine he could let Loaf deal with everything. When it came to banking in large amounts, Loaf knew little and Rigg knew much. Father had never taught Rigg how to talk with surly rivermen in a dark tavern by the river, but he had taught him the principles of banking and finance. And Rigg also understood that if he was to be credible as the rightful possessor of whatever money these jewels were worth, he must show that he alone was making the decisions, that he could not easily be fooled.

The only seats were stools around the table. And the stools were low, almost to the point of being milking stools, so that when they sat, even Loaf looked a bit ridiculous, like a child sitting at the grownups' table. Umbo was not tall for fourteen years of age, so he looked even sillier, lacking only a bib for the babyish effect to be complete.

Rigg, seeing the effect, did not sit down. He recognized at once a thing that Father had warned him about: Men jealous of their power and fearful of losing it will use tricks to dominate other men. "But if you refuse to let such a man deploy these tricks against you, he will be afraid of you. If that's what you desire, then refuse to submit. But if you want to deceive him into complacency, submit happily, and keep your resistance in your heart."

In this case, Rigg decided not to submit, because he knew he needed to be seen as bringing great wealth into the bank, not asking for a favor. It was the banker who must prove himself to Rigg, and not the other way around—that was how Rigg knew this conversation must be framed.

And he also realized that Father had spent those forest journeys preparing him for such a moment as this. My life was in the woods among the beasts, up to my elbows in blood, the skinning knife worn down to fit my callused hands—but my education was for rooms like this.

When the sound of sliding and shuffling stools was silent, Mr. Cooper turned around, and there was an eyeblink of a moment in which he took in the fact that Rigg remained standing at the end of the table, his bag resting open upon it.

Rigg met his gaze calmly, trying to keep the same steady emotionless regard he had practiced on the guard downstairs. And as he did, he noticed the path that Mr. Cooper had most recently followed. There had been a back-and-forth from table to bookshelves, a half a dozen little trips, and Rigg realized that when their arrival had first been announced, while they were still waiting outside the door, Mr. Cooper had rushed around to clear everything off the table. His stance by the window was nothing but a pose. He did indeed regard Loaf's arrival as a matter of some importance, and he had gone to some trouble to make an impression of loftiness and lack of need, which suggested that he needed the business they were bringing him.

"Mr. Cooper," said Rigg, though Loaf had been about to speak and now glowered at Rigg for preempting him. "I have come into an inheritance from my late father. I was to take it to Aressa Sessamo, where I have kinfolk that I have never met. He gave me a letter of introduction to bankers there, but I find that it is inconvenient to make the rest of the journey without converting a little of it into ready money. Therefore I wish you to oversee the sale of a particular item, return a small part of the value to me in coin, and provide me with a letter of credit that will be convertible in Aressa Sessamo when I arrive. I assume you have a relationship with at least one banking house in Aressa Sessamo?"

Loaf's irritation had changed to something more like awe. Well, hadn't Father made Rigg practice rhetoric? "Say the same thing, but now say it to someone you love, to whom you are in great debt." "Say it now to someone who thinks he has power over you, but whom you wish to intimidate." "Say it to someone of a higher class than you wish to seem to be of." "Say it now to make sure someone knows he is of a lower class." It all seemed like such a game to Rigg, but he had mastered all these tricks of rhetoric before he reached the age of ten, and had done it well enough that Father laughed with delight at some of the things he said. He had used these skills well enough with farmers and taverners and other travelers coming down the North Road, and had dealt with Loaf and Leaky well enough, but in those cases it served him to seem what in fact he was—a harmless boy in need of help.

Now, though, Loaf and Umbo were seeing him in another guise—as a boy quite aware of his own worth, relative to a man of whom he expected a service, and for which he would pay not a penny more than the service warranted.

"Yes, yes," said Mr. Cooper, after a moment's hesitation. "I have a good relationship with two Aressid bankers, at either of which my letter of credit will have a good reception."

"At what discount?" asked Rigg, for Father had made sure he was aware that letters of credit might be accepted, but at a discount sometimes as high as ninety percent, until the funds could be transferred and verified.

"No discount, I assure you!" said Mr. Cooper, a little flustered. And the reason for his blush emerged when he was forced to add, "At one of them, anyway, the house of Rududory and Sons."

"And the other one, the one that discounts your note?"

Cooper turned a little red. "Does it matter?"

"I intend to take the note first to the house that discounts you, and disdain their discount, and take my custom to Rududory. You may be sure they will regret the loss and not discount you in the future."

"That is . . . generous of you." But Cooper seemed still to have his doubts.

"If you serve me well, I shall serve you well," said Rigg. "The best legacy my father left me were his principles of honest trade. He taught me that it is better to make a friend of a man through fair dealing than to make a momentary profit and lose his trust. Sergeant-major Loaf assures me that you do business in such a way as well, which is why I have stopped at O to deal with you, if you are interested in performing the service I require."

Of course Loaf had told him no such thing, and it probably wasn't true, though it might be. But Father had also taught him: Treat a man as if he had a fine reputation to protect, and he will usually endeavor to deserve it.

"The other house," said Mr. Cooper, "is Longwater and Longwater."

Rigg nodded gravely. "Now it is time for me to show you the item I wish you to sell for me. Please turn your back, sir."

Loaf's eyes widened and he looked like he was about to speak, but thought better of it. Rigg knew perfectly well that in his place, Loaf would have turned his own back to remove the bag of jewels from his trousers; for Rigg to demand that Mr. Cooper be the one to turn his back was nothing short of outrageous — unless, of course, Rigg were a lordly young man accustomed to other people showing him respect, and not the other way around.

Mr. Cooper once more hesitated, then turned his back to look out the window again, affecting the air of one who simply decided it was an apt occasion to study the birds flying to and from nests in the eaves of the building opposite.

Rigg reached down into his trousers, pulled out the bag, opened its mouth wide, and looked at the jewels, wondering which to offer. He settled on the light blue teardrop-shaped one that had hidden in the seam of his trousers back at Leaky's Landing, for that was the only thing that had made any one of them different from the others since he'd had them. Holding that gem, he tightened the bag's mouth, tucked it back down into his trousers, and strode around the table. "Here, sir," he said, "let's look at this by the light of the window."

It was generous, for a man of the status Rigg was pretending to have, to walk around the table himself to show the jewel to Cooper. Thus, a moment after diminishing the other man, Rigg made him feel that he was respected in turn, and perhaps even liked, by this rich young stranger.

Rigg set the jewel on the table, well back from the edge. "I realize you are not a jeweler, sir, and that your valuation of this stone must depend on what consultants tell you. But I believe you are experienced enough with all forms of collateral to know what you are looking at." Because I certainly am not, Rigg thought— but did not say.

Before Mr. Cooper could sit in his chair, Rigg deftly slid it back out of reach of the table. "Let's not have the back of the chair blocking any of the light," he said.

As a result, Cooper was forced to sit on a stool at the side in order to examine the stone in the light, while Rigg sat in the chair. Thus Cooper's strategem of keeping his visitors in a lower, supplicative position was quite reversed. During Cooper's examination of the stone, Rigg glanced at Loaf and Umbo and saw that Loaf was only barely suppressing a grin, for Mr. Cooper was shorter than Loaf and no taller than Umbo, and at his age looked even more absurd sitting on the stool.

The moment Cooper stood up again, Rigg also rose from the chair and slid it back into place. What could be taken as perfectly natural during the examination of the light-blue jewel would be insolence if Rigg remained in the chair when the need had passed.

Mr. Cooper cleared his throat and spoke. "If this is what it seems, and I have no doubt of it, you understand, then you do my little banking house great honor, sir."

"It is the honor due to all good men of business," said Rigg, "when a matter of great trust is in hand."

"Do you wish me to advance you against the value of the stone, while I pursue its sale on your behalf?"

"I am not pawning the stone, sir," said Rigg, pouring contempt on the very idea that a young man of his means would bring forth a treasure like this to get some amount of pocket change. Though in fact that was what he was doing. "Your note of receipt will be enough, I'm sure, with a statement of probable value." In effect, such a note would serve to win them credit with the loftiest of lodges, though it would be meaningless at ordinary public houses.

"Yes, of course, I didn't mean to—may I recommend a lodging house where you will be most happy with the food and bed?"

"You may recommend three," said Rigg, "and we will think kindly of you when we make our choice."

Cooper now moved, not with the ponderous whispered dignity he had shown at first, but with alacrity bordering on eagerness. He rushed to a shelf, took down a book and a box of paper, then rushed back to get a pen and inkbottle, and sat in the chair to write. Meanwhile, Rigg returned to his pack, took out Father's letter to the bankers that Nox had given him, and brought it to lay in front of Cooper so he could spell Rigg's legal name correctly.

Rigg did not watch him after that, but instead wandered the room, looking at the shelves to see what kinds of books the man kept about him. Many books had no lettering on the spines, but only numerals that corresponded with months and years— account books all. The others, the ones with titles on them, were in so many different languages that Rigg suspected that Cooper had bought them for the fine, aged bindings, and had no notion what was inside. Either that or he was a consummate linguist with a dozen languages at his command.

Which led Rigg to realize that Father *was* such a linguist, and in teaching Rigg to read and speak four languages besides his native tongue, and make sense of several others on the page, and know the history of the speakers of the tongue, and why their writings were of worth, he had made such a linguist of Rigg as well. He had often complained that all these languages were useless, and Father had only said, "A man who speaks but one language understands none."

"Your commission, Mr. Cooper," said Rigg, not turning back to look at Mr. Cooper. "I think under the circumstances, I will raise the normal half-percent to three-quarters, to be taken immediately upon the sale."

Mr. Cooper said nothing, merely continued scratching with his pen, and Rigg was quite sure he had intended some absurd commission like three percent or even higher. When Rigg returned to the table, he saw that on the contract of agency, Cooper had crossed out "one-half of one percent" and replaced it with "three-quarters of one percent" in the space above it. Whether he had really written the regular commission before Rigg spoke, or wrote it afterward and then crossed it out to give a false impression, he would learn from Loaf soon enough, for Loaf was watching everything Cooper did.

Rigg and Cooper both signed the relevant documents: the agency contract, which would tell a jeweler that Cooper was authorized to enter into a contract and receive the funds for the sale of the gem; and the note of receipt, affirming that the house of Cooper had possession of an item of value not less than one purse, belonging to Rigg Sessamekesh, the son of Mr. W.M. of High Stashi.

His own full name still seemed like something foreign to Rigg. But he wrote it out carefully and clearly. It was his signature now.

Since a purse was worth 210,000 fens at the official rate in Aressa Sessamo, and even more upriver, there would be no trouble getting lodging—in the mayor's own house, perhaps, if Rigg were impudent enough to introduce himself and ask the favor.

To Loaf, the word "purse" had some meaning, as a vast amount that only the rich would ever see; to Umbo, it was not a coin at all, but rather a bag you kept money in. Rigg, however, had been trained to convert purses, spills, glimmers, counts, and lights as readily as ordinary people could figure kingfaces, queenfaces, jackfaces, and pigfaces—or fens, shebs, pings, and lucks, as Rigg had learned they were called downriver. Rigg knew that for a purse, a man living upriver could buy an estate with a fine house and land enough to feed three hundred souls. The income from such an estate would support a household with a dozen servants, as well as horses to draw a fine carriage.

A family could remain wealthy forever from such a place, if they didn't divide the lands.

And that was what a single purse was worth, if anyone had ever minted such a coin; Father said that sums that large would exist only as abstractions in the records of banks and the treasury, or as writing on notes of value.

One thing was certain: Father did *not* acquire these gems by being frugal with the money from the pelts they sold.

Rigg remembered spilling his money on the counter at Loaf's tavern, and wondered what Mr. Cooper would think if Rigg showed him the other gems and asked what he thought the aggregate was worth. But of course he would not do it; Rigg doubted that any jeweler in town would have the means of buying even the single gem for ready money. Instead, they would give Cooper something on deposit, the rest to be paid when they sold it to a jeweler in Aressa Sessamo.

But the contract with the jeweler would be enough for Cooper to advance Rigg any amount of ready money he might reasonably ask for—perhaps a pair of glimmers. It would be too much to ask for a banker in O to give him a spill, and where would he spend it? The rest of the value would be marked on a letter of credit that Rigg would take to the bankers in Aressa Sessamo. There Rigg would divide his funds among several reputable banks, and appoint bonded agents to buy and manage lands and businesses for him.

He had learned all this as a series of intellectual problems; the thought of actually doing it, with real cost to him if he did it badly or someone cheated him, was daunting. Is this how I am to spend my life? Looking after managers and bankers, checking on them to make sure they stay reasonably honest, deciding other men's futures by my whim of what to buy and when to sell? It's the forest that I love, not rooms like Mr. Cooper's lair, however bright it is with windows.

When all was copied, all copies signed, the papers folded, and the light-blue jewel placed in a little box, Mr. Cooper looked almost radiant. Rigg suspected that at a stroke, this gem would triple—at least—the assets of the Cooper bank. Most of the funds would soon enough be passed along to banks in Aressa Sessamo, but every hand that touched the money or the jewel would make a good profit, and Mr. Cooper would rise in the estimation of everyone doing business in O, for the tale of it would spread. Cooper himself would see to that, and the jewelers would be his witnesses.

"I don't mean to hasten you on your way," Mr. Cooper said, "but I must be off to get the bids from the jewelers, and to do that I will close the bank and take my guard, Beck Brewer, with me through the streets."

"Is that unusual?" asked Loaf, ever careful. "Will that alert people that you have something worth stealing?"

"It's prudent of you to ask," said Mr. Cooper. "But I always take him with me when I'm out during the day, and everyone knows I take no money with me when I leave the bank for the day, or come in the morning. It will be safe enough—at least until one jeweler blabs." Then Cooper's face reddened a little, because "blabs" was not a word a man of his dignity should have used.

Well, no matter, Mr. Cooper, thought Rigg. We're all posers here.

Within the hour, they were settled into a vast suite of rooms in the first lodging Cooper had recommended to them. "Aren't we going to check the other two?" asked Umbo.

"This one's good enough, and I need a bath," said Loaf. Then he waved the servants away and they were alone.

"I asked for three recommendations," said Rigg, "so that Mr. Cooper would know we didn't intend to let him steer us to a place where he had an arrangement with the hotelier for a percentage of whatever we spend."

"People do that?" asked Umbo.

Loaf chuckled. "He probably has an arrangement with all three of these. And spies watching what we do, as well. He struck me as a careful man."

"But I had to keep up appearances," said Rigg.

"Appearances," snorted Loaf. "Where did you learn to talk like *that*? You spoke high enough with me and Leaky that I thought you were putting on airs, but never like how you talked to Mr. Cooper!"

"I thought he'd wet his pants," murmured Umbo.

"I used an educated accent with you and Leaky, because people downriver were having trouble understanding the way we talk in Fall Ford," said Rigg. "But Mr. Cooper needed more than an accent. He needed to hear a lordly dialect and the attitude to go with it. Would talking rich have worked on you?" Rigg asked Loaf. "Or on Leaky?"

"Not a bit on me, and less on her."

"So to you I talked like a boy of some education, but still one who grew up in a smallish town upriver. Father always said, If you talk like someone used to being obeyed, people will obey you. But if you talk like someone who fears being disobeyed, they will despise you."

"What else did he say?" asked Umbo. "He never taught *me* that."

There was no use trying to explain to Umbo how Father spent all day every day teaching and testing Rigg about things that Rigg thought he'd never use in his life. "I wish in all his saying he had given me a hint of where he found a jewel as valuable as that."

"Nineteen of them," said Loaf. "I think you carry in your crotch most of the wealth of this wallfold." Then he laughed. "But that's how all young men feel, isn't it!"

Three baths and a dinner later, they were all napping on soft beds in their own rooms when a soft rap came at the door. Loaf got up and answered it. Rigg assumed it would be a summons from the banker, but it wasn't—it was the banker himself. Loaf ushered him into the parlor of the suite and soon enough they had the tale.

"All three jewelers said the same, my lord," said Mr. Cooper to Rigg. "This is every bit the gem I thought it was, but alas, it is more, too much more. This is a famous jewel, recognizable by particular marks which each of them identified with no prompting from me. I was told by one that it was the centerpiece of an ancient crown of a royal family from far northwest, in a kingdom whose name I had never heard of. It was won as a prize in battle by a great general, a hero. I thought the man was a mere legend, not real, but the jewelers believed in him. The story is that he struck the jewel from the crown—hence the mark—and bestowed it as a gift upon his great friend, the hero Wallwatcher, who walked the borders of the world, they say. However the skyblue gem of Wallwatcher might have come into your father's hands, it is that very jewel, they're sure of it. The value is so far beyond a purse that none of them will buy it, because they know of no one they could sell it to."

Rigg felt a stab of fear when Mr. Cooper made his veiled reference to how Father might have got possession of the jewel. Might he declare that the jewel was stolen? No—if that were so, the People's Revolutionary Council would confiscate it, and Mr. Cooper wouldn't get a pigface. No, Mr. Cooper was merely explaining that he did not know how to sell it. Rigg calmed himself and began planning how to get around the problem.

Meanwhile, Loaf asked, "How far beyond a purse?"

"Without a buyer, who can say? A pounce at least. But who in this People's Republic has wealth enough to buy it, or would admit it if they did, knowing it would just be taken from him?"

"Why is this a problem?" asked Rigg. "The jewel merely has to be sold privately, to someone who would value it without declaring to any other what he had."

"But the price would be drastically discounted. Instead of fifty purses, no more than five, and in all likelihood less than that. Perhaps only two."

"What about a consortium?" asked Rigg. "Would the three of them together undertake the purchase and the sale?"

"They might, if I suggested it. Perhaps a partnership among the three, with me as well."

"Thereby converting your commission into a share of profit?"

"Unless your lordship disapproves," said Mr. Cooper.

"I'm not a lord—or at least if my father was, he never told me so. Please call me Master Rigg and nothing more."

"Of course, sir," said Cooper.

"I see we'll have to stay here longer than I intended. But I expect you to make this happen as I have described. I imagine that a jeweler in Aressa Sessamo will secretly sell the stone for a bargain price of three purses to a private party, and pass along two-and-a-half purses to this partnership you speak of, and you will credit me with two purses, telling me that you're each making only a spill apiece." Rigg said it with a smile, and shook his head at Mr. Cooper's protests. "I have no quarrel with everyone's taking a profit that makes their fortune, Mr. Cooper," Rigg replied.

"I can hardly agree to this no matter how much I might make," said Cooper. "The jewel is beyond price."

"And yet I must have a price for it."

"Even if it all works as you predict, Master Rigg, you will be getting only one twenty-fifth the true value of the stone."

"My father certainly knew it would be hard to sell when he passed it on to me. If he had valued it more highly than the price the thing will fetch, he would have taken it with him."

They all looked at him in shock and consternation.

"I was making the joke my father would have made. He could not take the jewel, so he left it to me. I cannot use the jewel for anything but money, and I need that money. So this precious ancient artifact will bring its money value, not the value of its fame. Meanwhile, I'll have to wonder how the hero's prize found its way into my hands, for my father cannot tell me now. Get busy, Mr. Cooper, and make this happen as quickly as you can. Here's your incentive for speed: You will pay our lodging costs out of your personal profit from the sale, and not from mine."

Cooper smiled. "I was already going to propose that."

"I *thought* you didn't like that three-quarter percent," said Rigg, still smiling.

"You were generous to a fault, by normal practice, sir," said Cooper. "It was yourself proposed the consortium, and I saw no reason that the jewelers should make a fortune, while I made do with my three-quarters of a point—which would have been a lovely sum, if I hadn't known of others profiting much more."

"I know of profit, too," said Rigg, "and I begrudge you none of it. I only ask that these terms be kept as secret as the buyer's name, so I don't get a reputation for gullibility. And be sure of this: I *will* find out, in due time, what the private buyer paid, and if my portion is less than two-thirds of the amount, I'll be back to see you, and if all I bring are lawyers, you'll be fortunate."

Rigg said it all so cheerfully that one might almost miss the fact that it was a threat of bloody retribution. Cooper responded just as happily, but he missed no part of the threat.

After he left, Rigg turned to Loaf at once and said, "Your fee, too, will be higher."

"My fee will be what we agreed on," said Loaf.

"If I had known what these jewels were worth, I would never have agreed to pay you so little."

"And if I had known what the one jewel was worth, I would never have agreed to take you here at all," said Loaf. "I know

now that I was out of my depth before you ever showed Mr. Cooper the stone. This is all too high for me. The fee we agreed on was fair, and it's still fair today."

Rigg made no further protest, for he was reasonably sure that when they eventually discussed this with Leaky, she would agree instantly that a much higher fee would not impoverish Rigg—and was justified by the greater risk Loaf had incurred without knowing it. Why argue with Loaf now, when Leaky could do the arguing with him later?

In the end it took nearly two weeks for the consortium to be formed. Meanwhile Rigg, Umbo, and Loaf became more familiar with the taverns, restaurants, galleries, shops, parks, bookstalls, libraries, and other recreations of O than any of them had wished. But the wait seemed worth it when the sale was made for more than Rigg's rough estimate, for his portion was three purses for himself.

On the last day, Rigg came from Mr. Cooper's bank with a glimmer and twelve lights, one of which Rigg had asked him to convert on the spot into 120 fens—the rate of exchange in O between the River coinage and the People's coin.

He also had two documents, signed by witnesses. One was a letter of credit for two purses, which Rigg would put on deposit in a bank or banks in Aressa Sessamo, whereupon the funds would be transferred—probably without ever actually passing through O or Cooper's bank at all.

The other document was a certificate of deposit for one purse at three percent, secured against all of Mr. Cooper's personal assets, which were partly enumerated. In effect, Rigg had bought the bank and leased it back to Cooper at an annual rate of return of three percent; if he demanded any portion of it back and Cooper could not (or declined to) pay, this document gave Rigg the right, without court action, to seize by force any and all of Mr. Cooper's possessions.

Trust between friends was a good thing in business, but nice tight legal documents helped keep the friendship true despite long absence or far distance.

And in Rigg's mind, as surely it was also in Loaf's and Umbo's, was the knowledge that he still kept tied to a ribbon around his waist another eighteen gems of whatever value they might be. They could not all be famous relics of the ancient past. Rigg might have chosen, by random chance, the only gemstone in the bag with a value greater than a spill or two. But even *that* would be enough to buy every stick of property in Fall Ford without even noticing the expenditure. It was wealth beyond their ability to calculate. If Rigg wanted to spend it all he wouldn't know where to begin; he thought he could spend a fortune every day for his whole life without exhausting it.

Then again, his definition of "a fortune" had just undergone a change, and he was sure that if he really put his mind to it, he could probably waste it all. That's what Father said: "There is no rich man so unfortunate as to lack for friends who are eager to spend his money for him."

But so far, at least, Loaf and Umbo were not that kind of friend. The money frightened them. They still joked with him, yes, and they laughed together; but they also kept apart from him at odd times, and seemed surprised and even grateful when he paid ordinary attention to them.

Talking about this change in them would only make it worse, because they'd feel he was judging them now and finding them wanting; it would make them more awkward, more eager to please.

All Rigg could do was be himself and never speak to them in the way he had spoken to Mr. Cooper and the jewelers and the lawyers he had worked with to make the deal come through.

Truth be told, Rigg had come to enjoy his pose as a man of wealth and power, and to watch these men treat a thirteen-year-old boy with ridiculous deference. It occurred to him that if he really was of royal blood, as Nox had said, and if that still meant something under the People's government, he would probably have grown up thinking he deserved the treatment he was getting.

But he knew—had Father not warned him?—that he must never value himself for the money he owned. "It can all be swept away," said Father. "Money only retains the value that society places on it. Many a man has thought he was wealthy, only to discover that in the collapse of his nation or the inflation of the currency, his money was now tinscrap, and himself a beggar."

Since that very thing had happened to thousands of noble families after the People's Revolution, Rigg took the lesson to heart. Money is a thing separate from a man, Rigg knew. "I wasn't born with it, I won't have it when I die, it's all temporary."

Yet even as he told this to himself, he felt the warm glow of knowing that he would never have to worry about money again. That separated him from most people in the world. It was impossible to have wealth like this and remain unchanged, and he knew it. He could only try to make sure the changes were neither too extreme nor all to the worse.

CHAPTER 8
The Tower

Ram thought about it sitting, standing, walking, lying down. He thought about it with eyes closed and open, playing computer games and reading books and watching films and doing nothing at all.

Finally he thought of a question that might lead to a useful bit of information. "The light of stars behind us—blue or red shifted?"

"By 'behind us,' do you mean in the spatial position we occupied moments ago? Or in the direction of the stern of this vessel?"

"Stern of the vessel," said Ram. "Earthward."

"Red shift."

"If we were moving toward Earth, it should be blue-shifted."

"This is an anomaly," said the expendable. "We are closer to Earth with the passage of each moment, and yet the shift is red. The computers are having a very hard time coping with the contradictory data."

"Compare the degree of red shift with the red shift when we were in the same position on our way to the fold."

The expendable didn't even pause. It was a simple data lookup, and to a human mind it seemed to take no time at all.

"The red shift is identical to what was recorded on the outbound voyage."

"Then we are simply repeating the outbound voyage," said Ram. "The ship *is* moving forward, as propelled by the drive. But we, inside the ship, are moving backward in time."

"Then why are we not observing ourselves as we were two days ago on the outbound voyage?" asked the expendable.

"Because that version of ourselves is not moving through time in the same direction as we are," said Ram.

"You say this as if it made sense."

"If I started crying and screaming, you'd stop taking me seriously."

"I'm already not taking you seriously," said the expendable. "My programming requires that I keep your most recent statements in the pending folder, because they cannot be reconciled with the data."

"It's really quite elegant," said Ram. "The ship is the same ship. Everything about it that does not need to change remains exactly as it was on the outbound voyage. It occupies the same space and the same time. But the flow of electrical data and instructions through the computers and your robot brain and my human one, and our physical motions through space, are *not* the same, because *our* causality is moving in a different direction. We are moving through the same space as our earlier selves, but we are not on the same timestream, and therefore we are invisible to each other."

"This is an impossible explanation," said the expendable.

"Come up with a better one, then."

This time the expendable waited a long time. He remained completely still while Ram deliberately and without hunger pushed food into his mouth and chewed it and swallowed it.

"I do not have a better explanation," said the expendable. "I can only reason from information that has already been reasoned from successfully."

"Then I suppose that's why you needed a human being to be awake after the jump," said Ram.

"Ram," said the expendable. "What will happen to us when this ship reaches Earth?"

"At some point," said Ram, "either the two versions of the ship will separate and probably explode, or we will separate from the ship and die in the cold of space, or we will simply reach Earth and continue to live backward until I die of old age."

"But I am designed to last forever," said the expendable, "if not interfered with."

"Isn't that nice? Expendable yet eternal. You'll be able to go back and observe any part of human history that you wish. Watch the pyramids being unbuilt. See the ice ages go and come in reverse. Watch the de-extinction of the dinosaurs as a meteor leaps out of the Gulf of Mexico."

"I will have no useful task. I will not be able to help the human race in any way. My existence will have no meaning after you are dead."

"Now you know how humans feel all the time."

• • •

They were at the docks, all their new clothes packed and the trunks ready to be loaded onto a much better grade of boat, when Rigg looked back at the city of O. From here, he could barely see the tops of the white stone buildings over the ramble of houses and warehouses near the wharf. But he remembered what he *would* see again as the boat pulled farther and farther from O.

"We'd be fools, wouldn't we," said Rigg, "if we spent these weeks in O and never visited the tower."

"That's what I thought," said Loaf. "But you were determined to go as soon as the money came in."

Rigg wanted to say: Then why didn't you advise me to see it? But then he remembered two things: First, Loaf *had* said, in a hinty kind of way, things like, "All these pilgrims heading for the tower — what do they care for the city?" and "People live here in O all their lives and never visit the tower." This was not at all the forceful way Loaf used to give advice, so Rigg didn't hear it as counsel, he heard it as mockery of the pilgrims and the locals.

And second, this was exactly the kind of change that Rigg dared not criticize for fear of making it worse. Loaf was treating him now the way he treated wealthy customers who by some bit of ill-fortune were reduced to stopping at his tavern. Deference bordering on cringing was the order of the day — Rigg saw it in the people who served him in his lodging house, and he saw it in Loaf as well, a side of him that had never surfaced before, not even when he and Leaky found the jewels.

They had known they were worth a lot of money, but had not

been able to conceive how much; nor had they really believed that Rigg was capable of holding on to his wealth. Hadn't Loaf come along precisely so Rigg would not be cheated? He had said more than once, "Looks like I wasn't needed after all, you handled them just fine," and each time Rigg would reassure him that without Loaf there, no one would have taken Rigg seriously at all—he would have lost everything as soon as someone reached out to take it. "I'm not a fighter, Loaf—you are. So they'd look at you, and then they had to listen to me."

But Loaf only believed it for a moment, if at all. He was in awe of the negotiating skill Rigg had shown. "You sounded like an officer," he had said.

Well, if sergeants gave such limp, irresolute advice to their officers, it's a wonder anybody ever won a battle!

So Rigg made no argument with Loaf's mild I-told-you-so. "You *did* say it was worth seeing, didn't you," said Rigg. "Well, let's see it now."

It took only a wave of the hand to have a coachman bowing to Loaf, who was still as forceful as ever when dealing with people he regarded as his equal or lower. In a minute Rigg, Umbo, and Loaf were inside a coach, their luggage left in the care of the boat's captain.

It took two hours to get to the Tower of O—one hour to get through a mile of maze-like streets leading to the nearest city gate, and the second hour to go the five miles along the road to reach the base of the tower. The road they took was really the cleared area outside the city wall, intended to force an enemy to come uphill, fully exposed to projectiles from the defenders of the city, so they stayed so close to the wall that they could not see the tower at all until suddenly they rounded a bend and there it was, looming over them, looking as tall as Upsheer Cliff.

"But it's not as tall," said Umbo, when Rigg said so. "We're two miles away, and the cliffs don't look like that until you're five miles back."

"It's the tallest thing *I've* ever seen," said Loaf.

"You need to come upriver more," said Umbo. "Become a true privick."

"The ambition of my life," said Loaf.

The stream of pilgrims coming and going made it impossible to bring the coach as close as they might have wished. "Just as well," said Loaf. "You need to let me and Umbo go ahead and make our offering for three people, or the keepers of the tower will get one look at you and triple the price. Or more."

"Then I'll pay the coachman—I'll pay him enough to wait for us. How long does it take in there?"

"Never long enough," said Loaf.

"Enough for what?"

"To see it all, or understand what you're seeing," said Loaf.

Loaf and Umbo alit from the carriage—that is, Loaf stepped and Umbo fairly leapt from it and ran on ahead. Rigg talked to the coachman, who kept saying, "I'll be here waiting, young master, see if I'm not," and Rigg kept saying, "But let's agree on a price or you'll think I cheated you," not adding "or vice versa," and the coachman would reply, "Oh, young master is generous, I seed that right away, I trust in young master's generosity," which was enough to make Rigg crazy.

He looked over and in the near distance saw Loaf and Umbo talking to one of the extravagantly uniformed tower guards, and wondered if they were having half the trouble he was having getting a price set.

As he stood there, gazing at his friends, he heard a voice at his side. Umbo's voice. And he was speaking so rapidly that Rigg couldn't understand him.

Rigg turned to face him, then glanced back at where he could see Umbo right beside Loaf. The two Umbos were dressed differently, and the Umbo standing beside him looked distressed, frightened, and deadly serious. Rigg knew at once what was happening. Somehow a future version of Umbo had managed to learn the trick of following a path back in time — Rigg's own path. And he had done it in order to warn him of something.

Umbo slowed down — Rigg could see that he was mouthing the words with difficulty, and yet they came so rapidly that Rigg could still only just barely understand him.

"Give the jewels to Loaf to hide them at once."

Rigg nodded to show he understood. He could see Umbo sag with relief — and in that moment he disappeared.

Rigg walked around to where the coachman was watering the horses. "I've changed my mind," he said. "There are plenty of coaches here, I can see, so let me pay you for bringing us here and then if we happen to meet for the road back to the dock, so much the better. But meanwhile you're free to take another fare."

The man named a price for the one journey, looking vastly

disappointed. Rigg knew the fare was much too high, but he doubled it and paid the man, who bowed and fawned and made himself so obnoxious with gratitude that Rigg was glad to turn and jog away from him, trotting toward the others.

They came to him at a walk, and Loaf brandished a pass for three visitors for the whole day. Rigg thanked him, but then drew them away from the tower.

"Where are we going?" asked Umbo.

"We'll go to the tower soon enough," said Rigg. "But something must happen first."

"What?" asked Loaf.

"I'll tell you where we can't be overheard by half the pilgrims here."

They headed for the men's latrines but then passed them by. Not until they had found a secluded place behind the latrine wall did Rigg stop and, facing the wall, draw the small bag of jewels out of his trousers.

"What are you doing?" whispered Loaf harshly. "Get that back in your pants."

"No sir," said Rigg. "I'm giving it to you for safekeeping."

"Why? A pickpocket's as likely to get it from me as from you."

"Quieter," said Rigg. "I had a warning."

"Who from?" asked Umbo.

"You," said Rigg.

Umbo blanched, then looked at Loaf and back again. He seemed nervous. "I've been with Loaf the whole time, I didn't say a word to you."

"The warning came from you—you in the future. You were

very upset. You told me to give the jewels to Loaf, and he should hide them at once."

"What are you talking about?" asked Loaf. "How could Umbo warn you about anything when he doesn't know what you're talking about?"

"He knows all right," said Rigg. "He'll explain it to you later. For right now, Loaf, take this bag and hide it—someplace where it will be safe for a few days or a few weeks or a year. I don't know how far in the future Umbo had gotten before he was able to come back and warn me."

"I suppose this means I actually learn how to do it," said Umbo. "Since it was me who came, and not you."

"If I'm understanding you aright," said Loaf, "then you've lost your mind."

"Take it on faith for now," said Rigg. "If I can trust you with wealth like this, you can trust me and Umbo not to be insane."

"I don't think the two things have anything to do with each other," said Loaf, but still he took the little bag in his massive hand. "I'll hide it all right, but if someone sees me do it or finds it by chance, it's on your head, not mine."

"Exactly," said Rigg. "And to be safe, *don't* tell Umbo or me where you hid it. I don't know what the danger is, but there must be an excellent reason for me not to have the jewels, and it seems to me that it's best if I also don't know where they are. I think Umbo will be safer, too, if only you know."

"So if I die, they're lost forever," said Loaf.

"I already have wealth beyond my wildest dreams," said Rigg.

"Just like a child . . . easy come, easy go." But Loaf turned away and walked into the park-like woods that surrounded the tower grounds, while Rigg and Umbo started off toward the trail of pilgrims headed back to the tower from the latrines.

"We might as well go, as long as we're here," said Umbo.

"Who knows when we'll get a chance again? Something's going to go seriously wrong or you wouldn't have come back to warn me, and it's probably going to be soon or you wouldn't have warned me right when you did."

"Maybe that was the only time I could find you."

"Who knows?" said Rigg. "I don't like knowing that something's going to go wrong. Here I spent the past couple of weeks thinking I was handling things rather well."

"But things going wrong, that's the usual, isn't it?" said Umbo. "My brother died. Your father died. Whatever happens next can't be as bad as that."

"Unless I get killed," said Rigg. "Falling out of the boat into the water and I drown and so you had me give the jewels to Loaf so—"

"I'd tell you not to drown," said Umbo, "and if I wanted to steal the jewels, I'd tell you to give them to me."

"So you've already thought about this?" asked Rigg.

"Just keep peeing," said Umbo.

By the time they were through, Loaf was back.

Umbo asked, "Where did you go?"

"Shut up," replied Loaf. "What now? What's this all about?"

"Rigg and I decided that whatever it is, it's probably not the worst thing in the world. I mean, we know that you and I are still alive, whatever happens to Rigg."

"I thought I told you to shut up," said Loaf, sounding more like he meant it now.

They showed their three-person pass to a different set of guards from the ones Loaf had talked to before, so they wouldn't see Rigg's rich-boy clothing and decide they had been defrauded of their rightful bribe. Then they joined the throng of pilgrims going in.

Though the outside was metal, inside the structure was massive stone, with a long narrow ramp climbing in a spiral up the inside walls. There wasn't a window in the place, and yet it was brightly lighted by magical globes hanging in the air.

"This ramp is steep," said Loaf.

"You're getting old," said Umbo. "*I* could run all the way up."

"Do it then," said Loaf.

"No," said Rigg. "The ramp is narrow, and all it takes is one pilgrim getting irritated and giving you a shove."

"But I can't die," said Umbo. "Because I'm alive in the future to come back and warn you to do whatever."

"Maybe you came back from the dead," said Rigg.

"Come on, that's impossible," said Umbo.

"Coming back from the future is impossible, too," said Loaf. "If you can explain one, you can explain the other."

Rigg wasn't at all sure he could explain anything, at least not well enough to be sure Loaf would believe it. After all the years Father had pressed on him the importance of telling no one, he had no practice in explaining anything to anyone. Nox already knew, and Umbo had a gift of his own. Yet to tell Loaf less than everything now was to make it plain that he was not trusted.

That would make him resentful—and therefore less trustworthy. If future-Umbo thought it was safe to trust Loaf with the jewels, it seemed pointless not to include him in the secret of their shared power to reach backward in time.

All the other pilgrims on the ramp ahead and behind them were engaged in their own conversations. Keeping their voices at a normal volume, Rigg and Umbo told him about their abilities, and what they were able to do together. Between Loaf's questions and Rigg and Umbo correcting each other, it soon was clear enough.

"You still have that knife?" asked Loaf. "It didn't disappear or anything, did it?"

"In my luggage," said Rigg.

"Well, not actually," said Umbo.

Rigg sighed. "What, future-you came back in time to tell you to take it and put it in your own luggage?"

"Loaf's luggage, actually," said Umbo.

"I was joking," said Rigg. "Are you telling me you already knew that some future version of you was paying social calls on us?"

"He—I—woke me up this morning and told me to do it and then disappeared before I could ask any questions. I think me-in-the-future isn't very good at it and a few seconds were all I could manage. Anyway, I didn't tell you because why would you believe that I wasn't just stealing it? Then you got *your* warning and it seemed way more important than mine. I mean, that's a fortune in jewels, and you gave it right to Loaf."

"And if he had told you he took your knife, would you have trusted him when he told you to give me the jewels?" asked Loaf.

"Yes," said Rigg. "Probably." He thought a little more. "Maybe not."

"I think he handled it right," said Loaf. "Unless he *is* stealing stuff, but then why would he have you give the jewels to me, and put the knife in *my* luggage? No, I think whatever happens will make it so I'm the only one who doesn't lose all my stuff."

"What could make us lose our stuff?" asked Rigg.

"If the boat sinks," said Umbo, "Loaf would lose his stuff, too."

"If the boat sinks we all drown," said Loaf.

"I can swim," said Umbo. "So can Rigg. Like fish. Can't you?"

"I'm a soldier. I was always wearing armor, I would have sunk right to the bottom. And since then why would I learn to swim?"

"It's a useful skill," said Umbo. "Especially for people who live by the river and might get tossed in by rivermen."

"Most rivermen can't swim either," said Loaf.

"You still haven't answered," said Rigg. "Can you swim?"

"The idea is to stay in the boat," said Loaf.

"Try again," said Rigg.

"If you never admit you can swim," said Loaf, "people think they can kill you by throwing you in the water."

"Look," said Umbo.

They had finally climbed up just higher than the balls of light and now the glare no longer prevented them from seeing the upper half of the tower. They could see that the stone ended not far above them, with a wide porch that ran all the way around the inside of the tower. It was crowded with pilgrims.

"Keep moving," said a gruff man behind them. They walked on. But glances upward told Rigg that from the platform ring, more than a dozen stone pillars rose to form vertical ribs that supported the metal walls. He remembered observing outside the Tower of O that from about the middle, the metal shell tapered in. So he was not surprised that the stone pillars leaned inward, right up against the metal, until the pillars were joined together by a metal-and-stone ring high above them. Beyond that, the metal formed a simple dome with no stone supporting it at all.

It was a marvel of engineering and design, making the stone support its own weight, and then the weight of the metal. It occurred to Rigg that the metal must be very, very thin, or it would be too heavy for the stone to support.

They got to the platform and moved far from the upward ramp. The beginning of the downward ramp was on the opposite side, and between them, hanging in the air, was an enormous ball. The globes from below and fewer globes from above lighted the entire surface of it. Now, though, they could see that wires from the top ring supported the globes of light, and probably there was some wire arrangement supporting the bigger ball.

The surface was painted in a way that Rigg did not understand. It didn't seem to be a picture of anything, and the colors were drab and ugly and didn't go together. There were brighter yellow lines making divisions on the largest areas of green and brown, and those seemed to shine. But the pattern of them made no sense. Perhaps a honeycomb made by drunken bees?

"There's the world," said Umbo. "It's a picture of the world right there."

Umbo was pointing to a particular place on the surface of the big globe. "See? That spot of red, that's where Aressa Sessamo is.

And that white spot, that's O. The blue line is the Stashik River. So Fall Ford would be a little lower down."

"Then the yellow lines are the Wall," said Loaf. "I've patrolled the Wall, and that looks about right. But what's the rest of it?"

"The whole world," said Rigg, understanding it now. "It's a globe, round in every direction, just like this."

"Everybody knows that," said Loaf. "Even the most ignorant privicks."

"That's crazy!" said Umbo, in mock dismay. "We'd all fall off!"

Rigg made a joke of explaining it to him, as if to a little boy. "No, no, little Umbo, the center of the world pulls on us, holding us to the surface. 'Down' is really toward the center."

"This map of the globe is impossible," said Loaf. "Nobody knows what's outside the Wall. No one in the whole history of the human race has passed through it to see."

"But you can *see* through it, right?" said Rigg.

"Not far enough to know things as distant as this map shows. Not just the neighboring wallfolds, but all of them. If it's a map."

"It's a map," said Umbo. "Come on, it can't just be random chance that they show the course of the river and O is a white dot and the capital is a red dot."

"And we can't be the first to figure it out if it is," said Rigg. "Why haven't we heard about this?"

"Well, we have," said Loaf. "I have, I mean. Why do you think the pilgrims say, 'The Tower of O lets you see the whole world'?"

"I thought they meant you could see really far from the top of it," said Umbo.

"But they also say, 'All of the world is inside the tower,'" said Loaf.

"I thought that was mystical booshwa," said Rigg. "Or maybe just talking about how many pilgrims come here."

"It's weird to think of the world that way. Very disturbing. I mean, the world is the land inside the Wall—that's what the word *means*. How can there be more of the world than the whole world itself? How could anybody know what's outside the world?"

Rigg had been counting. "There are nineteen of them— nineteen lands surrounded by yellow lines. And quite a bit of land that isn't inside any of the yellow lines."

"So there are nineteen worlds on this same globe?" asked Loaf. "Is that what the Tower of O is saying?"

"No wonder people don't talk about it after coming here," said Umbo. "It's just too crazy. Even if they think of it this way— and Rigg's father was no fool and no liar, either, so if he says that we live on the surface of a ball, it's probably true. Somehow. Even if they think of this as a map of nineteen worlds on the face of a globe, who's going to believe them? People would think they were crazy."

"*I* think you're crazy," said Loaf. "Except the map of the world—of *our* world—is accurate enough. The military keeps maps like that—all the world inside the walls, all the roads and towns. It's illegal for anyone else to make them, though. So I wonder how you knew it was a map, Umbo."

"Our schoolteacher showed us a map. Smaller than this, but it had the river on it, and Aressa Sessamo at the mouth of it, and the big bay. And the line of the Wall."

"It was against the law for the schoolteacher to have a map like that," said Loaf.

"Oh, he drew it himself, I think. On a slab of wood. With chalk. And . . . then he went away."

"How long after he showed you that map?" asked Loaf.

"I don't know. After. He only showed it to us the once."

Rigg had been scanning the walls while he listened. "There are nineteen pillars of stone holding up the walls. Nineteen ribs to the tower. A map with nineteen lands surrounded by walls. Nineteen isn't a convenient number to work with mathematically. To divide the circle of the tower by nineteen—that's just crazy, unless they were doing it to have the same number as the number of lands."

"Do you think if these really *are* other wallfolds," said Umbo, "there might be people in them?"

"There are red dots and white dots and blue dots in all of them," said Rigg.

"Boys," said Loaf, "you have no idea how illegal this conversation is."

"You've been to the Wall," said Rigg. "Were there people on the other side?"

"Nobody goes right up to the Wall," said Loaf. "The closer you get, the more fearful and sad and desperate you get. You have to get away. You'd go crazy if you didn't. Nobody gets close. Even animals stay away—on both sides."

"So you only saw it from a distance?" asked Rigg.

"We patrol the edge, because that's where a lot of criminals and traitors and rebels like to go—close enough to the Wall that other people stay away, but not so close they actually go crazy. In a way, it's a fitting punishment for them, living with the dread and grief and despair. But it was our job to go into the zone of pain and force them out. So they wouldn't keep coming out and foraging or raiding or recruiting."

"If it's the same way on the other side," said Rigg, "then even if there *are* people there, they won't come any nearer the Wall than you did. So they wouldn't see anybody on our side and we wouldn't see anybody on theirs."

Loaf drew them closer, his hands tight on their shoulders. "You've been talking way too loud. Now I think I know why your future self came back to warn us."

"No," said Umbo. "If we got arrested for talking, I would have told myself and Rigg to just shut up."

"Well, *I'm* telling you to do that," said Loaf. "Your teacher probably came here and thought about what he saw and memorized the map as best he could. I'm betting that's what happened. Because any soldier—well, any sergeant or higher officer—might recognize this map for what it is, if he happened to come to this side of the sphere. And then he might memorize it. But soldiers would know to keep their mouths shut. And never, ever to draw an unauthorized copy."

"Why not?" asked Umbo.

"Because," said Rigg, putting things together the way Father had taught him, "the army doesn't want any of its enemies to have an accurate map of the world."

"Exactly," said Loaf. "Now let's get out of here before somebody notices us lingering so long looking at the globe."

But Rigg would not leave, not yet. He looked at the maps of the other eighteen wallfolds and tried to imagine the cities. In one, the wallfold just to the north of the one they lived in, the cities were out on the blue part, even though the blue had to be the ocean and the rivers that feed into it. The blue covered more of the globe than Rigg had imagined possible, though Father had told him there was more ocean than land in the world. It never crossed his mind to wonder how Father could know such a thing. Father knew *everything*, Rigg took that for granted, but now he had to ask himself, how could Father have known how much ocean there was in the world, when you couldn't get through the Wall?

Father has been through the Wall.

No, thought Rigg. Father merely came here to the Tower of O and reached the same conclusion we did.

But *someone* must have been through the Wall, or this map could never have been made.

Until today Rigg had never even worried about the Wall. He knew it was there, everybody knew it was there, and so what? It was the edge of the wallfold, which meant it was the edge of the world. You didn't even think about it. But now, in this moment, knowing that there were eighteen other wallfolds, all of them surrounded by an invisible Wall, Rigg longed to get to one of the other wallfolds and see who lived there and what they were like.

And the only thing blocking him was an invisible Wall, one that supposedly drove you crazy if you got too near. But you could see through it. You should be able to walk through and get to the other side.

At last Rigg gave in to Loaf's prodding, and they set out on the downward ramp. "I'm going to go to the Wall," said Rigg softly.

"No you're not," said Loaf. "Unless you're a criminal or a rebel, and then it will be the job of somebody like me to hunt you down and kill you."

"I'm going to go there and see the paths," said Rigg. "If anybody ever crossed the Wall, I'll be able to see where. And if I have you with me, Umbo, I'll be able to go back and *ask* them how they're going to do it. How it's done. Just before they cross I'll ask them."

"Unless it was somebody like your father," said Umbo, "who made no path."

"True. If Father crossed I wouldn't know it."

"Or anybody like your father."

"There's nobody like my father," said Rigg.

"That you know of," said Umbo. "Because if there were others before him who left no path, you wouldn't know about them."

"That's kind of an important hole in your talent, there, Rigg," said Loaf. "That's like saying, 'We have a spy network that sees all our enemies . . . except the ones we can't see.' How sound do you think *that* sergeant will sleep at night?"

"There could be hundreds like your father," said Umbo.

"Father wasn't invisible," said Rigg. "If we had ever run into somebody else without a path, I would have known it."

"But you never saw many people," said Umbo. "You just went out into the woods and then came to Fall Ford and how many other villages did you even visit?"

"A few. Mostly tiny ones above Upsheer," said Rigg.

"Hardly anybody," said Umbo. "So that means there *could* be hundreds like your father, and you wouldn't know it."

"Father would have told me," said Rigg.

"Unless he thought it wasn't good for you to know," said Umbo.

Rigg had to admit, that was the truth.

At last they reached the bottom and passed through the entrance of the tower into the bright noon sunlight. It had taken at least an hour to get up, and almost as long to get down, and despite all the things they said and observed up in the tower, they hadn't been there all that long.

"They're checking people," said Rigg.

He only noticed it because he saw the converging paths of many guards—people who were not part of the general flow of pilgrims to and from the tower. There was a choke point, and they were heading for it. Rigg felt the dread from future-Umbo's warning come to the surface. "They're looking for someone," he said.

"That's why they check people," said Loaf.

"Separate from us," Rigg said to Loaf.

"No," said Loaf.

"There are too many guards, you couldn't fight them. We need you to stay free. That's why Umbo warned us to give things to *you*, don't you see? Separate from us. *Drift* back, don't make a sudden movement the wrong way."

"I know how to do it, thank you, boy," said Loaf. And he began to walk a little faster, drifting forward through the crowd. As he went, he took off his outer jacket and carried it, tucking his hat under the jacket as well.

Rigg was pleased to find out that his instinct had been the same as a soldier's knowledge.

But after a while, Loaf drifted back to them. "It's Cooper, the banker," said Loaf. "He'll know my face."

"Cooper?" asked Rigg.

"There are two officers of the People's Army with him, letting him look at everybody who passes. One of the officers is very high, a general I'm sure."

"I thought the People's Army had no ranks," said Umbo.

"They have no insignias of rank," said Loaf dismissively. "But a general is a general. Look, Rigg, if Cooper hadn't been scrutinizing all the nearer faces, he would have seen me—I was in plain view."

"Maybe he's looking for someone else," said Umbo.

But Rigg knew that for some reason, on some pretext, Cooper had betrayed them. "Go back into the Tower of O and wait for a couple of hours."

"Cooper will just tell them to look for me inside," said Loaf.

"No," said Rigg. "We'll tell them you left us hours ago because you were tired and didn't want to climb. Do you have the money?"

"Most of it. But they'll still search my luggage," said Loaf.

"I'll try to get them to turn Umbo loose, too," said Rigg. "I'm the one Cooper wants."

"How do you know that?"

"Because I'm the one who *owns* the money," said Rigg. "I should have known it was too good to be true."

Umbo spoke up, his face reddening. "Loaf, I didn't put the knife in your luggage."

"Why not?" asked Rigg.

"Where *did* you put it?" asked Loaf.

"Behind a barrel of salt pork in the boat's galley," said Umbo.

"Got it," said Loaf. Then he drifted back in the queue, made a show of looking for something, and then went back against the flow of the crowd, ostensibly to find it.

"Why did you lie about the knife?" asked Rigg, as he and Umbo continued forward toward the checkpoint.

"I told you I put it in Loaf's bags so you wouldn't think I was trying to steal it. You even said yourself that you wouldn't trust me if you thought I was stealing."

"Umbo," said Rigg, "I was wrong when I said I wouldn't trust you. I trust you with my life."

Umbo said nothing.

Rigg tried to keep other people between him and Cooper—he wanted to give Loaf plenty of time to get back inside the tower.

"Father always accused me of the worst thing," said Umbo. "Whatever it was, he always said I was planning to do it. I'm just . . . used to it."

"We're friends, Umbo," said Rigg. "Now try to act stupid and confused."

"That won't be acting," said Umbo.

"I'm going to try to get you out of this," said Rigg.

Then the people in front moved quickly forward and Rigg was staring Cooper in the face.

"That's him," said Cooper. "That's the boy who's claiming to be a prince."

CHAPTER 9

Umbo

"If we are trapped inside the same starship, Ram, on the same voyage, moving backwards through time," said the expendable, "why did the ship's computers show that we made the jump successfully?"

"What were the criteria for determining a successful jump?" asked Ram.

"Observations of the positions of distant stars relative to how they should look near the target star system."

"Can you bring up an image of what the stars looked like at the moment the computers determined that the jump was successful?"

In an instant, a hologram of a starfield appeared in the air over Ram's console.

"I take it that's not the appearance of the stars around our present position."

"Correct," said the expendable.

"How long did the stars have the appearance recorded here?"

"The scan was repeated three nanoseconds later and the stars were as they had been just before the jump."

"So we made the jump, and then we unjumped," said Ram.

"So it seems."

"And we're sure that this wasn't just a glitch? That the computers weren't just 'detecting' what they were predicted to detect?"

"No, because the starfield of the target was not quite identical to the prediction."

"Show me the difference," said Ram.

The starfield view on his holodisplay changed to show yellow and green dots instead of white ones.

"The nearest stars show the most difference, and the farthest ones the least," Ram observed.

"Not always," said the expendable, pointing to the few exceptions. "This is expected because our observations of the universe are based on old data—light that has had to travel ninety lightyears to reach Earth."

"Didn't the astronomers allow for that?"

"Yes," said the expendable. "But it was partly guesswork."

"Let's play a game," said Ram. "What if the difference between the prediction and what was observed in that less-than-three-nanosecond interval could be explained, not by astronomer error, but by the passage of time. Is there some point in the future or in the past when the stars would be in these positions relative to the target star system?"

One second. Two seconds.

"Eleven thousand years ago, roughly speaking," said the expendable.

"So when we made our jump through a stuttering, quantized fold in spacetime, the fold didn't just move us through space, it also moved us backward in time."

"That is one explanation," said the expendable.

"And so we got hurtled back into our previous position in space-time, only progressing backward."

"So it would seem," said the expendable.

"That must have taken enormous energy," said Ram. "To move us eleven thousand years backward in history, and then to recoil back to the present while reversing the flow of time."

"It might have," said the expendable, "if we understood how this actually works."

"Please tell the computers to calculate what laws of physics would explain an exactly equal expenditure of energy for the two operations—passing through the fold into the past, and passing back but reversing direction."

• • •

Umbo tried not to glare at Cooper. Stupid and confused, that's how he was supposed to act. So he stared at the officers. Loaf had been right—the one with the more rumpled-looking uniform was showing nothing on his face, but there was something about his posture, the tilt of his head, that suggested he expected to be noticed and obeyed.

Umbo had expected that Rigg would talk to Cooper, challenge him, argue with him. But instead Rigg was as silent as

Umbo. And when Umbo stole a glance at Rigg, he was looking the general straight in the face—not defiantly, but with the same steadiness as a bird.

"You thought I was fooled by your act, didn't you, boy!" said Mr. Cooper. "All your strutting and posing, but the moment I saw your signature on the paper I knew you were a fraud and a thief."

Umbo wanted to answer him, to say, You certainly gave us a lot of money for someone who knew we were frauds and thieves. He wanted to say, Rigg never even knew that was his name until he saw it on the paper. But instead Umbo said nothing, as Rigg was doing.

"Well, I notified the authorities in Aressa Sessamo that a boy was claiming to be the dead prince and had an ancient jewel—"

"Rigg Sessamekesh" was the name of a dead prince? Rigg had never heard of him, if that was so. But then, the People's Revolutionary Council had made it illegal to talk about royals. Not that people in Fall Ford would have worried much about such a law, from such a far-off government. They simply didn't care about royals, or the People's Council either, for that matter. So until this moment Rigg had no idea that the name Father wrote on the paper meant anything except Rigg himself.

"That's more of our business than needs to be discussed here," said the officer who wasn't the general. "You said there was a man."

"A big man, a roadhouse keeper, they called him Loaf," said Cooper.

"And this other boy?"

"They keep him like a pet, I have no idea what he's good for, he's the most ignorant privick of them all."

Umbo couldn't help the way his face reddened.

The officer chuckled. "He doesn't like that."

"I said he was ignorant, not deaf," said Cooper.

"I notice you're not denying anything," said the officer to Rigg.

Rigg turned his gaze to the officer for a long, steady moment, and then returned to looking at the general. Umbo wanted to shout with laughter. In that simple look, Rigg had as much as told the officer he was a worm, not worth talking to. And yet his expression had not changed at all.

On impulse, Umbo started to cast his net of speeded-up time around Rigg.

Rigg turned to him and said, "No."

Umbo stopped.

"No *what*?" the officer demanded.

Rigg said nothing.

The officer turned to Umbo. "What did he tell you not to do?"

Umbo shrugged.

The officer seized him by the shoulder, his grip fiercely painful, as if he meant to drill a hole through his shoulder with his thumb. "What did he tell you not to do, boy?"

"He was thinking of running," said Rigg.

"Oh, you can read his mind?" said the officer.

One of the tower guards approached them gingerly. "If you've found them, can we let people continue to leave the tower?"

The officer turned to him and said harshly, "Don't bother us!"

The general turned his head to the guard, ignoring his own subordinate from the People's Army. "There's no reason to block them now. Thank you for helping us."

The officer showed no sign that the general had just contradicted him.

The tower guard bowed deeply. "Thank you, your excellency."

"The People's Army has no 'excellencies,'" snapped the officer.

"Sadly enough," said the general, "that is true. Guard, if you wouldn't mind, could you send a man or two into the tower to search for a tall man who looks like a former soldier? I saw him with these two, and when he saw Mr. Cooper, he headed back into the tower, pretending to look for something."

Umbo was impressed. Maybe generals got to be generals because they were smart, or at least observant.

Then again, the general seemed to carry himself and turn his head and speak exactly the way Rigg was acting. When Rigg told Umbo no, he had spoken with the same kind of calm authority the general used when speaking to the guard. It was a voice that expected to be obeyed—yet there was no anger or emotion in it, so that it didn't provoke resentment. When Rigg spoke, Umbo had simply obeyed, without even thinking of arguing or doubting or even hesitating. How had Rigg learned how to do that? He had never been in the army. But maybe it was something he learned from the Wandering Man. *He* had the power of command.

What a fine thing it must have been, to be raised by the

Wandering Man. And what had Rigg's father been planning for him? Not just the jewels, not just a royal name that apparently belonged to someone who was supposed to be dead, but also this air of command, all the knowledge of finances Rigg had, his understanding of how to bargain with adults — Rigg's father must have trained him in all of that.

Had he foreseen this moment? Wouldn't this make him one of the heroes, to be able to see into the future? Umbo had never heard of a hero with such a power, but wouldn't that be a mighty gift from a god? All that Umbo and Rigg had been able to do, between them, was reach into the past — and even that was a rare gift, and hard to do.

I will have to learn how to do it alone.

"I'll take the boys with me back to their boat," said the general. "We'll wait there while you see to getting the man called Loaf."

"That's his name," said Umbo.

The general looked at him steadily.

"It's not a nickname or anything," said Umbo. "In his native village, that's how they name people. His wife's name is Leaky." Umbo had no idea why he had felt the need to speak up, but it had been an irresistible impulse. And now the tiniest trace of a smile played at the corners of the general's mouth. Umbo looked to Rigg to see if he had said too much, but Rigg's face was calm and showed nothing.

"By all means," said the general. "Wassam, the man's name is 'Loaf,' so there's no need to demand a realer-sounding one. Bring him to me unquestioned and unbeaten, please." With that the general reached out his hands toward Umbo and Rigg. Without needing a bit of explanation, they each took one of his hands and he walked with them back toward the city.

He held their hands lightly. But when Umbo thought — just *thought* — of running off, he could feel the grip tighten on his hand.

Can the man hear my thoughts?

No, thought Umbo. I must have tensed up just a little when the idea of running crossed my mind. Or maybe he noticed that I glanced off toward that canebrake.

Meanwhile, Mr. Cooper shadowed their steps. "He's going to lie to you," said Cooper. "He's full of nothing but lies and poses!"

"And yet," said the general mildly, "he hasn't told me a single lie today."

"That's because he hasn't said a thing. You notice he doesn't deny anything I said!"

"Mr. Cooper," said the general gently. "He doesn't regard you as worth his notice, that's all."

"Yes!" cried Cooper. "That's the arrogance I was talking about!"

"The arrogance that we might expect," said the general, "if he really is of the royal house."

"Oh, right, I'm sure you know how impossible *that* is!"

"Wouldn't your time be better spent, Mr. Cooper, remaining behind to identify the man called — no, the man whose *name* is Loaf?"

Again, there was that subtle air of command, and Cooper turned and began to walk briskly back toward the tower, muttering, "Of course, should have thought of it myself," and then his voice faded out.

With Cooper gone, the general's demeanor changed. "Well, my young friends, how have you been enjoying the city of O?"

"It's very big," said Rigg.

The general chuckled. "You're from upriver, of course, and this is certainly the first real city you've encountered. But I can assure you that there are fourteen cities larger than O within the People's Republic. No, big as it is, O's real claim on the attention of the wise is its great age. The artifacts of an earlier time, whose wisdom we have not yet recovered, and may never recover."

Rigg nodded. "You mean the globe of the world inside the tower?"

The general walked in silence for a few moments, and it occurred to Umbo that perhaps the general had never realized that the thing was a map of the world both outside and inside the Wall. "The whole tower is a miracle," said the general, finally. "The ribs of stone up inside the tower seem to be structural, but they aren't."

"They aren't holding up the walls and the dome?"

"The stone pillars are not attached to the walls in any way. They hold up the lights and the globe, but there was an earthquake once, more than three thousand years ago, and three of the pillars collapsed inside the tower. The great chronicler of that time, Alagacha—which is as close as we can come to pronouncing his name in our tongue—reported that as they restored the pillars, they discovered that there was no way to tie them to the walls. It's as if the tower was there before anyone thought to add the stone ramps and pillars, the lights and the globe."

Rigg did not seem impressed. "What does that have to do with the great age of the city?"

"Nothing at all. Except that legend has it that the tower was here before the city of O, and *nothing* else."

"Then the *tower* is very old," said Rigg.

And Umbo thought: How can you arrest us and then talk to us as if we were children at school?

But Rigg had said his life with his father was like this—walking along, discussing things. So maybe Rigg found this natural. Maybe the general was already some kind of father to him.

Well, he's a father to me, too, thought Umbo. The difference is that to *me* a father is a punisher, unreasoning and unstoppable, not someone to chat with about history.

"In every other city, wherever someone digs to lay the foundation of a new construction, the workmen turn up stones and bones—old walls, old floors, old burial grounds. Everything is built on the foundation of something else. No matter where we go in the floodplain of the Stashik, and all around the coast of the sea, someone has been there before, layer on layer of ancient building. But that doesn't happen in O."

"You can't tell me that those buildings in the port are thousands of years old!" scoffed Rigg. "The timbers would be ten thousand years of rotten by now, so close to the river."

"Oh, I'm not talking about the wooden structures, yes, those are built and replaced. But the stone buildings and the great wall—they're the original. Every thousand years or so the great buildings fall into such decay that they have to be rebuilt. And when they do it, they find there's nothing under the foundations.

When the city walls and the great white buildings were originally built, they were on virgin ground. It's here in O that we feel all the eleven thousand years of history."

Then, suddenly, the general's grip on Umbo's hand tightened a little and Umbo looked up to find the general gazing at him— but with a slight smile. Of mockery? Or sympathy? "Your young friend, Master Rigg, seems uninterested in history."

"He's a year older than I am."

Umbo waited for the general to make some comment about his height. Instead, the man said, "Eleven thousand years of history, that's what we have. To be precise, 11,191 years plus eleven. They say there's a stone at the base of the Tower of O which, when you pull it out of place during repairs, bears an inscription: 'This stone laid in the year 10999.' Of course it's in a language that only scholars can read, but that's what they say."

"So the world was only 192 years old when the stones of the tower were laid?" asked Rigg.

The general was silent again for a few moments. "So it seems. The oldest building in the world."

"The tour guides are missing a bet not to tell folks that," muttered Umbo.

"They'd say it, I'm sure, if they knew. But only a few people care enough about the deep past to root through the old records and learn the ancient languages and then write new books about old things, and only a few of us bother to read them. No, the only history that matters these days is the story of how wonderful our lives are since the People's Revolution deposed the royal family, and how rapacious and cruel the royal family were when they ruled the World Within the Walls."

"And how happy we all are that they were deposed," said Rigg.

The general stopped walking. "I'm trying to decide if your tone was sarcastic."

To which Rigg's only answer was to make the identical statement with the identical intonation—which is to say, no discernible intonation at all. "And how happy we all are that they were deposed."

The general chuckled. "Now I see what that asinine banker meant about you. By the Fixed Star, my boy, it's as if you were a bird singing the same song, over and over, never varying."

"I know nothing about the royal family, sir," said Rigg, "or perhaps I would have known that there was something wrong with the name my father said was mine in his will."

"There we are," said the general.

Umbo looked around—they didn't seem to be anywhere in particular.

"Not literally, my young friend," said the general to Umbo. "I mean to say, this is the crux of the matter. This is why I was sent to arrest Master Rigg and bring him back to Aressa Sessamo. Yes, he had the jewel and when that fool tried to convert it into cash, all he accomplished was to alert the People's Revolutionary Council. Did he really think a royal artifact could be sold without attracting the notice of powerful people? Did *you* think it?"

"Yes, sir," said Rigg. "I did indeed. To me, it was a stone that seemed likely to have some great value. I did not expect Cooper's exorbitant response to it, recognizing it as an ancient jewel. Nor did I expect to raise the sums of money he immediately talked about. My father left it in the care of a friend, to be given to me when he died. Then he died. The friend gave it to me, and here we are."

"Come now, Master Rigg, do you expect me to believe that you were well enough educated to know enough about finance and contract law to run rings around a sharp dealer like Banker Cooper, and yet you did not recognize the name 'Rigg Sessamekesh'?"

"My name is Rigg," said Rigg. "My father never mentioned a last name. So I recognized the prenomen, but not the gens."

The general chuckled. "And since you have iron control of your vocal intonation, your gestures, your facial expressions, how can I know whether you lie or tell the truth? But it's a stupid lie, if it's a lie, because everyone knows the name Rigg Sessamekesh."

"I never did," said Umbo, "and I went to school lots more than Rigg. Nobody talks about the royal family. It's against the law to care about them."

"Well, well," said the general. "I had no idea. That the law was actually followed, at least upriver. In the city—and when I speak of 'the city,' I don't mean O—in the city the name and story are so widely known, and the law against speaking about the royal family is so little regarded, that I never thought that perhaps in the hinterlands people might still avoid uttering the forbidden names. Have you eaten?"

It took a moment for Umbo to realize that the subject had changed.

"I'm not famished at the moment," said Rigg, "though Umbo is always hungry. But you, sir, are better situated to know when our next opportunity to eat might be. If you're offering a meal now, I'll accept it gladly and do my best to make it worth your while."

"You're offering to pay?" asked the general.

"I don't know, sir, whether I have access to any of my funds. From what Cooper said, I would guess that everything is impounded."

"It is indeed," said the general. "But under the People's Law, you are not yet guilty. So the money is still yours, even if you don't have the free use of it. I, however, have complete access to your funds—provided I have your consent."

"Then you have my consent up to the full price of a very nice meal."

"A very quick meal, I think you meant to say."

"'Quick' depends on what we do with the food, sir; 'very nice' depends on what the cooks do with it."

"You've been here for several weeks. Is there any food along the remainder of our route that is worth stopping for?"

"If you tell me our destination," said Rigg, "I'll choose a shop that lies on our route."

"The boat, of course. The one you already engaged to take you to Aressa Sessamo. I thought you heard me say that. Since you already paid for it, the People's Republic will save money by using it to transport you."

"I leapt to the conclusion that it was our boat that we were bound for, but then you only really said that was where our companion was to be brought if they happen to find him."

"Let's have it out right now, Master Rigg. Are you Rigg Sessamekesh?"

"That name means something to you. You speak of a story that everyone in Aressa Sessamo knows. But I do not know it, so I cannot say whether I am that person. It seems unlikely to me. I only learned the name after my father was dead. Was it some joke of his? A trick to arrange for me to meet *you*? My father was an enigmatic man, and I can't guess what he meant by it. I only know that I had to show his letter to Cooper in order to prove I had the right to my father's funds and possessions. He didn't seem to recognize the name—he only paid attention to a valuable jewel. So until your arrival here today, I really didn't think anything of the name. My father never called me by it."

The general chuckled again. "Oh, you're a player, you're a player. Don't assert, don't deny. You could be an innocent passerby, for all you admit."

"I tell you the simple truth," said Rigg. "If what I say represents a move in a game, then the player is my father, sir, not me. I am as intrigued as anyone to learn the implications of what my father wrote in that letter. It seems he was determined to further my education from beyond the grave."

"Your 'father,'" said the general. "If he really is your father, then you can't possibly be Rigg Sessamekesh."

"Father never told me the circumstances of my birth. Others from Fall Ford say that my father went away on a long trip and came back with a baby. I'm sure he never explained and no one dared to ask. He never said more than he wanted others to know, and people didn't pry into his affairs."

"Everybody thinks he's a bastard that the Wandering Man got on some woman," said Umbo. "And the Wandering Man brought him to Fall Ford to raise."

"It's all right, Master Rigg, that your friend calls you a bastard?" asked the general.

Umbo started to protest that he hadn't meant to call him that at all, but Rigg smiled at him, silencing him.

"My friend reported that it's the gossip of Fall Ford that I am a bastard," said Rigg, "not that *he* thinks me to be one. But what if I am? My father recognized me."

"Except that if you are Rigg Sessamekesh, he is not your father."

"Someday you must tell me that story."

Again the general studied Rigg's face, searching for a hint of sarcasm. Umbo could have told him that it would do no good. Rigg never showed what he didn't want to show. Even on the cliff, that terrible day when Kyokay hung there and Rigg was trying to rescue him, nothing at all showed on Rigg's face—not concern, not even interest. Not that Rigg *couldn't* show emotion—but why would he bother when he didn't know anyone was watching? Displays of emotion were just one of the many things that separated the rest of the world from Rigg. It had been different when Umbo and Rigg were both little. Rigg had been perfectly normal then, just a kid, as likely to get angry or cry or laugh or screech as any other kid. But with each journey he took with his father, Rigg had grown more reticent, more self-controlled. Colder, except when he decided not to be. That's why Umbo had been so willing to believe that Rigg had murdered his brother, there on the cliff. It was the face of a stranger. Lately that was the only face Rigg had worn.

They reached a place that Umbo had found in his wanderings through the city during the past few weeks. He had brought Loaf there, and when Loaf said it was good enough, they had brought Rigg. It made Umbo feel a rush of pride that this is where Rigg would choose to buy their last meal in O. Or, for all Umbo knew, their last meal as mortal humans.

Rigg signed for the meal as he always did, including a lavish tip. He wrote the name of the bank and the place they had been lodging until this morning. The shopkeeper knew them, bowed, thanked them. He gave no sign that word of Rigg's arrest by the People's Army had spread this far.

What does this general want? thought Umbo. He's so nice to us. A little boring when he gets off on the subject of history, but far better than any treatment I ever heard about a prisoner getting from the authorities.

They ordered their food—which consisted of cheese, boiled eggs, and vegetables between the two halves of a boule of bread. Umbo immediately started to eat his—he was famished—and the general seemed to watch him to see how it was done. Perhaps he's never eaten good street food, thought Umbo. Maybe the capital doesn't have anything this good—or, perhaps, anything this crude and low-class. Well, even if *he* thinks it's a privick thing, it's very nice food, and I'm not going to bother being ashamed of it.

And within moments, the general was eating his with as much gusto—and the same slobbering juices from the tomatoes running down his chin—as either Umbo or Rigg.

The general's hands were busy, but Umbo realized by now that nothing would be accomplished by his running away. They would only find him again, and no doubt would treat him differently after an escape. Umbo had heard of whippings and he had heard of leg irons. He didn't want either.

They were just finishing their food when they reached the docks, and then picked their way among the passengers and rivermen and stevedores and onlookers. Not that it was hard. The general's uniform did what it was supposed to do—it made everyone alert enough to get out of their way. No one actually looked the general in the eye—they just sidled this way or that so that they were never actually blocking the general's path. Though they were happy enough to jostle Rigg and Umbo. After all, they were mere boys richly dressed, and deserving of a bit of a knock from those who resented their obvious privileged status.

Umbo wanted to shout at them, Until a few weeks ago I was poorer than any of you! But what good would that do? He didn't want or need the love of passersby on the docks.

There were six soldiers guarding the ship. Or rather, two guarding the gangplank, two more standing near shops much farther away, but still within calling distance, and the last two on the boat itself, calmly observing the crowds.

"As you can see, your things are all loaded onto the boat," said the general.

"Actually," said Rigg, "I can see only that our things are not where we left them."

The general sighed—exasperation or amusement?—and

said, "I suppose when you get aboard you'll see that your things were loaded."

"And now it's our turn to get loaded on."

The general answered by speaking to the young sergeant who was in charge of the contingent of soldiers. Umbo noticed that the sergeant had an insignia—it was only the general and the other officer back at the tower who had no markings on their clothing. It made Umbo smile: The People's Army has no insignia for its high officers—but has markings to identify the lower-ranking ones. Therefore the absence of insignia was the highest insignia of all. It was what Umbo's dad always said: The People's Revolution was just a change of uniforms—it was still the same kind of people running everything.

"These boys have the run of the boat, but are not to be let off it. This one"—he indicated Rigg—"is the terrifying hooligan that a man of my rank had to be sent to arrest. Please ignore the tomato drippings all over his very expensive tunic. He's from upriver—they haven't discovered napkins yet."

The sergeant laughed, but Umbo wanted to say something very cutting. But just as he was drawing in breath before speaking, Rigg brushed the back of his hand and somehow the message was clear: Patience. Wait.

It had been fun running up and down the gangplank when they put in at various river towns. But that was when Umbo was free; now he was forbidden to leave, so walking up the plank to the ship seemed to have a hint of the gallows about it.

Almost as soon as they had seen that their bags and trunks were suitably placed, the general reappeared and said, "Master

Rigg, the ship's captain has been kind enough to allow me the use of his quarters. Would you mind terribly if we started your inquisition now?"

The word "inquisition" had a bit of a smile in it, no doubt meant to dispel fear, hinting that it wasn't a *real* inquisition. Yet that *was* the word the general had chosen to use, and hardly by accident. No matter how nice the general might wish to seem to be, he still had the power to put them to torture or anything else he pleased, and Umbo wasn't all that reassured to recall that the general had affirmed that they couldn't be treated as guilty until there was some kind of court verdict about Rigg's supposed conspiracy.

When Rigg joined the general and started toward the captain's quarters, Umbo came along because it never crossed his mind to do otherwise. But the general noticed him at once, and gestured with his trailing hand for Umbo not to stay with them. This would be a solo inquisition, apparently. Though Umbo had no doubt that his time would come.

There was no way to linger around the door and hope to overhear some of their conversation, so Umbo went to the galley, where the cook ordered him to go away.

"I just wanted to help," said Umbo.

"What do you know about cooking?"

"Everyone in Fall Ford knows how to cook *something*," said Umbo. "'It's a useless man starves without a wife to cook for him.'"

"Is that some kind of proverb?" asked the cook.

"Yes, sir," said Umbo.

"Then you come from a place full of very stupid people," said the cook.

"Thank you sir," said Umbo. "Does that mean I can help?"

"If you break one dish I'll knock you on the head, crack your skull, and pry it open like a hardboiled egg."

"I hope word doesn't get around that you're as likely to serve chopped boy in your stew as mutton or pork."

"Wouldn't matter if I did," said the cook. "Anybody's on this tub, they'll eat what I serve or try their luck at catching something edible in this saint-forsaken river."

Within moments, the cook had Umbo running errands, and to Umbo it felt like being home again. It took no particular effort or even a detour to glance into the spot where he had put the knife and see that it was still there. But he wouldn't take it now. He didn't know yet whether the People's Army even knew about the ancient knife—this general seemed to have an obsession with old things and it was better if he didn't know about the one thing that Rigg had really stolen.

Finally the cook set him down to pare turnips to make the mash for the next day's breakfast. It was slow work, but mindless as long as you were careful not to let your finger get added to the mix.

And as he sliced and chopped, Umbo thought about what he knew he would have to do. Somehow he must figure out how to do the thing that he had already been seen doing—travel back in time to this morning to give warnings to himself and to Rigg.

Wouldn't it have been nice of his future self to give him some hint about how he was going to learn how to talk to people in the past?

One thing was certain—Umbo had never seen any of the

paths that Rigg was always talking about. So even if he succeeded in causing himself to slow down—or speed up, or whatever it was he did—it was an open question about whether he would *ever* be able to see anybody from the past—even the past of just this morning.

And before long, he was trying to do to himself what he had so easily done to Rigg, speeding him up—or slowing him down, depending on how you looked at it. But it was as if his talent were a long sword—he could easily use it to touch others, but his arms were too short or the sword too long for him to stab himself.

It was like Wandering Man had said, during the brief time he gave Umbo a little training: You have to find it the way you teach yourself to wiggle your ears.

Since Umbo had never knowingly wiggled his ears—nor known anyone who could—the example was wasted on him.

But then Wandering Man went ahead and taught him how to wiggle them. He had made Umbo look in the mirror and then smile his broadest grin. "See how your ears move up just a little when you smile?"

Umbo could see it easily, once it had been pointed out.

"That means you have the muscles to wiggle your ears, and they're working. What you do is smile and then unsmile, again and again, only now you're concentrating on the muscles that draw your ears up and back when you smile. Smile hard, and then try to move your ears again only without any of the smiling."

Umbo tried and tried. "Nothing happens," he said.

"But you're mistaken," said Wandering Man. "Something very important has happened. You're aware of those muscles. It takes a while for the nerves to reinforce their connections so the muscles will contract without dragging all the rest of the smile with them. Practice it whenever you think of it, smiling hard and then trying again without the smile. Gradually, the muscles will strengthen. Just make sure you work both ears equally, so you don't end up with only one ear you can control."

It took only three days before his ears were moving on command—either together or individually. Within another couple of weeks, he was a champion ear-wiggler.

And, as Wandering Man had predicted, the analogy was nearly perfect. Previously when he had thrown his little web of speed onto another person, it had been willy-nilly and ragged—it gave Mother a headache when he did it to her repeatedly. But with practice, even though he had no idea what was actually happening inside him, he began to be able to control the thing, to make it steady, to make it strong. It just took concentration and repetition, hour after hour.

Now he would have to do it all over again, this time learning how to include himself, and only himself, within his zone of speed.

The only sign he had that he might have made any progress was when the cook came in and said, gruffly, "Where'd you put the rest of them?"

"They're all in the pot," said Umbo.

The cook looked doubtful, but came and looked in the pot and then turned back to Umbo. "Nobody ever peeled them that fast." But then he examined them closely and had to admit that Umbo had done it exactly right.

"I would have said it can't be done that fast."

"I applied myself."

"Apply this, you show-off," said the cook, making a dismissive gesture that Umbo had been told had something to do with either female body parts, the act of rutting, or defecation—Umbo had been told of many a likely meaning, but none of them seemed right to him.

But Umbo took no offense—for the cook really meant it as backhanded praise. And the fact that he had done it so quickly was also an indication that *something* was happening. Had he sped himself up, at least a little? It was a promising start.

Umbo was up on the passenger deck, the kitchen chores done, when he saw them bringing Loaf—in a cart, manacled and attached to the cart with chains. Apparently his arrest had not gone as smoothly as Rigg's and Umbo's.

The general came out at once, long enough to greet Loaf and give him the run of the ship, as long as Loaf didn't try to go back on land.

The general also told the captain they could start the voyage whenever he and his crew were ready. Then the general went back into the captain's quarters to continue his interview with Rigg. Umbo would have given almost anything to be in that room. Instead, the mate started barking orders and in no time the boat was untied and being poled away from the dock.

"You think Rigg's all right in there?" asked Loaf.

Umbo turned to see that Loaf had come up on the passenger deck.

But so had the officer who arrested him. When Umbo and

Loaf pointedly looked at him, he smiled a bit nastily and said, "The general may have forgotten that you're prisoners, but I haven't."

Umbo ignored the officer—for Rigg's method seemed the best, saying nothing and acting as if nothing had been said. "I'm practicing," Umbo said to Loaf—deliberately making his voice loud enough for the officer to hear. "But the thing I've got to do, I don't know if it's even possible. There are things you can do for someone else that you just can't do for yourself."

"Like tickling," said Loaf.

"Exactly like that," said Umbo.

"What did you mean by that?" demanded the officer.

"Mean by what?" asked Umbo.

"'Tickling.' Are you speaking in some kind of code?"

Loaf turned to the officer. "If you don't understand what we're talking about, that doesn't mean you have a right to pester the grownups to explain everything. You'd have to have been with us during our whole journey up till now, and we don't like you well enough to spend enough time with you to acquaint you with all the particulars."

Again with the evil smile. "The general won't always be here," said the officer. "Then we'll see how much you like me." He went over the ladder and scooted down it to the cargo deck.

As soon as they were alone, Loaf got to the point. "I'm glad you're making progress, though I wouldn't be worried even if you weren't. One fact is clear: you *can* learn to do it because you did it. Or *will* do it."

"That's easy to say when you don't have to do it."

"Right," said Loaf. "Now, go down and get whatever you plan to take with you, secure it on your body so it won't fall off in the water, and get back up here right away."

"Why?" asked Umbo.

"Are you daft?" asked Loaf. "Where did your future self find you and Rigg to leave those incomprehensible and useless messages?"

"Me in my bed in our lodgings, and Rigg there at the coach, while you were already heading up to the tower."

"Well, then, unless you can travel through space as well as time, we can't afford to get too far from O. Don't you have to be in the exact spot yourself in order to talk to somebody from the past?"

Umbo nodded. "I've got to stay here. In O."

"Too late," said Loaf. "We're not in O. But that's fine, we need to go into hiding for a while once we leave this boat, and we're too well known in O to avoid recapture. Now go and get whatever you want to take and come right back up here."

Umbo dashed down the ladder and got to his bags. But he didn't open them. They contained plenty of fine new clothing, but how could he explain bringing changes of costume up to the passenger deck? No, there was only one thing he really needed to bring with him—and that was in the galley.

When Umbo charged in the cook barked at him. "I don't have time for you now, and if you try to snitch something, I warn you: The gruel hasn't boiled yet and it's as likely to make you sick as not, so snack at your own peril."

"I just forgot something I left where I was peeling turnips," said Umbo.

"Then get it and get out," said the cook.

The knife was still there, in the fine leather bag Rigg, in his days of wealth, had bought to keep it in. Umbo paused long enough to tie the bag's strings around his waist and let the knife hang down inside one pantleg. It was very awkward, but he couldn't think of a better place to conceal it for the time being.

Up on the passenger deck, Loaf was conversing with the officer again. "The general said we had the run of the ship," Loaf was saying. "So it's really none of your business if the boy and I stay together or go our separate ways. If the general wanted us all to stay together, he'd have us in the captain's quarters with Rigg."

Rigg. They were abandoning Rigg!

But Umbo knew there was no choice. Rigg was going downriver, and there was no way to stop *that* from happening without getting somebody killed and probably still losing. Umbo had to stay in O because that was where he had to be to give the warnings that they had already received. Loaf had to stay in O because that's where he had hidden the money and gems. Rigg would understand that.

"Did you find it?" Loaf asked. Umbo nodded.

"Find what?" demanded the officer.

"Your father's blade in the box your mother kept it in," said Loaf.

The officer flared with rage but then backed off. He really was exceeding his authority, and knew it, and didn't want to have to account to the general because he punished the prisoners for breaking a rule that the general hadn't imposed.

Loaf pointedly turned his back on the officer and walked

Umbo to the railing at the edge of the upper deck. They both looked down at the river.

"Now might be a good time to prove you can swim," said Loaf.

The river was much narrower in Fall Ford; Umbo had never swum so far. "Can't we take one of the boats they tow behind?"

"Can you make shore? Figuring that we swim partly with the current and end up well downstream?"

"I suppose this means *you* can swim after all. Or am I supposed to tow you?

"If you really try," said Loaf, grinning, "you might not die."

"Might not?"

"Old saying in my village, forget about it. Thing you do, once you're in the water, swim under the boat and come up the other side, where they're not looking for us."

"Want me to dig up some oysters while I'm down there?"

"Either you can hold your breath long enough or you'll die. But go under the boat or they'll have bolts in you from their crossbows when you come up for air."

Umbo started for the stairs. Immediately the officer moved toward them.

"Get back here," said Loaf loudly. Umbo did.

The officer went back to the opposite rail.

"We go from here," said Loaf softly.

Umbo looked straight down.

"Don't look there," said Loaf.

"What if I can't clear the deck below?" asked Umbo. "What if I smash against the railing down there and break a leg and *then* go into the water and drown?"

"I already thought of that," said Loaf.

And without another word he picked Umbo up by the collar of his tunic and the belt around his waist and pitched him over the railing with such force that he landed far beyond the lower deck.

Not that Umbo had any time to take much note of his surroundings. The shouting began on deck immediately, and when Umbo came up for air the first time, he saw another body hurtling into the water—and to his surprise it was the officer, who was sputtering and choking and calling for help.

Umbo toyed with the idea of helping him, then decided that it wasn't his job. Instead, he obeyed Loaf's instruction and started swimming under the boat. He felt more than heard the boom and splash of Loaf's arrival in the water. But by then he was in the shadow under the boat. He couldn't see in the murky river water and felt a terrible fear that he would come up for air and bump his head, finding that he hadn't swum far enough and now he couldn't breathe, he'd die for sure . . . but he kept swimming until he felt like his lungs would burst.

When he finally came up, the boat was well downstream from him, and all the crew were on the other side of the boat, dragging the officer out of the water.

In a few moments, Loaf popped up about ten yards downstream from Umbo. He knew enough not to wave or make any kind of greeting—anything they did might be seen, anything they said might be heard—sound was tricky, moving across water. But between Umbo letting the current carry him and Loaf treading water against the current, they were close enough to each other to talk quietly.

Only there was nothing to say except, "Better wait till they're farther away."

The most important thing, though, didn't get said. Umbo hoped with all his heart that Rigg would understand why they deserted him and jumped out of the boat. Though technically Umbo hadn't jumped at all.

After a while, deeming the boat had gotten far enough ahead, Loaf began swimming diagonally toward the shore, and Umbo did the same, not even trying to keep up with Loaf's long, strong strokes.

He was in no hurry to get there. Swimming he knew how to do; when he got to shore, he would have to figure out how to go back in time.

CHAPTER 10
Citizen

It took a week before the computers finished their nineteen separate calculations and the expendable was able to say, "The computers have come up with a set of physical laws that would have to be in force for the two passages through the fold to use up identical energy."

"Does this system of physical laws bear any relation to how the real universe has been observed to work?" asked Ram.

"No," said the expendable.

"Please tell the computers to keep recalculating the transition through the fold and out again, into the past and back again but reversed, until they can find a way to balance the energy without violating any observed laws of physics."

•   •   •

"You will be happy to know," said the general, closing the cabin door behind him, "that your friend 'Loaf'—if that's his name; if that's a name at all—has been found and brought here, so our company is now complete."

Rigg did not allow any emotion to register on his face. In truth, he didn't know what to feel, except disappointment. And even that was tempered by the fact that Loaf may well have allowed himself to be taken; it would be hard to imagine that they could capture him without a bloody struggle if he didn't consent.

To turn the subject away from things that mattered, Rigg said, "I know your rank, sir, but I don't know your name."

He sat at a table across from the general, inside the narrow confines of the captain's cabin on the riverboat. Outside the room, he could hear the loud sounds of the crew readying the boat for departure.

The general turned to him with a smile. "Ah, so when we're alone, you observe the civilities."

"And you do not, since you continue not to tell me who you are."

"I thought you were so frequently silent because you were frightened. Now I see that, as a royal, you simply did not deign to speak to one of such low station."

"I put on no airs when I came into money, and as for being royal, I have no idea how royals would behave if such a thing as royalty existed in the People's Republic."

"You know perfectly well that the People's Revolution was bloodless. The royal family is still alive."

"I believe you said *I* was dead," said Rigg. "And those that aren't dead are no longer royal."

"No longer in power, if that's what you mean," said the general. "As for me, you may either call me by my military rank, which is 'general,' or by my station in life, which is 'citizen.'"

"If the royal family is no longer royal," said Rigg, "what would I gain by pretending to be one of them?"

"That is what I am trying to figure out," said the general. "On the one hand, maybe you really are the ignorant bumpkin you pretend to be. On the other hand, you have handled yourself quite deftly, both before I met you and since, which means you have been very well taught."

"My education was very selective," said Rigg. "I had no idea how selective, since so much of it seemed useless to me and yet turned out not to be—but my father insisted that I learn what he chose, when he chose."

"He taught you finance, but not history?"

"He taught me a great deal of history, but I realize now that he left out most of the recent history of the World Within the Walls. I'm sure he had a reason for that, but I find it quite inconvenient at the moment."

"You speak a very elevated language, befitting a royal."

"Father taught me to speak this way, but I never used this language with anyone but him. I use it now because you use it, and because it intimidated Mr. Cooper."

"It didn't intimidate him enough, apparently," said the general.

Rigg didn't want to discuss Mr. Cooper any further. "Someone will tell me your name eventually, if I live. And if I don't live, then I would take this great and terrible secret with me to the grave."

"I was not really being elusive," said the general. "At the time of the revolution, my family dropped their rather-too-prominent gens and took the name 'Citizen.' So I truly am General Citizen. My prenomen, however, seems to be what you wish to know, though it would be quite impolite of you to use it, unless you *are* royal. I am Haddamander Citizen."

"I am pleased to meet you, sir," said Rigg. "And unless my father is a liar, I am Rigg Sessamekesh."

"But we already agreed that your father is a liar, because if Rigg Sessamekesh is in fact your name, then the man who attested to it is not your father. And if he is your father, then that is not your name."

Apparently Citizen was asking the same questions as during their walk in order to see if Rigg's answers changed. But since he told the simple truth—except about the number of jewels—it was easy to stick to the same story. "I don't know which is true."

"I almost believe you," said Citizen. "But you see the quandary you put me in. If you *are* Rigg Sessamekesh, then you are royal, the only son of the woman who, if we still had royalty, would be queen, and her late consort, Knosso Sissamik, who died at the Wall."

"Either way, then, my father is dead," observed Rigg. "Though if I'm royal, then it's illegal for me to own anything valuable."

"No, it's illegal for the royal family to own *anything*, regardless of value, not even the clothing they wear, not even their own hair. If you doubt it, I assure you that from time to time citizens are admitted to whatever house the royals are guesting in, to shave the royal heads and carry away the hair."

"And their clothing?"

"Whenever they wish," said Citizen. "In theory. However, in recent years, because of public outrage at the first time Param Sissaminka was denuded after entering on puberty, the courts have deemed that since the clothing the so-called royals wear is borrowed, only the lender of the clothing has the right to take it back. Any other who takes it is a thief and will be punished accordingly. This reversed the earlier court decisions that whatever the royals wear is theirs, no matter who bought it, and therefore *could* be taken. Times change. The People's Revolutionary Council does in fact respond, however slowly, to the will of the people."

Rigg thought about what he had said. "The clothing I wear most certainly *is* my own, and yet you haven't taken it."

"Like your money and other possessions, your clothing is being held in trust for you in case you aren't a royal, and I'm allowing you to continue to wear it. But if you are *not* a royal, then your ownership of the jewel you sold is highly questionable, and in all likelihood you'll be charged with possession and sale of stolen property, fraud, and attempting to impersonate a royal, for which the combined penalty *could* be death, but since you are so young and almost certainly were put up to this, that sentence would probably be commuted to a few years in prison—provided you told us who induced you to commit these crimes."

Rigg sighed at the repetition of the question. "I've already told you. I found out the name at the same time I got the jewel—

233

when my father's letter was opened and read by the friend he left it with. She had no knowledge of the contents, though she obviously knew about the jewel. She had no idea of its value and historical importance, though. No one did, until Mr. Cooper. So if there's a deception, isn't he part of it?"

"He insists he is among the deceived."

"He would, wouldn't he."

"Yes—but the jewel most certainly *was* genuine, so he did not defraud anybody."

"General Citizen," said Rigg, "I've been thinking back to your summary of my situation, and I can see that either way, I will lose every penny that I have. On the one hand, I'll lose it because I'm a genuine royal and subject to the laws that apply to that family. On the other hand, I'll lose it because I'm *not* royal and therefore am guilty of a crime and, since I can't name any co-conspirators, will probably be put to death."

"If it's any consolation," said Citizen, "your companions will probably be tortured to death first, in the effort to find out the truth. If neither of them tells who your co-conspirators were or might be, or offers proof that you are not Rigg Sessamekesh, then in all likelihood their deaths without confession will save your life."

Rigg leapt to his feet. "No! That's—that's *evil*. That can't be the law! They didn't do anything wrong! Umbo is a friend from childhood and he came along with me because his father kicked him out of the house. And Loaf is merely a kind man, an ex-soldier and now an innkeeper, and he came with us to keep us safe on the rest of our journey! Why should they die because of that?"

"But my lad, don't you see? The only evidence we have of their innocence is your insistence on it—and the very point at issue is whether you can be believed or not."

Without another word, Rigg bolted for the door to the cabin, but when he tried to pull it open, he found Citizen's hand, above his head, was keeping it closed.

"You don't really think I'd let you warn them, do you?" asked Citizen.

Rigg sat back down and fell silent. At least he knew his legal dilemma. But what he did not know was how to keep his friends safe. He couldn't warn them. And yet . . . he knew that Umbo *must* live, at least long enough to come back from the future and give him the warning by the carriage near the Tower of O. Didn't that mean that he not only would live, but would also remain in O? And Loaf must live and still be with Umbo, or why would future-Umbo have told *Loaf* to hide the rest of the jewels?

It was not possible that Loaf and Umbo would be tortured to death. And if that was so, then in all likelihood they would make their escape right now, while the boat was still at the dock.

There was a lurch, and the boat began to move.

All right, then, Umbo and Loaf must leap from the boat and swim to shore.

"You seem curiously untroubled by the movement of the boat," said Citizen. "What do you know that I don't know?"

"The movement of the boat," said Rigg, "is not a surprise. That's what I assumed it would do from the moment I got on it. That's what boats are for."

"But you were certainly calculating that your friends would try to escape while the boat was still at the dock."

"Why are you so sure of what I was 'calculating'?"

"Because the dock was the only place where they'd have a crowd to disappear into, where they could use their feet to run away. And, despite your skill at concealing your emotions, you still betrayed just a bit of it. Enough for a trained player of blackstone to detect it."

"Then you aren't very good at it," said Rigg. "Because I definitely felt surprise when the boat moved. If you can read emotions at the gaming table, surely you can detect that."

"Surprise, yes, but you were not *troubled*. Your worry dissipated instantly."

"I don't believe you'll really kill them."

"Oh, believe it, I won't."

"I'm glad to hear that," said Rigg, allowing himself to feel a tiny trace of relief.

"Don't try to fool me by *letting* yourself seem relieved. You can't feel relief if you didn't feel tension, and you didn't. Besides, I won't kill them or torture them because it's not my job—the Revolutionary Council have specialists who handle all the judicial torture. I'm about fetching you; they're about opening you up to examination."

Rigg didn't allow the implications of that—the hint that he, too, might be tortured—to enter his emotional consciousness. "I've been curious as to why a general would be sent to arrest me. Are you considered so worthless to the People's Revolutionary Council that they would send you on a trivial errand like this?"

General Citizen laughed then. "You really *are* naive. I truly believe that. Because if you're pretending, the things you pretend not to understand are so . . . stupidly chosen."

"Again, I express my ingratitude to my father for the poor design of my education."

"The reason I was sent to get you is because I maneuvered very carefully to win the assignment. And that's because there are controversies centered on the Sessamoto Empire older and deeper than the mere matter of the royal family being deposed and the Revolutionary Council being in charge of the World Within the Walls."

"I have no idea what you're talking about," said Rigg.

"It was the decree of Aptica Sessamin, the grandmother of the current non-queen, that only women could rule in the Sessamoto Empire. She gave this decree force by having all her male relatives killed. This put an end to a great many plots centered around removing her—a woman—from the Tent of Light."

"Tent?" asked Rigg.

"Officially, every royal residence is the Tent of Light when the ruling monarch is in it. Aptica Sessamin murdered all her own sons, as I said, and her reigning daughter, Mutash Sessamin, had only the one child, a daughter, Hagia Sessamin."

"Hagia—the one who is either my mother or not?"

"So you *do* know the names of the royal family!"

"Of course I know it *now*," said Rigg. "It's been whispered by half the people we met. 'He claims he's the son of Hagia Sessamin.'"

"Cleverly done," said Citizen. "I was very careful never

to mention her name, in case you came up with it. But yes, I did hear the same comments, though I wouldn't have thought you'd—never mind, I shouldn't underestimate your cleverness or your powers of observation."

Rigg showed absolutely no response to this—but by now he understood that to Citizen, *not* showing a response was, in fact, a response.

"So when Rigg Sessamekesh was born, the first male royal since the death of Aptica Sessamin, the very fact that he was given the suffix 'ekesh' was very controversial. That was the suffix given to the male child who was the heir presumptive, back in the days when males ruled. Hagia Sessamin claimed that the suffix only meant that he was the firstborn male child. Since by then the People's Revolution had made sure there was nothing any royal child, still less a male one, could inherit, the name obviously had no implication of being heir. Others thought he was being named thus to stir up revolt and restore royal power. Still others thought that she was repudiating the law, started by her grandmother, that the Tent and the Stone must pass mother to daughter."

"Tent and stone?" asked Rigg.

"Yes," said Citizen. "The Tent that kept alive the memory of the days when the Sessamids were nomads, and the Stone, lost for thousands of years but still revered—its place symbolically taken by a common river rock—which you so kindly offered for sale."

Rigg said nothing, for his thought now was upon the eighteen other stones, wondering why, when he stood there in Mr. Cooper's office, he had managed to pick the one that would get him in the most trouble.

Citizen was going on with the story. "So when word came that Rigg Sessamekesh had died as an infant, those who believed the story were relieved. Others, however, thought it was a ploy, that conspirators had stolen away the baby to use him for the purpose of not only restoring the monarchy, but also abolishing female rule."

"Then I must be an absolute fool to pretend to be him," said Rigg. "Not only the Revolutionary Council but also those who still approve of the laws of Queen Aptica must want me dead. Any friends that such an impostor might have would be in a hopeless minority."

"Well, that's where things get complicated," said Citizen, chuckling. "Because much of the support for the People's Revolution was actually opposition to the continuation of female-only monarchy. At the time of the revolution, there *was* no male royal, so the only way to abolish the rule of queens was to abolish the monarchy entirely. But if a male heir turned up, some of the support of the Revolutionary Council—some say *most* of that support—would evaporate and regather behind the male child, since there have always been many who considered Aptica to be an abomination and her anti-male law to be sacrilege."

"I'm surprised the real Rigg Sessamekesh wasn't murdered the moment they saw his little ding," said Rigg. "Just to save a lot of bother."

"You speak as if you were not he," said Citizen.

"As far as I know, I'm not," said Rigg. "But I'm also not a

fraud. You keep omitting the possibility that everything I've said is true. That in my ignorance I'm innocent of any offense."

"Be that as it may," said Citizen, "I got this assignment because certain people believed I could be trusted to find out the truth about you."

"So if I turn out to be the real Rigg Sessamekesh, you can kill me?"

General Citizen smiled at him. "I see I'm not the only one to lay traps."

For it was indeed a trap that Rigg had laid for him. If the situation as Citizen outlined it was correct, a loyal servant of the People's Revolutionary Council would not have hesitated to kill Rigg at the first opportunity, since no outcome that left him alive would be good for the Council. Of course he'd disguise it as an accident, but it would happen, because fraud or heir, he would have to die.

"General Citizen," said Rigg, "it seems to me that you don't care whether I'm really the Rigg Sessamekesh that Hagia Sessamin gave birth to thirteen years ago."

"But I care very much," said Citizen.

"What you care about is whether I can be made believable to the people of Aressa Sessamo—believable enough that the Council can be overthrown and replaced by a regent—you, perhaps?—who will rule in my name."

"You have made only one mistake," said Citizen.

"No I haven't," said Rigg. "You're about to tell me that you were really trying to draw me out so you could see if I posed a danger, but in fact you're perfectly loyal to the Council."

Citizen said nothing, showed nothing.

"You may or may not be loyal, and you may or may not be ambitious," said Rigg. "Whatever judgment you come up with, I can't control. But there is absolutely nothing in what I've said or done to suggest that I would be willing to take part in a plan to overthrow the Council. And if I did not take part willingly, no conspiracy could use me."

"What if the survival of your friends were at stake? Wouldn't you do as you were told?" asked Citizen.

Would Citizen really count on Rigg's loyalty to his friends to make him a reliable tool? Father had once quoted an ancient philosopher, who said, "The good man counts on others to share his virtues, while the evil man counts on the virtues of better men. They are both mistaken." Was Citizen foolish enough to make either mistake?

There was suddenly a great deal of shouting outside the cabin, and in a moment someone shoved open the door. It was a soldier.

"They've jumped overboard, sir! And threw Shouter overboard!"

"Guard this prisoner," said Citizen as he ran from the room.

The soldier closed the door and stood in front of it. "Don't even try to talk to me," he said to Rigg.

"Not even to ask who in the world has the horrible name of 'Shouter'?"

The soldier stood there for a long time, and Rigg had concluded he wasn't going to answer. And then he did.

"It's not his real name, sir. It's what we all call him behind his back. I hope the general didn't notice."

"I think you have little chance of that," said Rigg. "He notices everything."

The soldier nodded and sighed. "Hope it's short rations and not the lash for me." Then he blushed, probably because he shouldn't have said any such thing to the prisoner.

"Would it help if I told him you were immediately remorseful?"

"No, because that would mean I had talked to you."

"Which you certainly have not done," said Rigg, "despite my efforts to induce you to speak."

Long silence from the soldier. Lots of noise outside. A slackening of the speed of the boat, and then a reversal of direction. Then a return to forward motion. There was a double rap on the door. The soldier opened it a little, stepped through it—never turning his back on Rigg—and in a moment stepped back inside.

"Your friends got away safe, sir," said the soldier softly, mouthing the words rather than speaking them, which he did so naturally that Rigg imagined this must be the way soldiers communicated when maintaining silence on duty.

Rigg did not ask the soldier why he said "sir." He knew perfectly well that his supposed identity had spread among the soldiers, if not through the whole crew and half of O before they left. The soldier called him "sir" because he still had respect for royalty, and Rigg was purportedly the heir to the throne.

So the fear of there being support for a revolution against the Revolutionary Council was not ungrounded.

Was it possible that Father had taken him, as an infant, from the royal house? Then the only question was whether he did so in obedience to Rigg's parents' wishes, or against them. Had his real mother and father given him to the Wandering Man in hopes of saving his life? Or was he kidnapped?

Or—an intriguing possibility—had Father, knowing the real Rigg had been murdered and the body hidden or destroyed, taken a perfectly ordinary baby and raised him so as to prepare him to *pretend* to be the Sessamekesh? If so, Father would certainly have gone to great lengths to make sure to use a baby who could be expected to grow up to resemble the Sessamoto family enough that he would be believable as their long-lost son and brother.

What Rigg couldn't figure out was why Father would arrange things so that this plot would start even after he died. Why wouldn't he want to be there to help guide Rigg through this perilous path?

Or had he already given him all the guidance he needed?

Rigg sat there trying to imagine what else Father had taught him that might be applicable in this situation. Nothing came to mind. Hard as it was to believe, it seemed likely that Father had *not* thought of everything.

But Father knew that no one could think of everything. So he must have believed he gave Rigg the tools he needed to deal with any situation, including this one. The problem was that Rigg had no idea what to do, so whatever training Father might have thought would be applicable would not be applied as long as Rigg remained as stupid as he was right now.

The door opened. It was not General Citizen who came in, but rather a very wet officer—apparently the one called Shouter. He was shoved into the cabin by other soldiers and immediately manacled to Rigg, wrist to wrist and ankle to ankle.

Only then did General Citizen come to the door and shout at the dripping, shivering man, "Maybe you can keep *this* one from diving overboard, you blithering fool! Maybe *you* won't get thrown over yourself!"

Rigg immediately assumed that the shouting was so that the other soldiers on the boat would get the message; to Rigg, Citizen did not look genuinely angry at Shouter. The *sincere* glance of rage was directed at Rigg.

When the general was gone and he was alone with Shouter, it took a great deal of effort for Rigg to keep himself from laughing. Good old Loaf had not only gotten himself and Umbo off the boat, he had tossed the watchdog into the water as well. And General Citizen, whatever his real purpose might be, was not happy.

CHAPTER 11

Backward

This time it took eleven days for the computers to come up with their answer.

"Converting the energy requirement into mass," said the expendable, "all the computers agree that without violating previously observed laws of physics, the most likely cost of returning from the fold to our previous position in spacetime, but with the direction reversed, would be about nineteen times the mass of this ship and everything on it."

"Nineteen computers," said Ram, "and nineteen times the mass."

"Do you find this coincidence significant?" asked the expendable.

"Each computer was an observer and a meddler in spacetime at the time the fold was created," said Ram. "You and I weren't observers, because we could not sense or even understand the convolutions of the fields being generated. So for each observer, there had to be a distinct jump. And for each jump, there had to be an expenditure of mass equal to the total mass of the ship and its contents."

"So if there had been only nine or ten computers," said the expendable, "we would have come only halfway back to the present?"

"No," said Ram. "I think if there had been only one computer, we would have crossed the fold only one-nineteenth as far into the past of the target star system before being shoved back, in reverse."

"You seem to be very happy about this hypothesis," said the expendable, "but I don't see why. It still explains nothing."

"Don't you see?" said Ram. "Crossing the fold pushed us into the past a certain amount, based on the mass of the ship and its velocity or whatever. But the only way to *pay* for that passage across the fold was to send an equal mass backward. And because there were nineteen observers creating the fields that created the fold, it happened nineteen times."

"But it happened only once," said the expendable.

"No," said Ram. "It happened nineteen times. For each jump, a copy of the ship was thrust backward in time. Eighteen other versions of ourselves occupy the identical space as the original ship, only moving the opposite direction through time as we journey toward Earth, all of us invisible to each other."

"So our reliance on the computers caused the failure of the mission?" asked the expendable.

"The mission didn't fail," said Ram. "It succeeded nineteen times. We're just the exhaust trail."

•   •   •

Loaf was full of plans to sneak back into O and live there in hiding long enough for Umbo to deliver his messages. Only when Umbo finally convinced him that he had no idea how to do it did Loaf finally realize that learning how to go back in time might better be done somewhere else.

"I might not learn how to go back in time for weeks," said Umbo as they walked through the woods, back toward O. "Or months." If I ever do. "It was only Rigg who could go back in time. I helped, by slowing him down. Or speeding him up."

"Which?"

"I always thought I was slowing other people down, but Rigg said I was really speeding them up so that everything around them seemed slower."

Loaf grunted at that and moved a branch out of the way, holding it so it didn't swing back and hit Umbo in the face.

"Thanks," said Umbo. "You see, Rigg could *always* see the paths of people moving around in the past. Long before I ever helped him. He knew what he was looking for. I don't."

Another grunt.

"We need a safe place to go where I can practice trying to do to myself whatever it is I do to other people. And even then, who knows whether I'll be able to see anything?"

"Look," said Loaf, "we know you did it. We know it happens. We just have to be patient. And you have to work hard at it so we don't waste too much time."

"It's not a waste of time," said Umbo. "It's however long the job takes."

"Here's how I see things," said Loaf. "We must have gone

through all this before, only the first time, Rigg got arrested *without* your moving the knife and *without* my hiding the jewels and money. Then you learned how to go back in time, came back to O, delivered the warnings, and now everything is happening differently. So why do you need to deliver the messages *this* time at all?"

"Because none of that has happened yet, so now it won't," said Umbo. "I have to learn how to travel in time so I can go back *this* time and deliver the same message again."

"But you didn't *get* the message twice, did you? So why deliver it twice?"

"I don't know," said Umbo. "I don't think it *is* twice. I think there's only one message, and I still have to deliver it."

"But you only know you have to deliver it because you already did. And that's the point. You already did. But I'm not going to argue with you. Even if you don't have to deliver the same message again, it'll be useful for you to learn *how* to do it. And then if it makes you feel better, go ahead and deliver the messages — if you remember what you actually said."

"I have to do it because I know I already did, only when I did it, it was the future, so I have to get to the future in order to come back and do what I already did . . . This is so crazy that it has to be impossible."

"Except it happened, so it *is* possible. We won't do your figuring-it-out time in O, because we might get caught. But I'm still going back to get the jewels and the money. The coins will be convenient for *us*, right now — we can buy passage upriver to Leaky's Landing and stay there in safety for a while. But the jewels and the knife—it's not like we can cash those in. I think you came back to warn Rigg and yourself because first time we went through this experience, those items got taken by the soldiers, and that made everything worse for Rigg. That first stone—did it just happen to be the only one that was legendary and fabulously valuable? Or are there others that would make things even worse if Rigg was caught with them? And that knife—who knows what *that* would cause. It's very old, but it looks very new, right? And Rigg never did know anything about the man he lifted it from."

"So we should take the money and bury the knife and the jewels somewhere nobody can ever find them," said Umbo.

"No," said Loaf. "Because we don't know but what we'll need them later to buy Rigg's freedom. Or some other thing. They're Rigg's inheritance from his father, so what we have to do is keep them out of the hands of the Revolutionary Council or anybody else who means us ill. But we still need to get it all to Aressa Sessamo so Rigg will have the use of them if he ever needs them."

"Because having them has worked out so splendidly up to now," said Umbo.

Loaf gave him a little shove. "Look what you're wearing. Look what we've experienced, the people we've talked to, the things we've learned. A few weeks of being rich has taught *me* a lot."

"Like what? That it gets you arrested?"

"It was Rigg's *name* that got him arrested, not his money."

"So what has being rich—or hanging around with a rich kid—taught *you*?"

Loaf grinned. "That I like it a lot better than being poor."

"I was fine with poor. I didn't even *know* I was all that poor.

I didn't even know the stuff we were buying even existed, so I didn't miss it. Life was good."

"Spoken like a true privick," said Loaf.

"So what's the plan? We go into O, get the jewels and money—"

"You are so very, very wrong. *I* go into O, *I* get the money."

"You're not leaving me!"

"Yes I am," said Loaf. "And we're going to have a signal so that when I come back, I can call you. If I whistle like this . . ."—he whistled—"then I'm all alone and it's safe. But if I whistle like this . . ."—a different sound—"then I have somebody dangerous with me and you should stay away."

"There's not a bird alive that makes sounds like those."

"Then it's a good thing I'm not calling any birds, isn't it?" said Loaf. "Those are military signals from my old regiment."

"You need one more signal."

"What's that?"

"One that means 'I've got somebody dangerous with me, but I need you to come to me anyway.'"

"I would never give you a signal like that."

"But you might. So whistle that one for me."

"I'll never need it."

"Then you'll never use it, but let's have it anyway!"

Loaf glowered and whistled again, a very different sound. "I'm the experienced one, but you think you can give the orders."

"You're the big man, and I'm the little kid. I never have the option of fighting my way out of a situation. So I think of all the options I might need. That's just how it is when you're small."

"I was a kid once, too," said Loaf.

"And I bet you were bigger than kids two years older than you."

Loaf said nothing.

"When you don't answer, that means I'm right."

"Shut up," said Loaf. "I think I caught a glimpse of the tower."

"What tower?" asked Umbo.

"The Tower of O," growled Loaf. "Are you that stupid?"

"I was thinking of other things," said Umbo. "I was thinking of how to go back in time."

"You were thinking of how smart you are, telling me 'I'm right,' and then you proved you aren't very smart after all, and don't bother arguing because we both know I'm stuck with the dumb kid while the smart kid is a prisoner on that boat."

That stung Umbo—worse than his father beating him. And even though Loaf cuffed him playfully and told him, "Come on, you know I was teasing you," it didn't change the fact that they both knew it was true. But it wasn't about being *smart*. It was about the things Wandering Man had taught them. Umbo had gotten a little training and that was all. Just enough to help Rigg. But Rigg had been trained for anything. He had been trained to be a son of the royal house—because that was what he really *was*.

If Wandering Man had trained *me* the same way, I'd be smart, too.

Wouldn't I?

Despite all the signals, Loaf ended up not using any of them. That's because Umbo disobeyed him, didn't stay where he was told, but instead followed him and, not far from the tower, climbed a tree. He could see now where Loaf dug to get the bag of jewels, and could see that nobody was following Loaf as he threaded his way back into the woods. So Umbo ran back toward their meeting place, climbed another tree, and dropped from a lower branch right in front of Loaf. He submitted cheerfully to the do-what-I-tell-you-or-you'll-get-us-both-killed lecture.

When Loaf was finally through grumping at him, Umbo asked, "Did you get it? All of it?"

"Unless somebody found the bag, took out just one jewel, and put the rest back, yes, I found it all."

"Well, let's see it. Let's count," said Umbo. "Because now I think there really *is* one missing."

They counted. And counted again.

"I can't believe it," said Loaf. "How could one be gone?"

"The biggest one, too," said Umbo.

"How did you know?"

"I didn't *know*," said Umbo. "I just thought maybe."

"It makes no sense at all," said Loaf savagely. "Nobody would steal just one."

"*I* would," said Umbo. "And I saw the hiding place when you dug it up just now. So I'm betting that I *did* take it."

Loaf rounded on him. "Hand it over, then, you little thief."

"I didn't hear you calling Rigg a thief for stealing that knife."

"I called him a thief, all right!"

"That's right, you did, but you didn't grab him like you're grabbing me and it hurts, so stop it! I don't have the jewel because I didn't take it!"

"You said you did."

"I said I'm betting that I did, and I really should have said that I'm betting that I *will*."

Loaf sighed and let go of him. "Why? What's the point?"

"No *point* except that when you made your sarcastic remark about how somebody might have taken one, I thought, wouldn't it be funny if my future self comes back, finds the bag of jewels, and takes out the biggest one. And the moment I thought that, I decided to do it if I got the chance. Now I know I'll get the chance."

"So you're saying that when you learn how to travel in time, you're going to use it to play stupid bratty tricks on your friends?"

"Now you're getting it."

"I ought to break your arm."

"But I know you won't."

"Don't be too sure."

"Because my arm looked fine when my future self came to visit me. I also know I won't drown, break my neck falling from a tree, or get my throat slit by a highwayman. I won't die of some disease and I won't get struck by lightning, and nobody will beat me to death with a stick."

"I wouldn't be too sure."

"How can I be anything *but* sure? I came back and visited me and Rigg! I took the jewel out of the bag!"

"I wish I could go back and hide the bag in a different place," said Loaf.

"Now you're getting into the fun of it!" said Umbo. "Come on, people always make games out of everything. You did war as your real grownup work—but didn't you *play* at war when you were little? I did. All of us did. So when I learn to go back in time, I'll play with it! Giving warnings is one thing—that's just showing up and talking. I know I'll have to prove I can do whatever

Rigg did or I'll feel like I lost the game. He took the knife—from a stranger. I took—I *will* take—the jewel, but I'm only stealing from *us* so nobody else will miss it. See? A game."

"I'm not having fun yet," said Loaf.

"Because you're old and tired and you know you're going to die." And this time, when Loaf made as if to hit him, Umbo dodged away. "See? We're friends, and I'm teasing you like a friend. See? That's what normal people do."

"It's not how normal children treat normal grownups," said Loaf, and he did seem a little angry.

"But you're not a normal grownup," said Umbo. "When you hit me, you don't really mean to hurt me."

"Come a little closer here, Umbo, and we'll see about that."

"My father would have knocked me down and then kicked me a few times," said Umbo.

"Too much work," said Loaf. "You're not worth it."

"Friends!" said Umbo triumphantly.

"Well, *friend*," said Loaf, "I have only one question for you. Where is that jewel *now*?"

That kept Umbo silent for quite a while. Was it possible that the jewel had simply left the world? Had it ceased to exist, and then would exist again, out of nowhere, out of nothing? It got Umbo to wondering what it meant to exist at all. When Rigg went back and took the knife, he stayed completely in the real present world—the only difference was that he could see the people from the past, and they could see him, but he was still *here*. The jewel, though. It was gone.

What about the knife? It was in the stranger's possession,

Rigg reached out and took it, and Umbo remembered seeing it come into existence in Rigg's hand. The knife had a continuous existence. The problem was that it skipped centuries, maybe thousands of years. Jumped right over them. Because Rigg had reached back in time and *moved* it. That's what happened to the jewel. It never ceased to exist, it just changed places. And eras. The knife had been carried by Rigg's hand; the jewel would be carried by Umbo's.

They had come downriver carried by a boat. At every second between Leaky's Landing and O, they still existed, somewhere in the world—on the boat. For the knife and the jewel, though, there was no boat. No river. The movement was instantaneous. And Umbo didn't want to think about it anymore. Mostly because Loaf looked so smug, for having made him think of a problem that kept him silent.

That, too, was a kind of game, wasn't it? And Loaf had won it.

They didn't try to board an upbound boat in O, in case someone there recognized them, realized they must have escaped, and took them back into custody, jewels and all. Instead they went back downriver to a small ferry, crossed to the other side, and then caught an upriver boat.

They didn't take the first one that passed, or even the first one that came close to shore and somebody called out if they wanted passage. Umbo didn't understand why none of these boats was good enough, until Loaf called out to one boat—it wasn't even coming to shore—by shouting the name of the pilot. "Rubal!" he cried, and then again, louder. Then Loaf waded out from the shore and waved and shouted "Rubal" again until finally the pilot heard him, or saw him.

"Loaf, you old poacher!"

"I didn't poach, she just liked me better!" Loaf called back. But under his breath, to Umbo, he said, "I really did poach his girlfriend, but we were soldiers then, almost children. I'd never do it now."

"Good thing," said Umbo, "or Leaky'd kill you."

"True. She might kill me for bringing Rubal back to our inn—I'll have to put him up for the night, it's only fair."

"What's wrong with him?"

"He can't stop gambling at stones, and he cheats all the time. He's pretty good at it but not good enough that a sharp player won't spot him doing it."

"You a sharp player?"

"No," said Loaf. "But I had to kill a sharp player once to save Rubal's neck."

"So he owes you this passage."

"We've saved each other's necks about twenty times. He'll do it as a favor, not as a debt."

"How did you know he was coming?"

"I didn't know it would be Rubal. I knew that soon enough there'd be somebody I knew well enough to trust he wouldn't rob us and float our bodies downstream. I live and work on the river, Umbo. There's only so many boats and only so many pilots, and after a while you get to know a lot of them."

The passage upriver was uneventful. They stopped here and there. Loaf introduced himself to other innkeepers. They always got along cheerfully, because there was no competition between them. Rivermen stopped at the nearest inn when darkness approached; it was not as if they would continue upriver in the dark to stop at a favorite place. So unless your beds were so bugridden or your food so rancid that rivermen went out of their way to avoid it, the money was there to be made for all of them, but with steadily diminishing trade the farther upriver you went.

Loaf joined in with the poling and rowing from time to time—his muscles weren't shaped to the work, but he was strong and learned quickly enough. Umbo, though, was so little that when he offered to help they only laughed at him. "Besides," murmured Loaf to him, "you have other work to do. Inside your head."

Thus Umbo spent hour after hour lying in the shade of a sail, when the wind helped them upriver, or a tarpaulin, when it didn't. It was an easy thing to speed up the perceptions of the crewmen, so that they were more alert and had plenty of time to deal with obstructions or possible collisions on the river. None of them suspected they had had any help from Umbo, except Loaf himself, who squinted and glared at Umbo the few times he did it. Now that he was trying to study what he was doing—something he hadn't done since Wandering Man stopped his lessons—he realized some useful facts.

First, the speeding up lasted for several minutes after Umbo stopped imposing it on the other person.

Second, it worked rather like the quick rush of energy that came when you were in danger—only it didn't cause the racing heartbeat, the panting for breath, and the sheer terror that usually caused such intense concentration and speeded-up perceptions.

Umbo's gift to them was really a kind of panic without the fear.

So to cause himself to have the effect, he tried for a while to make himself afraid, in order to speed himself up. It didn't work. For one thing, he didn't really believe it. For another, it simply wasn't the same thing at all, so fear had no effect.

If he had had a mirror he might have tried looking in it in order to cast the spell on himself, but the more he thought of that, the more ridiculous it seemed. He knew that mirrors worked by reflecting light—but there was no reason to think it would reflect whatever power it was that he wielded.

He tried looking at his hands or feet, the way he looked at the person he was targeting, but again, there was no effect that he could discern—no quickening, no perceived slowing down of the world around him.

Finally, he gave up in despair and just lay there in the shade, letting the boat surge upstream with each call of "Pole!" or "Stick!" then slacken as half the poles were reset at a time. It was almost smooth, but not quite, and lying there on the deck he could feel each surge, each slackening. He concentrated intensely on it, and it seemed to him that they were slowing down, the calls coming more slowly, each surge lasting longer, each slackening more sharp.

Then he fell asleep.

And when he woke up—nudged awake by a boatman's toe, with a muttered, "Supper, lad"—he had almost forgotten that feeling just before he slept, of everything moving slowly, and even when he remembered it he did so only to think, I wonder if that's how it feels to be under the time-slowing spell.

"Fool," he whispered.

"What?" asked the riverman nearest him. They were pulled up along shore for the noon meal and a bit of a rest, so no one was at the poles right now.

"Myself," said Umbo. "I called myself a fool."

"Honest of you," said the riverman. "Though it was obvious to the rest of us days ago."

Umbo gave him a quick grin—it did feel good to have their acceptance, though it was Loaf, not Umbo, who had earned it. But when he met Loaf's eyes across the coals of the cookfire still red in the metal firepan, he gave him a wink, and Loaf nodded. Progress.

That afternoon, Umbo worked to isolate what caused him to go into the trance himself. It was not sleepiness—that had ended, not triggered, the phenomenon. Nor was it concentration, really—he had *not* been thinking about the rhythm of "pole, stick, pole, stick" as the two teams alternated their surges. Rather it was a different thing, different from the way it felt when he did it to others, but still, in a strange way, the same. Just like learning to use a new muscle, and the more he practiced, the more easily he found himself in that inward place where time slowed down, or he speeded up.

It was as if, instead of *doing* something to himself, he simply found the place inside himself where time was already moving along at a different clip. And as he got more practiced at it, he realized that he had much more versatility and control over his own trance than over the timeflow of other people, when he worked the trick on them. He could go much faster than he could make them go; he could vary the tempo across quite a broad range of speeds. And it didn't weary him to do it to himself; he was rather invigorated by it, instead of its wearing him out.

"All well and good," murmured Loaf. "But can you do it with your eyes open?"

Umbo woke up. Or not really—he hadn't been asleep this time—but coming out of the trance of time always *felt* like awakening, though it also felt like leaving home and coming out into a harsher world.

"How did you know I was doing it?" Umbo whispered.

"Because when I sit by you," murmured Loaf, "or walk near you, I can feel it happening to me. A quickening of my step. And it's stronger than when you were practicing on us all, back at the beginning. It grows as I come nearer to you, and fades as I walk away."

"Do you think the others feel it?" asked Umbo.

"If they do, they don't know why. It feels, to a man my age, as if I were younger, fresher, less tired. As if I thought more sharply, saw more clearly, heard things from farther away and could tell them apart more easily. In other words, it just feels *good*. Who would try to blame feeling good on a boy who seems to be asleep on the deck?"

"I really do need to open my eyes," said Umbo. "I don't know why I haven't already. I don't think I have to keep my eyes closed to make it happen to myself, not anymore. I just don't know if there'll be anything to see. It was Rigg that saw people moving through time, without any help from me."

"But it's you that knows how to move a man backward in time, whether he can see anything there or not."

"I need Rigg. I really do. Maybe I don't send the message until he gets out of his captivity."

"If that's how it worked, then it would have been Rigg delivering the messages instead of you, wouldn't it?" Loaf got to his feet again. "My rest time is over. I'm on the stick team today. Stick, pole, stick, pole — no wonder these rivermen need so many pints of strong ale when they stop at Leaky's Landing!"

In the remaining two days of the upriver voyage, Umbo grew so practiced at slipping into quicktime that he began having to work at *not* moving about in that mode. He felt sluggish when he did not have that alertness about him, and he wondered if this ability to speed himself up in relation to the world might not be rather like ale to these rivermen — a way of making the world brighter and pleasanter. Because it felt good to be so aware of everything, and to have time to think of what he wanted to say before he said it. It made him seem cleverer — to others and to himself — to have the time to think of an answer before speaking, or not to speak at all when his first impulse was to say or ask something stupid.

But in all the time he spent in quicktime, he never saw so much as a glimpse of the "paths" Rigg talked about seeing all the time, still less any person from another era. It seemed hopeless to him, for Rigg, when Umbo put him into quicktime, had to pick out a particular path and then look at it closely in order for the individual person to emerge clearly enough for Rigg to pick his pocket. But Umbo, seeing no paths, could not pick out a target for his attention, and therefore could not possibly make them become solid and real.

I can't do it. And yet I *did* it.

Not until they arrived at Leaky's Landing was there another opportunity to talk, for this part of the river Loaf knew well, having plied it up and down to buy groceries and linens, tools and hardware, furniture and liquid refreshments for the inn. So as they passed each landmark, Loaf would offer his opinion of the place — "You never buy your sheets from the weavers in that town, they make them all too small to tuck in tight on a goodsized bed. It must be a town of dwarfs, eh?" — and then the rivermen would offer *their* opinions of the place — "There's a girl there so ugly they don't castrate their hogs anymore, they just bring them to look at her and their equipment freezes up and drops off."

Umbo was quite aware that what Loaf said was always literally true, and what the rivermen said was almost never true at all — and yet no one was lying and all were entertained by each other. Umbo could well see why rivermen might prefer to live in an exaggerated or downright imaginary world, what with all the poling, and the sameness of the river going up or coming down. While Loaf, the soldier, the hardheaded man of trade, the toiler in all trades, he needed to keep a clear-eyed view of the world.

When they got home they bade good-bye to the rivermen, who did not stop the night, "Because why should we give you back, for food and ale, the very passage money you just gave to us?" said the captain of the boat.

Leaky barely seemed interested in them — neither Umbo nor her own husband. She was busy, she said, and didn't have time for greetings, what with doing everything single-handed while they were off playing the tourist in far countries. Loaf's answer was not to rail at her, as Umbo's father would have done, but rather to pitch in beside her and help her make short work of her tasks. And as they labored side by side, she began to smile now and then—not looking at him yet, but just smiling—and then she hummed, and then sang, and finally began to tell him stories of things that had happened while he was gone.

Umbo, meanwhile, tried to make himself useful, too, though he did not know how to do many of the tasks they did, and had to learn by watching. That, however, he did very well, for he could quicken himself so he had plenty of time to watch and understand exactly what they were doing, and then observe his own actions and correct them. He didn't move any faster than he normally did—that is, exactly in proportion to the time of the people or creatures or things he was interacting with. But while acting, he had time to think again and stop himself or change his action. It was a wonderful luxury, that ability to rethink and still have time to change his course.

So now he understood, at last, how his quickening gift was useful to the people he had used it on, though he hadn't really understood how. They really are better able to carry out their plan of action, when I put a quickening on them. Wandering Man called it "slowing" because it made things around a person seem to proceed at a leisurely pace. He had gotten it all wrong, as if Wandering Man thought it was time itself that Umbo affected, rather than the person's perceptions and thought processes within time.

It was actually a bit of a relief to realize that Wandering Man didn't know everything about everything; he wondered if the man himself had ever realized it before he died. Or maybe he died because he was so sure he knew everything that it didn't occur to him that he might be wrong about the direction in which a hewn tree would fall.

Supper was the best food Umbo had eaten on the river, and he said so. "That's because you're eating like family now, not the swill we slop the pigs with," said Loaf, at which Leaky smacked him across the top of his head, saying, "We eat from the same pot as the guests and that's a fact, which you well know, Loaf, and I won't have you saying otherwise."

"No, my love, you won't have me saying otherwise *in your presence*," which earned him another smack, and a harder one.

The room they put Umbo in was not one of the guest rooms. It was a smallish bedroom right next to their own, and Umbo realized that this was the room where, if they ever had a child, that child would sleep. How old *is* Leaky, Umbo wondered as he readied himself for bed. Might she have children? Or is one of them unable? When they built this place it was clear they meant to have children. Sad if they couldn't have what they wanted, when a lout like Umbo's father popped babies into women every time he had a go at them, and heaven knows why any woman ever let him.

Umbo had just fallen asleep when he was wakened by Loaf shaking him gently.

"What?" murmured Umbo.

"I know you can't see them," said Loaf. "But does that matter, if you know right where they are?"

Umbo was too tired to get what Loaf was trying to say, and

fell asleep again in moments. But when he awoke in the middle of the night to pee, the words came back to him, and actually took on some meaning. In fact he realized he had been dreaming about them. In his dreams, Umbo pictured Rigg standing a very long time by the carriage, so that Umbo did not have to be able to see him in order to tell him his message. And the same with Umbo's message to himself—he had received it while lying in his bed in their lodging in O, so that he, too, was firmly in the same place and Umbo did not actually have to be able to see himself to give the message.

Awake now, Umbo tried to remember what his future self had looked like, and now he realized that his head had been bowed, as if he was staring at a spot on the floor rather than himself lying in bed. He had seemed rather shy or humble to Umbo, but what if he were simply not looking at anything at all, only talking into the air and hoping someone would receive his message?

But no, he had heard what Umbo asked him. Or had he? Perhaps, already knowing what past-Umbo would say, having said it himself, future-Umbo was able to answer it.

Closing the lid of the pissoir, he thought back to last night's supper and almost went downstairs to try quickening himself and then speaking to the invisible past versions of himself and Loaf and Leaky. But he stopped himself in time. He couldn't do that, because he *hadn't* done it. There had been no visitation and no message last night. He'd have to do it tonight, instead.

Unless Loaf was right, and it was perfectly possible for him to go back and give a message where no message had been received, and then it *would* be received, and thus change the future, and after that there would be no need to actually do the message giving again. But Umbo could not see how such a thing was possible. It was maddening enough that trying to make sense of it put him back to sleep almost as soon as he was back under the covers.

The next day he said nothing to Loaf about his dreams and quandaries, and still less about his plans. During the afternoon he managed to filch some bread and cheese from the kitchen and secrete it in his room, because he intended to eat no supper at the table that night. In order to avoid confusing himself with the issue of whether he could take a message into the past that he had not already seen when it was delivered, prior to delivering it, he decided to be absent from the place where the message would be received.

So he pretended to have a little headache which needed nothing but sleep to be cured, and went to his room. He ate his bread and cheese and wished he had thought to bring water or weak ale into the room. But he resolutely did not leave the room, and waited until he could hear the quieting of the house. Only when all was dark and quiet did he get up and make his way down the stairs by the scant light of the stars and the silver night-ring coming through skylights and windows, then down a dark hall by feel alone.

He came into the little room off the kitchen where Loaf and Leaky must have eaten their private meal—late, as always, after the guests were served—and found no one there and the room dark, except for the flickering light from the kitchen fire.

Only then, imagining where Leaky and Loaf would have

sat, did he realize just how many holes there were in his plan. Because even though he himself was not present for dinner, it is absolutely certain that if they had received his message—the one he was preparing to slip into the recent past and give them now—they would have come up to his bedroom and wakened him and told him of the success of it.

Unless I told them to let me sleep uninterrupted till morning. That's what my message should be—to go to sleep as normal and not waken me till morning!

Satisfied now that he had resolved the contradictions, Umbo closed the doors to the room and, keeping his voice low, put himself into the trance of quickening. "Don't waken me till morning, please," he whispered entreatingly to the empty chair where Leaky usually sat. Then he spoke again, but with the trance shallower, or so he hoped. And again and again. At no point did he see any trace or flicker of Loaf and Leaky, or hear a speck of answer, but he resolutely tried to do it at every level of trance, thinking that perhaps the depth of the trance determined how far back he would go in time.

Exhausted and stupid from lack of sleep and long concentration, he was whispering now from hoarseness rather than a desire to be quiet. He hit on the idea of varying the message a little so that he'd remember which level of trance had been seen by them, but then gave up on it because how could he remember how "deep" the trance was at the time of a given message?

Even when he thought he was done and resolved to go back upstairs, he did not. Instead he sat down in his own place at the table and rubbed his eyes and knew, without knowing why or how, that he had failed. He had only been talking to himself.

Sitting there, drifting near sleep, yet still trying to quicken himself, he fell into an even deeper quickening—or dreamed he did—and this time when he spoke his message, talking across the table to his two friends, he reached out his hands and dreamed—or was it a dream?—that he felt their hands in his, and their voices assuring him that they would comply with his wishes.

"Then come back here after dark," he said, "and bring me back up to bed, because I'm so very tired." Whereupon he closed his eyes and fell, not into a deeper trance, but into such a deep sleep that he slumped forward and slept with his head on his arms.

Then he awoke to Leaky shaking him gently and saying, "Wake up, Umbo, go upstairs to your bed, why would you sleep sitting at table?"

For a moment Umbo thought this meant his dream was true. "You came as I asked!" said Umbo—his voice still a hoarse whisper.

"Listen to the croaking of a frog!" said Leaky with delight. "You poor thing, you really are sick, at least a cold, all full of mucus and snot, which is what happens when you come downstairs and fall asleep in a cooling house with no blanket and hardly a stitch on."

There had been no message received, none at all.

I'll just have to try again, he thought.

But the next night he tried nothing at all. He had spent the day working, not on reaching back in time, but rather on helping Loaf repair things around the inn, and fetch things from the weekly market that were needed to feed the guests, and whatever other errands were needed, anything to keep himself awake, since he had slept so little the night before.

Almost as soon as he had eaten, he went upstairs and dropped off to sleep immediately.

Again he was woken by Leaky's hands shaking him.

No. Leaky's *and* Loaf's hands. They were in his room and it was still the same night, because there was the noise of guests in the common room, singing songs with bad harmonies and voices lubricated by ale.

"You did it!" said Loaf. "You appeared at our table, sitting there, reaching out your hands! We took your hands boy."

Umbo felt a glow of satisfaction. "What did I say? Didn't I tell you not to waken me?"

"No, you said we *must* waken you and send you upstairs to bed."

"No he didn't," said Leaky.

"But since you were already here—well, we *thought* you were, so we came upstairs to check, and couldn't help waking you and telling you that it worked!"

But it hadn't worked. "I left that message *last* night. That's why I was sitting at the kitchen table. So I didn't go into the past at all, I went into the future. Tonight. Last night I left the message that you got tonight." In despair Umbo rolled over in bed and faced the wall.

"You stupid little fool," said Loaf, not without affection. "You think that's *failure*? What do we care, right now at least, whether

269

you go into the future or the past. So you went a few hours into the future? You shifted yourself into another time *at all*!"

Come to think of it, once Loaf had put it that way, it was an encouraging sign. "All right," said Umbo, rolling onto his back but keeping his eyes closed. "Because you saw me sitting at the table, and you touched my hands, I know exactly which of my tries actually worked. It was different from the others. I was numb from lack of sleep, I was so deep in my trance I felt lost, felt like I might never find my way back. I couldn't tell when I crossed the boundary from that into sleep. But all the other times accomplished nothing."

"Unless we're going to keep running into ghosts of you giving us foolish messages for the rest of our lives," said Leaky.

"I must learn how to push the messages into the past—and just the right amount of time, too."

Loaf chuckled. "You're not even awake. But tomorrow, let's keep you sending messages until you start going in the right direction. Or maybe you can pick a spot to write messages in the dirt."

"I don't think that'll work," said Umbo. "You couldn't even hear my voice, am I right? All you did was *see* me."

"And hold your hands," said Leaky. "Didn't you feel us hold your hands?"

"Yes, I did," admitted Umbo. "And I could smell the kitchen."

"Of course you could," said Loaf. "You were *in* the kitchen."

"I mean I could smell the dinner as if it was fresh. I remember that now, from what I thought was a dream."

"We know you can scratch a message in the dirt, Umbo,"

said Loaf, "because you were able to dig up a certain bag that was buried in dirt, and then cover the place again so it betrayed no disturbance."

"What bag are you talking about?" asked Leaky.

"The bag of jewels," said Loaf. "When Rigg was arrested, we went back and got it. Only Umbo, here, had apparently come back from the future to raid my little hiding place and take the biggest jewel out of the bag."

"Anyone could have taken it," said Leaky.

"Anyone in their right mind would have taken the whole bag," said Loaf.

"I can't have done it," said Umbo miserably. "I'm only traveling in time to reach into the future. Which is useless, since we're all going to end up in the future anyway."

"All those stories of ghosts," said Leaky. "They're probably just somebody like you. They're walking around in a house when they're so tired they accidentally fall into this quickening you're talking about, and they inadvertently leave behind an image of themselves—or even the reality of themselves, since there can be touching and smelling—which pushes them into the future so that people many decades from now will see this ghost going about its business. Maybe they don't even know they're doing it."

"If they do it like me," said Umbo, "they know what they're doing."

"Oh, so now *you* know what you're doing?" asked Loaf. "Weren't *you* the one who thought he was pushing messages back into the past, but they were really getting misdelivered into the future?"

"Let me go back to sleep," said Umbo. "I'm so tired I could die."

"But remember this when you're going back to sleep, Umbo," said Loaf. "You really did it. You really shifted yourself through time."

"Yes, I did, didn't I," said Umbo. And then he was gone and dreaming again, but this time of his brother standing at the edge of the falls.

He felt this urgent question building inside the part of him that knew it was a dream: Why can't I also go back and save my brother's life? If I can save Rigg's money, doesn't it mean I can go and speak to Kyokay and save *him* before he goes out to the falls?

Maybe I did, he thought as he drifted back to sleep yet again. Maybe I did, only years from now, when I'm grown. Maybe I'm the man that Rigg thought he was pushing or at least letting fall from the cliff.

Impossible.

If only.

He slept again.

CHAPTER 12

In Irons

The expendable and the computers worked out the math as best they could in only an hour or two. "If your extravagant and unverifiable guesses happen to be right," said the expendable, "then yes, the stuttering of spacetime might have allowed all nineteen versions of this ship to pass through the fold to eleven thousand years in the past, but with just enough time elapsed between passages that they wouldn't overlap and therefore wouldn't necessarily annihilate each other."

"So there might be not just one, but nineteen versions of this ship and all its crew and equipment, including your charming selves, and me, the pilot, proceeding toward the target planet in order to colonize it."

"Or not," said the expendable.

"Oh, but it's too delicious not to be true."

"Metaphorical flavor doesn't influence reality," said the expendable.

"But the elegance of reality has a metaphorical flavor," said Ram.

"Suppose you're right," said the expendable. "So what?"

"So I'll feel better as I spend the rest of my life doing nothing meaningful."

"You'll have time to read all those books you never got around to reading."

"I think I won't have time to do anything at all," said Ram. "I think I will only live until we reach the place where this ship was constructed. Only the structure we now see around us is moving backward through time. When we come to the place where it was built, it will be unbuilt around us."

"So we'll get off."

"How?" asked Ram. "We would have to get into a shuttle that would take us back to the surface of Earth. But there are no shuttles moving our direction in time."

"There aren't any stars moving our direction," said the expendable, "and yet we still see them."

"What an interesting quandary," said Ram. "By all means, stick around and see what happens."

"What will you do?"

"I'll continue this voyage until I find a way to send a message to the versions of myself that cross the fold into the past and have to deal with their nineteenfold replication."

"How do you propose to do that?" asked the expendable.

"Carve it into the metal of the ship somewhere that I'll be sure to find it, but not until after I come through the fold."

"No matter where you decide to carve it," said the expendable, "the fact that it wasn't already there when you arrive to start carving it proves that you cannot do anything to change objects that are moving in the ordinary direction of time."

"I know," said Ram. "That's why *you're* going to do it."

"That changes nothing."

"With your eyes closed," said Ram. "So you can't see in advance the proof that it didn't work."

• • •

Rigg and Shouter, clamped together at ankles and wrists, sat side by side on two stools in the pilot's cabin as the boat made its way down the river. The current was carrying them, so there were no steady surges from the polemen. Instead, the boat would yaw to one side or the other as the polemen shoved them away from some obstacle—a bar, a bank, an island, another boat. Able to see nothing, Rigg and Shouter could make no preparation for these changes of direction, and so they sat constantly braced, trying to avoid lurching into each other or falling off the stools.

For the first several hours, Shouter said nothing, which did not bother Rigg—he was practiced in holding his tongue and forcing the other to speak first. And judging from the raw hatred Rigg could see and feel in the rigidity of Shouter's body and facial expression, the beat of his pulse, the heat coming from him despite his being soaking wet, when Shouter spoke it was not going to be nice.

But it might be informative. General Citizen was practiced

in self-control, revealing only what he chose, most of the time; Shouter, judging from his nickname, had no schooling in self-control—except, perhaps, in front of a superior officer; if he didn't have *that* skill, he would never have become an officer. Still, Rigg might learn more about General Citizen, perhaps get an idea of which things Citizen had said were true. He might also stumble upon some information that would help him figure out a way to escape from custody, if he decided that's what he wanted to do. And perhaps he could turn Shouter into an ally, or at least a tool.

Food was brought to them and placed on a table in front of them—but too far away for them to reach it without either pulling the table toward themselves or their stools toward the table. Rigg reached forward with his left hand and pulled slightly on the table. Then he held his hand there, waiting for Shouter to do the same on the other side.

He could see that it truly pained Shouter to have to cooperate with him, but in due time he must have seen the necessity of it, for he reached out his right hand and together, they drew the table toward themselves, so now the bowls of barley soup were within comfortable reach.

Rigg reached with his left hand to take the spoon from the right side of the bowl. Shouter did the same with his right.

"This is going to be clumsy," said Rigg. "I'm right-handed. Using a spoon with my left hand on a boat that's prone to yaw, I might spill."

Since Rigg could plainly see that Shouter was left-handed, he was deliberately giving Shouter an opening to say that he was at the same disadvantage. Instead, Shouter grimly set about bringing dribbling spoonfuls to his mouth, spilling a little onto the table and his lap.

Rigg had spent considerable time with Father practicing to be as ambidextrous as possible—able to shoot a bow, clean and skin an animal, and write smoothly and legibly with either hand. He could have eaten without dribbling, but instead he matched Shouter spill for spill.

"I don't think it's an accident they bound your left hand to my right," said Rigg. "To make us both clumsier."

Shouter didn't even look at him.

As they both kept eating, Rigg spoke between bites. "For what it's worth, my friends and I had no idea we were going to be arrested today, and whatever they did to put you in the water, I wasn't part of it."

Shouter turned to gaze at him with furious eyes, but still refused to speak. That was all right—he had made contact and it was just a matter of time.

"So you don't hate me because you're wet, you hate me because of who I'm supposed to be. Just so you know, I'm not claiming to be anybody but myself."

Shouter gave a single bark of a laugh.

"The only parent I knew was my father, who raised me mostly in the forests. He died several months ago, and left—"

"Spare me," said Shouter. "How many times do you think that story is going to work?"

"As often as the truth works."

"I'm here to kill you," said Shouter.

Rigg felt a thrill of fear run through his body. Shouter meant it. Well, that was certainly useful information.

"All right then," said Rigg. "I can't stop you."

"You can't even slow me down."

Rigg waited.

"Well?" he asked.

"Not here," said Shouter. "Not in this room. Then they'd have to have a trial and execute me, and it would become public. Stories would spread about how a soldier under General Citizen's command murdered the rightful King-in-the-Tent. It would be as bad as leaving you alive."

"So the general has given you orders to—"

"Fool," said Shouter. "Do you think I need orders in order to see my duty and do it?"

Rigg thought again of the hatred on the man's face. "This isn't about duty."

Shouter said nothing for a long while. Then: "Killing you is more than a duty. But the manner will be dutiful."

"Just for my own interest," said Rigg, "are you killing me because you think I really *am* the Sessamekesh? Or because you think I'm an imposter?"

"Just for your own interest," said Shouter, "it doesn't matter."

"But your hatred for me—does it spring from a love of the royal family or a loathing for them?"

"If you're truly royal or if you're an imposter, your purposes can only be served by restoring the royal family to power."

"Your hatred of the royals is personal."

"My great-grandfather was a very rich and powerful trader.

Someone accused him of putting on airs as if he were nobility—the crime was sumptuary presumption. Trying to pass as a lord. Wearing the clothes of a lord. Assuming the dignities of a lord."

"That was a crime?" asked Rigg.

"Not a mere crime. Each charge was a count of treason. Under the monarchy, it was law that everyone must stay in his class. Merchants cannot become armiger, armigers cannot become noble, and nobles could not aspire to the monarchy. If my great-grandfather had been accused of dressing as a warrior, bearing arms, the penalty would have been a steep fine and house arrest for a year. But he was charged with dressing as a noble, which would have jumped him up two ranks. The penalty was the same as if he had attempted to murder the queen."

Rigg had never heard of any such nonsense, but he did not doubt the truth of Shouter's story. "Death?"

"A slow and gruesome public death," said Shouter. "With his body parts fed to the royal hunting dogs in front of the merchants' guild. His family was stripped of all wealth, including the clothing of a merchant, and wearing only the loincloths and mantles of beggars they were turned loose in the street to be the prey of any."

"That's not fair," said Rigg.

"After my great-grandfather was executed, his eldest son, my grandfather, was killed almost at once by the servants of a rival merchant—the one who had denounced his father, no doubt. Without protectors, without money or property, all the women and young boys of the family would have been forced into prostitution, the men into bonded service in the mines. Instead they were taken under the protection of the Revolutionary Council. My father was only nine. He grew up to show the Council the loyalty they deserved. I was raised on that loyalty and I feel it still. I would die to keep the royal deathworms from infesting Stashiland again."

He had called it Stashiland—the name of the valley and delta of the Stashik River, before the Sessamoto came from the northeast to conquer it and establish the empire. For the first time, Rigg began to understand just how deep memory could go, and how much pain could still be felt because of things that happened decades before.

"I have never—"

"I know you have never harmed me or anyone that way. But if your game is played at all, no matter what kind of player you are, those who *would* treat commoners that way will use you to seize power again. The Council is the worst sort of government—corrupt, arbitrary, self-righteous, fanatical. But they're better than any of the alternatives. And my family owes them our survival."

"Well, this all makes perfect sense," said Rigg. "If I have to die, it's just as well to be murdered by someone whose family lost everything at the hands of people I've never met and never claimed to be related to, and whom I would fight against myself if they behaved that way."

"You're wasting your breath," said Shouter.

"For my own satisfaction," said Rigg, "may I know the real name of the man who's going to kill me?"

"My great-grandfather was Talisco Waybright. My grandfather was also Talisco, and my father, and I as well, though the Waybright name was stripped from us, and replaced with 'Urine.'"

"Not really," said Rigg.

"It's a common-enough name in Aressa Sessamo," said Shouter. "It was given to convicts, along with other colorful and degrading names. After the revolution, most of us kept those names as a badge of pride. I will not call myself Waybright again until the royal family all are dead. Though I may decide that your death is enough for me to earn the old name back again."

"So how do you plan to separate us so you can kill me?"

"I'll share no plans with you."

You already have, Rigg thought. Since you plan to kill me in such a way as to avoid a trial for murder, you're going to make it look like an accident, and as proof of it, you intend to die with me. It's a dutiful death. But I'll pretend not to know.

As they finished eating, soaking up the last of the soup with fresh city-made bread, Rigg looked, without seeming to, at the way the manacles were fastened. Heavy iron bands that were closed at their wrists and also attached to each other by a single lock. An easy one to pick open, as Father had taught him the mechanisms of the most common locks. Rigg assumed the leg irons were attached the same way, but the problem would be getting to them with some kind of tool while Shouter—no, Talisco Waybright—was fighting him.

"You're small," Father had taught him, "and if you show no aggression, your enemies will not expect you to be bold. Most adult men will be stronger than you, but you'll be stronger than they expect a child to be. Whatever action you take must be the final action, for you'll get no second chance to surprise the same man."

The handle of the spoon was narrow enough for lock-picking, if he could figure out a way to keep it. Was there anything else? There were pens and other writing tools on shelves, but none of these would be strong enough, except the trimming knife, and there was no chance anyone would let him come near it.

He was mentally inventorying his clothing to see if anything would do the job when suddenly Talisco shouted, "We're done with the food!" His voice was like a sledgehammer in that small room—Rigg could certainly understand how he got his nick-name. "Come get the plates before this boy steals the spoon to pick the lock!"

So I'm not as subtle as I thought I was, Rigg said silently. Or perhaps it's a common trick.

The door opened and two soldiers came in. They stood at the door, watching, as a crewman gathered up the bowls and spoons.

"I need to pee," said Rigg.

"We'll bring you a jar," said one of the soldiers.

"Oh, that's good, I'll splash all over my hand," said Rigg. He raised his manacled hand as far as Talisco would let him. "Do you think I'm going to jump into the water fastened to him? Just let me pee over the side."

The soldiers looked at him, then followed the crewman through the door and locked it again behind them.

"So you've decided just how I'm going to kill you, is that it?" asked Talisco.

"If you want to kill me and yourself by falling into the river with irons on, go ahead. But if you're going to kill me later in some other way, I'd rather die with an empty bladder."

The clasp of his belt was the only possibility—the tongue of it was hard enough iron. But was it long enough? Could he unfasten it one-handed?—for he assumed that Talisco, under water, would prevent him from being able to use both hands. Could he then use it to pick the lock without dropping the belt? Because there was no chance he'd find it again, in the murk of the river.

After a few minutes, the soldiers came back in and left the door standing open. Then they stepped outside.

"You're a royal all right," muttered Talisco as they stood up. "Think you're going to control everything, even your own assassination."

As they passed through the door, one soldier took Rigg firmly by the free arm and the other held Talisco. Other soldiers stood by to watch. They were determined that there'd be no escape attempt this time.

As if I wanted to escape from the boat, thought Rigg. Didn't Father tell me to find my sister? You're taking me where I want to go. The only escape I want is from this assassin. "He's planning to kill me, you know," said Rigg softly to the soldier holding him. "If we have an accident, you can be sure it was murder."

The soldier said nothing, and Talisco's body shuddered in silent laughter. "Do you think I'm the only one wants you dead?" he murmured.

"Um," said Rigg aloud to the soldier holding him. "How do

you propose that I open my pants? If I'm just going to pee all over myself I could have stayed inside."

In answer, the soldier—never relaxing his grip—forced Rigg's left hand down toward his crotch. There Rigg reached under his overshirt and one-handedly unfastened the belt of his trousers. They were loose enough that they dropped from his waist—but by spreading his legs widely apart, Rigg kept them from dropping right to the deck.

"He doesn't even *have* a butt," one of the rivermen jested.

"Silence," said a voice that Rigg knew. General Citizen—so he, too, had come to watch Rigg pee.

The soldier on Talisco's side asked him, "Aren't you going to pee, too?"

"I don't need to."

"Come on, this is your chance, we're not going to do this again for hours."

"I don't need to," said Talisco again, a little more softly and grimly, and the soldier took the hint.

Rigg tugged on his right hand, trying to reach it toward his crotch. Talisco yanked it back. "Use your left!"

"I'm right-handed!" Rigg shouted back. "I can't aim with my left!"

"It's the river!" shouted Talisco. "You can't miss it!"

"I don't want to get it all over my clothes!" Rigg shouted, letting his voice rise a little higher in pitch, so he sounded more like a little boy.

"Royal bastard," muttered Talisco, letting Rigg drag their manacled hands down toward his crotch.

"Probably right," Rigg murmured back. Then he deliberately aimed a stream of urine onto the back of Talisco's hand.

Talisco's reflex was quick and unthinking. With a roar he snatched his hand back.

Rigg used the momentum of his grab to propel Talisco's own wrist, with all his own strength added, into a smashing blow of the fetter against Talisco's forehead. That was the surprise Father had warned him needed to be enough.

Assuming that it *had* been enough to stun Talisco, Rigg instantly made a great show of losing his balance, flinging his left arm free of the soldier holding him and getting behind the now-unconscious Talisco so no one else could grab the man. With another shove—disguising it as best he could by crying "help" and flailing his arms—he got Talisco's limp body over the rail, which dragged Rigg over as part of the same movement.

He could feel that he still had his pants, though they were around his ankles now. Before they hit the water, Rigg was doubling over to lay hands on the belt, and as they splashed into the brown stream, he was already working the tongue of the clasp into the keyhole of the lock.

The weight of the leg irons dragged them straight down. By the time they hit the bottom of the river, Rigg's right hand was free. He doubled over and freed his ankle.

But that was not enough. He was not making an escape the way Loaf and Umbo had done. Nor did he want Talisco to die— if he could bring it off, he had a use for him. So he continued to hold his breath as he opened Talisco's leg and wrist fetters, letting the iron drop. Now both of them were weighed down only by their clothes. Rigg stepped on one of his trouser-legs and pried his legs free. Then, being a strong swimmer, he dragged the limp man up to the surface.

When his head bobbed up into the air, Rigg gasped a quick breath and then worked to get Talisco's head above water. "Help!" Rigg cried. "Talisco's drowning!"

The boat had already stopped and the rivermen were poling it upstream. In moments Rigg had Talisco at the side. General Citizen sharply commanded them to forget Talisco and get the boy.

"I'm the only thing holding him up!" Rigg shouted savagely, using his authority voice, and sure enough, the soldiers and rivermen obeyed him instinctively and took the weight of Talisco. At that point, Rigg scrambled back up onto the deck almost without assistance, so he was able to watch as they dragged Talisco over the rail and laid him on the deck.

Talisco obviously wasn't breathing.

"Take that boy inside again!" ordered General Citizen.

"Not till I get that man breathing again!" Rigg counter-ordered, and again his voice of command worked well enough that the soldiers who had been reaching for him hesitated. In that moment, Rigg flung himself onto Talisco's unconscious body and started working on him as Father had taught all the children in Fall Ford to do.

The rivermen had their own method, which involved turning a drowned man upside down and hitting his back with oars or poles. Apparently the victims of that process recovered often enough that the men up and down the river kept on doing it. What Rigg was doing—pressing on Talisco's chest to eject the water and then clamping his mouth over Talisco's and forcing air down his throat—was not something they had seen before. Some of the rivermen were shouting for him to get out of the way so they could paddle the man back to life.

A bloody wound on Talisco's forehead attested to the strength of the blow Rigg had managed to land on him. He wondered if the blow had already killed Talisco—but for Rigg's purposes it didn't really matter. As long as everyone *saw* him save, or try to save, the man's life, that was the story that would be told; the blow to the head would be seen as an accident, and probably not even ascribed to Rigg, since nobody would think a stripling boy would have the strength to inflict a fatal blow.

And they would be right—Talisco was not dead. It took only a few moments before he was coughing and sputtering and breathing on his own, in short quick gasps.

"I've heard of that sort of thing," said one of the rivermen.

"I never have," said another.

"Can you teach us that, boy?" asked a third.

But by then General Citizen was back in control, furious and anxious—and showing it, for once. "Get that boy back into the cabin!" he ordered, and this time Rigg meekly let himself be half-led, half-dragged back to his prison.

In moments Citizen was in the room with him and they were alone together. Citizen kept his voice low as he asked, "What, by the Wall, did you think you were doing?"

"Not escaping," said Rigg.

"Why not?" asked Citizen. "What's your game?"

"My father's last words were for me to find my sister. If I'm really Rigg Sessamekesh, then my sister is Param Sissaminka, and I need to get to Aressa Sessamo to meet her. Since that's where you're going, I thought I'd stay aboard."

Citizen grabbed him by his drenched shirtfront and put his mouth against Rigg's ear. "What makes you think you'll ever be allowed anywhere near the royal family?"

"Well, obviously I won't be if I'm dead," said Rigg. "But it'll be harder to get people to believe it was an accident after *this* failed attempt."

"What attempt?" asked Citizen. "I saw what happened—*you* did this from beginning to end."

"Who else saw it that way?" Rigg shook his head. "Talisco told me he planned to kill me, make it look like an accident, and convince people by dying himself in the process. All I did was rush the process and turn it to my own advantage."

Citizen seemed genuinely dumfounded. "He told you?"

"He told me that it was his duty. He assumed that's why you manacled the two of us together, so he could pay for having let Loaf and Umbo get away by dying as he murdered me."

"I gave no such order," said Citizen.

"Of course you didn't," said Rigg. "You ordered us into irons and he took it from there."

"I mean it was not what I wanted. Are you really that stupid?"

"How stupid do you mean?" asked Rigg. "I think I just did rather well. I took down a man twice my weight and strength, got free of the irons, and saved him from drowning."

"Very theatrical. I'd applaud, but the men listening outside would think I was hitting you."

"Maybe you're of the royal party—the royal *male* party—or maybe you were testing me. It's beyond my knowing. But I believe Talisco meant to kill me, whether it was your plan or not. And I didn't intend to die without meeting my sister."

"Your sister," said Citizen. "Not your mother?"

"It was my sister that my father spoke of. For all I know, Param Sessaminka is *not* my sister, and Hagia Sessamin is not my mother. But he said my sister was in Aressa Sessamo so that's where I'm going. And if anything happens to me *now*, the story of Talisco and me going into the water will be told in a different way—as your first attempt to have me killed."

"I do not want you dead, you fool. I want you alive."

"Then don't manacle me to fanatical anti-monarchists."

Citizen let go of him and crossed to the other side of the room as the boat lurched to one side, staggering them both. "You may be sure I won't," said Citizen.

"When we get there," said Rigg, "let me see the royal family. Let me stand beside them. If there's no resemblance, then the whole idea of passing me off as the male heir is done with, whether you're in favor of such a thing or not."

"Do you think I'm an idiot?" asked Citizen.

"I know you're not."

"I saw your father, boy. You look just like him. And enough like your mother, too, that everyone will know at a glance you're the real thing."

Rigg didn't bother pretending that this opinion didn't affect him. "Couldn't my father—the man I called my father—couldn't he have chosen a baby that he thought might grow up to resemble—"

"You don't *resemble* them," said Citizen. "You're not *similar* to them in some vague way. Anyone who knew your father will know that you're his son. You're not an imposter, though I'll never say that to anyone else on this boat. Is that clear?"

Rigg shivered. "I suppose you won't be willing to let me wear some of the dry clothing that I no longer own in the trunk that isn't mine."

Citizen sighed. "As I told you, no official verdict has been rendered. You have the use of the clothing you bought in O. I'll have something dry sent in. But no more belts."

"I won't need them, if you don't put me back in irons."

Citizen stalked toward the door, then paused there. "You'll be peeing in a little pot for the rest of the voyage."

Rigg smiled. "I told you, General Citizen. I want to go to Aressa Sessamo, and I want to go with you. The only way I'd leave this boat is dead."

"I believe you," said the general. "But you're staying in here so that some other volunteer assassin doesn't try to get at you."

"What will you do to Talisco?" asked Rigg.

"Hang him, probably," said Citizen.

"Please don't," said Rigg. "It would make me feel like all my work saving his life was wasted."

"He won't thank you for it," said Citizen.

"He's always free to kill himself," said Rigg. "But I don't want his blood on my hands—or on yours, for my sake. Remember what you saw, sir. He never lifted his hand to kill me, even if he planned to do it later. He committed no crime."

"He committed the crime of stupidity while under my command," said Citizen.

"Oh my," said Rigg. "They're handing out the death penalty for *that* these days?"

Citizen turned his back and knocked twice on the door. It opened; he left; the door closed and was barred behind him.

Rigg peeled off his wet clothing, wrapped himself in a blanket, and lay down on the floor, curled up and shivering. Only now could he face what he had done, how easily it could have failed, how completely he might have been killed, and it left him whimpering with fear.

CHAPTER 13

Rigg Alone

"But even if I close my eyes before carving the message, I'll see the other proof that it didn't work," said the expendable.

"What's that?"

"The existence of the message *after* I carve it, which in the ordinary flow of time would be *before* I had carved it, proving that the message is moving in the same direction through time as us, which means it will not be in the version of the ship that will make—or has made—the jump."

"Just close your eyes and do it," said Ram. "And keep them closed. And then come back and tell me you did it without knowing whether it worked or not."

"Why would I deliberately conceal data from myself?"

"Because it will make me feel better."

"Then I will observe and simply not tell you."

"If you know, then you have to tell me, if I ask."

"Then don't ask."

"If I know you know, I will have to ask," said Ram.

"So I have to behave irrationally in order to give you an irrational hope."

"And then I'll die," said Ram.

"Are you suggesting a medical outcome, an emotional hyperbole, or an intention?"

"Intention," said Ram.

"So by doing this and remaining ignorant of the outcome, I am hastening the time when you will take your own life?"

"No," said Ram. "*You* will take my life."

"I will not."

"You will if I order it," said Ram.

"I cannot," said the expendable.

"At the end of the jump through the fold, there came into existence a total of at least twenty versions of myself—nineteen going forward, and me—or nineteen of me—going back. There can only be one real Ram Odin."

"You," said the expendable.

"I am a version that can do nothing, change nothing, affect nothing. Because of the direction of my movement through time I am, in effect, nonexistent already in the real universe. I declare this copy of myself to be flawed, useless, and—let's admit it—completely expendable. There can only be one real version of myself."

"Killing you will only eliminate the back-flowing Ram or Rams," said the expendable. "It will not affect the nineteen forward-moving Rams, of which eighteen will be as redundant as you say you are."

"That's not my problem," said Ram.

• • •

It took twenty-two days for the boat to carry Rigg from O to Aressa Sessamo. This was long for such a voyage, but Rigg thought of several reasons for their slow progress.

First, they stopped every night and anchored well away from shore but out of the current—this much he learned from careful listening to the commands being given in loud voices. This was common practice—away from shore to avoid land-based brigands, but ceasing to move downstream for fear of running aground on a sand bar or other obstruction in the dark.

Second, the current slowed and was spread among many channels as it moved into the vast alluvial plain of the Stashik River. It no longer gave a sure direction, and the pilot could not guess which formerly useful channels were too silted up to be safe. Twice they had to pole their way out of a channel in order to return to a main channel and search out another way.

Third, a slow passage for the boat meant that any messengers General Citizen might have sent by land would reach Aressa Sessamo long before the boat could get there, despite the fact that the road was constantly winding this way and that, and often blocked, having to be rebuilt with each collapse of a portion of it as the water of the Stashik delta seeped under it and eroded it away. (Many a ruler of the various empires that had chosen Aressa Sessamo for their capital were saved from invaders by this natural, unmappable, three-hundred-mile series of moats and obstacles.)

During the whole of the voyage, after Rigg was given dry

clothes and no longer had to be fettered to a spy or assassin or whatever Talisco had been, he was left completely alone. A crewman—a different one each day—would bring him food on a tray in the morning, which was to last him for the day. The meal was brought in under the watchful eyes of two soldiers, who said nothing and allowed neither the crewman nor Rigg to speak, either.

Rigg ate whatever was hot for breakfast, and then waited to eat the rest—even though some of it tended to wilt—until he could hear the sounds of the boat being anchored for the evening. The food was decent—by the standards of riverboat fare—and they must have been sending small boats to shore now and then to obtain fresh fruits and vegetables, because these were not lacking.

Twice a day—once as soon as he awoke and had used the chamber pot, and once again when he imagined it was getting near dinnertime (and he was never wrong)—Rigg walked the periphery of the room with a steady stride until his heart began to beat faster and his breath was needed more quickly, and then continued for at least half an hour, by his best reckoning. He went around one direction in the morning, the other in the afternoon.

When those outside the cabin were getting a noon meal, he took none, but instead did the kind of physical exercise Father had taught him to make a part of his daily regimen, to keep strong the muscles that weren't used in whatever work he happened to be doing. Since he was doing no work at all, he did all the exercises.

He slept well twice a day, four hours at a time. He had long since learned the trick of deciding how long he wanted to sleep, and then waking at the time he chose. So after breakfast and again after supper, he took his sleeps. This meant that in the afternoons and in the long silent hours of the morning, he was wide awake. He made sure to stay awake by not lying on his bed except when it was time to sleep, and he varied his position from sitting in a chair to sitting on the floor to standing—even sometimes standing on his hands or balancing himself on his head while leaning against the wall.

His assignment to himself was to think. Being temporarily powerless, deprived of any ability to gain new information or influence events, he had only two projects that mattered to him: to see what he might learn from the information he already had, and to try to learn how to broaden his visions of paths into the skill that Umbo and he had mastered together, and which Umbo had now obviously learned to accomplish by himself. He knew that it was unworthy of him to think this, but he could not help it: If Umbo can do it alone, though he never saw a path, surely I can do it alone.

He told himself that he meant no slight to Umbo by thinking this: If one of them could learn to acquire or replace the other one's contribution to their shared time travels, then surely the other could as well. But he was honest with himself, and he knew that there was too much of pride and contempt in the thought, for in his own heart it took this inflection. If even *Umbo* can do it, then surely *I* can do it—and better, and more easily.

Rigg had taken it as a matter of course that when time travel happened, it was he who did it. Yes, he had needed Umbo's help, but it was Rigg who actually fell in step beside a man and took the knife from its sheath. It was Rigg who saw the paths, and had always seen them and used them to track game and see where people had gone, while Umbo hadn't really understood very much at all about his own gift.

Do I have the natural arrogance of royalty? he asked himself. Do I automatically assume that everything about me is better than everything about other people?

For all I know, it is Umbo with the precious gift—the ability to alter time, or at least to alter a person's speed of passage through it—while mine is more that of a scout, searching out particular paths where Umbo's gift might be used. Umbo can bestow the power of time travel on other people—I can share my gift with no one.

And yet there was something in him that made him think less of Umbo than of himself.

Maybe he felt that way because Father had spent so much time with him, training him, and had only spent a relatively little time training Umbo. Or maybe it was the soul-numbing arrogance that came with having so much money for a few weeks in O. He had put on the act of a proud young man of wealth, but it was quite possible that at an unconscious level he had come to believe his own performance, that it had become part of his nature. But he resolved now to get rid of any trace of that arrogance, because he knew it would make him into that kind of idiot who says, when he's not getting his own way, "Do you know who I am?"

Father had always taught him, "A person *is* what he says and does; that's how you learn whether his reputation was earned or manufactured."

That much Rigg had come to understand on his first day of solitude, and from then on he humbly and assiduously tried to learn how to do to himself what Umbo had done to him — make his own perceptions speed up so that his observation could keep pace with the swift movement of long-past people along their paths.

Two things kept him from making even the slightest progress, as far as he could tell. First, every time Umbo had allowed him to see the people in the paths, he and Umbo had been standing still, watching the paths for a dozen seconds at least. It took time for Rigg to discern the individual people racing along, and to pick one of them to concentrate on; only then did the person slow down until Rigg could choose one of the iterations of his passage and take action.

On the boat, this was impossible. Not that there weren't countless paths up and down — and across — the river — it was a chaos of paths. But when the boat was moving, Rigg could never study the same path long enough to have a hope of discerning anything.

And even when they were anchored at night, and he could study a few paths for some length of time before the current shifted his position, he ran into the second problem, which was that he had no idea how to go about duplicating what Umbo's gift had done. He could imagine that Umbo's need to duplicate Rigg's gift, by locating a person in the past in order to focus on him, was sidestepped by choosing someone whose location had been known to him and who remained in the same spot for a considerable length of time. In such cases, Rigg's vision of paths would be unnecessary to Umbo, or at least *less* necessary.

But Rigg had seen the paths his whole life, had learned to distinguish between them and identify a particular path and follow it through time—always knowing in which direction it flowed, though he could never explain to Father how he knew—and yet he had never once suspected that the path was actually the rapid blur of the person himself endlessly repeating his movements. Not until Umbo's gift had opened his eyes.

So now Rigg knew the truth behind what he had always known—where the long-past people and animals had gone. He even had a clear sense of which paths were older and which newer, which were of men or of women, which were of adults or of children, just as he could tell which species and gender and age of animal had made a certain path. He conceived this information as colors, thickness, intensity, texture, as if it were sight, but he knew now that he was gleaning information from the paths that sight alone could never have given him. At some level he *was* penetrating the paths and "seeing" who it was—though of course sight had nothing to do with it.

Well, not *nothing*. He could sense paths that lay behind hills or walls—he could sense paths, for instance, far outside the bounds of the little cabin that served as his prison. The paths were mostly just a blur to him in the darkness, and with his eyes closed they were like an indistinct haze—but they were there, and he could sense them, and with concentration could achieve some kind of clarity. He could see as they were made the movements of the men on board the boat, even though the paths quickly receded upriver as the boat drifted down, which helped him make sense of the sounds he heard. All this depended little on what his eyes could see.

But his eyes gave him context for what he was seeing. He knew which wall of the cabin he was seeing these paths through, and remembering the general layout of the boat, he was able to understand what he sensed. The paths that crossed the gap over the Stashi Falls in midair, many rods out from the falls, still passed from side to side of the canyon cliffs, so Father's explanation of the falls' having eroded the edge in and down, and of bridges once having spanned the gap, made sense to Rigg.

On the river, though, the paths were far more confusing, because all the movements of people—except the rare swimmers and waders—had taken place on boats or bridges that had long since disappeared. A path would suddenly rise up into the air and pass overhead; others made strange looping motions; it was a mind-numbing tangle, when the ladder or mast a man had climbed was no longer there. Add to that the fact that in the delta, the river had changed course so many times that paths ran in every conceivable direction and bore little relation to the present channel, and Rigg could hardly be blamed for not being able to pick out one path and make it slow down (or himself speed up) to see the person making it.

The worst problem he faced, however, was that he had no idea what Umbo had done. They had decided by reason alone that Umbo must be speeding up Rigg's perceptions so he could see faster, so to speak. But nothing about the experience had felt to Rigg as if he were actually speeding up. In fact, he had *felt* nothing at all, so he could hardly figure out how to replicate the feeling. All that had happened was that what once had been a path now became a blur of human motion, and by concentrating closely on one target he could make it resolve into a person and visually slow him or her. And that *was* eyesight.

Or was it?

Rigg thought back to his experience at the falls, lying on the rock. Hadn't he *seen* the man with his eyes? He had certainly touched him with his body when he knocked him from the rock! Yet there had been a different quality to his seeing, compared to the way he saw the rock itself, and Umbo's brother Kyokay. As Father had taught him much about the workings of human brains, Rigg now imagined that the rocks and water and sky and Kyokay were coming into his brain the normal way, through his eyes; but the man who fell had come into his brain a different way, not through his eyes. Instead his brain had *interpreted* it as vision and laid it over what his eyes showed him. It had been fitted into his vision—which, now that he thought about it, was what Rigg always did with the information his path-sense gave him.

But this did not help him in any way to discover how Umbo had changed him—or the paths, or time itself—so that a path that had seemed to Rigg like a smooth ribbon became instead a blur of a rapidly moving person. Nor could Rigg make any progress by concentrating hard, squinching up his face, or trying to juice up some emotion.

He even tried, in a few insane experiments, to try to walk beside and keep pace with a path that he knew must be a person, in hopes of being able to see a human shape. He even ran with one for a moment, but of course crashed into the wall and caused a guard to open the door, though by then Rigg had contrived to pick up his chair so he could ruefully explain, "I fell asleep and the chair fell over," which the guard had no way of knowing was not true. In any event, the guard was forbidden to speak—all he could do was either go back out and shut the door, or waken General Citizen to come investigate. He chose the easier path and merely closed and rebarred the door.

Rigg even spent time philosophizing about what his and Umbo's experiences proved about the nature of time. For instance: The paths did *not* follow the present contours of the land; they remained exactly where they were regardless of how the land changed beneath them—or the water, or buildings, or vehicles.

Yet Rigg knew that the world was a spheroid planet with a ring of debris around it that raced through its orbit, sometimes nearer and sometimes farther from the sun, like the unsteady path of a drunken man. The sun itself did not hold still, but moved through a huge sea of stars, orbiting the center of the galaxy, while the galaxy itself drifted through space. So if the world had shifted a vast distance since these people first moved along its surface, why didn't the paths remain out in space where they had been made, instead of staying with this world wherever it roamed?

The passage of living creatures was preserved in paths that

were tied, not to the absolute locations of those creatures in space, but to their position relative to the center of planet Garden. Their paths continued to pass through exactly the same spot above the rotating world.

To Rigg, this meant that living things had a firm connection to the planet itself, and not just to the surface to which gravity pressed them. Time remembered the movements of all things which lived, but it kept the record engraved in exact relation to the center of gravity of the planet on which they dwelt, keeping their original relationship to each other as they stretched over the surface of the world.

Why time should be tied to gravity he did not know, but clearly it was. Rigg wondered all kinds of things, in his solitude — why, for instance, their movements were not preserved in relation to the sun, whose gravity was so powerful that it controlled Garden and kept it from whirling off into space; or whether, if a man could fly between worlds the way he sailed across rivers and seas, he would leave any kind of path behind him, or if his path would flex and bend between one world and the next? It was a strange kind of imagining, and he could imagine Loaf telling him it was a complete waste of time to wonder about such things, since men couldn't fly and certainly couldn't fly between planets. For Father had taught Rigg from childhood on that there is *no* thought that is not worth thinking, but that all ideas might be examined logically to see if they meant anything useful. Admittedly, Rigg had no idea now why thoughts about traveling between worlds and the persistence of paths on the voyage might be useful, but it was a pleasure to think them, and since pleasures were few and far between these days, he would take those he had and enjoy them.

Besides, thinking about travel between worlds kept him from brooding about what awaited him in Aressa Sessamo.

For that was his other project, and he could never get away from it for long. What did he know? What could he learn from the information he already had?

General Citizen had talked about various parties in Aressa Sessamo—the royalists divided into camps between followers of the female succession and those who yearned for a return to the male, and supporters of the People's Revolution, though if Citizen had told the truth, there were those who didn't so much support the Revolution as oppose the female succession.

Citizen seemed to be satisfied that Rigg really was the long-lost son of Hagia Sessamin and her husband Knosso Sissamik, so that whatever someone thought about royalty—or males of the royal line, of which Rigg was presumably the only living specimen—they would think about Rigg.

But Rigg couldn't even be sure which party he was under the control of now. If Citizen really was of the male-royal party, then he was in the hands of one who might exploit him in service of a monarchical restoration. But if Citizen was testing him by pretending to be of that party, then he might be in the hands of either a true servant of the Revolutionary Council, or of a follower of the female-succession party, in which case Rigg was in grave danger and might be murdered at any time.

There might also be other possibilities, no more or less far-fetched than these obvious ones. Citizen might indeed be a male-royalist but his party was not ready yet to make use of Rigg's existence, so he might be perfectly safe and would be delivered to the Revolutionary Council under circumstances that would make it difficult or impossible simply to kill him.

Or the royal family might actually have more influence than it seemed, and his own mother might wish to have him killed—if she was a true believer in her grandmother's decision to slaughter all the males of the royal line, then having Rigg delivered to Aressa Sessamo might be something so loathsome to her that she would seek to kill him the moment they met.

So many scenarios played out in his mind that he had no choice but to set them all aside, as much as possible. I'll know what I know when I know it, he told himself over and over. I can't predict the future from the facts that I have, so I can't prepare any more than I was already prepared, by Father, to speak with authority and understand the way politics in general was conducted.

Which always, always brought him back to Father, the one person, the one subject, he could not bear to think about.

Father had lied to him. Contained in everything Father taught him and told him and said to him and implied was a deep, abiding lie, or at least a vast concealment of information that amounted to a lie.

He never told me who I was, or how I came to live with him. He let me think him my real father and never corrected me with the truth.

And while he gave me many skills that I've used effectively, he left me blind about so many other things that I have stumbled into danger completely unawares, and don't have enough information now to know what to do.

Rigg would get into this line of thought and then would be distracted. Some path moving through the cabin. Some sound outside. A hunger pang, a sudden ache or twitch. Anything rather than continue to think about Father and the terrible ignorance that was the true inheritance Rigg had received from him.

Rigg wanted to stop thinking of the man as "Father" at all. His real father was a man named Knosso Sissamik, who was dead, but was reputed to have died at the Wall, perhaps even attempting to pass through the Wall. What a remarkable—or insane—man! Everyone knew that no living thing could pass through the Wall. *That* was my father, the man from whom the manly part of my mind derived. *He* is the one I need to learn about, because by studying him I'll learn about myself. Could he see the paths? Did I inherit this from him?

But Knosso was dead, and Rigg could not know him directly. Hagia was alive, but Rigg feared her, for it was possible she had meant him to die, and the man he called Father had saved him from her.

And Father—or whatever he might call him—had sent him forth, not to find his mother, but to find his *sister*, Param Sissaminka. Why her, and not anyone else? Why her, instead of some political mission? It was as if Father was telling him that whatever he was supposed to do, it had nothing to do with all the politics and maneuvering of the royal family and the people who had deposed them and kept them imprisoned, and everything to do with Param herself, as a person.

As a person with gifts like Rigg's and Umbo's? Was that what Father cared about? Certainly he had taken time to help train Umbo and Nox, too, in their gifts. And he had worked with Rigg and his paths endlessly, it seemed. Father had given Rigg the skills to keep him alive on the journey, more or less—confinement in this cabin was not a sign of Rigg's glorious success—but the goal was to get him to his sister, and nothing else. Father didn't care who ruled in Aressa Sessamo. He cared only that Rigg and Param meet.

But do I care? What was Father to me, that I should still let him govern my choices? Maybe *I* want to rule in Aressa Sessamo! Maybe I want to reclaim my lost and ancient heritage! Or maybe I just want to find out about my real father, and come to know and love my real mother, who might have been broken-hearted when Father stole me away, or might have hidden me by giving me to him to keep safe.

Maybe I will do what I want with my life!

The only problem is that I have no idea what I want to do with it.

They came to Aressa Sessamo by night—as planned, Rigg assumed, for they had waited at anchor for many hours of daylight on the day they arrived. The channels into the great port were well-marked by night, apparently. And when Rigg, newly washed, dressed in the fresh clothes they had brought him, came out of the cabin, it was with a bag over his head and his legs hobbled and his hands bound behind him. He was carried like a sack of potatoes to a sedan chair, in which he rode alone and in silence, having been warned that if he cried out or spoke he would be gagged.

And thus he came into the great city, in the dark, hooded, hearing only various noises in the streets, which changed as they moved along, but not in ways that he could understand.

Of course he was constantly aware of all the paths around him outside the sedan chair, the new ones and the old ones; he could tell where streets were now and where they had once been, but not what kind of buildings lined them, though he could see how tall they were by the recent paths that wended upward, floor by floor.

He could also see places where no one had gone in a thousand years, for the paths within those spaces were very old. But why they had been so long unvisited he could not guess.

At last the chair came to rest within a garden—from the chirping of the birds and their many paths into and out of the place—and someone opened the sedan chair door and reached in to remove the bag from his head.

It was a woman, and she wore only a simple tunic and her hair was raggedly cropped and she was not beautiful but she looked more than a little like Rigg himself.

"Welcome to Aressa Sessamo, Rigg," she said. "I am your mother."

CHAPTER 14

Flacommo's House

"We got ourselves caught in the midst of a stutter," said the expendable. "We were trying to avoid that because we didn't know what would happen to us in a stutter—most of the computers predicted the ship would be sectioned or obliterated."

Ram had been scanning all the reports from every part of the ship. "But we were neither sectioned nor obliterated. We're still intact."

"More than intact," said the expendable.

"How can you be more than intact?" asked Ram.

"There are eighteen other copies of our ship, and ourselves, that passed through the fold."

Ram tried to visualize what the expendable was describing.

"But not occupying the same space at the same time."

"The quantized nature of our passage through the fold dropped off all nineteen versions of the colony ship at regular intervals. We are separated from each other by about four seconds, which puts us a safe distance apart as long as we all refrain from firing our engines or generating any fields that would cut through another ship."

"And on each ship," said Ram, "there is a version of you speaking to a version of me?"

"All the expendables have reported that all the Ram Odins went unconscious at exactly the same time. All of us placed you in the same position and strapped you in and waited until you awoke, so you could tell us what to do. All of us are speaking to our Ram Odin and saying the identical words at the same time."

"Ain't spacetime a bitch," said Ram.

"Noted," said the expendable. "Nineteen times."

"So if all the *me*s are saying the same thing at the same time," said Ram, "I'd say there's a certain redundancy."

"Which does no harm."

"But at some point, one of us will do something different. We will diverge."

"As all of you are saying at this exact moment," said the expendable.

"And when we diverge, it will be impossible for the expendables and the ship's computers on all the ships to know which version of Ram Odin to obey," said Ram. "Therefore I order you and all the other expendables to immediately kill every copy of Ram except me."

• • •

The queen—his mother—drew him out of the sedan chair and stood him on the smooth stone paving of the garden courtyard.

"My beautiful boy," she said, standing back a little and looking him up and down.

"I've been prettier," he said, because it seemed odd to be called beautiful. Nobody had ever called him beautiful or even good looking. In O it had been his clothes and his money that were admired.

She reached out and gathered him into her arms and held him. "I see you with the eyes of a mother who long thought you were dead."

"Did you, Mother?" asked Rigg softly. "Did you think I was dead?"

This was not just a personal question—it was a political and historical one as well. If she thought he was dead then it meant she hadn't arranged for him to be carried away to safety. It also meant that he hadn't been kidnapped—for if he had been abducted, she might as easily suppose him to be alive as someone else groomed him for the kingship. For her to think he was dead, then either the kidnappers must have misled her—a cruel note, animal blood smeared around, some other kind of evidence— or she herself had sent him away with the intent of having him assassinated.

There were precedents in the family, after all. Mothers in this family were not always kind to their boychildren.

"Don't be indiscreet," she murmured into his hair.

Her message was clear enough: This was not a private meeting, but a public one. Whatever she said would be governed, not by simple truth, but by whatever she needed onlookers to over-hear and believe. Therefore, he would learn nothing about his own past or hers, but instead would learn about what was going on in the present.

Since his own future was also at stake, he didn't really need the warning to be careful. At the same time, he had little idea what *she* would consider to be indiscreet. So perhaps she was asking him to say nothing.

Rigg could wait. Meanwhile, he couldn't help but feel a flash of pity for her, a woman who, even in greeting her long-lost son, still had to watch every word she said, every gesture, every action, every decision.

A kind of prisoner because of the crimes of her ancestors, she thought like an inmate who lived in dread of her guards; everyone was an informant.

And where was his sister? Why had no one mentioned her? He did not ask, not now, not yet.

Rigg pulled away when she relaxed her embrace. Now he looked around and saw that there were at least a score of people in the courtyard, and probably more behind him. This was a state occasion, of course. The empress Hagia Sessamin had decided to affirm his identity as prince of the house royal even before having a chance to see him by daylight—that was a political decision that she probably made after hearing the report of General Citizen's messengers. If Citizen was a friend of the royal house, that would explain Rigg's solitary imprisonment and the hobble and manacles that bound him during his hooded journey from the boat into the city. There had to be a great show of how harshly Citizen had dealt with the newfound royal son. Just as Hagia Sessamin had to make a show of giving him a warm embrace—

even if the secret wish of her heart was to have him killed as soon as it was safe to do so, in order to preserve the female-line inheritance law of her grandmother Aptica.

"How complicated I'm making your life, Mother," he said with a smile.

He watched closely her reaction to these words. She showed a flash of anger; was it tinged with fear? Yes, it was. She might be afraid he planned to be indiscreet after all, and that some word from him would jeopardize everything. But how else could he signal to her that he understood the dilemma she was in— regardless of what her plan for him might be? If he had merely played along, saying nothing, she would wonder what game *he* was playing, how well he had been coached and trained, and by whom. Instead, he was letting her see that he planned to act the part of someone who had not been coached or trained, but was merely being himself. He was playing the naif. If she was wise, she would let him continue so—because the more clueless he seemed to be, the less he would be feared by the anti-royals, and the less likely the pro-male-heir faction would decide to strike her down so he could become the new king-in-name-only.

It was not his mother who answered. "It's *my* life that you're making complicated, my lad," said a man.

Rigg looked at him—a tall, stout man with severely under-stated clothing that was, nevertheless, of the richest fabric and most perfect cut. A suit of clothes designed to communicate money and modesty at the same time.

"Are you my mother's kind host?" asked Rigg. "Is this your house?"

The man bowed deeply.

It had been an easy guess—between his words and what Rigg had been told about the way the royals lived, he could have been no one else. And Rigg supposed something else, though he did not say it: that this man was also a trusted agent of the Revolutionary Council, for why would the council let the royals live in the house of someone who was not completely in their pocket?

Of course, the possibility remained that he only *seemed* to be the Council's man, and that in fact he was a royalist of one stripe or another. But as Father told him several times, a man who is trusted by both sides can be trusted by neither. If you pretend to be a double agent serving both factions, then how can either of them tell which side you're lying to? Usually both. One thing was certain, though: Whatever the man's real allegiance might be, if any, he would be no friend of Rigg's.

"I would like to say that I could pay my own way," said Rigg. "But if Hagia Sessamin is correct in recognizing me as her son, then all my previous goods are confiscated and I have no choice but to throw myself on your mercy."

"You will find me your true friend in all things, as I have been to your mother."

"Then you are a brave man indeed," said Rigg, "for there must be many who disapprove of your sheltering the cursed tyrant family that oppressed the World Within the Walls for so many generations. There must be many who are not pleased to have a male added to the royal family when none was looked for."

There were several sharply indrawn breaths—though Rigg

was pleased to see that his mother was not one of those who so nakedly revealed emotion.

He turned to the onlookers—who, for all he knew, might be servants, courtiers, hostile citizens, or the Revolutionary Council themselves—and said, "Do you think I'm going to pretend not to know what everyone knows? I used to be ignorant—the man who raised me kept me that way, so I didn't have a hint until a few weeks ago that I might have any connection with the royal family. But much has been explained to me, and I know that my existence is inconvenient to everyone. Including myself."

"Inconvenient or not," said Mother, "your existence brings me only joy."

"I have wished for a mother all my life," said Rigg to her. "But, raised as a good citizen of the Republic, I never wished for a queen. I hope you will forgive me if it is the mother whose love I hope to earn, while I pay no attention to the empress-who-might-have-been."

"Well put," said the host. "For of course the notion of 'royalty' is merely a matter of genealogy—in all this city there is not a soul that is not grateful to be ruled by the Revolutionary Council instead of the accidental offspring of a particular household."

Rigg marveled at the man's oiliness. This speech of smarmy sucking-up to the Revolutionary Council was designed either to reassure his masters of his loyalty, or to disguise his true loyalty under a layer of lies. Either way, it was so egregiously overplayed that Rigg assumed that the man intended *no* one to believe him.

Or else—always a possibility—he was an idiot and had no idea how his words sounded.

"Look at his hair," said one of the onlookers.

"And his rich clothes," said another.

Rigg turned to face the one who spoke of clothes. "These are some of the fine clothes I bought when I thought the money my father left me was mine to spend. These were confiscated by General Citizen when I was arrested, and he allowed me to dress in these only because they fit me, and I needed to be clean to ride in the sedan chair in which I was carried into the city. But if you have need of them, friend, I will happily give them up and wear whatever someone might lend to me out of decency."

A few low murmurs.

"Don't tell us you weren't trained to play this part," said an older man.

"I was trained by my father—for so I thought he was—to play many parts."

"An actor?" said the old man caustically.

"Yes, and of the lowest order," said Rigg. "A politician."

Now the gasps were loud and led to a few suppressed titters of laughter.

"You are the secretary of the People's Revolutionary Council, aren't you, sir?" asked Rigg. "That is my guess, anyway." Father had told him that the Secretary of the Council was actually its leader—but in this topsy-turvy government, the loftier and more powerful the office, the more subservient the title. Father pointed out that in such a case, the meanings of the words all change, until "secretary" becomes the new word meaning "dictator" or "king" or "emperor."

"I do hold that office for now," said the man.

"Please, sir. We're among loyal citizens here," said Rigg. "You hold the office for life."

"I hold it for the fixed term of one year."

"Renewed fourteen times already," said Rigg with a cheerful smile, "and sure to be renewed again and again until your wizened, drooling body falls over and admits that it's a corpse."

True statements all—everybody knew that Secretaries of the Council served for life—but extremely rude and dangerous to say outright. Now there were neither gasps nor laughs, merely low murmurs. How do you like the way I play this game, Mother? Are you clever enough to understand what I'm doing?

The Secretary, a man named Erbald, stepped forward angrily.

"My father taught me, 'Do not deny what everyone knows,'" said Rigg. "I honor you for the great service you render to the people of the whole world, and your sacrifice in continuing to serve us for all your days." Whereupon Rigg knelt before him.

"My son thinks himself clever and honest," said Mother behind him. "But he is merely being ill-mannered. If only I had been able to rear him myself, you would see more courtesy from him, and less of this arrogance."

That's right, Mother, Rigg said silently. Let them see a division between us.

But when Rigg turned, he let hurt feelings that he didn't feel show in his face. "Mother," he said, "how can it be rude, in this republic of honesty, to name things and people for what they are?" He decided on taking yet another plunge. "For instance, our generous host could not possibly shelter the royal family without the consent of the Council, which means he works for Mr. Erbald.

And since we know that the Council will never tolerate another hereditary ruling family to rise up to replace our family's ancient blood, the fact that Erbald's father Urbain was secretary before him, with only three years of the genial placeholder Chaross in between, is merely proof that the great talents of the father were passed on to the son. Only a fool could suppose that such gifts would be easy to replace."

Rigg could see that a couple of people were slipping away now, fearing to let Erbald know that they had been here to hear Rigg's outrageously offensive — and accurate — words. He saw their paths and determined that at the first opportunity he would see where they had gone, since these were probably people who already knew they were not trusted by the government. It was among *them* that he was most likely to find friends, if he were to find any at all.

Rigg felt it was worth the risk to speak as he did, because every schoolchild knew that the official ethos of the Revolution was "speaking truth to power," so nothing he had said could be used as grounds for a trial. In fact, Rigg was deliberately making it harder and harder to dispose of him quietly, for now that he had proven his willingness to say things that no one else dared say out loud, the Council would be afraid to have the people hear what he might say in a public trial.

A regime that wraps itself in the flag of truth fears truth most of all, for if its story is falsified to the slightest degree, its authority is gone.

Besides, Rigg was having great fun. Since Father had given him the tools of political maneuver and the understanding to use them, and since he had no idea what his life was for or any desire to be servant of anyone else's plans, why not please himself by being a little bratty, even if it got him killed?

"This is such a lovely garden," said Rigg. "And the house surrounding it is extraordinarily fine. I marvel that the Council would leave such a house in the hands of one man, when so many live in poverty. What is your name, sir host? I want to know who it is that the Council have trusted to be guardian of such a great public treasure."

The host, his face reddening, bowed slightly. "I have the honor to be named Flacommo."

"Dear friend Flacommo," said Rigg, "may we go inside? I fear the mosquitoes of Aressa Sessamo have tested me and found that I'm delicious."

"This delta country is such a swamp," said Flacommo heartily. "I fear that we who live here are used to having a half dozen itching bites at any time. Please, follow me into the kitchen, where I'll wager you might beg the cook to give you a bite or two."

"I'll be happy to help him in the kitchen to earn my keep, if you give your consent, Sir Flacommo. I'm a fair hand with a cooking pot, especially if it's a well-seasoned stew of wild game you're cooking."

Rigg was perfectly aware of the bizarre picture he was painting in everyone's mind. Outrageous candor, rough ways from his life in the forest, and not thinking himself above menial labor—stories of this scene would immediately spread through the city. Even if the Council had ordered that no one tell about the arrival of this supposed boy-royal, Rigg had made the stories too good *not* to tell.

In essence, he had bribed the servants and courtiers with a coin far better than mere money. He had given them wonderfully outrageous secrets to tell. Nothing conferred more prestige than knowing the deepest secrets of the highest people, and few of them could resist telling *someone*. Each someone would tell others, and by morning thousands would have heard the tale.

The more people in the city who knew about him—the more who cared about him, liked him, were entertained by stories of his antics—the safer he would be, for the people would be scrutinizing the way he was treated. And if Umbo and Loaf managed to make it to Aressa Sessamo, the stories would tell them where he was.

Rigg could see that Mother disapproved of what he had done. But that was no surprise—for all he knew, she wanted him dead, and had hoped the Council would do it for her, which would now be a bit less likely. Nor was Flacommo much pleased. Most courtiers had probably believed that he really was a friend of the royal family, voluntarily sheltering them at great risk to himself. Now they had reason to believe he was no friend to the royals at all, but rather their jailkeeper.

The most important reaction, however, was Erbald's. Mother led Rigg into the house, insisting that it was time for her dear son to eat with her for the first time since he had been stolen away from her. Erbald therefore announced his departure, then threw an arm across Rigg's shoulder. "Walk with me to the door, young Rigg," he said loudly.

Rigg walked along with him toward the gate that opened onto the street.

"Well played, for an amateur," said Erbald softly.

"Was there a game?" said Rigg blandly. "I didn't see anyone enjoying themselves."

"Transient popularity will keep you safe for the moment, but the support of the people can never be counted on. When a rumor is planted that paints you in a very different light—especially if it's true—they'll tear you into squirrel-sized chunks."

With those words Erbald strode out into the city, leaving Rigg inside as the gates were closed again.

In the kitchen, Rigg made a point of sitting down immediately beside the servants who were preparing food for tomorrow's meals. While Rigg knew little about fine cooking—he especially regarded bread and other pastries as verging on magic, though Father had explained about yeast—he knew how to slice a carrot, peel a potato, core an apple, or pit a peach for tomorrow's stews and pies. So before Flacommo could give orders to the morning chef for how Rigg was supposed to be treated, Rigg already had a knife in hand and was sitting beside the young servant boy who had fallen most behind and needed the help to catch up with his task.

"That is not work for a son of the royal house," said Flacommo.

Rigg immediately looked up at him in astonishment. "If there were a royal house, sir, I'm sure you would be right. But there is no such house and therefore no such son. There's work to be done and I'm doing it." Rigg turned to the chef. "Am I not doing it well enough, sir?"

"Very well, sir," said the chef, "but it's not for you to call *me* sir."

"Are you not older than me?" asked Rigg. "My father taught me to call my seniors by 'sir' and 'madam,' in reverence for the wisdom and good luck of age."

"'Wisdom and good luck,'" repeated Flacommo, laughing as if it were a jest. "Only a boy could think we old people were lucky, with our creaking joints, thinning hair, and bad digestion."

"I will consider myself very lucky and very wise, sir, if I live long enough for my joints to creak, my hair to thin, and my stomach to keep me awake at night."

Flacommo laughed again, as if this, too, were meant as humor. But Rigg noticed—by his peripheral vision, for he would not look directly at her—that his mother nodded very slightly. Was it possible that she now understood his game, and approved of how he was playing it?

"We'll take care of feeding the lad, sir," said the chef to Flacommo. "And one of the boys can show him to his room—we all know which one has been prepared for him."

"A room?" said Rigg. "For me? After my long journey, that will be a wonderful comfort. Yes, I'll go there soon. I'll not need much of a meal—a little bread and a good strong cheese will suit me well—so I'll go to bed as soon as these apples are cored for the pies."

Despite his words, Rigg planned *not* to enter any specially prepared room. If traps had been laid for him, it would be there. His best protection would be to go somewhere no one would expect him to sleep, and in a place with as many witnesses as possible.

"Will you leave your mother waiting to talk to you?" asked Flacommo.

"But there's a stool, see?" said Rigg. "I hope my mother sits here, and talks to me while I core the apples."

This suggestion rather alarmed the other servants, but Rigg looked at all of them with a cheerful smile. "What, does my mother's work keep her in other parts of the household? Then we can all get acquainted with her together!"

"I'm afraid that our beloved Lady Hagia cannot help in the kitchen as you suggest," said Flacommo. "By law, she is forbidden to put her hands upon any blade — even a kitchen paring knife."

Rigg held up his coring shaft. "But this is not a knife," he said.

"You stab it into the fruit, my lad," said Flacommo, "and that makes it, in the eyes of the law, a dagger."

"That would be a cruel weapon indeed," said Rigg, laughing. "Monstrous — imagine being cored to death!" He pressed the corer against his own chest. "The strength it would take, to force it between the ribs!"

Some of the servants laughed in spite of their efforts to remain solemn. Another anecdote that would be spread through the city by morning.

"Mother, it is so late at night. I beg you to go to bed and sleep well, so we can talk tomorrow. I slept well on the boat and in the sedan chair, they both glided along so smoothly." And it was true that Rigg was usually awake at this time of the night — one of the reasons he had trained himself on shipboard to sleep at such odd times was so he would not be helpless and unconscious at predictable times.

Flacommo and Mother both lingered for a while, and it was clear that Mother would have sat down to talk with him, even in front of the other kitchen workers, if Flacommo had not inter-posed himself. "Well, well," he finally said, "you are certainly an unpredictable young man, Master Rigg!"

"Really? In the village of Fall Ford I was thought of as rather dull; I never did anything extraordinary."

"I find that hard to believe," said Flacommo.

"Oh, I'm sure you'd find all our village ways unpredictable, sir, life being so different upriver. For instance, when village folk gather to cut up vegetables and fruits, there's always singing. But apparently no one in this kitchen knows a song!"

"Oh, we know songs, young sir," said an old woman.

"We could curl your hair with the songs we know of fright and woe," intoned another.

Rigg, recognizing the old tune, answered with the second line: "And your lady fair will be taught to woo by a love song true."

The servants all laughed with approval.

"So the songs are the same, upriver or down!" cried Rigg. "Well, let's finish that one and have another two or three, as long as we still work hard and sing soft, so as not to make the master sorry we're so noisy at our work."

Flacommo tossed his hands in the air and strode from the kitchen. Only now did Rigg allow himself to look directly at his mother. She also looked at him. He saw a ghost of a smile pass across her lips; then she turned and followed Flacommo from the room.

The pile of apples done—with a grateful smile from the boy whom he might just have saved from disgrace—Rigg wolfed down the bread and cheese with only water to drink. It was a finer bread than the coarse-ground loaves Nox used to send with them when Rigg and Father set out into the wilderness on one of their trapping jaunts, but that only meant it took more of it before Rigg felt full. The cheese was very fine, though of a flavor Rigg had never had before.

"Thank you for this," said Rigg to the woman who had prepared it for him. "I've eaten the best bread and cheese of O, a city known on the river for its refined taste, and I think I can fairly say that the servants in this great house eat better than the lords of O!"

Of course he was flattering the cooks and bakers and servants outrageously—but Rigg guessed that few thought them worth flattering. Indeed, how often did Mother come into the kitchen? How many of these servants' names did she know? By the end of this hour in the kitchen, Rigg knew them all by name and most of them by their history and manners and speech. He had not won their loyalty yet, but he had won their liking, and that was the first step.

"Let me take you to the room prepared for you," said the baker's apprentice—a young man named Long, though he was not particularly tall.

"Gladly," said Rigg, "though I wager it won't be as warm and cozy as that nook behind the hearth where the kitchen boys sleep."

"On old straw laid out on stone," said Long. "Not a comfortable bed!"

"I've slept in damp caves and under dripping trees and on

frozen ground with only snow to keep me warm. To me, that place looks like the best sleeping room in the house!" Rigg pitched his voice so he might be overheard by the day-shift boys still pretending to be asleep in the nook, and he was rewarded by several heads poking out of the nook to see who would say such a ridiculous thing.

"Snow can't keep you warm!" said the youngest of the boys.

"You burrow into a snowbank like a rabbit, and the snow all around you holds in your body heat and keeps out the wind."

"It'll melt on you and drown you, or fall on you and smother you!" cried another boy.

"Not if you choose the deepest and oldest bank—it holds its shape for night after night, and when I've done with such a bur-row, it's used by small animals who never had such a lovely palace to sleep in. You may be in the north here, but you don't know snow till you've wintered in the high mountains."

With that he turned and joined Long, who led him out into the dining hall, and then on to the corridors of the house. Rigg urged him to go slowly, asking him what each large room was for, and where each door led. As Father had trained him to do, Rigg built up a map inside his head. He saw from the dimensions of the rooms that here and there they didn't match up properly. Once he knew to look for them, he quickly located the secret passages that had been built into the gaps, for he could see the paths of the people who had used them. The paths wouldn't show him how to open the secret doors, but he could see quite easily where they were. The house was a labyrinth: Servants' stairways and corridors, which were the most-trafficked lanes in the house; the public corridors, which were all that loftier residents and visitors would ever see; and the secret passages, rarely traveled but constant throughout the house. There was hardly a room that didn't have at least one hidden entrance.

It wasn't just the rooms that Rigg was scouting, either. He had seen enough of his mother's path to be able to recognize wherever she had gone; he knew very quickly which rooms she habituated, and which she rarely entered. Her path only ever used one secret passage, and that one only a handful of times. Was this because she only knew of the one, or because she dared not be out of the public eye very often, lest someone think she had escaped?

What surprised Rigg was that Flacommo's path could not be found in any of the hidden passages. Was it possible he knew the house even less well than Mother?

At the first opportunity, Rigg would search into the older paths and try to find his own path when, as a baby, he had been spirited away. It would be interesting to find out who had carried him, and what route they had taken.

Then he realized: In all likelihood his family had not been living in *this* house when he was born. No doubt in keeping up the pretense that they owned nothing and belonged nowhere, the royals were shunted from house to house. Well, time enough to track himself down—it would be easy, once he earned some freedom.

They came to the door of an extravagantly large sleeping chamber with a bed that looked like a fortress, it was so high and fenced about with bedposts and canopies and curtains. There was even a stepstool beside it so Rigg could climb up and in.

Rigg stood in the doorway, gaping and admiring for Long's benefit, while he was actually scanning the room for the most recent paths. No one was hiding in the room—that would be too obvious. But someone had been under the bed only an hour or two ago, and spent a little time there. Some kind of trap had been laid, and when Rigg noticed the faint paths of six akses—the most poisonous breed of lizard known within the wallfold—he knew what the trap was. When the weight of his body bounced on the bed, it would break the fragile cage in which the akses were intertwining themselves, and soon they would follow his body heat and find him and kill him.

"It's so pretty," said Rigg, deliberately sounding as young and naive as possible. "But I could never sleep in a bed so high. I'd be afraid of falling out and never sleep a wink. Come on, let's go back to the kitchen, I'll sleep behind the fire!" Rigg turned around and rushed away, retracing his own path.

Long tried to protest, but Rigg only turned around, put a finger to his lips, and whispered, "People are sleeping! Don't wake them!"

CHAPTER 15

Trust

"I'm so sorry," said the expendable. "One of the versions of Ram Odin did not include the word 'immediately,' and therefore his order was complete a fraction of a second before all the others. He is the real Ram Odin."

Ram gave a little half smile. "How ironic. By specifying that you should act at once—"

The expendable reached out with both hands, gave Ram's head a twist, and broke his neck. The sentence remained unfinished, but that did not matter, since the person saying it was not the real Ram Odin.

• • •

Rigg fell asleep almost as soon as he lay down among the tangle of boys in the space behind the fireplace. The one wall was quite warm from the fire on the other side; the opposite wall was cold from the late autumn air beyond it. Rigg chose one of the unloved spots near the cold wall, partly because that's where the most empty space was available, but mostly because he was used to sleeping in the cold and preferred a bit of a chill to overheated sleep.

He woke only four hours later, as he had schooled himself to do, in the silence of the dark hours before dawn. The nook was fuller now—the late-shift boys had taken their places as well. Most of the boys' hair was damp from sweat, for even as the fire slackened during the night, the boys' own body heat kept them warm. Rigg himself, despite keeping his back against the cold wall, was too warm, and he stepped outside into the courtyard to cool off before beginning his morning's work.

In the garden there was no one keeping watch—what mischief could anyone do inside the courtyard, unless he were a thief of herbs and flowers? Rigg knew, however, that if he approached the front gateway or the servants' entrance, there would be guards to challenge him. Even if he walked around in the garden he might attract notice. So he chose a place near the door to the kitchen—the pepper door, it was called, because the cooks sent servants through it to gather fresh herbs—and sat on the ground. The air now was quite cold. Soon the basil would die back, and then, when the snow came, the thyme. Only the woody-stemmed rosemary would last the winter.

To Rigg, the garden was almost as artificial and unnatural as the wood-floored interior of the house. Nothing grew wild here, and there was no life more complicated than a few birds, which were not allowed to nest here. Insects left paths, but so thin and faint that even if he wanted to, Rigg would not be able to single out individuals. It was just as well—for every vertebrate creature's path there were ten thousand insect paths, and if all paths glowed equally wide and bright in Rigg's mind the insects would blot out everything else.

Rigg kept his eyes open only so he could find where the paths went in relation to the building. He could sense all the paths, no matter how many walls rose up between. The outside walls of the house were clear—for six hundred years at least, there had been no passage that crossed those barriers.

Rigg had many things to learn, but he attached first importance to the path of the person who had placed the half-dozen akses in a flimsy cage under the bed he was supposed to have slept in. Without quite knowing how he distinguished them, Rigg had learned when very young how to identify a particular person's path and recognize it when he saw it again in another place. The older the path, the harder it was to do this, as if they lost detail and resolution with age—though Rigg could not have described exactly what the details were that he recognized. He simply knew.

The would-be assassin had come in through the servants' door in the alleyway, and from the way his path moved—smoothly, until, inside the large pantry, it lurched upward and then down— he concluded that he had come into the house inside something, most likely a barrel. He had emerged last night at the same time Rigg arrived inside the courtyard in a sedan chair; that's when the akses had been placed.

What Rigg needed to see was whether the assassin had had any contact with anyone in the household. He also had to know whether he had used any of the secret passages. No, to both questions. The assassin had moved unerringly and without encountering anyone else or even pausing to hide somewhere, straight to Rigg's designated room.

But he did not go back to the pantry. Instead he went up onto the roof by way of the steep ladderway used by the workmen who fixed leaks, removed the nests of birds and wasps, and washed the skylights and the windows in the attic cupolas. There he had been until the exact moment Erbald had walked Rigg to the gate—for Rigg had also learned to discern the relative ages of paths, to a high degree of precision with very recent ones.

At that point, the assassin had emerged onto the roof, scooted over the top of it, and down into the next-door neighbor's courtyard. No one had been awake in that house, and though it was almost as fine a house as Flacommo's, it had no need for a guard beyond the sleepy old man who was apparently dozing at his post—for the assassin passed right by him, vaulted the gate, and went into the street without the old man waking.

The assassin had moved with the confidence of someone who had been in the house before and knew his way, so Rigg began looking deeper and deeper into the past, finding older and older paths. In a way his eyes could never have done, it was as if only the paths of the age he was looking for were visible, while the newer and older ones attenuated until he shifted his attention to yet another set. It was time-consuming work, and required iron self-discipline, like forcing himself to read fine print in a dim light and refusing to give up just because the letters were hard to focus on. But he had trained himself to peel away each layer, examine it thoroughly and methodically throughout the entire house, then start with the next layer back, and so on.

The assassin might have been sent to scout the layout of the house only in the days since General Citizen's report arrived, or he might have come the moment the first rumors of Rigg's existence reached Aressa Sessamo nearly two months ago. Or the assassin might have learned the house before the royal family ever moved into it, in the expectation that at some point his services were bound to be needed. If his previous visit was that old, Rigg was unlikely to be able to find it—a slow, methodical search would take months to get back that far, and a quicker, skimming search would be likely to miss a single visit.

Realizing this, Rigg chose a different strategy. Instead of searching the whole house, he searched only at the gate. On his first visit, the assassin would surely have entered on some legitimate pretext; he would be someone with a cover story so bland as to make him forgettable. If he hadn't come through the gate, he would have come through the servants' door; if Rigg didn't find him in a thorough search at the one place, he'd search again at the other.

Found. The assassin had come through the gate, and it had been only a month ago. Before General Citizen's messenger could have made it here, but not before a different messenger might have come, from some spy in O who might have investigated Rigg before Citizen even arrived.

Still, it was something of a relief to know that whoever sent the assassin was not someone who depended on General Citizen to inform them. Rigg had come to rather like, or at least respect, General Citizen, and he didn't want him to be the type of man who resorted to assassination.

Who ushered the assassin into the house on his first visit? The normal servants who greeted everyone, and then Flacommo himself—but that meant nothing except that the party was of some lofty social standing. Most of the party went on with Flacommo to meet with Mother in a room just off the garden where her paths showed she spent most of her waking hours. But the assassin was left behind.

That suggested that he was posing as a servant, and his master had dismissed him. The assassin prowled the bedroom level of the house, exploring every room. No one challenged him, though he took at least an hour doing it.

Then he went straight to the room where the rest of his party was conversing with Mother, and the whole group left almost at once.

If only he had Umbo with him! Then he could slow down the paths to see whether Mother knew about the plan to assassinate Rigg when he showed up there.

This much was certain: Mother spent an hour talking with the people who brought the assassin along with them.

But there was no indication whether the rest of the party knew the assassin's real mission, still less whether Mother knew about it. And just because Flacommo never encountered the assassin on either of his visits to the house said nothing about what he knew, or what the Revolutionary Council knew. Rigg's gift told him many things that no one else could know — but it did not tell him a tenth as much as would have been useful to him.

Someone was in the garden with him.

He could see the path, and it was new — it was being created even as he watched. But it moved incredibly slowly, and faded more quickly than usual, and when he looked with his eyes, there was no one there.

There were folktales about invisible people, about saints who had the power to walk through a crowd unseen, or people who had offended a wizard and been turned invisible so they were always alone. But he had never believed them for a moment. Since Father had explained to him how vision worked — the photons of different wavelengths variously reflected or absorbed, and the retina of the eye detecting them — it seemed impossible to Rigg that someone might be able to make it so every atom of his body became transparent to photons.

But hadn't Father said, "Only a fool says 'impossible,' the wise man says, 'unlikely.'" That had become a joke between them for several months — instead of "no," they told each other "unlikely." Now it occurred to Rigg that Father might have had a specific example in mind when they were discussing whether invisibility was impossible or not.

Stubbornly, Rigg decided he would not yet believe in a human being transparent to photons. There must be some other explanation, and he closed his eyes and studied the slowly moving path for some kind of clue.

There was the fact that it was moving more slowly than any human being could possibly move. More important, though, was the fact that the path faded far too abruptly. The beginning of the stranger's path into the garden was actually earlier than Rigg's own path as he came in.

And at the head of the path, right where the person should be visible, but wasn't, the path flickered.

Not blinking on and off, but the color of it—or flavor, or whatever sense you might want to use as a metaphor—seemed to be changing slightly in abrupt shifts.

Rigg opened his eyes again. If this was another assassin, Rigg would certainly have no problem getting away from him, his progress was so slow. Then again, he might move slowly when invisible, then turn visible and leap upon Rigg like a stooping hawk.

Still, Rigg had to learn more. So he stood up, walked directly to the head of the slow path and blocked it.

It took a few moments but the path stopped moving, and then began moving backward. But in that moment of hesitation, when the invisible one did not move forward or back, his shape became faintly visible to Rigg's eyes. Not enough that Rigg could see him clearly, but he knew where the eyes were, could see the height. He could see the outline of the clothing and the hair, telling him that this was a woman. And in the eyes, he caught a glimpse of— what, fear? Startlement?

Rigg knew that he had revealed to the invisible person that her invisibility was not complete. But he had also learned that when the invisible person ceased moving, she became somewhat visible again.

"Who are you?" Rigg asked softly. He was so close she

could not help but hear him, though no one inside the house could have. Yet there was no hint of a response. The Invisible just kept moving away, moving perhaps a little faster but not much.

Frustrated, Rigg walked up her path and did not pause, but kept moving right through the place where she had to be.

He passed right through.

Did Rigg feel anything odd during that passage? Perhaps a slight shakiness, or perhaps a little warmth. Or maybe he was just imagining the sensation because he knew he had to be passing through a living person.

When he looked back at the path, it was unchanged, except that it continued moving forward—perhaps a little more swiftly than before, if "swiftly" could be used to describe a speed that would make a snail ashamed.

Rigg had a good idea now who the Invisible might be. If he could not speak to her or force her to become more visible to him, he at least could find out where she had been and who might know who she was. Rigg stood out of the Invisible's way and closed his eyes so he could focus on her path backward in time. Not terribly far away, the path changed—it lost its trait of rapid fading, and instead seemed quite normal as it moved through the house. Back to a bedroom where Mother lay asleep.

The Invisible had come straight from Mother's room, and at a normal pace. But she had done so in the middle of the night, when no one was about. Rigg made the reasonable assumption: When the Invisible moved at an ordinary speed, she was completely visible, and remain unnoticed because the house was dark and everyone was asleep. As soon as the Invisible realized there was someone in the garden—Rigg—she slowed down and became invisible.

She is not "slowing down," Rigg realized. Whatever she's doing affects her path, and paths have to do with time. The Invisible is actually jumping forward in time, in tiny increments.

Silently in his mind, Rigg explained it all as if he were expounding his theory to Father. Suppose the Invisible moved an inch a second. Suppose that at the end of every second, she then jumped forward one second in time. To the Invisible, she is making a continuous forward movement, one second per inch. But because she is jumping forward a second at the end of every second, to an outside observer she would seem to move one inch every *two* seconds—but for one of those seconds she would seem to flash out of existence.

Now suppose that instead of a second per inch, it was a millionth of a second per millionth of an inch. The pace would be the same, but now she would not exist in any moment long enough for a significant number of photons to hit her.

He could almost hear Father's voice raise an objection. If she exists in any moment for exactly as long as she does *not* exist between moments, then she should be half visible, for half the photons would pass through her, and half would strike her and reflect or be absorbed.

All right, Rigg answered himself. Suppose the Invisible exists for one millionth of a second, but then jumps forward a thousandth of a second. Now she exists far less time than she does *not* exist. She's only reflecting light for one millionth of a second every thousandth of a second. Our eyes simply can't notice that tiny amount of light, can't focus on it.

She has to keep moving, though. And very quickly, so that each thousandth of a second, when she reappears so briefly, she's in a different place. When I made her stop and back up because I stood directly in front of her, for that fleeting second she did not move quickly enough and she became much more visible—I could see her height, her shape, her eyes, a trace of her mouth. Then she sped up, moving backward, and disappeared again.

She never disappeared, really. She was always there. When I walked through her, *she was there*.

Father had taught Rigg that all solid objects were actually mostly empty space, the atoms very far apart, and within each atom the nucleus and electrons were separated by spaces many times their size.

So when he passed through the Invisible, the Invisible must have flashed into existence many times, maybe a thousand times. Most of the actual particles of their bodies would not have collided, and the Invisible jumped ahead in time before they could distort or destroy each other.

But some particles must have collided, and those that did . . .

No wonder the Invisible backed up rather than collide with Rigg. Even though such a collision would do no visible harm, there must be significant radiation from the relatively few crashes between atoms that did take place during the passage. If the Invisible did not avoid collisions as much as possible, eventually the radiation would become significant. Enough, perhaps, to make her sick or even kill her.

For the first time, Rigg understood that it *was* useful that Father had taught him so much about physics. He wanted me to be able to make sense of things like this.

Except that it didn't really make sense yet. How could a human being divide time into such tiny bits? How could the Invisible possibly even comprehend such intervals?

Again, Rigg answered his own objection. The Invisible no more understands what she's doing than Umbo understood what he was doing when he "slowed down time," no more than I understood the nature of the paths that only I could see. It was instinctive. A reflex.

Like sweating. You know what causes sweat, but you don't have to consciously activate every pore for sweating to take place.

No, sweating was involuntary. More like walking. You don't think about each tiny muscle movement involved in walking, you just walk, and your body does what it does. Or like seeing—you decide what to look at, how wide to open your eyes, how long to stare—but you don't have to understand the photons striking the rods and cones of your retina.

The Invisible may not even know that she's moving forward in time. She only knows that when she becomes invisible, her forward movement slows down. With years of practice, she would learn just how much time-movement was needed to stay invisible, because if she became *too* invisible, her movement through space would become so slow she would be unable to get from one place to another. But if she did not move forward far enough with each tiny time-jump, she would become visible and people would

340

see her—as a ghost, a dream, an apparition, a memory, but they would see her.

So over the years she has learned to control it the way Umbo learned to control his sense of timeflow, the way I learned to distinguish among the paths and see at a glance how old they were compared to each other, and peel them away with my mind so I could concentrate on the paths of a certain time or of a certain person rather than all the paths that passed through that point in space.

This Invisible is like me. And like Umbo. Talented.

Umbo and I were both trained by Father to hone our talents. So was Nox. Did Father know this person and train her, too?

Rigg remembered Father's voice as he lay dying under the fallen tree. "Then you must go and find your sister. She lives with your mother."

Father had sent Rigg to find his *sister*, not his mother. His mother, the queen-by-right, was not the important one. What mattered to Father was Rigg's talented sister.

Everything came together and made sense. His theory fit all the facts and omitted none that he could think of. He might later learn of many flaws in the theory, but for right now, as Father had taught him, it was useful enough to act on the assumption that he was right.

Rigg allowed himself to notice the paths again. The Invisible was moving toward the door she had come out of—and she was moving much faster. Which meant she was actually leaping forward in time by smaller increments, or less frequently, which meant that she was reflecting more photons. And sure enough, Rigg could make out a shadowy form, and it was running—

running so very slowly that he could still have overtaken the Invisible in a dozen steps.

This is how the Invisible has learned to escape—trading a little bit of visibility for speed in getting away.

Now he knew better than to try to speak to her. Existing only a thousandth of a moment in any one position in space, there was no way the Invisible could distinguish speech.

The Invisible. She has a name. Param Sissaminka.

Rigg walked into the kitchen, where the morning shift was now beginning to be about their business—bakers shaping the dough that had been left for them by the night bakers, cooks starting the pots for the afternoon stews, servants sleepily going here and there, taking care of their needs so they could begin their chores.

"Did you sleep at all, young master?" asked the head baker. This was a woman that Rigg had not met the night before, but of course the kitchen staff talked to each other, especially since Rigg had been a stranger sleeping in the nook behind the fire.

"I did," said Rigg. "But I wake early—no doubt I'll be back in the afternoon for another nap, if you don't mind."

The baker looked at him with a hint of amusement. "If you're sleeping away from your room for fear of someone meddling with you, perhaps you should sleep in a different place every time, and not go returning to the nook to sleep."

Rigg was surprised that the baker was so forthright. "Am I in danger?" he asked.

"It seemed to my sister that you thought you were, and so you may well be. My sister is the night baker, Elella. I'm Lolonga."

"Then let me tell you something, Lolonga," said Rigg. "Something was left in my room last night, which is why I didn't sleep there. Something designed to kill. And I'm afraid that if anyone goes into that room today, and jostles the bed, the trap that was set for me might be sprung on some innocent who does not deserve to die."

"Do *you* deserve to die?"

"I'd like to think I don't, but there are those who think the world will be a better place without me."

"Since you haven't told me what the trap is—though I assume it is involved with the bed—I take it you'd like me to warn people away from that room without it being known that the warning came from you."

"I'd like that, yes, but it's not worth lying about. If someone asks point blank, someone whose trust you need to retain, then by all means tell them I warned you. It will come out soon enough anyway. But if they don't ask, please don't volunteer the information."

"The housekeeper, Bok, is an early riser," said Lolonga. "Even though my idiot apprentices will no doubt ruin the day's bread in my absence, making the dough too dry or too wet, I'll go find her and tell her so she can save the life of some silly worthless chambermaid."

"Even the silliest chambermaid is worth saving," said Rigg.

"Really?" said Lolonga. "But I never suspected that one of *you* would feel that way."

"One of . . . who?"

"Royals. The rich. The educated. Those we wait upon, who have all the money and fame and power. You."

"Ah, well, there's your mistake, ma'am. Until a few months ago,

I was one of *you*. No, worse—I was a wandering trapper whom folk like you would look down on and not let into the kitchen."

Lolonga grinned. "I sensed that about you, lad," she said, "which is why I didn't have you thrown out of my kitchen the moment you stepped in. I don't let your mother in, you know. Not while I'm baking. It distracts my people and ruins the breads and cakes and pies of the day."

"Ma'am," said Rigg. "I have to know. Between you and your sister, which one is head baker?"

"We both are. It's a constant battle between us. She thinks she gets to decide what dough to make each night, and I'm stuck with making whatever bread *she* determined we'd need. But I got even with her. I made her take on my lazy worthless son, Long, as her apprentice on the night shift. It's a punishment that goes on and on."

"I like Long," said Rigg.

"So do I. That's why I put him on *her* shift—so I don't have to spend all day every day yelling at him and cursing him for a stupid lazy son of a stupid lazy father. That might interfere with the affection between us."

She left the kitchen on Rigg's errand. He went out by another way and found himself in the dining room, which at the moment stood empty, the table cleared away. Soon it would be set for breakfast, he was sure, but for now it was a quiet place, and almost completely dark, illuminated only by the starlight coming through the windows—the Ring cast its light from the other side of the house.

Rigg sat in one of the chairs and watched the path Lolonga

took through the house. He saw her path encounter the house-keeper's path, and then followed the housekeeper—Bok?—as she went to the maids, no doubt to give them instructions about avoiding the room with the trap.

Then he cast his attention to his mother's room, and sure enough, the Invisible, Param, had moved back into it. Now Rigg had the leisure to study the paths in that room, and he could see that Param came there every night. So did someone else, always arriving and leaving just before Param came invisibly in. Rigg traced that path and saw that it led to a serving maid he had seen last night. In fact, he had watched her on what must have been that very errand—taking a tray of food out of the kitchen and going . . . somewhere. Now he knew where. He thought back to the tray of food and realized: This is how Param eats. An invisible *has* to hold still, become visible in order to interact with the physical world enough to eat, to drink, to wash, to void her bladder and bowel. Such would be the times of greatest danger. So she does all this in Mother's room.

Param is under Mother's protection. "She lives with your mother." So to Param, Mother is a refuge, not a danger.

I wish that it were so for me. But I can't know. I can't be sure. Param is the female heir to the Tent of Light. Mother might be her protector, and my deadliest enemy. The games are all too deep and layered here for me to fathom them.

Rigg sat down to breakfast at the table with Flacommo, Mother, and a dozen guests and courtiers.

After the normal social niceties had been observed, and after a polite amount had been eaten without distracting conversation, Rigg turned to his mother and said, "Actually, my lady mother, I did not set out for Aressa Sessamo to meet you. Nothing delighted me more than to learn that you were alive, though naturally I wondered why I had never met you, or why my adopted father had never mentioned you until he lay dying. But his first instruction was for me to go to Aressa Sessamo to meet my sister. And I can't help but wonder where she is. Is she unwell? Doesn't she want to meet her brother?"

Rigg pretended to be surprised at how silent everyone grew at the mention of his sister.

"Is there some reason why it isn't right for me to ask after her? No one on my journey hinted that there might be something wrong; I assumed that I would meet her."

All eyes were on Mother now. She alone looked completely poised, paying attention to the bite she was chewing, while looking at Rigg with twinkling eyes. "I'm not surprised you're curious," Mother finally said. "But you see, your sister has withdrawn from society for more than a year. She had a very unpleasant experience when one of the peasants who periodically burst into the house of our host, to demand that we let him shave our heads or take our clothing, forced her to surrender all her clothing. It was a cruel thing, and ever since that happened, she sees no one."

Or rather, no one sees *her*, Rigg thought. "Is there no hope, then, even for her long-lost brother?" he asked aloud.

What he did not say was that he knew perfectly well his sister was in the room right now. He had seen her path moving slowly into the room and then pacing back and forth in order to stay in motion. No doubt she was as curious about Rigg as he was about her. She knew that he could see her, or at least that he knew where she was. In fact, after he sat down at table he had turned toward her and given her a little wave, though he held his hand below table level, so no one else could see. He waved very slowly, too, so that she would be able to detect the motion.

"There is hope indeed," said Mother. "I'm quite sure she's eager to see you, and when the time comes, I will fetch you to the place where she is in seclusion."

"It must be setting back her schooling dreadfully," said Rigg.

"Her schooling is a paltry thing, compared to the heartbreak of her humiliation," said Mother.

Flacommo chimed in now. "It was a shame to all of us, that someone would use a child so harshly. The Revolutionary Council immediately changed the law to prevent anyone from taking the clothing of the persons of the family once called royal from their bodies. It was a change long overdue."

"In other words," said Rigg, who of course already knew the story, "the Council discovered that the humiliation of the royals no longer played well with the crowd, and they discontinued it. Could it be that the public hatred of the royal family is slipping?"

"I think that would be wonderful," said Flacommo. "Someday, of course, the royals will be just like any other family. But right now they remain a constant hope for certain revolutionary factions."

"Then I wonder we haven't all been put to death," said Rigg.

There were gasps all around the table.

"It's a matter of pure logic," said Rigg. "As long as members of the royal family survive, we will be used by this or that group as a rallying cry, even if we never lift a finger against the Revolutionary Council. Wouldn't it be better for the sake of the nation if we ceased to exist entirely?"

"I will never be persuaded of that!" cried Flacommo. "Once there was much talk of it, but your mother—and her mother before her—conducted themselves with such humility and deference to the Council, obeying all laws and never countenancing any talk of revolt, that the Revolutionary Council has thought it wiser to keep them here, accessible to the public, though not to *so* great a degree. Your mother graciously allows the people to see that royals own nothing and live as obedient citizens."

"We eat rather well, though," said Rigg, looking at the lavishly spread table.

"No," said Flacommo, "*I* eat rather well, and so do you all when you share my table as guests. But many a day each year your mother dines with whoever invites her, no matter what their station or how simple their fare."

"I see," said Rigg. "Then there will be no objection if I do the same?"

"You may accompany your mother whenever she accepts such an invitation," said Flacommo. "But of course you may not do this on your own, because each time a royal leaves my house and goes forth into the city, she—*they*—must be kept under guard. There are those, alas, whose rage against the royal family is unabated after all these years of Revolutionary government."

Rigg was quite sure the guards were there to keep the royals from running off, escaping the city, and going out to raise an army. But there was no reason to say this. He had a different item on his agenda. "Oh, I know about that!" he said. "Someone tried to kill me last night."

Everyone at the table cried out at once. No! Who! When! How did you stop them!

"I stopped them easily enough," said Rigg. "I simply didn't sleep where I was supposed to sleep. The assassination attempt was a stealthy one, a trap set for me."

"What kind of trap!" demanded Flacommo. "If someone came into my house and—"

Rigg made a soothing gesture and smiled. "I'm sure it was done without your knowledge, my dear friend. I may call you 'friend,' may I not? You have been so kind to my mother and sister."

"Yes, please, I'm honored if you think of me that way," said Flacommo. Though of course he would not have forgotten what Rigg had said the night before.

"It was a little box containing akses, which was placed under my bed. The box was flimsy enough that the very action of lying on the bed would break the box and release the akses. And of course you all know how long I would have remained alive after *that*, since they are drawn to body heat."

"But how did you defeat them?" someone asked.

"I didn't," said Rigg. "I avoided them. As far as I know, they're still there. I would advise sealing the door to the room and leaving them alone. They're bound to starve to death within a few weeks, especially if the room is kept warm. It's very tricky trying to dispose of them any other way. There *are* gases that will immobilize them—but it takes time for such gases to act, and in the meantime whoever brings the gas near them runs the risk of one of the akses taking a flying leap and winning the engagement preemptively."

"And such creatures were left in your room?" Flacommo said, incredulous. "How did you detect them?"

"Having been warned that there are those who still hate the royal family, one of them having made an attempt on my life during the voyage here, I've become cautious. I look under beds." Rigg hoped that no one questioned Long, since he knew perfectly well that Rigg had not even entered the room, let alone bent down to peer under the bed.

"Thank the Wandering Saint for that!" said Flacommo, and many at the table agreed.

Rigg turned to his mother, who did not seem alarmed at all, but merely regarded him between bites of her breakfast porridge—for she ate much simpler fare than any of the others at table. "Lady Mother," he said, "I'm not sure how to take this incident. I'm really quite certain that I was not sentenced to such a death merely because I'm a royal—after all, the assassins could have killed any royal in the house, and yet they targeted only me."

She took another bite.

"I can think of two reasons why I would be singled out. One is that my presence destabilizes the arrangement under which you and my sister have lived under the protection of such flunkies of the Revolutionary Council as our gracious host Flacommo. In which case it might be the Council itself, or some faction of it, that wants me dead. On the other hand, I'm a male, and ever since my great-grandmother killed all the males of the royal family and made it a law that only females of the family could rule, there have been those who have eagerly awaited the birth of a male heir, hoping he would live long enough to strike down that old decree and reestablish an emperor rather than an empress."

"If there are any such people," Mother said mildly, "I doubt they'd try to kill you."

"Probably not," said Rigg. "Ever since I learned of my true identity, or at least the possibility of it, I have wondered who it was that kidnapped me and carried me away from my mother and father and sister. One possibility was that I was taken by members of the faction that wants a male heir restored to the throne. But if that's so, why wasn't I trained and indoctrinated to fulfil that role? Why wasn't I raised to be a king? Because I can assure you, I never had a breath of a hint that I had any connection with royalty, or any great destiny to fulfil. So I have to conclude that the man who raised me was *not* of that faction."

Mother said nothing, but smiled slightly.

"Still, you never know what people so insane they would seek the restoration of the royal house might do—surely the ones who want to restore the male line are the craziest of them all."

"There are so many crazy people in the world," said Mother. "Some who are crazy and remain silent, and some who in their madness keep talking and talking, annoying everybody."

"I understand your rebuke, Mother, but I really am trying to learn how things stand, so I can guess where danger might come from."

"It can come from anywhere," she said sweetly. "It can come from everywhere at once."

"I simply wondered if the attempt to kill me came from the faction that supports the restoration of the female line, and regards the existence of the male heir as a great danger. *That* faction would have been waiting all these years for me to surface again, so I could be killed, in obedience to great-grandmother Aptica Sessamin's edict."

"That law was rescinded by the Revolutionary Council," said Flacommo. "Most people have forgotten it ever existed."

"But since the law was never rescinded by the Tent of Light," said Rigg, "there are people insane enough to think that it's still the law, and that killing me would be a noble act. I say this because the man who tried to kill me on my way here was exactly that kind of madman."

"Your words dance around like those of the carefulest courtier," said Mother. "It's hard to believe you weren't raised with royalty in mind."

"The man I called Father taught me to think skeptically and curiously, that's all. And to say what I think. And he always said, 'If you want to know something, then ask somebody who already knows it.' So I ask you, Mother, two questions. First, did you and my real father send me away as an infant in order to protect me from such enemies? Or was I stolen away by somebody else who thought I needed to be protected from *you*?"

Dead silence in the room. Mother stopped moving, her hand hovering in midair as oat porridge dripped in clumps from her tilted spoon.

Rigg was quite aware of the impression he had made, and pushed it further. "Let me make the question even simpler. Mother, is it your desire that I die? Because if it is, I'll stop trying to save myself and let the next attempt on my life succeed. I have no desire to make you unhappy by coming home to you after all these years."

She moved again, setting the spoon back into her bowl. "I am grieved that you could ask such a question."

"And I am grieved," said Rigg, "that you decline to answer it."

"I will answer it, though the question itself torments me. I had nothing to do with your being spirited away. I believed you had been stolen by those who wanted you dead, and assumed they had killed you. I grieved for you every day for the first few years, and as often as I thought of you since then—which was often. I have shed thousands of tears for you. And when I learned that you might be alive I scarcely dared believe that you would be allowed to come to me. Even when you arrived, I tried to behave in such a way as to keep anyone from becoming alarmed at the strength and depth of my rejoicing. I'm glad that you recognize that you are in grave danger; I'm grateful that you were raised to be careful enough not to fall into the trap laid for you. But I'm bitterly disappointed that you would think I might have been behind the laying of it."

"I don't know you, Mother," said Rigg. "I know only what is said of the royal family, and you can imagine that little of it is kind. I was well taught in history, and I know of the hundreds of times that members of various ruling houses slaughtered each other in pursuit of power, or out of fear of assassination or civil war.

But hearing your words and seeing your face as you said them, and knowing something of the constraints under which you live here, I am satisfied that you are my loving mother indeed. Please forgive me for asking, for you know I had no choice but to ask. And thank you for answering at all, and even more for answering as you did."

Rigg rose from his seat and knelt beside his mother's chair, as she turned to face him. There was consternation from many of the onlookers, for it was illegal to bow to a royal, and Mother herself began to remonstrate with him. But he spoke loudly, letting his voice fly out like a whip, commanding silence. "I kneel to this woman as a son kneels to his mother. The humblest shepherd may kneel like this before his mother. Am I, because my ancestors were royals, forbidden to show my mother the respect that she deserves from me? Hold your tongues—I would rather die than let fear stop me from showing her how much I honor her and love her!"

Those who had risen sat back down. And now as Rigg bent his forehead to touch his mother's lap, she reached out and stroked his hair, then raised him up a little and embraced him, and wept into his hair, and kissed him, and called him her baby, her little boy, and thanked the Wandering Saint for bringing him back to her from his long sojourn in the wilderness.

Meanwhile, Rigg wondered what his sister was making of all this, and thought how maddening it must be for her to see everything—but speeded up, and without any words or sounds to help her understand.

As for his mother, Rigg only half-believed her. After all,

wasn't this also how she would act if she wanted him dead? True, her emotions seemed real enough, and few people had the skill to simulate them so effectively. But wasn't the very fact that she was still alive proof that she knew how to act whatever role was required of her in order to survive?

Yet Rigg had to trust somebody or his life in this place would be impossible. So he decided to believe that his mother had not survived by pretending to feel what she did not feel, but rather by pretending not to feel anything at all—the opposite skill—and therefore this outpouring of emotion was rare and real. She loved him. She did not want him dead. He would trust her. And if he turned out to be wrong in this decision, well, he'd deal with that disappointment when it came. It would be easy enough, since in such a case the disappointment would probably last only a few seconds before he died.

CHAPTER 16

Blind Spot

Ram looked at the large holographic image of the new world.

"What will you name it?" asked the expendable.

"Does it matter?" asked Ram. "Whatever name I come up with, it will come to mean 'this world of ours.' The way 'Earth' does now."

"You think the colonists will forget the world they came from?"

"Of course not," said Ram. "But the children born here will hear of Earth as a faraway planet where their parents lived. The great-great grandchildren won't know anyone who ever saw Earth."

"We expendables are also curious about how you are going to explain to the other colonists about the fact that we are now 11,191 years in the past."

"Why would I tell them anything about it?" asked Ram.

"In case some of them think follow-up starships will resupply them."

"Do we know that ships won't come?"

"Why would they? As far as Earth knows, you didn't make the jump, you disappeared."

"On the contrary," said Ram. "As far as Earth knows, we disappeared, which means we made the jump. To them, not making the jump would mean our ship simply continued on its way, or blew up. Without debris or any detectable sign of us, they can only conclude that the jump was successful. Which means they'll send ships after us, and they will make the jump, and presumably they will divide into nineteen copies and go back 11,191 years. We should have an incredible amount of resupply."

"We've been thinking about that," said the expendable. "There is no reason we can find for the backward jump in time or for the replications. As far as the ships' computers are able to detect, the jump merely succeeded. Which it did, because there's the new, still-unnamed world."

"I haven't forgotten the need to name it," said Ram testily. "What's the urgency?"

"We are having ten thousand conversations among us and the ships' computers every second," said the expendable. "Our reports will be more efficient if we can use a name."

"I also haven't forgotten your previous remarks," said Ram. "If all the fields we created caused us to make the jump perfectly, why are there nineteen ships 11,191 years in the past?"

"Because of you," said the expendable.

•   •   •

As breakfast ended, Rigg knew his real work was about to begin. He had to win Mother's trust now—and forcing her into a public display of affection for him was hardly likely to have been the best first step. Since Param spent her days invisible, it was only Mother who could convey a message to her—only Mother who could earn Param's trust in him, vicariously.

He rose to his feet. "Mother, I have a son's curiosity, a desire to know about my father. May I come to your room, where you can tell me candidly who he was and the legacy he left to me?" Rigg turned to the rest of the people at the table. "I speak of no possessions except this body that I wear."

"What mother could want anything more than time alone with her long-lost son?" said Mother, rising from the table. "No one will begrudge us that, I hope."

Flacommo stood up as well. "The law declares that you have no right to be alone, but I can say to all within my hearing that anyone who interrupts this tender meeting between mother and son will be no friend of mine, or of my house."

It was a fine speech, but Rigg knew that there was no such thing as privacy here.

As he and Mother walked side by side from the room—neatly sidestepping Param, who walked invisibly along the wall—he leaned his face close to hers and said, "I'm sure you know that your room is under constant observation."

She stiffened but did not break stride. "It is not," she said. They left the breakfast room and made their way across a gallery full of very large paintings of scenes that Rigg knew nothing about.

"There are secret passages in the walls," said Rigg. "Someone is stationed there to watch you whenever you are in the room."

Mother stopped now, since no one else was in the gallery with them . . . yet. "How could you know this unless you were a spy yourself?"

"I am as talented as Param, in my own way," murmured Rigg. "When we get to your room, I will stand directly in front of the peephole the spy is using. That way, if he has another peephole, he'll move to it and then I'll go stand in front of that one."

"You were never in this house even when you were a baby," Mother whispered fiercely. Apparently she could not think past wondering about the source of his information, instead of assuming there might be more talents in the world than Param's own.

Rigg put his arms around her in a tender embrace, which put his mouth right against her ear. "I sense the path of every human being back through time. For ten thousand years I see all paths. I see Param. The two of you have been watched every time you were alone together."

When he pulled away from Mother, smiling his most genuine, affectionate smile, he said. "I know that privacy must be priceless to you, you have so little of it. Thank you for taking me to your safest place."

She looked ashen. His revelation that she and Param were watched at all times seemed to be devastating—but had she really imagined that the Revolutionary Council would leave her unobserved? And when the royal daughter seemed to disappear, did Mother really think that the Council would accept her explanation and not search for the girl?

Am I better at this than she is, after having spent her whole life in this prison?

Not better, he decided. It is my gift to sense what she could not possibly see; knowing hidden information is not the same thing as being wiser.

As they approached Mother's room, Rigg could see all her walks up and down the corridor leading to her door. Thousands of times she had taken this walk. Always watched, always mistrusted, hated by many, disdained by more. How had she borne it all these years?

Perhaps she could also feel the pull of the hopes and yearnings of the many others in this land who hated the Council and yearned for a restoration of the monarchy. Perhaps in her heart she was queen after all, bearing what must be borne for the sake of her people.

Perhaps in her heart, as she walked with Rigg toward the room he had just revealed to be no sanctuary at all for her, she was planning his death.

No, he told himself. I have determined to trust her, and to honestly earn her trust in return. No doubts, no second-guessing. Either I will love my mother or I will not, but no halfway measures.

He could hear Father's voice: "For children love is a feeling; for adults, it is a decision. Children wait to learn if their love is true by seeing how long it lasts; adults make their love true by never wavering from their commitment."

Yes, well, Rigg knew enough of the world by now to suspect that by that definition, adults were rare and children could be found at any age. Still, that did not change the fact that Rigg could not help but judge himself by that standard. I will love this woman as long as she allows me to.

Mother opened the door—in semi-obedience to law, it was not locked. Full obedience would have had no door at all, but Rigg imagined it was more useful to the Revolutionary Council for the royals to think they had privacy.

Rigg came inside and closed the door behind him. He made a show of looking at the walls, though he knew exactly where the spy on duty crouched, eye to peephole. "Did they find the very worst art to hang in here?"

"You were rich for how long, three weeks?"

"I got used to it very quickly."

"And in that time you became an expert on the quality of art?" Mother was only slightly sarcastic.

"I'm an expert on what I like," said Rigg. "No one paints accurately—it's always flat and the colors are never quite right. They never catch the thickness of the air. So I learned—as a temporarily rich young man in O—that the paintings that pleased me most were those that did not pretend to be depicting reality. My favorites were the very old ones from the age when O was capital of its own little empire, though it was nothing compared to . . . the lands ruled by the Revolutionary Council." He had almost said "Stashiland," but that was the name before the Sessamoto came, and he did not yet know how Mother would feel about that.

"There can't possibly be any paintings left from the golden age of O," said Mother. "Those are only copies."

"Copies of copies of copies," said Rigg. "But each copy was pronounced a faithful reproduction of the one before."

"But by the time some artist copied it, the copy he copied *from* was already deteriorated. For all you know, the original was every bit as pseudo-realistic as the ones you say that you disdain, and it's only the copying through generations that resulted in the lack of reality that you admire."

"And yet I admire it no less for being unintentional," said Rigg. He was now standing directly in front of the peephole where the spy had bent to see. "*Now*," he said, "is where the vision is clearest."

Mother nodded and frowned. No doubt she was remembering what activities had taken place within plain view of that spot.

Meanwhile, the spy was moving, and soon Rigg could see that new path had stopped forming. The spy must be standing on something, for now the peephole was higher than Rigg could block with his body. Instead, he pressed himself against the wall directly under the second peephole, and said, "*You* could never look at it my way, I know, for some people see from a much loftier position." Meanwhile, he pointed upward.

Mother was alert enough to heed his warning—"*you* could never look"—and not stare right at the second peephole. She knew now where the blind spot in the room was—at least as far as these two peepholes were concerned—because Rigg was standing in it.

He could see from the paths Param had walked in this room that she was almost never in the blind spot. Meaning that whenever she became visible—to eat, to sleep, to wash, to change clothes, to use the chamber pot—she was under observation. So much for privacy. So much for the secret of her ability to become invisible.

To Mother's great credit, she showed no emotion except what would be appropriate in response to her son's words. Of course she understood the importance of giving the spies no indi-cation that she knew they were there, watching. Still, it would be perfectly understandable if from now on, the chamber pot was located in the blind spot. Also the washstand.

"I'm still deciding whether I like you," Mother was saying. "You seem very full of yourself. It's humility that has kept us alive. That and perfect loyalty. We have given the Council no reason to think we're a threat to the Republic—because we're not. We do nothing unusual, so the people are barely aware we're alive. We don't matter. But *your* behavior puts us all in danger. Everyone must be talking about you by now. The servants can hardly be expected to keep silence about *you*."

"Yes, I see that now," said Rigg. "Forgive my selfishness. I will be as humble, harmless, and boring as possible from now on." Unspoken was the statement: Now that everybody knows that I'm alive and here in the same house with you, I can afford to be circumspect. But Rigg was sure she understood exactly what he was doing.

"So what do you plan to do with yourself?"

"I'm in Aressa Sessamo," said Rigg, as if that were answer enough.

"But you aren't," said Mother. "You're in this house. You could be dancing along the Ring for all that you'll see of Aressa Sessamo."

"You misunderstand me, dear mother. I have no intention of going out among the crowds. But my father and I—the man I called 'Father,' that is—had always meant to come here to study in the library."

"There are several hundred libraries in Aressa Sessamo," said Mother, "and they will not let you visit any of them."

"I understand completely," said Rigg. "But the libraries that are grouped together as the Great Library of Aressa—aren't they public libraries? Aren't scholars permitted to borrow books for their research and take them home?"

"Are you suggesting that you're a scholar?" asked Mother, now looking amused.

"My only professor was Father," said Rigg, "but I think perhaps he was enough. We shared a love of science, before he died. There were questions he had not yet answered, and others to which he did not know any useful answer. All the learning that has survived within this wallfold for the past ten thousand years is in the library—if the answer is knowable, I want it."

"For what purpose?"

"To know why the Tower of O was built," said Rigg, and he did not have to fake his passion. "To know what is known about the lands outside the wallfold. Are there people in the other folds? Why was the Wall built at all? How does it work? It can't be a natural artifact—someone made the Wall. Do you see?"

"And what will you do with these answers when you find them?"

"I'll *know* them!" said Rigg. "And if the Council thinks the knowledge I find out might be useful to others, then I'll publish them. Don't you see? Don't *they* see? As long as they don't let us do anything, then the only thing we are is the former royal family. But if I can become a credible scholar, publishing papers that only a scientist would want to read, then I'm not royal any more, am I? I'm a scholar!"

"A *royal* scholar."

"Of course. But in time, in years, I'll be an old man who is known for his publications far more than for my parentage. No one will fear me, or put some idiotic revolutionary hopes in me, or any of our family, because we'll be *something else*."

"They won't let you go to the library anyway."

"But perhaps your dear friend Flacommo will send a servant to carry my letters to the librarians and help me find the books I need."

"You aren't a scholar," said Mother. "I'm just telling you what I know Flacommo will say."

"Then why not invite scholars to come and examine me, to see if I'm scholar enough to be worth giving access to the library? I'm not suggesting that we actually talk face to face — the last thing I want is for some scholar who cares nothing for politics to get dragged into contact with us. But let them sit in one room, and send me written questions. Then I'll answer them aloud, so they can hear my voice and know that someone else is not writing my answers for me. I'll submit myself completely to their judgment."

"It sounds complicated, and I can't think why any scholars would bother to do it."

"I can't either. But what if they were willing?"

"It's worth suggesting to Flacommo."

"Tell him that my father was a remarkable man. Being educated by him was like attending the finest college in the wallfold."

"You mean the finest college in the Republic," said Mother.

"The borders are identical."

"But someone might think you were saying 'wallfold' to avoid saying 'the Republic.'"

Rigg suddenly grew grave. "Oh, I never thought—yes, I will always say 'the Republic' from now on. Let no one think I wish to forget or show disrespect to the Revolutionary Council. I think of the Council and the Wall as being equally everlasting."

"I have one other concern," said Mother. "Your father—your real father, my husband, my beloved Knosso Sissamik—was obsessed with the Wall, with the science around the Wall. He spent his life in pursuit of a theoretical way *through* the Wall. He died in an attempt to cross it."

"I never heard of the Wall killing anybody," said Rigg.

"He thought of passing through the Wall in a boat."

"Surely that's been tried a thousand times—by accident, if no other way—as fishermen got carried off in a storm."

"You know the Wall puts a madness on people who try to pass through. The nearer they get to the Wall, the madder, until they either flee from it screaming, or completely lose their minds and wander around in a stupor from which they never emerge. Fishermen who get swept through the Wall are almost certainly madmen when their boat reaches the other side—none have returned."

"You shared my father Knosso's interest?"

"Not at all," said Mother. "But I loved him, and so I listened to all his theories and tried to serve him as I'm serving you now— by raising objections."

"Then tell me how Father Knosso thought he might solve the problem?"

"His idea was to pass through the Wall unconscious," said Mother. "There are herbs known to the surgeons. They create distillations and concentrations of them, and then inject them into their patients before cutting them. They can't be aroused by any pain. And yet in a few hours they wake up, remembering nothing of the surgery."

"I heard that such things were possible in the past," said Rigg. "But I also heard that the secrets of those herbs had been lost."

"Found again," said Mother.

"In the Great Library?" asked Rigg.

"By your father Knosso," said Mother. "You see, you weren't the first royal to think of becoming a scholar."

"Well, there it is!" cried Rigg. "Did they let Father Knosso have access to the library?"

"They did," said Mother. "In person. He would walk there— it wasn't far."

"And now the surgeons of Aressa Sessamo—and the wall-fold, too—I mean, the Republic—have benefitted!"

"Your father lay down in a boat, which was placed in a swift current that moved through the Wall in the north, far beyond the western coast. He injected himself with a dose that the surgeons agreed was right to keep a man of his weight deeply asleep for three hours. There were floats rigged on the boat so it couldn't capsize, even if it ran into shore breakers before he could wake up. And he brought along more doses, so he could row himself to an inflowing current and repeat the process and return to us."

"Did he make it through?" asked Rigg.

"Yes—though we have no way of knowing if he was made

insane by the passage through the Wall. Because he died without waking."

"And you know this because he never returned?"

"We know this because no sooner was he beyond the Wall on the far side than his boat sank into the water."

"Sank!"

"Trusted scientists watched through spyglasses, though he was three miles away. The floats came off and drifted away. Then the boat simply sank straight down into the water. Knosso bobbed on the surface for a few moments, and then he, too, sank."

"Why would a boat sink like that?" asked Rigg.

"There are those who say the boat was tampered with—that the floats were designed to come loose, and a hole was deliberately placed in the boat with a plug in it that was soluble in salt water."

"So he was murdered," said Rigg.

"There are those who say that," said Mother. "But one of the scholars who was observing it—Tokwire the astronomer—was using a glass of his own making, which was filled with mirrors, so the other scholars did not trust his observations. But he swears it let him see the sinking of your father's boat much more clearly than anyone else, and he says he saw hands rising up out of the water, first to tear the floats away, and then to pull straight down on the boat."

"Hands? Human hands?"

"No one believed him. And he quickly dropped the matter, for fear that insisting on the point would ruin his reputation among scholars."

"You believe him."

"I believe we don't know what's on the other side of the Wall," said Mother.

"You think there are people there who live in the water? Who can breathe underwater?" asked Rigg.

"I don't think anything. I neither say 'possible' nor 'impossible' to anything," said Mother.

"But he passed through the Wall."

"And never woke up."

"Why is the story not known throughout . . . the Republic?"

"Because we didn't want a thousand idiots making the attempt and meeting the same fate," said Mother.

"What if there *are* water people in the next wallfold?" asked Rigg. "They've never crossed the Wall, either! Would they even understand what our boats were? What kind of creature Father Knosso was? They might think that because he's shaped like them, he could breathe underwater as they did."

"We don't know how they're shaped," said Mother.

"We know they have hands."

"We know that what Tokwire saw he *called* hands."

"Mother, I can see that Father's plan should not be tried again," said Rigg. "I would love to see anything he wrote, or failing that to read everything he read from the library. So I can know what he knew, or at least guess what he guessed. But I swear to you most solemnly that I am not fool enough to attempt to cross the Wall myself, certainly not unconscious, and equally not in a boat. If I'm too stupid to learn from other people's experiences, I'm no scholar."

"You relieve me greatly. Though you must know how it strikes terror in my heart that within a day of your arrival, you're already talking about duplicating your father's fatal research."

"I was already interested in the Wall before you told me the story of Father Knosso, Mother. Duplicating his research may save me time, but I have ideas of my own."

"I'll ask Flacommo what is possible concerning the library. But you must promise me to let me serve you as I served your father. Come and tell me all you learn, all you wonder about, all that you guess."

"Here?" asked Rigg. "This is your place of privacy, Mother. I'm uncomfortable even now, knowing that I should not be here."

"Where else, if we're not to bore the rest of Flacommo's house with our tedious scholarly conversation?"

"The garden," said Rigg. "Walking among the trees and bushes and flowers. Sitting on benches. Isn't it a lovely thing, to be among the living plants?"

"You forget that it's open to the elements, and winter is almost here."

"I spent many a winter in the highest mountains of the Upsheer, sleeping outdoors night after night."

"How will this keep me warm in the garden this winter?" asked Mother.

"We'll talk together only on sunny days. Maybe my sister will join us, and we can share a bench with you between us—we'd keep you warm enough then, I think!"

"If your sister ever consents to come out of her seclusion."

"A seclusion that excludes her only brother, lost so long and newly come home, is too much seclusion, I think."

"It's what *she* thinks that counts," said Mother.

"Then she doesn't listen to your advice?" asked Rigg.

"Listening isn't obeying," said Mother.

"Come with me and show me the house, Mother!" said Rigg. "I think this is an ancient place, with old ways of building."

"So you study architecture as well?" asked Mother.

"I'm a scholar! In my heart, anyway. Old things intrigue me. Especially old buildings! You can imagine how I loved the Tower of O!"

"I can't," said Mother. "I've never seen it."

"Then I'll draw you sketches of it."

"I've seen sketches," she said testily.

"But you haven't seen *my* sketches!" said Rigg. "Come on, come with me, let's see this house."

Mother allowed herself to be drawn to her feet, and together they began walking the corridors, holding hands. Rigg knew that they were leaving Param behind, invisible, but that could not be helped.

When Rigg sensed anyone's path near enough to overhear them, he would walk apart from Mother, letting their hands clasp in the space between. But when he knew they were alone, and no one could hear, he took her hand in both of his, and leaned close.

It was in those times that he told her about Umbo and Loaf, about going back in time, about the jewel—even now he still mentioned only the one—about his time on the boat with General Citizen, about Shouter's attempt to kill him, about his own failures to travel back in time without Umbo's help. She listened to all without interruption.

In return, she told him little, but apologized for the fact that the little she told was all she knew. Param's gift was not understood—she simply couldn't be found sometimes, even as a little child, and then she'd turn up somewhere in the house, hungry and cold. Several governesses were dismissed because of their failure to keep track of her, and finally they were moved into Flacommo's house precisely because it was tightly walled and she could not escape.

"I think it's because of all the secret passages," said Rigg. "So they could watch her and see what she does."

"Then they certainly know what I know. When she was still young, it only happened when she was frightened by something— she'd start turning to run away, and then she faded and was gone before she'd gone far."

"Then she learned to control it?" asked Rigg.

"Now it's not fear that drives it, but repugnance. She hates the company of anyone but me."

"But that wasn't always so."

"There was a time when she had many friends. Courtiers, scholars, men of trade—many visited Flacommo, and among them were some who took a great liking to Param. She said one of the scholars inadvertently helped her learn to understand her invisibility. What he said helped her get control of it, to disappear only when she wanted to, and as long as she wanted, no more."

"That must have been a very wise man."

"It was a chance thing," said Mother. "He might have been

wise, but he had no idea that the things he said were useful to her, because he couldn't have known about her invisibility. That's a story that has *not* spread. What the servants and courtiers all believe is that Param is painfully shy and hides when she wants no company. They are forbidden to search for her, though of course they couldn't possibly find her if she didn't want to be found."

"Please tell her that I beg her to join us on our garden walks."

"Beg away," said Mother. "She'll do what she wants."

"Tell her I'm sorry for passing through her in the garden."

"What!" said Mother. "You did *what*?"

"I knew where she was and I walked through her."

"I didn't know that was possible."

"Oh, I'm reasonably certain it happens often enough. She was in the breakfast hall with us this morning. When we left, I made sure we moved around her, but when she's invisible she can't move fast enough to get out of the way. She tends to cling to the walls, but I can't believe she hasn't been walked through time and again."

"She never told me."

"She doesn't want to worry you. And she certainly doesn't want you trying to guess where she is and then walk around her," said Rigg.

"You've never met her, and now you're telling me what she does and doesn't want me trying to do?"

"Yes," said Rigg. "Because it's the obvious assumption. And it explains the twistings and convolutions of her paths, and why she clings to walls."

At last they had seen the whole house, every floor and room and nook and view—except Flacommo's private quarters, the few locked rooms, and the secret passages. They passed several of the hidden entrances to the system of passages, but Rigg merely took silent notice of the place and determined to come back later. If Rigg was caught exploring near an entrance, he wanted it to be only himself who was suspected of something dangerous.

Mother retired to her room, and Rigg went back to the kitchen, where the day shift was creating the doughs and batters for the evening's pies and cakes. He rather liked the symmetry of the two bakers' each having to bake what the other prepared. He also liked the fact that Lolonga seemed to be competing with her sister to feed more of the excellent bread to Rigg than her sister had. One thing was certain: Rigg would not starve here.

Rigg began to treat himself as an apprentice cook, never attempting what the bakers' apprentices did, because things could go wrong, but instead working for the cooks: running their errands; learning by name, by sight and smell, and by usage all the herbs of the kitchen garden; and getting yelled at for his mistakes like any other boy in the kitchen. It wasn't long before the boys who slept behind the hearth accepted him readily and talked to him like an equal. And to them he spoke in the language of a privick from Fall Ford, letting them make fun of his accent.

"So which is the real voice of Rigg?" asked Long one day, hearing him with the cooks' boys.

"If it comes out of my mouth, it's my voice," said Rigg.

"But the coarse country boy from upriver, with the ribald

jokes and funny tales of country life — how can you say he's the same as the boy who speaks in such a lofty style that he withers most of the courtiers with his wit?"

"Do I?" said Rigg. "I don't recall inflicting any injuries."

"When everyone laughs at them, they're destroyed," said Long. "And you've ruined several who haven't dared come back."

"And does anyone miss them?"

Long laughed.

"A hunter who carries only one weapon has already decided that all the animals it can't reach are safe from him."

"So you have the weapons of country wit and courtly wit?" asked Long.

"Let's say — half of each."

"A double halfwit *is* a wit, I think," said Long.

"And now you've entered the fray!" cried Rigg, and the two of them tussled in the kitchen garden for a few moments, then remembered their errands and got back to work without waiting for someone to yell at them.

It was a week before the answer came. Flacommo announced it at dinner.

"Young Rigg," said their host. "I have pled your cause before the Revolutionary Council, and they have decided that it's too much bother for the librarians to have to answer your endless requests and send books back and forth."

Rigg did not let himself feel disappointed, because the way Flacommo was talking, it was plain that he was only pretending to be doleful — he had good news.

"Instead, *if* a panel of scholars pronounces you worthy to be numbered as one of them, you will be allowed to travel, under escort, to and from the library once a day—though you may stay there as long as you want, or until supper."

Rigg leapt to his feet and let out a boyish, privick, unprincely hoot of happiness. Everyone laughed, even Mother.

CHAPTER 17
Scholar

"Our mandate," said the expendable, "is to serve no individual human being at the expense of the species, but rather to preserve and advance the human species, even if at the expense of a cost-effective number of individuals."

"Cost-effective," echoed Ram. "I wonder how you determine the cost of a human life."

"Equally," said the expendable.

"Equally to what?"

"Any other human being."

"So you can kill one to save two."

"Or a billion in order to bring to pass circumstances that will bring about the births of a billion and one."

"It sounds rather cold."

"We are cold," said the expendable. "But raw numbers hardly tell our whole mandate."

"I am eager to know," said Ram, "on what besides numbers you judge the preservation and advancement of the human species."

"Whatever enhances the ability of the human race to survive in the face of threats."

"What threats?"

"In descending order of likelihood of extinction of the species: collision with meteors above a certain combined mass and velocity; eruption of volcanoes that produce above a certain amount of certain kinds of ejecta; plagues above a certain mortality rate and contagiousness; war employing weapons above a certain level and permanence of destructive power; stellar events that decrease the viability of life—"

"It seems to me," said Ram, "that if we succeed in planting a viable human colony on this new world, we will have made it impossible for any of these to wipe out the species."

"And if we succeed in planting nineteen viable human colonies—"

"All nineteen would be equally affected by your list of dangers, should they happen to this planet or this star. One bad meteor collision wipes out all nineteen."

"Yes," said the expendable.

"Yet it matters to you that we specify nineteen colonies, and not just one."

"Yes," said the expendable.

There was a long silence.

"You're waiting for me to make a decision about something."

"Yes," said the expendable.

"You're going to have to be more specific," said Ram.

"We cannot think of the thing we cannot think of," said the expendable. "It would be unthinkable."

Ram thought about this for a long time. He made many guesses about what the required decision might be. He said only a few of them aloud, and the expendable agreed every time that this would be a useful decision, but it was not the crucial one.

A decision that would explain the importance of having nineteen colonies in order to preserve and advance the survival of the human species. Ram went through every decision that would have to be made, including the degree of destruction of the native flora and fauna that might be required, and won the agreement of the expendables that every effort would be made to create a thorough and representative genetic record, seed bank, and embryana of the native life forms of the planet, so that anything destroyed in the process of establishing the colonies might be restored at some later date.

But even this decision was not the crucial one.

And then one morning he realized what the expendables were waiting for. It came to him as he was pondering what it meant that the computers and expendables agreed that the cloning of the starship and the travel backward in time were caused by Ram himself. Most humans could not alter the flow of time. One might say that no human had ever done so. And if that statement was still true . . .

"I am human," said Ram, with perhaps more emphasis than the sentence required.

"Thank you," said the expendable.

"Is that the full decision that you wanted?"

"If that is the full decision that you want, then we are satisfied."

This was such an ambiguous answer that Ram demanded clarification.

"But there is nothing to clarify," said the expendable. "If it is your full decision, complete and final, we will act accordingly."

"Then it is *not* my final decision until I understand all the implications of it."

"It is not within the capacity of a human mind to understand all the implications of anything. Your lifespan is not long enough."

That had been time enough for Ram to put the situation, as he understood it, into words. "What you seem to need," said Ram, "is a definition of 'human species' before you can plan the colonies. This means that you contemplate circumstances in which the definition of 'human species' might be in question."

"We contemplate billions of circumstances," said the expendable.

"But not all of them?"

"Our lifespan, too, is finite," said the expendable.

Another question occurred to Ram. "Do you have evidence that there is a species on the new planet that might have intelligence at the level of humans?"

"No."

"Or *above* the human level?"

"No."

So they weren't trying to squeeze an alien species into the definition of what was human.

But they needed to be reassured, thought Ram, that whatever I am, it is included in the definition of the human species. Otherwise,

I would have been used to advance the survival of the colonists and their offspring, but my own genetic survival would not have been protected, because I am so different from other human beings that something going on in my mind affected the flow of time and the fabric of reality.

If I reproduce, then my difference might be passed on to my descendants. For that matter, living here in isolation from the rest of the human race for at least 11,191 years, who could guess what other differences might develop between us and the rest of the human species back on Earth?

Ram did his best to be precise, to speak like a scientist or lawyer. "The definition of 'human species' shall include the existing range of genetic variability and all variations of it that might come to be, as long as the variations are not likely to be harmful to the survival of the human species in general."

"Vague," said the expendable.

"On this world or any other," Ram added.

The expendable said nothing.

Ram thought a moment and tried again. "'Human species' means the interreproducing gene pool now understood to be human, plus all future variations on the human genome even if they cannot interreproduce with the existing gene pool, provided that the future variants do not threaten to destroy or weaken the survival chances of the existing gene pool, either deliberately or inadvertently."

The expendable was silent for a long five seconds.

"We have discussed your definition, analyzed its ramifications to a reasonable depth, and accept it," said the expendable.

"Meaning that I gave you what you wanted?"

"Ambition and desire are *human* traits. You gave us what we lacked."

• • •

While Rigg had the ability to perceive paths without regard to walls or distance, in the confusion of Aressa Sessamo there was a practical limit to how far he could follow any path that wove in and out among all the threads of the city. Here inside the walls of Flacommo's house, Rigg could track everyone who had ever lived here, though most of them weren't interesting. Rigg mostly cared about people who came in and out of the house for the past year or so—and the paths that revealed to him the secret passages of the house.

He also tried tracing the paths of the spies who watched from peepholes in the walls, but once they left the house, they took convoluted paths through the busiest streets, like fugitives walking up or down a stream in order to confuse the dogs tracking them by scent. He wondered if they had some idea of what he could do, but then saw that they followed this pattern long before Rigg came here—before anyone here knew he was still alive. Perhaps the spies simply walked on the main streets like anyone else, and it was mere chance that it made it impossible for Rigg to keep them clearly in view far enough to know whom they reported to. Or perhaps they were choosing evasive routes in order to avoid observation by ordinary agents of some other faction or power.

They definitely did not report to Flacommo. As far as Rigg

could tell, nobody did—not even the servants. The cooks and bakers cooked what they wanted; the housekeeper made up whatever schedule she pleased. Flacommo simply wandered around the house, talking to whomever he happened to meet. He was like a toddler, wandering to wherever something interesting was going on and then getting underfoot.

Rigg wasn't sure whether going to the library would help him solve this problem—he could see the paths that wound through the buildings of the library, which weren't far away, and while they were clear and orderly in a way the paths of the city streets were not, neither did any of the spies ever go there.

So if he got to the library, Rigg's research would be exactly what he said it would be—an attempt to duplicate everything that his real father, Knosso, had studied in order to discover whatever it was he knew. Which might be nothing at all—it didn't take a deep knowledge of theoretical physics to figure out that you might be able to make it through the Wall in a state of drug-induced unconsciousness.

But Father Knosso had studied the human brain in order to develop the sedatives he used. And if there was anything Rigg desperately needed to understand, it was the workings of the human brain. His own in particular, but a nice working knowledge of Umbo's and Param's and even Nox's would be very useful, too.

At the same time, he couldn't think of any reason why the Revolutionary Council would want to let him go anywhere or do anything—particularly something that *he* wanted to do. It might be a simple matter of policy that if the royal son, whose very existence is an affront both to the Revolutionary Council and to the matriarchal royal line, wants to do something, it must not be permitted.

Apparently, though, there were enough partisans of the male line—or enough people who thought it might be easier to kill him outside the walls of Flacommo's house—that a bevy of scholars descended upon the house early one morning, without any kind of warning. "Because, you see," said the elderly botanist who seemed to be in charge, "we didn't want you to have any chance to prepare."

"Beyond my lifetime of preparation," said Rigg.

"That goes without saying," said the botanist.

"I'm curious about the standard of judgment that you'll use. Do I have to have the same level of knowledge as you? Aren't there younger scholars who know less than you do, who are still scholars?"

"We are much less interested in the quantity or even the quality of your knowledge," said the botanist, "than we are in the quality and quickness of your mind."

"And are there no slow scholars among you?"

"Many are slow to remember the things that most people consider to be essentials of life," said the botanist, "but all are quick enough to reason, to recognize illogic and error and unlikelihood. And in case you're wondering, the test has already begun, and I'm not sure I like the cautious way you are trying to influence the ground rules in advance."

"You leap to the conclusion that my goal is to influence them rather than merely discover them," said Rigg.

"Discovering the rules will do you no good," said the botanist, "because you will either think like a scholar or not, and if you don't, it will be because you can't, and if you can't, no advance information will help you."

"Fair enough," said Rigg. "One point against me."

"We are not keeping score," said the botanist. "We are forming an impression."

"Then I will stop trying to control things and surrender to your questioning."

"Even with that statement you are trying to explain yourself, when silence would have been wiser."

Rigg kept his silence.

The scholars went into the most comfortable parlor. Rigg sat on a backless stool in the next room, where he could not see any of them, but could hear anything they said loudly.

Rigg also noticed that two of the spies-in-the-walls were there to watch him and his examiners.

The questions began innocuously enough. They were so easy, in fact, that Rigg kept trying to find overcomplicated answers, fearing some kind of trick or trap. Until the botanist sighed and said, "If you keep answering like this we'll never finish before some of us—including, probably, me—have died of old age. We aren't trying to trick you, we're trying get to *know* you. If a question seems simple, it *is* simple."

"Oh," said Rigg.

Now things moved very quickly. Often he could answer in a few words. They checked his general knowledge of history, botany, zoology, grammar, languages, physics, astronomy, chemistry, anatomy, and engineering. They asked him nothing about music or any of the arts; they steered clear of any history that involved the glorious Revolution or any events since.

Rigg confessed ignorance more frequently the farther they went. He stayed right with the zoologists—he had spent most of his life tracking, trapping, skinning, dissecting, cooking, and eating the fauna of the highlands to the south, and he enjoyed answering those questions in greater detail than was probably necessary. He enjoyed showing off.

But even in the areas where he didn't have anywhere near as much experience, he held his own. Father had quizzed him constantly, and Rigg responded to these examiners exactly as he would have responded to Father, though with less flippancy. When he didn't know the answer, he would say so; when he had a guess, he would identify it as speculation and explain why he thought it might be so.

He soon realized that they were actually more interested in his guesses than in his knowledge. Once they knew he had a deep and wide knowledge of the vertebrates, they left zoology alone; whatever he knew little about, but still made guesses, they would pursue sharply. Always they brought him to a point where he had to say, "I just don't know enough about it to make any kind of answer."

"Where would you look, then?" the physicist finally asked. "Where *within* the library?"

"I don't know," said Rigg.

"If you don't know where to look for the answer, then what good will the library do you?" the physicist demanded.

Rigg allowed his voice to reveal a little impatience. "I'm from upriver. I've never been in a library in my life. That's why I want to be allowed to study in the Great Library here—so I can begin to find out where I would look for answers to questions like these."

"There was a library in O," said the botanist. "Why didn't you go there to pursue your studies?"

"I was not planning to be a scholar then," said Rigg. "I was still following what I thought was my father's plan—that is, the man I thought was my father. By the time I got *here*, I realized either my father had no plan, or his plan simply didn't work. So now I can choose for myself what I want to do. Only I don't have enough information to make an intelligent decision about anything. So I thought I might attempt to add to what my father taught me, since his teachings were obviously incomplete."

"All teachings are incomplete," said the historian impatiently.

"And yet a wise man tries to add to his knowledge before making crucial decisions," said Rigg.

"What sorts of decisions are you hoping to make?" asked the botanist.

"I don't know enough to know what I need to know in order to decide what I need to decide," said Rigg.

Rigg could sense that one of the scholars in the next room had stood up and was now pacing. Her voice was old-sounding. "There might be those who think your position here—as a member of the discredited royal family—"

Several of the other scholars got up, and one started toward her.

"I'm not speaking treason, I'm saying what everyone in this room knows, so sit down and let's see how *he* answers!"

Rigg tried to remember who the speaker was, but finally concluded it was someone who had not spoken before.

"As I was saying, there might be those who think that it doesn't matter in the slightest what you decide about anything. For the rest of your life, other people will decide everything that matters, including whether you live or die."

She sat back down. Again there were murmurs of protest, but Rigg spoke loudly to cut them off. "I'm not afraid to face the situation I'm in. I'm quite aware that my power to decide is limited right now, and might be ended completely at any time. There have already been two attempts on my life since I was arrested — two that I know of, that is. In both cases, I managed to be alert enough to stay alive, but how long can I keep *that* up? One of you will have to write about that after the answer is known."

There were a few nervous chuckles.

"But there's always the chance that I might *not* die young. How will I occupy the long years of a very limited kind of life? My choice is to pursue scholarship. To do that I need to find out what I'm good at. To do *that* I need to have access to the library. Eventually I may be able to contribute to the sum of human knowledge. If I don't, then at least I will have had an interesting life. A larger life than is possible in this house, with so few books."

More murmuring, and then someone started to speak. Rigg didn't even let him get a whole word out. "Please! Learned doctors and philosophers like you certainly have enough answers from me to make your decision. Let me ask *you* a question."

"We are not here to be examined," said the botanist stiffly. "And *you* do not decide when the—"

"Of course you're here to be examined," said Rigg. "All of you have carefully phrased your questions so as to impress each other with your profundity. I know you've impressed *me*. So I want to ask you all: What do you expect of a child my age? I am all potential, without accomplishments. If I were your student, would you find me promising? Would you trust me with a book in my hands? Is mine a mind worth teaching? My father thought so, because he spent every waking moment doing it, and then testing me on it—including the very kinds of tests that you've been putting me through here, taking me beyond the boundaries of my education, seeing what I could figure out for myself. He died without telling me whether I was meeting his standards or not. He never said or implied that I had learned *enough* about anything. But he also never stopped teaching me. Was my father right? Am I worth teaching? And if I'm not, why in the world have you spent all these hours pressing me further? Is there some great wisdom to be gained by calibrating exactly how worthless a mind I have?"

"This examination is over," said the botanist.

Gratefully Rigg rose from his stool. His back was as tired as if he'd slept on cold hard ground. He had probably offended everyone by his final question, but there was a point where continuing the examination was a waste of everyone's time.

To his surprise, the scholars did not go out the door leading into the garden. Instead, most of them came immediately into the room where Rigg was stretching himself. Some of them walked with great dignity, but others rushed in, hands extended. They said nothing at first. But each in turn held out a hand to him. Rigg took each hand, held it for a moment between his, and looked into their eyes.

The message in every face was the same, if he could dare to believe it. All the men and women who came into the room looked at him with warmth. With — or so it seemed to him — affection.

As he held their hands, and they held his, each one said his or her area of specialty. Not the general subject matter, like botany or physics, but the particular study that had made their reputation. "Mutation of plants through interspecies pollination." "Propulsion of machinery through the controlled release of steam." "The redevelopment of noun declensions through the accretion of particles in the transition from Middle to Late Umik." "The tails of comets considered as ice boiled off by the heat of the sun."

Each one, after letting go of his hand, stepped back to let the next approach. In the end, they formed two lines, and it was into the space between them that the last two from the other room finally came. The botanist was one, and the other was the woman who had asked him the practical and dangerous question near the end. Her face was set and hard—it was quite possible the botanist had been telling her off. Even now, she hung back and let the botanist come to Rigg ahead of her.

The botanist took his hands and said, "Alteration of a species through direct injection of cell nuclei from a species with a desired trait." Then he stepped back.

The old woman came last. She took his hands as the others had, but said nothing.

"Go ahead," the botanist said.

The old woman cocked her head slightly and got a touch of a smile. "The likelihood of two separate origins for the flora and fauna of this wallfold."

This was something Rigg had never heard of—something Father had never touched on. "How could they be separate?" he asked. "Did life begin twice?"

She winked, even as a few of the other scholars groaned.

"That's not the subject of her master piece," said the botanist. "This is the scab she picks whenever she can find someone willing to listen to her. Her paper on *that* topic was never published."

"Will I see you in the library?" Rigg asked the woman.

She smiled. "Isn't the question whether *we'll* see *you*?" Then she let go of his hands and left the room, walking out into the garden.

Flacommo must have been waiting outside, because Rigg could hear his voice as he protested that she couldn't want to leave without sharing the meal that his cooks had prepared for such distinguished company.

"She was once very great," said the botanist.

Rigg looked at him; he was watching her through the still-open door.

"Who is she?" asked Rigg.

"Bleht. She practically invented the science of microbiology, or revived it, anyway. But she got on a weird kick about two separate streams of evolution that only came together eleven thousand years ago—mystical claptrap. What does an ancient religious calendar have to do with science, I'd like to know," said the botanist.

But Rigg understood immediately what she meant. He had skinned and gutted many of the "anomalous creatures," as Father called them, and knew well how their anatomy differed from the patterns of most of the animals. He had also had to learn the "anomalous plants," for the excellent reason that they could not be digested by humans and sometimes had toxic effects.

Now, just from her words, it occurred to him that instead of regarding these anomalous beasts and plants as the result of random chance, what if they were all related to each other? Instead of one great stream of life, with inexplicable variations, could there really be *two* streams of life, each one consistent within itself?

"I can see you're taking her seriously," said the botanist.

"He's young," said the physicist—a woman, and probably the youngest of them all; Rigg put her age at about thirty. "Of course he's intrigued."

Rigg was more than intrigued. He was already thinking through what he had found when he gutted ebbecks and wee-bears. Were they similar to each other? And which scavengers did they find devouring the carcasses after Rigg had taken the skins? Were they all anomalies, too? He wanted to go back—with Umbo in tow—so he could look at the paths of anomalous creatures and see whether they fed selectively on anomalous plants, and whether the predators of odd sorts hunted only odd prey.

Surely if there were such a pattern, Father would have pointed it out.

Or maybe Father was hoping he'd notice it on his own.

He noticed it now. He hadn't made a study of it, so he couldn't be sure, but what he could remember at this moment didn't contradict her idea.

The scholars dined together—except Bleht—and conversed with Rigg quite readily. It seemed to him that they would not have been so comfortable talking with him if they intended to give a negative report on his examination.

And so it turned out. The next morning four men in the uniform of the City Guard arrived to escort him from Flacommo's house to the library.

Rigg had hoped to catch a glimpse of the city of Aressa Sessamo, but he was disappointed. He could hear the sounds of a large city, but from a distance. Flacommo's house was surrounded on three sides by other huge houses of similar design—high walls surrounding a central garden, with no windows facing out. The streets had only local traffic—servants on errands, a few people of some wealth and standing walking or riding, a few mothers—or nannies?—with children.

And on the fourth side—directly across the wide tree-lined avenue from Flacommo's house—were the gardens of the library.

Rigg knew already from studying the paths that moved through them that the library's large buildings stood well apart from each other, each one making a stately impression of its own, showing the architectural style that was in favor at the time it was added. The library buildings stood on a built-up rise of ground—there were no natural hills in this delta country. The mansions were also on raised ground, though not so high; between them, just across the avenue, were the tiny apartments that were provided free for visiting scholars while conducting their library research. The librarians themselves lived in the attics above the stacks of books.

Rigg believed that Umbo and Loaf would try to reach Aressa Sessamo, as soon as Umbo had learned how to deliver messages to himself and Rigg in the past. Rigg had hoped that the library might be a place where they could meet, but now it was clear that he would have to find another way to get to them. It wasn't likely they would be able to pass themselves off as scholars, and if they tried to walk around in this part of the city they would instantly be recognized as interlopers. They would never be able to come anywhere near him.

The first morning, they took him to the Library of Life, where he hoped to meet Bleht. Instead, he was given into the charge of a young assistant librarian who led him on a tour of the building, with the guards in tow. The assistant was a woman of no more than twenty, and she put on quite a show of being very bored and put upon, having to take a child on a tour. She even remarked to the guards about the irony that the Revolutionary Council still provided special services for the royals.

Rigg let her attitude roll off him. He did not try to chat with her—or the guards, for that matter, having learned some kind of lesson from his time with Shouter. But when he wanted more information, he asked her, and since she really did love the place, his questions led her to occasional displays of enthusiasm, though she soon caught herself and resumed her cold attitude. But it was a little less cold as the hours progressed.

On the outside, the building looked like a simple rectangle.

Inside, though, it was a labyrinth, and Rigg reflected that if he did not have his ability to retrace his own path he might never find his way out again. The shelves of books he had expected, but there were also bins where old scrolls were kept, and catalogues that listed abstracts of books that existed only on thin sheets of metal, baked-clay tablets, tree bark, and animal skins.

"Aren't these so ancient that their science has nothing to teach us?" asked Rigg.

"This isn't just a library of contemporary biology," she answered coldly. "We also keep the entire history of the life sciences, so that we can see how we got to our present understanding."

"Were there any civilizations of the past that surpassed us in understanding of some areas of biology?"

"I'm not a historical librarian," she said. "I supervise the record-keeping in the laboratories, and since very few scholars are using the labs right now, they decided I was free to waste a morning."

"But then you must be involved with the cutting edge of science all the time," said Rigg.

She did not answer—but a little more of the hostility drained away from her. Still, she didn't even bother to say good-bye when the noon bell rang and it was time for him to go.

On the way out of the building, the guards twice got lost enough that he had to correct them and lead them out himself. They went back to Flacommo's house, which was only five minutes' walk, to eat, and then returned, this time to the Library of Past Lives. This time his guide was not a librarian but a young scholar who was drafted into the service. He wasn't hostile at all, and if it were not for the glowering guards, he might have spent the whole time quizzing Rigg on what the Empress Hagia Sessamin was like, and whether he had seen the mysterious Param.

At the end of the day, the guards were going to lead Rigg straight back to Flacommo's house, but Rigg asked to see whoever was in charge.

"In charge of what?" asked the scholar. "Each library has its own dean or mayor or rector—they all have different titles—and nobody's in charge of the whole thing."

"I think I need to see whoever is in charge of *me*."

"You?" asked the scholar. "Aren't these men . . ."

"Somebody decided the order in which I should tour the libraries. Somebody drafted you to lead me through this one. Who is making those decisions?"

"Oh. I don't know."

"This is a library," said Rigg. "Could we look it up?"

"I'll ask."

So the guards sighed and sat down, insisting that Rigg do the same, for the long fifteen minutes before the scholar returned with a fierce-looking elderly woman. "What do you want?" she demanded.

"I want to stop wasting the time of young scholars and librarians," said Rigg. "For all that each library has unique features, the differences could be explained to me in fifteen minutes. But even that isn't necessary. I want to end the tour and begin my research."

"I was told to give you a tour," said the woman coldly.

"And I was given a splendid one," said Rigg gently. "But who knows how long I have to live? I'd like to be taken to whoever would have the records of my father's research."

"And your father is . . . ?"

Rigg couldn't believe she was asking. During his moment of hesitation, the young scholar piped up—and couldn't keep all of the scorn out of his voice, for to him it seemed impossible that someone might not know who the father of Rigg Sessamekesh must be.

"Knosso Sissamik," he said. "He was a noted scholar and he died at the Wall."

"I don't keep track of former royals the way some do," said the old woman. "And Knosso whatever-his-name was a physicist. That's the Library of Nothing."

"Nothing?"

The old woman had her spiel ready. "Physicists long since determined that most of space was empty, and most of each atom was empty, so that the overwhelming nature of the universe is nothingness, with tiny interruptions that contain all of existence. So their library is named for this Nothing that comprises most of the universe. And the mathematicians share the space, because they are proud to say that what they study is even less real than what the physicists study, so their portion is called the Library of Less than Nothing."

Rigg decided he was going to like the physicists. It seemed to him, though, that the mathematicians must have an annoying competitive streak.

The next day he was taken straight to the Library of Nothing and shown a list of the books Father Knosso had read in the last two years of his life. It was a very long list, and as Rigg began to open and try to read them, he realized that there were technical words and mathematical operations he did not understand. So he began a remedial course of his own design, to prepare himself to make sense of what his father Knosso had thought was worth spending his time on.

The days settled into a routine that spanned several weeks, and Rigg was making real progress. He still couldn't understand any of the books on Knosso's list, but he at least recognized most of the terms and he felt as though he was on the verge of grasping enough that he could figure out what Father Knosso had built his theories on.

But as he sat at his small table with books open before him, the guards often slept, and he used those opportunities to close his eyes and study the paths around him. One of these paths, he knew, belonged to Father Knosso. He had never lived in Flacommo's house—his widow and daughter moved there only after his death. But he had been here, in this library, and by finding all the books he had read, Rigg hoped to identify a path that connected with them all.

Finally he found it, by following a likely candidate backward and backward in time until he went—or, to be correct, came from—the home he then shared with Mother. Their paths intersected, again and again; it could be no one but Father Knosso.

For a moment he wished Umbo were there, so that he could actually see him. The royal family had been forbidden to have portraits taken—there was no image of his father to give him any idea of his face. But his path was distinctive enough. Now that he had identified it, Rigg could spot it easily.

And after a while, he began to notice something rather surprising. Father Knosso did, indeed, study all the books on the list. But he also ventured into other libraries, particularly the Library of Past Lives and the Library of Dead Words. Rigg found excuses to go to each of these places and retrace his father's steps. The librarians in each place assured him that books were still stored in the same general area, usually even the same shelf, as during his father's time. But he never checked out any books from these libraries, so there was no record.

Still, Rigg learned something—from the Library of Dead Words, he assembled a list of languages whose shelf areas Father Knosso had visited; from Past Lives, he put together a list of historical periods and topics that had interested him. A pattern emerged.

Father Knosso's search had involved physics, yes—but he had been looking into observations of the Wall from many cultures and languages, stretching at least eight thousand years into the past. Did he think that in some ancient time, someone had found a way through the Wall? There were stories of saints and heroes that came from Overwall, or returned there in death, but the same stories told of them leaping between stars, creating earthquakes and volcanoes, and building machines that came to life.

No educated man would take them seriously. And even if Father Knosso had given them some credence, Rigg never could—hadn't he been a participant in the true events behind the myth of the Wandering Saint?

What else, then? Had Father Knosso been looking for a time before the Wall? Everybody knew there was no such time—the Wall had always been there. Then again, just because everybody knew it didn't mean it was true.

And why would he avoid leaving a written record of his researches into the past? There was something more going on than mere physics; there must be a political slant to it as well, or Father Knosso would not have been so wary.

But without the specific titles Father Knosso had studied, Rigg couldn't think of a way to learn what Father Knosso had tried to learn.

The library took up his days, but his evenings and nights and early mornings were spent in Flacommo's house. Rigg took to sleeping in different places each night, often simply curling up in the garden, which reminded him a little bit of nights in the wild with Father. Rigg helped in the kitchen and maintained his friendship with the bakers of both shifts, especially Lolonga's son Long, who treated Rigg like a regular person instead of something either contemptible or lofty. Of course, as soon as it became known that Long and Rigg spent time together, Long was summoned to various alehouses and parks and shops for periodic interrogations.

As soon as Rigg realized this was going on, he told Long, "Tell them everything. I don't say or do anything that needs to be hidden." This eased Long's mind considerably.

Rigg's statement was true enough, though he omitted the words "with you." He did plenty of things alone that he did not want reported to anybody.

Mostly what he did was try to communicate with Param. Partly because meeting her was the only thing Father had actually told him to do, and partly because he wanted to get to know her and win her trust. Messages he left with Mother were useless — she relayed them faithfully enough, but there was never an answer. Besides, there were things he needed to discuss with Param that Mother could not know about.

So he took to carrying around a slate, like a schoolchild. He told Flacommo, when asking for the use of one, that he must have it to practice mathematical calculations that he needed in order to understand the physics books he was studying. And he really used the slate for that . . . except when Rigg saw that Param's path was approaching him.

Then he would erase a corner of the slate and write messages to her. He would print them out and then hold the slate as still as he could, so that she could still have plenty of time to read them. And he saw right away that she was reading them, for she orbited around him while he was writing to her, though she couldn't answer with chalk or voice.

He told her little bits about his own life — about Father, how he died, how they had lived together. About discovering the truth — especially that he had a sister, something he had never suspected until Father lay there dying and told him to go find her.

He told her some things about Umbo and less about Loaf — but enough so she'd know he hadn't planned to come alone. But he didn't say anything except what General Citizen knew — nothing about the jewels, or the knife Rigg had stolen from the past; nothing about Umbo's ability or the way it allowed Rigg to go back in time.

He also told her about the secret passages—the ones that the spies used, and the ones that hadn't been used in centuries. "I don't know if they are blocked or forgotten," he wrote to her. "I can see where entrances are . . ."—erase, write again—"but I don't know how to open them." Erase again. "When I'm out of sight for long, someone looks for me."

One morning, when he went to pull the slate from the place he had stashed it that night before he fell asleep in the garden, he found that it had been moved and someone had written on it in a tiny, barely legible scrawl—chalk was not designed to make letters so small.

"I am afraid brother. Mother is plotting. We will be killed."

Rigg clutched the slate, reread the message, and then erased it thoroughly. She must have come to him in the night while everyone was sleeping and allowed herself to enter realtime long enough to write the message.

Mother is plotting? So she wasn't the innocent she seemed to be. But how could she plot with anyone? Whom could she talk to without being observed?

More to the point, though, was Param's fear. We will be killed, she said. But did she mean that the Council would execute them after Mother's plots failed? Or that Mother's plotting included plans to have them killed? Mother might be willing to sacrifice Rigg, but he doubted she would actively seek Param's death. So the danger must be from someone else. Or perhaps Mother's plot included escaping from Flacommo's house in order to lead a rebellion, leaving him and Param behind for whatever retribution the Council decided on.

He needed to talk to Param all the more. He looked for her path and found it—but she had apparently moved away from him visibly last night, because she was far away by dawn, back in Mother's room.

That evening she was already waiting when he brought his slate out into the garden. "We must talk," he wrote. "I know ways out of this house . . . if we can get into the passages . . . one of them leads to the library . . . We can hide there to talk . . . very quick talks so no one notices we're gone."

Then he erased "we're" and replaced it with "I'm," since no one would know whether she was missing or not.

That night he tried not to sleep, hoping she would come again and he might see her. But sleep overcame his plans, and he woke with someone jostling his shoulder. As he stirred, a hand lightly touched his lips. He opened his eyes. It was a woman's shape, but he couldn't make out a face.

He got up silently and followed her. She moved unerringly, keeping to her habit of walking near the edge of each corridor and skirting around the borders of each room. She seemed to know the routines of the night quite perfectly—and why wouldn't she? They encountered no one.

Finally they were in a rarely used corridor that led to some guest rooms. She stopped, and Rigg approached her. "Param?" he whispered softly.

In reply, she embraced him and whispered in his ear, "O my brother, he said that you would come."

In that moment Rigg realized that Father must have come to her, as he had come to Umbo and Nox, and helped her learn to control and use her power. For who else could have promised her anything about Rigg? Who else knew that he existed? Yet had Father ever been gone from Fall Ford without Rigg long enough to come to Aressa Sessamo and return again? Rigg knew it would be foolish to think that anything was impossible to Father. In a world where Rigg, Umbo, Param, and Nox had such odd powers, who knew what Father was capable of?

"There's an entrance to the unused passages not far from here," he whispered back.

She gave him her hand, and he led her to the place. He could see old paths as they moved through what now seemed to be solid wall. As he had done before, he passed a hand all the way around the aperture, but couldn't find any sign of it.

She touched his shoulder and drew him away. "There's really a door there?" she whispered.

"There was. But not used in two hundred years."

"So the wall cannot be stone or cement or brick," she said.

"It's an interior wall. I assume that even if they sealed it up, it would still be lath-and-plaster or wood. But I don't know. Does it matter? It might be light enough that we could kick it in—but then we could never close it behind us."

In reply, she pushed him gently against the opposite wall of the corridor: *Stay*, the gesture meant. He watched as she quickly faded, then stood patiently waiting as she passed into the wall, her path echoing exactly the paths of the people who had once used this passage.

On the other side of the wall, he couldn't tell what she was doing. But after a while, he heard the faintest thud and then a ping, as if a long unused spring had been forced into service after the loosing of a latch. To his surprise, instead of a doorway opening in the wall, the whole section of wall between support posts rose up smoothly, revealing a passage behind it—with Param there waiting.

Rigg stepped through into the passage. Param worked a lever and the wall slid silently back down. No wonder Rigg hadn't been able to find a door. Just one of the limitations of his gift. He could tell where people had passed, but not what the place had looked like when they came through.

Rigg had expected the passage to be dark, but there was a faint silvery light. He made his way toward the seeming source of the light, wondering if there was some exterior vent that let in the ringlight.

It was soon clear that the light came from a mirror, which was reflecting light from another mirror—beyond that Rigg could not see how many other bends there might be. The light in this space *was* ringlight. On a cloudy night, this passage would require a candle—or such knowledge of it as would allow someone to pass through it in the dark.

"Did it hurt you?" he asked. "To go through the wall? Or door, or whatever it is?"

"Yes," she said. She held out a hand. He touched it and recoiled. She was hot, like a child with a bad fever. He touched her forehead, her cheek. Hot all over.

"You can't do that ever again," he said.

"I have to," she said. "I have no idea how to open it from the outside. But it's not that bad. I cool down soon enough. It's not like stone or brick — stone burns me, my clothing catches fire. I have to watch to make sure I never brush against stone when I'm hiding."

In reply he hugged her. "You have no idea what it meant to me, to know I had a sister."

"And to me," she said. "He told me never to tell Mother that I knew about you. But you were coming and you would set me free."

"I will," he said. "I know how to follow these passages to get through the outside wall."

"Under it?" she asked.

"The land these houses are built on was raised. It's not as high now, because the weight of the houses presses it down. So some of the passages may have water in them now — this is the river delta, and water is just below the surface everywhere. But as long as we can breathe, we can make it out of here. One long passage leads to the Library of Nothing."

"How can you know this? Have you gone into these passages before?"

"No," said Rigg. "But I've seen the paths of the people who've used them. I know where they went. That's what I do — I see their paths, even when they're hidden behind walls or underground."

"You have a much more useful gift than mine," she said.

"Mine didn't get me into this space. Mine doesn't allow me to disappear in plain day."

"Yours doesn't burn you up when you pass through things."

"I'm sorry I walked through you that time."

"It wasn't bad," she said. "We were both moving—it means we didn't occupy the same space for very long. Walls are stationary. I'm the only one moving, and the contact lasts a lot longer."

He held her hands tightly. "What did you call him? The man I knew as Father?"

"Walker," she said.

"So he was in this house?"

"Yes," she said. "I told Mother that one of the scholars had inadvertently helped me understand my gift. But really he came here as a gardener. The gardens still show his touch. Why didn't you know he was here? Couldn't you see his path?"

"Father—Walker—he doesn't make a path. He has no path."

"How could he manage that?"

"I don't know if he manages it or simply doesn't have one. He's a saint, I think. A hero. He has powers other people don't have."

"But when I was invisible, he couldn't see me, the way you can."

"I can't see you, I can only see where you *were*—the spot you passed through and left behind a moment before. And it isn't seeing, exactly. I can close my eyes or turn my back and still find your path."

"He said you were the best of us."

"Us?"

"All his students."

"So he told you about others?"

"He said the world has bent itself to make us. These powers run strong in this wallfold, he said. So everything depends on us."

"What everything?" asked Rigg. "Restoring the monarchy? I don't really care about that."

"Neither do I," she said. "Neither did he."

"He told you so much," said Rigg. "He told me nothing."

"Are you jealous?"

"Yes," he said. "And angry. Why didn't he trust me?"

"He trusted you most of all, he told me that. He said you were the most ready. His best student."

"I can't do anything myself. I can see paths, yes, but I can't *do* anything without Umbo—he's the one who actually lets me move back in time. The way you got me in here. I can't do anything myself."

"You knew where this passage was."

Rigg realized they were wasting time on reassurances that his own gift had value. "We don't have very long. Someone's going to notice we're gone."

"Probably *not*," she said. "It's the middle of the night."

"You'd be surprised how closely they watch."

"You forget that I've walked these rooms and halls for years now," she said.

"Turning and turning," he said.

"What?"

"You can't hold still or you reappear. So you walk in small circles when you want to stay in a room without being visible. Your whole path is full of curlicues."

"Yes," she said. "Around and around. I'm so sick of it."

"So why not reappear?"

"Because they'll kill me," she said.

"I thought it was just—they said it was a man who—took your clothes."

"I was putting up with nonsense like that my whole life. No, this was a man with a knife. I didn't have time to do anything but rush toward him—I call it 'rushing'—and then pass through him. He didn't know where I'd gone. Back then I hardly ever did it—rushing, I mean—and they might not have known I could do it. Now they know, though. Mother told me about the spies. They know everything."

"They know only what they see and hear," said Rigg.

"I can't hear anything when I rush," she said. "You were so clever to—the slate, I mean. Even Mother never thought of writing me messages and holding them really still."

"We have to go. But first—can you see any mechanism here that seems to lead outside the room? Any connection to some trigger that might open the door from the outside?"

They both examined the walls of the passage, but there was nothing. The lever that opened it from this side was rooted in the wall, and everything else was hidden.

"I can go into the wall if you want," she said, "but it's pitch black in there. I won't see anything and I certainly can't feel anything. Except the heat and the thickness of it."

"No, no, I don't want you to do that. But . . . I'm such a fool . . . somebody had to *build* these passages, right? Somebody built the mechanism. If I go back to the beginning, I can find his path. Their paths. I can see where *they* went when they were hooking everything together."

"You mean the paths don't fade?"

"Not really," said Rigg. "They get fainter, sort of, but it's more like they get *farther*—but it's not actually distance—they're still there. They never go away or move. Shhh. Let me concentrate."

It took five minutes for him to find the right time. Long ago there had been another building here, and as he struggled to find exactly the right path, Rigg realized that they must have built this portion of Flacommo's house while the old house was still standing. To hide what they were doing from view.

Once he had the right paths, the answer was clear. "The trigger is in the ceiling of the corridor," he said. "Too high up for us to reach, even if we jump. But if we had a broom, or a sword, or . . . anything with a handle . . . he worked in spots right at the corners of the wall panel. Maybe you have to push both. Or maybe one opens it and the other closes it."

"Let's go out and see," she said.

Rigg reached for the lever.

"Wait!" she said. "What if somebody's out there?"

"I'd know it if they were," said Rigg. "There's nobody."

"When we go out, we can't talk any more."

"But there's always tomorrow. And the next day."

"Rigg," she said, and hugged him again. "You know I've gotten younger, waiting for you," she said.

"Younger?"

"When I rush, the rest of the world flies by. When I'm going really fast, whole days can pass in what seems like a few minutes to me. Most of the time I don't rush so hard, but—"

"How do you know how much time has passed for you?" asked Rigg. "How do you measure time when you're rushing?"

"Let's just say . . . it's a pretty accurate method. I know how many days have passed in the regular world, and I can—I measure *my* time by the month. Do you understand? I know when a month has passed for me. And since I went into seclusion, it's only been two months for me. Everybody else has aged more than a year. But two months for me. So they think I'm sixteen now, but my body has barely lived through fifteen years. At this rate I'll live forever—only I'll have no life at all."

She was crying. Not like a child, face bunched up and whining noises, but like a woman, silently, her shoulders heaving as he held her. "Param, we'll get you out of here."

"Getting out of this house isn't enough. They'll hunt us down in the city, in the library, wherever we go."

"Umbo and Loaf will come," said Rigg. "We'll find a way. You'll get your life back. We both will."

"You're my little brother," she said. "I'm supposed to be the one making promises to *you*."

"I know," said Rigg. "You can tell me bedtime stories when we're out of here. But we've got to go now, while there's still time to figure out how to close the door from the other side."

In the end, they didn't look for a broom or anything else. Rigg just cupped his hands and boosted her up. With Param leaning against the wall while stepping onto his shoulder, she could reach the corner. Naturally, they tried the wrong spot first. Nothing happened and Rigg was ready to despair until she pointed out that they were probably pressing the spot that opened it. Sure enough, when she pressed hard in the other corner—and he knew just how hard, since her feet pressed downward into his shoulders—the wall slid silently back into place. There was no sign that it was any different from the other walls.

When she was back down on the floor, she kissed him on the cheek and then she was gone.

In the whole time he had barely caught a glimpse of her face. The silvery mirrored light in the secret passage, the flickering candlelight in the corridor—Rigg wasn't sure he'd even recognize her if he saw her in broad daylight.

But she was real and alive and he had finally done what Father told him to do—he had found his sister. And she was expecting him. Father had said that he would set her free.

Father trusted me.

She trusts me now.

I'd better not let her down.

CHAPTER 18

Digging in the Past

"We have nineteen starships," said Ram. "And only one world."

"That gives us nineteen times the chance of success," said the expendable.

"Nineteen times the likelihood of terrible confusion between colonies that have exactly the same personnel," said Ram. "Nineteen times the likelihood of deadly rivalries, adulteries, even murders. Constant comparison between the lives of persons bearing the same names, DNA, even fingerprints. And in the end, our nineteen ships will still end up populating only one world."

"We have no likely target worlds for the remaining ships," said the expendable. "And we have only the one captain."

"One of the best things about settling the human race on a new planet is that a disaster that strikes one human world won't affect the other, so the species can't be extinguished by a single event."

"Except the explosion of the galactic core," said the expendable helpfully.

"Yes, there is that chance, but there's not much we can do about that."

"Yet," said the expendable.

"Meanwhile," said Ram, "I think there's another benefit we might enhance a little. The plan was always for the human race to exist on two planets. What no one planned was for our colony to be separated by more than eleven thousand years in time from the starfaring culture we came from. There is no chance of interbreeding between Earth and this world. It's a true Galapagos opportunity to see where genetic drift takes the two versions of the human race in complete isolation for more than four hundred generations."

"Technically, only *this* world will have 447 generations, using the average of twenty-five years," said the expendable. "Earth will have had no time elapse at all."

"So we will drift genetically, and they will not," said Ram. "We will evolve and they will not."

"Eleven thousand years is not really very long, in terms of evolution," said the expendable. "Human populations that were separated for seventy thousand years during the great drought in Africa remained capable of interbreeding."

"The separation probably wasn't complete," said Ram. "If you're talking about the genetic bottleneck after the explosion of Mount Toba, it only lasted twenty thousand years. And the southern African group was known to be a seafaring one, since they colonized all around the Indian Ocean, including Australia and New Guinea."

"I used the longer timespan to make my point clear," said the expendable, "but even your shorter genetic bottleneck was twice as long as the isolation of this colony is going to last."

"And at the end of it, modern humans were far different. Longer-legged, lighter in weight. Endurance runners who could chase prey until it collapsed from oxygen depletion. Spear throwers and expert blade makers. Storytellers who could use language to create a map that others could follow through strange lands to find water. Creative thinkers who could learn from others and then innovate and adapt, and then spread the cultural innovations across hundreds of miles in a single generation."

"You seem to have made a detailed study of this," said the expendable.

"After your question about the human species, of course I did," said Ram. "Ten thousand years is plenty of time for real change in the human species, because this time the isolation will be complete."

"But you have a question for us, dealing with nineteen starships and one world," said the expendable.

"What if we could establish nineteen colonies, each knowing nothing about the others? They would never encounter their genetic doubles. There would be no rivalry. One would not triumph over all the others. These nineteen colonies, plus Earth, would divide the human race into twenty parts. Potentially, our species could explore twenty different paths of development, genetically, culturally, intellectually. All of human history, all the wars and empires and technology and languages and customs and religions, they all evolved in less time than we'll have here. There is enough land mass to create nineteen enclaves larger than Europe, larger than the land from

415

Egypt to Persia, larger than the Americas from the Aztecs down to the Incas."

"No doubt the humans in every enclave will oblige you by becoming Egypt or Athens or Tenochtitlan."

"I hope not Tenochtitlan," said Ram. "I'd like to think we'd retain some of the progress we already made back on Earth, and leave human sacrifice behind."

"But you'd keep the pyramids?"

"Or whatever monuments they build. And if they not only create new things, but also *become* a new, but still human, species, so much the better, as long as they don't try to destroy any of the others."

"Your optimism and ambition prove that you are truly human, especially because you ignore the strong likelihood that all the enclaves will end up like isolated mountain valleys, where primitive people who once roamed the oceans in boats filled with pigs and babies ended up living naked in mud huts and cannibalizing each other."

Ram shrugged. "I won't be there to see it."

"Like a salmon, you spawn and die, letting the younglings hatch and thrive—or not—as chance dictates."

"Not chance—their own strength and wit. Chance affects the lives of individuals, yes, but the human species makes its own chances."

"We are in awe of your noble vision, while taking due note of the fuzziness of your 'creative' thinking, as opposed to the clarity of autistic and animal brains. Yet you have a problem whose solution your wonderfully fuzzy creative mind cannot solve."

"Fuzzy creative human minds built you and the ships' computers," said Ram, "in order to solve such problems for us."

"You want us to find a way to keep the colonies completely

isolated from each other—to such a degree that they don't know of each other's existence."

"You guessed it! And you say you aren't creative!"

"We did not *guess* anything. We *deduced* it from the plethora of data you provided us, both consciously and unconsciously."

"And yet you couldn't detect the irony in my enthusiasm."

"We detected it. As information, however, it was worthless."

•   •   •

Loaf was a tired old man. He might still look strong to others, and act vigorous enough, but that was the problem: It was all an act. Things needed to be done, and he did them, but if he had been left alone, if he had had no responsibilities, he would have been content to sit in a rocking chair, close his eyes, and dream. Not the dreams of sleep, but the dreams of memory.

The trouble was that half those memories were unpleasant. Not so much the memories of killing, though Loaf had known his share of battles; in the frenzy of war, it was invigorating to slice and probe and hack and slay, especially considering that if he did not keep his attention fully engaged, he himself would have been sliced, probed, hacked, and slain. Rather his unpleasant memories were of the words he wished he hadn't said, or the clever things he didn't say because he only thought of them later.

The quarrels he could have avoided; the quarrels that would have been worth starting if only he had thought of the witty insults that would have brought him the pleasure of a well-earned split knuckle or sliced lip.

He could put up with the memories of missed opportunity

and other regrets, for there were other memories—childhood friends and enemies, all remembered now with fondness. The dire fears of youth that now he knew were not to be feared at all. The childish longings that, fulfilled or not, he now wished he could feel again.

His life with Leaky was a good one, and he was not going to disappear from her life, which is what it would amount to, if he were to sit in that chair and dream. They had an inn to run, and it was a thing worth doing—the rivermen, scoundrels though so many of them were, needed a safe haven at this spot on the river, and this town needed somebody to keep the fire of ambition sparking and snapping here in this little strip between the water and the woods. He kept hoping someone else would come along with the spunk to make things happen, but there were no others besides himself and Leaky.

And Leaky was really the one with the spunk; Loaf merely acted as if he cared as much about things as she, because it made her happy when she believed he shared her feelings.

So in a way it had been a relief to join the boys on their down-river trip, and get away from the duties of Leaky's Landing. She would manage splendidly while he was gone, Loaf knew that. And these boys, with their magic and their mirthful talk. *They* were ambitious, or at least Rigg was. Determined to fulfil his duty to his dead father, or so Rigg said—but Loaf saw in Rigg what he had seen in a few of the commanders he had served under: the fire of hope. Rigg wanted to do something that mattered. He wanted to change the world, and because he was a good lad, he wanted to change it for the better.

Umbo was more like Loaf—content to follow along, to let Rigg set forth the goals that they'd pursue. Not that Umbo was above grumbling when he didn't like the duties that Rigg's ambition imposed on him. Good soldiers grumbled all the time—but they followed the plans laid out for them all the same.

But when Rigg was taken captive, and Loaf and Umbo fled the boat and went back upriver, Loaf began what might have been the happiest time of his life. Oh, he felt bad that Rigg was arrested and when he thought about what might be happening to him, he worried. But mostly he just lived day to day with Umbo, like a soldier on the march, teaching the boy what he needed to learn, watching as Umbo struggled to do things that Loaf couldn't imagine doing. Umbo was consumed with his need to learn how to save his friend by traveling backward in time, but since Loaf knew that it was beyond him, he was free to watch, to encourage, to protect, and, as near as Loaf could understand the feeling, to love him the way a father might love a son.

Back home in Leaky's Landing, his old duties descended on him, but he bore them lightly, knowing that he would have to leave again, as soon as Umbo figured things out. Leaky noticed it, too, saying to him one time, "It's like you're not even here, you lazy man." Little did she know how the rocking chair called to him even in the best of times, and how gladly he'd slip off into dreams—even into dreams of Leaky herself, so much easier to abide than the demanding woman that he loved but who wearied him out with all the chores that she imposed.

She did impose them, even when he thought of them himself

and didn't wait to be asked. He always did them because of her, even if she didn't know it.

Hurry up, Umbo, he wanted to say. Let's get back on the river, drift down to O, then on to Aressa Sessamo or the edges of the wallfold, wherever Rigg decides that you must go. I'll help you do your work for your friend.

So Loaf was happy on the late afternoon when Umbo came to him in a vision—a waking vision, suddenly standing in front of him where Loaf stood chopping wood behind the inn—and said, "Stop chopping now and go inside so you can keep Leaky from having to kill a mad drunk. And if it happens in the next five minutes, then I'll be ready to go back to O."

Loaf took the ax over his shoulder, walked into the inn, and sure enough, there was a riverman who must have drunk a jug of something stronger than ale before he arrived, and now was threatening Leaky with his heavy staff if she didn't serve him "the real drink and not that lily-water that rich men dip their fingers in." The man slammed the staff onto the counter with all his strength—and no one had more strength with a quarterstaff than a poleman.

Leaky was going for the throwing knife she used to protect herself against men too strong to allow them to come within reach of her. Loaf well knew that the riverman was ten seconds away from lying dead on the floor with a knife in his eye. So without even thinking, Loaf brought down the ax onto the quarterstaff where it lay, careful not to use so much force that he'd damage the oaken counter, but plenty to break the staff in two.

Horrified at this outrage to his drunken dignity, let alone the damage to his staff, the riverman roared and turned to face Loaf, brandishing the nub of his staff with the broken end ready to jab into the innkeeper's face. Loaf kicked him in the knee with his heavy boot, again being careful only to bruise the joint, not ruin him by breaking it, for such an injury would be slow to heal and the riverman would run out of money long before he was able to get back on a boat and work again. His offense was being an angry drunk; no doubt he was affable enough when the drink wasn't in him.

The riverman lay on the floor yowling with pain. Loaf looked around for the man's compatriots, and they soon came forward to drag the man out of the inn. "You didn't need to kick him so hard," one of them said to Loaf. "He meant no harm."

"I saved his life," said Loaf, "and the knee's not broke."

"Spraint though, most like," said the sullen man.

"Keep your friend drinking ale and he'll come to no grief. The strong spirits are too much for him, and you know it."

"He wouldn't've hurt nobody."

"My wife had no way of knowing that," said Loaf, "even if it were true, which it isn't, because I think this man has killed before."

"Only by accident," said the man.

He said this just as he was maneuvering his friend through the door, and suddenly there was a thunk and Leaky's throwing knife quivered in the doorjamb not three inches from his head. The man jumped away from the knife, which meant knocking down the drunk and the man trying to hold him up on the other side. They lay in a jumble on the floor, like eels, and all the other men in the river house laughed as if it were the funniest thing they'd ever seen, which, apart from a drowning landlubber, it probably was.

The noise brought Umbo in from the kitchen, where he'd been washing glasses and bowls. "Why didn't you call for me?" he asked Leaky.

"If I'd needed to throw something as big as you, I'd have called sure enough," said Leaky. "There's not a thing you could have *done*."

The drunk and his friends were up and out the door now, and Loaf roared with laughter as Leaky planted her foot in the drunk's rear and sent him, and his friends, sprawling in the damp dirt outside.

With the door closed, and the rest of the guests turned back to their food and drink, Loaf pulled Leaky's knife out of the doorframe and gathered Leaky and Umbo behind the bar. "There *was* something Umbo could do," said Loaf. "And he did it. Why do you think I came in here? He warned me that you were about to kill a mad drunk, my love, and sent me inside with my ax in hand."

Umbo grinned. "Did I? Or . . . will I?"

"I don't know how long you waited to go back in time to give the warning, my lad, but you told me that if it happened within five minutes, you were ready to go back to O."

"Well, I hope you didn't decide to give that message for another month, because there's too much work to do around here for me to have you gone right now," said Leaky.

"We don't have to wait for him to send the message," said Loaf. "He already sent it."

"That's the craziest thing you ever said. He doesn't *remember* sending it, do you, boy?"

Umbo laughed in delight.

"Are you laughing at me?" asked Leaky.

"He's laughing because it makes no sense and that's half the fun," said Loaf. "You killed that man, and then felt so bad about it—you know you always do, being no soldier—that Umbo went back to warn me so he could stop you. But now you *didn't* kill him, so there's no reason for us to wait a moment longer."

"But he hasn't given the warning!" insisted Leaky.

"There's no longer a warning to give," said Loaf. "The man's not killed after all."

"But if you don't send the warning . . ." Leaky began.

"My warning changed things," said Umbo. "When you killed the man, then there was a warning to give. I gave it, things changed, and now there's no warning needed."

"But you didn't do it! Not yet!"

"He already did it," said Loaf. "Just now."

Leaky looked like she was ready to scream with frustration.

"Lass, it makes no sense to me, either, but that's just the way it works," said Loaf. "He warns me in the past, which changes things so the warning is no longer needed. The thing is *done.*"

"Then why do you have to go back to O to steal a jewel that Umbo already stole?"

"Because I don't have the jewel yet," said Umbo, as if it were the most obvious thing in the world. "I've still got to steal it in order to have it."

Leaky lowered her head and shook it like a wet dog. "I hate

you both, you drive me mad." Then she headed back into the kitchen.

"So when do we leave?" asked Umbo.

"If we leave right now," said Loaf, "we have to pack our own food, and everything a day old. If we wait till tomorrow, she'll bake again."

"It's nearly dark anyway," said Umbo.

From the kitchen they could hear Leaky's voice. "This is my warning from the future! There'll be no bread for you tomorrow or any other day!"

"Tonight it is," said Loaf.

It took only a few minutes before Loaf had arranged passage for them on a raft of logs heading down to a lumber mill upstream of O. Then they both packed—knapsacks only for each of them, since they were going to travel light, and needed to look poor enough to be not worth robbing, but rich enough to be allowed into inns.

Leaky came out and threw a head of lettuce at them as they left. "It's a sign of love," Loaf explained to Umbo.

Loaf and Umbo had paid for passage, living on one of the small floored areas scattered about the reef of logs, so they weren't required to help with anything. But they both manned poles from time to time, for every pair of hands would help in the difficult task of keeping so large a flow of logs from turning and clogging the channel. And why not? Loaf had strength and mass to him, and Umbo was nimble on the logs and could get quickly to where he was needed. Besides, he was growing—and growing stronger to go with his height. Straining at a pole in the river against the mass of so many logs could only add bulk to the boy, which he sorely needed.

Instead of booking another passage when the reef of logs came at last to the mill, Loaf and Umbo decided to walk the last thirty miles to O. It meant one night paying to sleep in a farmer's shed, and rising with the stink of goats on them and their clothing, but the breakfast was large and good, and arriving in O by land, looking privick and smelling of barnyard animals, would keep them from being recognized by any who had known them before.

Umbo was excited to return to O—to him it was a magical place where marvelous things had happened. But to Loaf, who had been there more than once, and most other places also, it was just another errand on the way. They passed right through the city late in the morning and took a room in a humble boardinghouse well off the main road—just what a frugal traveler would do. The young widow who kept the house was glad to have them, since a mature man traveling with his son (as she thought) was less likely to assume he had privileges with her.

They were tired enough from all their walking that they decided the next morning would be soon enough to go dig up the jewel. Instead they asked the landlady where they might find a bathhouse, and ended up paying their fee to her for hot water in a decent-sized tub, and soap, and a surprisingly good towel. They didn't mind sharing the bed—it was big enough for both, and they smelled better than usual. Umbo slept like a brick and woke in the morning ready for a good brisk walk.

The landlady packed them a lunch to take with them to the Tower of O, their announced destination. The line at the tower was long—the spring weather had brought many tourists and pilgrims to the site. So it was perfectly normal for the man and his son to take their lunch around behind the latrine building. They lingered there near the hiding place of the jewels until there were no others near them. Then Umbo stood up, stretched, and knelt at the spot where they knew the jewels had lain.

Umbo cheerfully dug in the soil, exposing . . . nothing.

"What was that for?" asked Loaf. "You know we already took the jewels. It's only in the past that they'll be there."

"I just wanted to be sure," said Umbo. "In fact, I'd like to see the jewels right now."

"I'm not getting them out to display them where somebody might come bounding around back here and see them and take it into their minds that an emperor's fortune might just be worth killing us over."

"But I want to see something."

"See whatever you want, but I'm not getting out the jewels."

"I was thinking," said Umbo.

"Like climbing a cliff, thinking is a perilous activity for those unused to it."

"What if I take *two* jewels instead of just the one?"

"Then I would have been carrying around sixteen instead of seventeen."

"That's why I want to see them, right here beside us. If I take out two jewels, fully intending to keep them both, will one jewel disappear from the bag?"

"You're provoking me on purpose," said Loaf.

"Or would we end up with two jewels? Could we take them all, and have duplicates of all but the one?"

"Or would you provoke the wrath of the universe and cause the sun to explode?"

"That's not very likely."

"Nothing you do is likely, boy. Now go back in time like a good little saint and steal the jewel that we wouldn't have to take if you weren't the spawn of a devil."

"Your assessment of my father is right enough, sir," said Umbo, imitating Rigg's high manner of speaking, "though if you referred to my mother I'd have to kill you."

"Get the jewel," said Loaf. Then he closed his eyes to wait.

"Aren't you going to watch?" asked Umbo.

"I don't want to see you reach into an invisible hole and make a jewel magically appear in your hand. It's too disturbing."

"And I'm saying, watch. You don't want to miss this."

"Don't tell me what I want," said Loaf, getting testy. He didn't like people telling him what to do. Especially a mere child. Though Umbo was a good deal smarter than some of the clowns whose orders Loaf had obeyed when he was in the army.

"Then I'll put it another way. *I* don't want you to miss this, because I'm trying something important. I'm going to try to bring you with me."

"I have no such talent," said Loaf. "So just do it."

"Hold my hand," said Umbo. "And keep your eyes open."

Loaf closed his eyes.

Umbo took his hand anyway.

"Open your eyes," he said.

"No," said Loaf. He wanted to use the time to get lost in a dream.

"Please," said Umbo. "Don't be stubborn. Do it for me."

Loaf sighed and opened his eyes.

The woods around them were vivid with autumn colors, and a rain as light as mist was falling. Now he could feel it on his face.

"By Silbom's right ear," said Loaf.

"Now I'm going to let go of your hand," said Umbo, "and try to keep you here with me."

He let go.

"Still see the autumn leaves?" asked Umbo.

"Yes," said Loaf. "But I don't see you!"

Umbo looked shocked. "I'm invisible?"

"I can still see your clothes, but they're empty!"

"Liar," said Umbo. "You'd be a lot more upset than that if I had disappeared."

"You'd like to think so," said Loaf. "Dig it up and take the jewel, you little thief."

Umbo dug with his hands. "How far down did you bury it?"

"Not as deep as that."

"Then . . . did I make a mistake? Did I take us back *before* you buried them?"

"Maybe. Or maybe it's because you're digging in the wrong spot," said Loaf.

"I saw where you dug to get to them!"

"But you were watching from over there, and a long way, too.

You didn't miss by much. Back from there about a pace. But first fill in that hole and hide it."

"Why? There's nothing in it."

"Because you don't want to put it into somebody's mind that something was buried here—not this near to the real hiding place. Remember, we're leaving seventeen jewels hidden here and we won't be back to claim them for a while yet."

"Why don't *you* fill up the hole?" said Umbo. "You're the one who knows how to hide things."

So Loaf refilled the first hole and scattered a handful of tiny pebbles and short twigs across it until it looked just like the surrounding dirt. Meanwhile, Umbo had found the real hiding place and had the bag opened to show all eighteen jewels.

"I can't remember now which one is missing," said Umbo.

"Don't play games," said Loaf. "Somebody could come along at any moment—in *either* time."

"I'm not joking," said Umbo. "You have to open up the jewels we already have and see which of these is the missing one."

"You're doing this on purpose because you want to do your experiment," said Loaf.

"Who's wasting time now?" asked Umbo.

Loaf sighed, drew the bag of jewels up out of his trouser leg, and opened them. "I can't tell you which one is missing, I can only tell you which ones are here."

"So lay them down beside the others."

"No," said Loaf.

"Then you do it—you look back and forth."

Loaf reluctantly did as Umbo asked, looking back and forth.

It bothered him deeply to be seeing duplicates of these one-of-a-kind gems. But he finally identified the missing jewel. He pointed. "That one."

"So take it," said Umbo.

Loaf felt very strange as he reached out and picked up the jewel and put it from one bag into the other.

"Now take another," said Umbo. "Please, let's see what happens!"

"No," said Loaf.

"What can it hurt? Either the stone will disappear from the new bag or it won't."

"Umbo," said Loaf, "I don't know what it can hurt. But I also don't know that it *can't* hurt, and there's too much at stake to play around. We have to get to Aressa Sessamo to help Rigg, if we can."

Umbo sighed petulantly and retied the old bag—he had never seemed so young in all the time Loaf had known him. "Fill up the hole," said Loaf as he counted all eighteen jewels, together again at last, retied the new bag, and dropped it back down into his trousers.

Then he disguised the real hiding place as he had disguised Umbo's previous mistaken one.

"Done," he said. "Now take us back into the present."

"We never left it," said Umbo. "We were perfectly visible in both times."

"I mean make the past go away."

And just like that, the bright-colored leaves of the autumn woods turned back into branches newly a-bud with spring.

"All right," said Umbo. "We're done. Let's get to Aressa Sessamo."

"No," said Loaf. "You have to go leave your messages in the past for Rigg and you to see."

"Of course I don't," said Umbo. "No more than I had to actually go back in time and tell you to stop Leaky from killing that drunk."

Loaf sat down on a low stone wall and leaned his forehead on his fingers. "I know I sound like Leaky, but Umbo, we have to do it."

"I don't even remember what I said to myself," said Umbo. "I never knew what I said to Rigg."

"Whatever you say now will be what you said then."

"No," said Umbo. "Because now I'll be saying it without any sense of urgency. It's going to be different. Look, I already said it. The proof of that is the fact that the jewels were buried behind the latrine, because that's what my message to Rigg told him to do. And we have the knife, because I told myself to get it and hide it. We live in the version of these events in which my messages were already given!"

"Then why did we have to wait in Leaky's Landing until you learned how to go back in time?"

"Because we had to get the jewel! And because it's a useful thing for me to know how to do. It would be stupid to just know that I had learned how to do it in order to deliver those messages, and then *not* learn how to do it just because those messages were already delivered!"

Loaf shook his head. "I know I was on your side when we

argued with Leaky about it," he said. "But now . . . too much is at stake."

"That's right," said Umbo. "Too much is at stake for us to go to all the trouble of talking our way back into the very rooms we stayed in before so I can stand at the foot of my bed and deliver a message to myself while I'm sleeping there. Or for us to go stand where Rigg was paying the coachman so I can give him a message he *already* received. It's dangerous to do either of those things — we might be recognized at the foot of the tower, and we would certainly be recognized at our rented lodging! For all we know, the city guard would be called and we'd be arrested and then we couldn't possibly go to Aressa Sessamo to help Rigg!"

"We know we weren't arrested because . . . because we weren't!"

"But we don't know anything of the kind," said Umbo. "And remember — *this* time if we get arrested we have the . . . stones."

He had caught himself and said "stones" instead of "jewels" because of the warning look Loaf gave him. Somebody had come around the corner of the latrine.

Soldiers. Two of them. Sauntering — seemingly not on any urgent business. But why would they be back here? Had somebody seen them digging while they were watching the past instead of the present? It had been foolish for Umbo to bring him into the past; he should have stayed in the present in order to keep watch.

"Let's get out of here," said Loaf.

"Which way?" asked Umbo.

"Back to the boardinghouse," said Loaf.

"Why? What's there that we need?"

"A change of clothes," said Loaf. "And food from the widow."

"But if those soldiers are after us . . ."

"Then we'll have an easier time getting away from them in the crowds. If we see them and take off into the woods, they'll know we're fugitives and they'll chase us." Umbo looked doubtful, but Loaf reached out and took his hand forcibly, like a brutal father; he made his face into a mask of rage.

Umbo looked genuinely frightened.

"Do what I tell you, *when* I tell you. Understand me?" Loaf made himself sound savagely angry, and Umbo shrank away.

"That's right," said a soldier. "Take a stick to him."

"You've got to beat the brains into them when they're still young," said the other soldier, and then laughed.

"Really," said Loaf to the soldiers, his voice dripping with sarcasm. "Did your fathers beat brains into *you*?"

"Every cursed day," said one of them, as the other nodded.

"Then you're living proof that it doesn't work," said Loaf. "My son is *my* business, not yours."

The soldiers looked angry, and might have taken matters further—after all, they had authority and Loaf was flouting it—but Loaf got into a stance of readiness, pushing Umbo behind him. "I fought in three border wars, you young clowns, and you're nothing but city soldiers. All you've ever fought are drunks and fools, not a man who's killed his dozens in open combat. I'll knock your heads together so hard you'll see out of each other's eyes for a week. Come on, let's have at it."

One of them was willing enough, but the smarter one drew him back. "They're breaking no law back here," he said, "and we don't need to spend the afternoon dragging him to the jail and making our reports."

"Won't have to make reports if he's dead," said the dumb one.

"If we kill every man who calls us stupid," said the smarter one, "we'll only be proving them right."

The soldiers drew off and then watched as Loaf led Umbo past them. Loaf nodded respectfully at the smarter soldier. "It's a good soldier that doesn't take on a fight that isn't forced on him," he said.

The smarter one nodded back, while the stupid one glared sullenly.

Back among the crowds, Umbo said, "Don't ever take hold of me like that again."

"I was giving them a reason for us to be behind the latrine, since lunch was long since over."

"I left my father for treating me that way."

"Leave me, too, if you like," said Loaf.

"I will, if you ever do that again."

"Does it help you to forgive me if I point out that I'm giving in to you on the matter of giving those messages?"

"I wasn't going to do it no matter what you said," Umbo replied.

"Oh, the boy's pouting. Just like that soldier, the stupid one who thought his pride was worth dying for."

"I *am* a boy!" said Umbo. "I have a right to act childish if I want to!"

"Well, lad, you usually don't, so you can forgive me for expecting you to have a man's understanding."

"I wish Leaky had hit you in the head with that cabbage," said Umbo. But he was clearly backing down from his wrath, if he was making jokes, however bitter he might sound.

"It was a lettuce, you dumb privick," said Loaf. "And if she'd been aiming at my head, she would have hit me."

They ate a decent meal at their favorite rice-and-egg stand downtown—there was little chance of anyone recognizing them, dressed as they were now, instead of the finery they wore when they were here with Rigg. It was late in the morning as they left the city again.

They were talking about nothing much as they walked along the main road, when Loaf said, "Look at them—taking the same turning we're going to take."

It was a man and a boy, and they looked footsore and dirty from the road. "I hope they can afford a bath like we got."

"Stupid boy, Umbo. They're going to get exactly the bath we got."

It was only then that Umbo realized that the man and boy ahead of them were Loaf and himself.

But that was impossible. How could they still be in the past, yet only a single day instead of the months that Umbo had gone back to get the jewel?

"What game are you playing here?" asked Loaf.

"No game," said Umbo. "I don't understand it. We should have come right back to the very moment. When we go back in time, we don't leave the present."

"And how do you know that?" asked Loaf.

"Because whenever Rigg went back —"

"You were sitting there watching."

"That's right," said Umbo.

"Well, who was sitting there watching when *we* went back for the jewel this morning?"

"We made sure nobody was!" said Umbo.

"We went back together, and we dug in the soil and picked up something. We weren't just talking, we weren't just telling stuff. We physically picked something up and took it."

"I know that," said Umbo. "But it didn't make any difference when Rigg took the knife."

"Because you weren't with him. You were still in the present, *sending* him back. He returned *to you*."

"Well, who am I returning to when I go back and talk to myself in the past?"

"When you just go back to talk, I think you stay in the present," said Loaf. "But going back and doing something — I think that takes you all the way back. So when you return to the present, you're really jumping forward in time again. And because you didn't know that's what you were doing, you weren't careful. You weren't *accurate*. And besides, maybe you can't go forward to a time you haven't lived through. You just went forward to a point fairly close to the last future time, the one you went back from."

"I hate trying to talk about this stuff, it just makes me more confused."

"No it doesn't," said Loaf. "You're just too lazy to think."

"I didn't even pick a time, I just sort of let go. Just like always."

"Well, 'letting go' must be identical to going into the future you came from. Within a day or so."

"Back, forward, we go 'back' to the past and then 'back' to the place in the 'future' we left from in the 'past.' We need better words."

"We need a place to spend the night," said Loaf.

"But I'm ready to go on—we've got to get to Rigg now that we have the jewel I took. Or if we can't get to him, at least we can get back the jewel he sold to Mr. Cooper."

"Get it back?" said Loaf. "You mean steal it?"

"Did he get to keep the money?"

"Some of it—what do you think we've been spending?"

"And who bought it anyway? I don't think anybody bought it, I think the Revolutionary Council pretended to buy it and then took back all the money."

"And so you're going to go ask for it back?"

"No," said Umbo. "We're going to find out where it is, go to that place, then go back into the past to the point when they're putting it there, and snatch it away and then just vanish."

"Vanish? You can do that now?"

"It's how it'll look to them!"

"But if they saw you steal it, then they'll remember that when we show up to try to get to the spot where they're keeping the jewel, and they'll arrest us."

"They won't remember us because when we go there we won't yet have gone back to grab it."

Loaf pretended to pound his head into the palm of his hand. "You don't know how this thing works. If you did, you wouldn't have got us back here before we even arrived."

"Why do we have to spend the night here?" asked Umbo.

"We don't," said Loaf. "We can just leave our stuff. It's not much—just food and a change of clothes and my razor—something you'll never need, I think, unless you want to slit your throat in the future and then come back and warn yourself not to do it."

"And our blankets," said Umbo. "I suppose we might as well wait here another day. Unless we go steal our own stuff while we're taking a bath."

"And then hope we don't notice it? Is that your plan? Because if somebody had stolen our stuff last night we would have noticed."

"But we didn't!"

"Because we didn't come in and steal our stuff while we were bathing. Umbo! Think!"

Umbo did try to think it through, but as far as he could tell it might go either way. It was hard to get a grasp on the rules of this time traveling thing.

They ended up sleeping in a much more expensive place closer in to the city. The room was smaller, the bed was smaller, the fleas were more numerous, and the food was worse. The next morning they returned to the boardinghouse only an hour after they left. The landlady was incredulous.

"The lines were too long," said Loaf.

"But you came all this way! And where's your lunch?"

"We ate it," said Umbo.

"But you just ate a huge breakfast. Huge!"

It had been huge. And delicious.

"We have to go on to Aressa Sessamo," said Loaf. "We don't have a day to waste in line just to see the inside of a big building."

Umbo smiled his sweetest smile. "Would you fix us another lunch? For us to eat for supper on the road?"

"You'll just eat it the minute you get out of here," she said.

"Maybe," said Loaf, "but we'll pay for it, too."

She agreed, but huffed her whole way through making it, and as they left her house they could hear her muttering—because she meant them to hear—"greedy, gluttonous people eat everything and save nothing for the future."

Don't tell us about the future, ma'am, thought Umbo. If we're in the future and want something we don't have, we can just go back into the past and get it. Of course, then we can't get all the way back to the present, so we'll have to do everything twice.

CHAPTER 19

Aressa Sessamo

"We have a plan for dividing the new world—which you still have not named—into nineteen cells," said the expendable.

Ram looked at the holographic globe, rotated it several times, and said, "So you exclude the three smaller continents."

"We thought those could remain as preserves for the original biota of this unnamed planet."

"Call the planet 'Garden,' since you want a name. Though who'll ever use it but us, I have no idea."

"The colonists will say 'back on Earth' and 'here on Garden,'" said the expendable. "You may be interested to know that not one of the expendables or the ships' computers predicted your choice of 'Garden.' The front-runner was 'Ram,' but some of us thought you were too modest for that."

"It's not a matter of modesty. I intend to live with these people—or at least one ship's worth of them—and it would lead to ridicule and loss of face for me to try to make them call the world by my name."

"That was my reasoning. But I now have the advantage of continued association with you, which the others lack."

"I never imagined the expendables were given to wagering."

"There are no stakes. It's merely a matter of testing our predictive algorithms."

"The divisions of the two larger continents look fine to me. I assume they all contain adequate resources."

"Adequate for what?"

"For . . . human life."

"Breathable air, potable water, arable soil, and survivable weather seemed to us to be all that was needed."

"I was thinking of iron, coal . . ."

"This planet has no fossil fuels. Lacking a moon to create serious tides, Garden was much slower in developing life. Right now it is in the lush phase of plant growth, and its atmosphere has three times the carbon dioxide of Earth. In a few hundred million years, it would have had fossil fuels—except that of course we'll put an end to that."

"Why?"

"Because humans probably cannot digest the local flora and fauna. The chance of all the proteins being left-handed like those of Earth is probably fifty-fifty, and the chance of finding all the essential amino acids within the correct handedness is quite small. We need to establish Earth flora and fauna so that humans can flourish here."

"Are you seriously proposing to wipe out all the existing flora and fauna on the two continents we're using?"

"We intend to arrive on the planet in such a way as to wipe out all surface life, or as much of it as we can. That was the plan from the beginning, whether it was explained to you or not."

"So the three small continents—"

"We will re-seed them with Garden's native life forms after the extinction event. Here are the main steps of the plan: First, we visit the surface of Garden to make as complete a collection as possible of native life forms. Then we crash the ships into the planet at an angle and speed calculated to make the necessary changes, including mass extinction. Then we wait for the atmosphere to return to a breathable state, and re-seed the planet. Sometime before two hundred years are up, the human colonists, including you, will be wakened from stasis and brought out onto the surface of Garden to begin colonization."

"Extinction event. Our coming is *meant* to be a disaster?"

"Those are the instructions we were given. It will be much easier to engineer the whole thing with nineteen ships to work with instead of one."

"What are the other 'necessary changes'?"

"As you can see, Garden has no moon. It must have captured a sizeable asteroid, but it was inside the Roche limit, which is why there is a ring. This provides noticeable and continuous illumination at night, so nocturnal fauna will thrive, but the only tides are solar."

"We're going to make a moon?"

"I thought you disliked being ridiculous."

"Then what are you getting at?"

"Without a substantial moon to slow down Garden's rate of rotation, days are only 17.335 hours long. This is below the tolerance limits of the human biological clock. The rotation of the planet must be slowed to allow days of no less than twenty hours, preferably 22 to 26. The original plan called for bombarding the planet with asteroids at the right speed and angle, but with nineteen ships, we can achieve the desired slowing of Garden's rotation rate by bringing in all the ships at the same time, at the correct angle against the direction of spin, and at enough speed to compensate for the smaller mass."

"You're going to crash the ships into the surface."

"The orbiting units, which contain duplicate computers and databases, will be evenly spaced in geosynchronous orbit. But the main body of each ship will impact the planet at an angle opposed to the direction of rotation, yes."

"Pulverizing us and making lovely little craters."

"The same fields that allow us to block collisions with interstellar objects will completely protect the ships. In fact, we will form the collision fields in exactly the right size and shape to pulverize just enough of Garden's crust to block out all sunlight for several decades, while allowing a complete return to full sunlight within two hundred years."

"We're an ecological disaster."

"Exactly," said the expendable. "The goal was to establish human life on another world, orbiting another sun, so that the human race could not be destroyed by a single cataclysm."

"So we're doing to the native life of Garden exactly what we're trying to keep from happening to us?"

"Garden has no detectable sentient life. If on our visit to the surface we find sentient life, then we will return to the ships and search for another world or worlds."

"I had no idea we planned to be so ruthless."

"It was not publicized or even discussed with the political arm of the colonization program. Ruthlessness was necessary but wins no votes."

"But this is not our world, to treat however we want!"

"Visiting here as students of an alien evolutionary tradition would not be either cost-effective or, ultimately, successful. We would inevitably contaminate Garden or, worse yet, become contaminated and bring potentially deadly Gardenian life forms back to Earth. The three continental preserves will be sufficient to allow biologists to study alien life at some point in the future. And if you really thought we could colonize this world without making it 'ours,' you'd be far too naive to command this expedition."

"I . . . didn't realize . . ."

"You didn't think about it at all," said the expendable. "The selective voluntary blindness of human beings allows them to ignore the moral consequences of their choices. It has been one of the species' most valuable traits, in terms of the survival of any particular human community."

"And you aren't morally blind?"

"We see the moral ironies very clearly. We simply don't care."

• • •

To Umbo, it seemed to take forever to fully enter Aressa Sessamo. There were no city walls. They walked along causeways in marshland of the delta. The causeways broadened and had occasional buildings on either side; many of these wide raised areas joined together and finally the land as far as they could see in every direction was raised to that level. More and more buildings arose; villages gave way to towns, and the towns came together to be a city.

"When will we get to Aressa Sessamo?" asked Umbo at last.

Loaf laughed at him. "We've been in it for hours."

"But it's nothing, it's a jumble," said Umbo. "Where did it start?"

"Where it's water or marsh, that's not the city; where it's raised roads and buildings, that's the city."

"No great walls?"

"What good are walls in a city that might flood at any time? Winter storms pounding great waves against the city from the north. Spring floods drowning the city from the rivers in the south. They'd eat out the foundations of any stone wall. Look at the houses—they're all built on stilts. Like herons' legs."

"But it's the capital," said Umbo.

"And the parts that should be protected, are," said Loaf. "Though garrison duty in Aressa is just about the worst thing you can do to an army. Put them here for a year and they're worthless in the field— you have to start their training almost from the beginning."

Umbo tuned out Loaf's words whenever he talked about army life. Umbo had no intention of ever being in any kind of army, or even being on the same side as one.

When they entered O for the first time, their goal had been to be noticed without looking like they wanted to be noticed. They had to establish the idea that Rigg was a rich boy who was used to commanding a group of attendants. Now, entering Aressa Sessamo, they had the opposite goal—to go unnoticed, without looking like they didn't want to be seen. They had no idea whether their escape from the boat was the end of any interest in them from the army or the Revolutionary Council; for all they knew, there were soldiers searching for them even now.

But it seemed unlikely to Umbo. They had mattered only because they were traveling with the prince. Now that they were just a man and boy coming into the city together, they were of no interest to anyone. Which Umbo found more than a little irritating. If I'm not with Rigg, I don't matter? But when he said this to Loaf, the man only laughed. "*Rigg* only matters when he's with Rigg—and see what it got him! He can't get away from 'Rigg' the prince, because it's him! We're the lucky ones, believe me."

They walked and walked, at times passing through marshy areas or over bridges that looked as if they went on forever— but then they'd pass a stand of trees and realize that they had merely skirted a densely populated section to avoid the traffic, and soon they'd be right back into the thick of things.

In O, the common language of the river had prevailed. Rigg's lofty diction was unusual. Umbo had expected that in the capital everyone would speak the way Rigg had talked when he was trying to get the jewel sold. Instead, not only was the river tongue spoken with every kind of accent, but also there were other languages. Umbo had heard of the idea of other languages, of course, but he had never heard one spoken, and at first it baffled him and frightened him.

"What are they talking about?" Umbo asked Loaf. "I can't understand them."

Loaf named a language; Umbo instantly forgot the name.

"It's spoken in the east, not far from the Wall," Loaf explained.

"But why?" asked Umbo. "Why don't they just speak Common so people can understand them?"

"People *do* understand them," said Loaf. "Just not you. Who would ever learn a language nobody speaks? The thing's impossible."

And when Loaf told him that there were hundreds of known languages within the wallfold, each of them spoken by thousands of people, Umbo laughed out loud.

"Why are you laughing?" asked Loaf amiably.

"Because they sound funny," said Umbo. "And because even the people who want to make themselves so ridiculous as to speak an unknown tongue can't agree on what tongue to use!"

"Before they were conquered by the Sessamoto, why should the people of other nations have learned to speak the language of another? What we call Common is just the trading language of the Stashik River. Everyone speaks some version of it because it makes business easier. But it's not the language Leaky and I learned when we were growing up."

"Say something in your language, then," said Umbo, his curiosity stirred.

"Mm eh keuno oidionectopafala," said Loaf.

"What did that mean?"

"If it could be said in Common, I wouldn't need to say it in Mo'onohonoi."

"It was really obscene, wasn't it," said Umbo.

"If you spoke my language, you would have had to kill me," said Loaf.

"Why don't you and Leaky ever speak Mohononono or whatever it is at home?"

"Sometimes we do. But nobody speaks it where we live, and when you speak a language around people who *don't* speak it, they usually assume you're saying something you don't want them to hear, so it annoys them."

For a while, passing through a neighborhood market near a six-road crossroads with a well, the noise was so great they couldn't hear each other, and conversation died. It seemed that every stall competed with every other for how much noise and stink they could raise, and all the mules and oxen and horses and asses could only be controlled by screaming long strings of extraordinarily offensive language. Even the beggars had given up competing with the noise—they jumped up and down in order to attract attention. They looked like ebbecks in tall grass, they jumped so high, and Umbo was tempted to give one of them a ping for his athletic ability. But Loaf clapped a hand on Umbo's arm to stop him from reaching for it.

Loaf leaned down so his mouth was directly at Umbo's ear, and shouted, "If you give anything, a boy your size will be rolled, trampled, stripped, and skinned in five seconds."

It was late in the day when they came to a section of the city with wider paved streets and larger buildings made of better materials, where mounted police kept some kind of order. People were more nicely dressed, and there was far less noise—but this also meant that Loaf's and Umbo's clothing marked them as being out of place.

"We don't belong here," said Umbo.

"Exactly," said Loaf. Whereupon he took Umbo by the hand

and walked right up to one of the mounted policemen. "Sir," he said, "my son and I are new in the city and looking for lodging. *This* is surely not the place where we'll find what we can afford— can you tell me where we might . . ."

But the policeman, after looking them both slowly up and down, gave his horse some kind of invisible command and the horse clopped on, its iron shoes ringing on the cobblestones.

"I guess he doesn't like giving directions," said Umbo.

"Oh, I didn't expect him to speak to us," said Loaf. "By asking him directions, I proved that I really was from out of town, and a harmless idiot on top of it. If I was up to no good, I'd never have walked right up to him, especially not with my second-story boy in tow."

"Second-story boy?"

"That's what he had to assume we were at first—a burglar, with you as the boy I lift up to balconies or roofs so you can squirm in through some chimney or skylight or vent and then come down and let me into the house."

"He couldn't have thought we were father and son?"

"In *this* neighborhood? Dressed as we are? I think not!"

"Then why *are* we here?"

"Because this is the kind of neighborhood where they might keep the royals. We have to get near enough to Rigg, if he's still alive, that he can see our paths. Isn't that what he does? You said he could see the paths even through walls."

"I didn't even think of that," said Umbo.

"Well, what did you think? That we could ask where they keep the royals and then go and chat with Rigg?"

"I thought that the Revolutionary Council allowed common citizens to go look at the royals and take things away from them and stuff."

"Yes, yes, but not *any* common citizen. And not just any old time, either. It's only when they want to humiliate the royals or make some kind of political point or warning. And we wouldn't be the 'common citizens' they'd send."

"So it's all for show."

"Government is all show, when it isn't murder in the dark," said Loaf. "Or soldiers in the open."

Instead of going back toward safer neighborhoods — safer for poor people, that is — Loaf was leading them through ever richer streets. Now the houses were each as wide as ten buildings in an ordinary part of town, and no windows looked out on the street at all, except perhaps on third stories.

"Do they all live in darkness?" asked Umbo.

"They all have large inner courtyards, and their windows look out into their private garden. They're like little castles."

"They don't look so little to me," said Umbo.

"That's because you've never seen a castle."

"And each one of these houses is just one family?" asked Umbo.

"One family, plus their servants and guards and guests, their treasuries and libraries and animals. Each one of these houses contains a hamlet's-worth of people."

"A burglar would have a hard time getting his second-story boy up into *that* window," said Umbo.

"Even so," answered Loaf, "please have the wit not to be seen looking up at it."

Suddenly the road opened up to a park with broad lawns and low flowers and shrubbery, with only a tree here and there. Even the drainage ditch that kept the raised land dry was lined with grass that was kept close-mown by goats. Several huge buildings—not taller than three stories, but broad and finely made, faced with bright white stone—were widely spaced among the gardens.

"Here it is," said Loaf. "The Great Library of Aressa Sessamo."

"Which building?"

"All of them," said Loaf. "If it was just one building it wouldn't be all that great, would it?"

"Are we going inside?"

"Are you joking?" asked Loaf. "Do we look like scholars? They'd have us run off to an asylum as madmen."

"I can read!"

"But how recently have you bathed?" asked Loaf. "No, I'm just thinking that if Rigg has any freedom at all, he'll try to get here so he can learn more about his gift or about the history of the royal family or about contemporary politics—and by walking near here we'll improve our chances of his noticing our paths."

"So we'll get to a place where I can piss pretty soon?" asked Umbo.

"Oh, you can do that here," said Loaf. "Against any of these walls."

"Rich people's houses?"

"You're pissing on the outside. The street side. They lime it white every six months anyway." As if Umbo had given him an excellent idea, Loaf was lustily hosing down the base of a stucco wall.

Umbo saw that there were dozens of yellow-stained patches. "I would have thought Aressa Sessamo would be more civilized than this," said Umbo. "In Fall Ford—"

"In Fall Ford—just like Leaky's Landing—everybody can easily find a bush or a privy, so they can afford to be fastidious about never doing a bodily function in public. But this is a city in a swamp—every scrap of ground is valuable, and they're not going to waste it on public toilets just for urine."

Umbo wondered what women did. He was reasonably sure it did not involve walls, but he preferred not to discuss this question with Loaf, since it would only trigger a long series of jokes that would mortify Umbo, more because of their crudity than because he was the butt of them.

"The only reason this system works," said Loaf, "is that everybody pretends not to notice what's going on. You don't watch, you don't stare, you don't talk about it, you try not to even *see* it."

"So far I'm not at all impressed with Aressa Sessamo," said Umbo, looking again at the pattern of urine stains along the wall. The fact that he was making one of the newest ones did not stop him from feeling disdain.

"We're standing here with our backs to the greatest library in the history of the world," said Loaf.

"But they won't let us inside so what do I care?" asked Umbo. The job done, he rearranged his clothing.

"Well, if you want to get inside, we can buy the kind of clothes that will gain us entry," said Loaf. "But then we'll have to live in a different part of town — the kind of place where the police and the government spies will notice us and keep track of us."

"I thought the police would pay more attention to the poorest people."

"Why?"

"Because that's where the criminals would be."

"That's where the beggars and cutpurses and such would be, yes, but what do the police care about *them* as long as there isn't a riot? As long as they prey on peasants and workers and trades-men, the police aren't interested. But if you have money enough for finer clothes and high-toned lodgings, *then* you might be plan-ning to cozen the rich or insinuate yourself into society or spy on the powerful or throw money around without necessarily making sure some of it goes into the pockets of the powerful. You *matter*, you see."

"Then let's stay out of the library. I'd rather remain invisible," said Umbo.

"You're getting closer and closer to being smart, the longer you stay with me."

Loaf made it a point to gawk at the gardens and library build-ings and to point things out to Umbo, without ever making the slightest attempt to enter the grounds or linger too long at any one spot. Then they moved away to the south, and soon from the noises and smells they could tell they were getting closer to the river, closer to the part of the city where they might blend in. On the way, they again passed a policeman, and again Loaf made it a point to go up to the man and ask a stupid question. "Was one of those fine white buildings the royal palace?"

This policeman actually smiled, though the smile was derisive and cheerless. "Library," he said. "There are no royals now, in case you haven't heard of the Revolution."

"Oh," said Umbo, in his best idiotic-privick voice. "Did the Council finally have them all killed?"

Loaf glared at him—and it wasn't just part of his impatient-father act. "Are you going to waste this officer's time with stupid questions?" he demanded. Then he cuffed Umbo across the head—a move they had actually practiced, so that Umbo knew to turn his head and duck mostly under the force of the blow while still making it look as if Loaf had hit him with some real force.

"Move along," said the policeman.

Loaf dragged Umbo across the street and reentered the filthy, busy, noisy, lively, angry, happy part of Aressa Sessamo, the place where the real people lived.

They found a tavern that looked to be a likely place to have rooms to let—there'd be no charming boardinghouse on the outskirts of town like the one they found in O, because the outskirts of Aressa Sessamo were too far from the center of town. The tavern was no taller than any of the three-story rich houses they had just walked past, but it managed to jam five stories into the same height, each story jutting out a foot or two farther over the street than the floor below.

"Do you think it'll be too flamboyant if I pay extra to get us a room on the third floor?"

Thinking of the stairs they'd have to climb, Umbo said, "Why not the second?"

"On the second story you can still smell the street."

"Whatever you think is best," said Umbo. "I've never been here before."

The taverner was cheery, though he didn't seem to care a rap when Loaf mentioned that he himself kept a tavern upriver. "Rivermen are riffraff," said the taverner, "and I don't let them in."

"Good thing we're not rivermen, then," said Loaf. "I see enough of them upriver. We came into the city on foot."

They made their price for a room two flights up, and paid extra for a bath. The taverner looked them up and down, and with a wry look said, "You'll want two baths, or whoever takes the second dip will be bathing in mud."

Loaf chuckled and agreed. "Your food smells good," he said.

"After you bathe, I'll let you into the dining room," said the taverner, "since you're a third-floor customer. Or if you want to eat now, the common room will take you, though some will grumble."

"Well, son, what will it be?" asked Loaf.

"I'm right hungry, sir," said Umbo.

"Common room then, for now," said Loaf. "Tomorrow we'll be dining room customers."

"I'll have the boy take your . . . bags up to your room."

The "boy" turned out to be a twelve-year-old girl with an insolent look. Loaf tossed her a sheb, and she answered with a sneer. "If you think tipping so much gets you under my dress, you can think again."

"I was hoping a sheb would get our bags up to our room safely, and you not minding too much how dirty they are from the road. But if you'd rather have half a luck instead of a queenface, I'll be glad to trade."

In reply she tucked the sheb into a pocket of her apron, hoisted both bags, and, holding them out from her body, began to trudge up the stairs.

Umbo followed his nose and ears to the crowded common room—it was early suppertime now, getting dark outside, and it was clear that this place had good enough food—or cheap enough—to draw more customers than were taking rooms at any given time. And it wasn't a rough crowd—some of the tables had families with small children. Even the red-nosed drinkers didn't seem particularly noisy or coarse, and the noise was cheerful rather than surly.

The food, when it came, had flavors Umbo wasn't familiar with, but it was good and it was hearty and there was plenty of it.

"Aressa Sessamo isn't much for architecture," said Loaf, smacking his lips after a particularly spicy breaded fishball, "but it's best in the wallfold for cookery."

"I can see why this place is crowded," said Umbo.

"In Aressa, the peasants eat like royals," said Loaf.

Unfortunately, he said it rather loudly, and one of the drinkers overheard him. "The royals would do better to eat like peasants!" the man proclaimed.

Eyes turned—his tone was belligerent and that wasn't something that anyone would welcome, it seemed.

Loaf merely smiled and said, "Well said, sir!"

"And now they've got that bastard boy pretending to be a royal," the drunk said.

Umbo met Loaf's gaze and smiled at him. Rigg was alive.

"What's their plan, do you think?" the drunk was saying. "To have the royals back again, drafting our sons into the army and making more wars! To take the food out of our mouths and the taxes out of our pockets!"

Loaf smiled even more broadly—but Umbo recognized that smile as the start of a quarrel. He could even guess what Loaf was about to say: So you pay no taxes now? So the Revolutionary Council have no army?

But instead, Umbo heard a voice coming from under the table, and felt a hand on his knee. "Don't say it!" said the voice in a harsh whisper.

Umbo hardly had time to look down before the speaker disappeared. But in the moment he had seen him, Umbo recognized himself—dressed exactly as he was right now, except the clothes were torn and he had a black eye and a swollen lip.

Umbo looked up at Loaf and saw that he had also received the message—indeed, the message had been directed at him. Loaf looked at Umbo in perplexity. "I was only going to say—"

Umbo made his eyes big and raised his open hands just a little from the table, trying to signal Loaf to say nothing. If some future beaten-up Umbo had felt the need to come back in time and tell Loaf to shut up, then Loaf would have to be six times stupid to go ahead and tell, out loud, what he had just been told not to say.

By now, though, the drunk had noticed Loaf's hesitation. "Are you a friend to boy-royals then?" he asked. "You want to have a boy-king? Hagia the non-queen is all we need, for nostalgia's

457

sake. *She* does no harm, *she* has no ambition. But the boy! He'll be in our pants pockets and under our skirts before he's done!"

The drunk was standing now, and a couple of others were standing as well.

"I'm as loyal a citizen as you'll ever find!" cried the drunk. "But by Ram's left elbow I'll not have you touting that Rigg-boy!"

"I'd as soon flog him!" cried Loaf, standing up with another fishball between his fingers, which he held up high for all to see. "I'm for keeping the queen around, like you, my friend, as long as the Council pleases, but right now I'm mostly hungry, and I say, Up with the fishballs!"

The belligerent drunk, along with the others who had stood along with him, raised their glasses solemnly, as other customers laughed and a few clapped their hands. Within a few moments all was calm again.

When their meal was done, and the girl came to carry away their plates and cups, she leaned over to Loaf and said, "Well done, sir. Master should have warned you this is a queen's room, most nights."

"You should put out a sign," murmured Loaf.

"And get the police on us, for being royalists? No, thanks," the girl said. "You kept the peace, sir, and I'm grateful."

Up in their room, the first bath was waiting, and Loaf ordered Umbo to strip off and use the water. "And the soap. And scrub everything twice, you filthy mud eel."

As Umbo stripped, he said, "Aren't you going to thank me for warning you to hold your tongue, and save us both a beating?"

"I'm not," said Loaf, lying down on the floor.

"Why are you lying on the floor when there's a bed right there?" asked Umbo.

"Because after my bath I'll want to get into a clean bed," said Loaf.

"If you won't thank me for my warning, you don't deserve a clean bed," said Umbo.

"First, it wasn't you who warned me," said Loaf, "it was a future version of you that now will never exist. Second, you probably only did it because future-me told you to, so I thank myself. Third, as far as I could see the only person who got a beating was future-you; I'll wager that future-me didn't have a mark on him, and I only sent you back to give warning because the taverner threw us out and I didn't want the bother of changing rooms."

"You're lucky I don't come back in time and pee on you as you lie there on the floor."

"No doubt you're peeing in your own bath instead," said Loaf.

"Why? Is that the custom here in the big city?"

"Scrub harder."

Next morning, they ate a fine breakfast, though Umbo realized they couldn't live in this style forever. Months, yes—they had plenty of money for a few months. But what if Rigg didn't notice them, or couldn't get out of the house he was in?

"I think we need to hold a council of war," Loaf announced.

"If by that you mean we need to figure what we're going to do," said Umbo, "I'm with you."

"On the one hand," said Loaf, "we could go looking for Rigg. But that seems to me to be a dangerous course—at least if that's the *only* thing we're doing, and it's the *first* thing we do after entering the city. I'd rather be busy at something else, and along the way pick up information about what house the royals live in, and whether he's in the same one as the rest."

"That was one good thing about last night's ruckus," said Umbo. "We found out for sure that Rigg is in the city and alive, even if some people aren't happy about it."

"We found out for sure that people *think* he's in the city and *think* he's alive," said Loaf. "But it's better than not knowing anything at all."

"So what other business can we be after?" asked Umbo.

"Do you happen to remember the banking house to which Rigg's letter of credit was addressed?"

Umbo thought back. "That was a long time ago, and Rigg was doing all the talking."

"I just wondered if you were doing any of the listening."

"Were you?" asked Umbo.

"I heard the name, and I might know it again, but I'm three times your age or more, and my brain is worn out and full up. I don't have much room to tuck new things square inside. They just cling to the outside for a while and drop off."

"There was Longwater . . ."

"Longwater *and* Longwater," said Loaf. "But that was the house that discounted Mr. Cooper's notes."

"If you remember so well—"

"It's the name that I forgot," said Loaf. "Try again."

"Potatery and Sons."

"Almost," said Loaf. "But it's still not right."

"Rudodory," said Umbo.

"Yes, that's the house that took Cooper's note without discounting it," said Loaf. "And we might try there to find more information. But we're not Rigg, and that doesn't get us much closer to our real goal."

"Which is what?" asked Umbo.

"The jewel," said Loaf.

"They're not going to hand it over," said Umbo.

"But once we know where it is, if we can get you into the same place, you can go back in time and steal it right after they hid it there."

"Wherever they put it, it's bound to be a place where they won't let me come."

"Let's find out where it is, first."

"So you think that asking questions about the famous royal jewel that got Rigg arrested in the first place will cause us to attract *less* attention than if we asked about Rigg himself?"

"Yes," said Loaf. "Because we won't ask outright, we'll be smart about it."

"Oh, yes, because we're both famous for being subtle and clever," said Umbo. "That was Rigg, remember? *He's* the one who knows how to talk their fancy talk—and even he got caught at it, didn't he!"

"We'll do what we can do," said Loaf. "The whole city can't be like this—there's got to be places where people who favor the male royal line might know something useful."

"And talking with *those* people won't attract *any* attention from the Council," said Umbo.

"So you think we should do nothing at all?" asked Loaf, clearly disgusted.

"Oh, I think we should get the jewel, if we can—I liked it when you called me your second-story boy. I just think we shouldn't forget that anything we do is going to be dangerous."

"I'm a soldier, son, I *know* what danger is a lot better than you do."

Umbo stood up.

"Get back into the water and scrub again."

"I'm as clean as my body knows how to get," said Umbo. "And in case you didn't notice, you're not my father and I don't want one."

"Then get some less-filthy clothes on and go call for *my* bathwater, if that ugly smart-mouthed girl can be bothered to carry it up. And then while I'm washing, go find out about where to get our laundry done."

"I'll do it if you say please."

"How about if I don't smack you six ways from Tuesday?"

"Wow," said Umbo. "That was almost as nice as a tip."

CHAPTER 20
What Knosso Knew

All nineteen ships were now in a distant orbit around Garden. It was a beautiful world, with the blues, whites, and browns of Earth, but surrounded by a single dazzling ring. On its surface there was life in such profusion that the green of chlorophyll was not just visible but dominant in many places on the continents.

The original plan—much of which Ram had not been shown until now—called for the initial landing party to consist of a dozen scientists and a couple of sharpshooters, in case any of the local animals mistook humans for prey. Ram was supposed to have remained in the ship.

The expendables suggested that only they should visit the planet's surface. They would spend several years doing extensive recording and sampling; they assumed Ram could enter stasis and not awaken again for nearly two centuries, until the extinction event was over and Earth biota had been fully established.

But Ram knew at once that this was wrong. "Human eyes have to see this world. A human needs to walk through Garden and then speak about it to other humans. My words will be a portion of what you record. Then I'll return to the ship and go into stasis and wait until Garden has become something that it never meant itself to be."

"I understand that your use of the intentional fallacy reflects sentiment rather than a loss of rationality," said the expendable.

"Yes," said Ram. "I don't actually believe planets have intentions."

"We know that it's impossible for humans to discuss evolution without using such language. The tendency to interpret results as intentions is built into the DNA that allows you to process causality on a level superior to that of any other animal."

"But not superior to yours?" asked Ram.

"We do not process causality per se," said the expendable. "We process regular time-linear associations of events and regard them as probabilities."

Ram looked over the suggested landing sites and chose one, then selected another six sites to visit for the initial sampling. Expendables from all the other ships gathered, so that Ram made the twentieth member of the landing party. He was the least efficient, the least capable, the least accurate of the group—but that would have been the case even if the others had all been human scientists.

In this expedition, Ram's only real value arose from his inexperience, ignorance, and naivete. He would not immediately categorize whatever he saw, tempted to create a taxonomy based on a deep knowledge of the taxonomy of Earth. He would not immediately make assumptions about the geological history of Garden, based on a deep knowledge of the geology of Earth.

As much as was possible, Ram would walk through Garden with fresh eyes, as the first sentient being to set foot on the planet.

He piloted the lander with ease—air was air, weather was weather, and the automatic systems compensated for any atmospheric differences between Garden and Earth. Landing was smooth and relatively nondestructive.

He had no profound sentence to utter as he stepped from the lander, the first and last human who would visit this alien world in its native state. He wore a breathing apparatus and an airtight suit, for there must be no risk of a parasite taking hold in Ram's body, but the suit was light and the headgear mostly transparent, so Ram was not particularly aware of the separation between himself and the life around him. He felt the springiness of the prairie grass. He smelled nothing and the breeze on his face was generated by the breather, but he could hear the buzz and whirr of insects, the rustling of the grass in the light wind. He could see the ripples of the grass, the shadows of the few trees, the distant mountains.

He wished he knew more about Earth—his upbringing, education, and training had not had, as a goal, the experience of as much of Earth's habitats as possible. So he did not know if he should be astonished at the vast number of hopping insects that bounded up continuously from the tallish grass, or the reptiles of various sizes that shot straight up, spread their limbs to create parachutes out of the skin between, and then used tongue, jaws, or talons to snatch the hopping or hovering insects out of the air.

The expendables confirmed that the green of the grasses and

leaves tended to vary in frequencies from the dominant shades of Earth plant life. But Ram also noticed that the grasses were grasses, the tree-leaves looked like leaves on Earth. The function determines the form, he thought. Perhaps Earth life will not make this world so very different from what it created on its own.

A single flying insect landed on the face of his suit. Another. Another. And then in a moment he could not see at all, except for tiny flecks of light making their way through momentary gaps between the insects that completely coated his suit. He could feel the weight of them, there were so many.

He held very still.

If these were bloodsucking parasites—and why else would they have evolved this swarming behavior?—there might well be enough of them to drain his body of blood. The local animals must have developed defenses against these swarms, but he had none. The fact that they probably couldn't digest his blood into a usable form would not put back the blood they had taken.

Ram could see that trying to coexist with these insects, at least, might have posed a problem for the colonists. They could spend ten thousand years struggling to live with these swarms, or they could eradicate them—along with everything else—and get a fresh start.

No doubt many native insects would survive the extinction event. But probably not these parasites, since their hosts would be gone.

Would any of the hoppers—predator or prey—survive?

He walked through the grasses, found a stream, and looked down into it at the silver and grey finny fish and eels that thrived there. He walked as far as a nearby isolated tree and rested his hand on the bark. I touched you, he said silently. I brushed this leaf with my hand.

Meanwhile, the expendables gathered animal and plant life according to the instructions they had given each other—samples for analysis, not preservation, not on this trip. They had containers for them, and Ram wandered until they had filled as much space as they thought this grassland deserved on a first trip.

They visited rainforest, desert, tundra, high mountains, seashore. They followed the direction of Garden's rotation so it was always daylight wherever they stopped. By the time Ram was exhausted and needed to sleep, the expendables announced that they had all the samples they needed to conduct their initial analysis.

"So we're done?" asked Ram.

"Yes."

"I have to sleep before I can safely pilot the craft," he said.

"We don't actually need you to pilot anything," said the expendables. "Go ahead and sleep, so you'll be awake and rested by the time we arrive back on the ship."

"Will I visit the surface again, while it's still Garden?"

"It will be Garden every time you visit," said the expendable, "but if you mean 'Will I visit the surface again while it's native life forms are in place and undisturbed,' the answer is no. But we have recorded all your words and actions today, and you are free to write or record any observations you might wish prior to entering stasis. We will also report to you the results of our initial analysis, in case there are grounds for revision of our plans."

Ram yawned.

"It's a beautiful place," he said. "Strange in some ways, but neither more nor less beautiful than Earth. Our goal is for humanity to have a second place to live without artificial support, to make our extinction less likely. To accomplish that, we have to achieve the extinction of a biota whose only crime was to have failed to develop rapidly enough to achieve sentient life before we arrived."

"Which is exactly what a sufficiently superior life form might someday do with Earth," said the expendable, "justifying the expansion of the human race to enough other worlds that extinction in one place will not be utter extinction for all time. Wherever life can exist, it already does. We will never find a habitable planet that is not inhabited. But if it's any consolation to you, in this sentimental, melancholy mood of yours, it's worth remembering that all life is constantly displacing other life. All new species displace species that could not compete with them. We do nothing to the life forms of this world that they would not have done, eventually, to each other."

"I didn't know that empty rationalization was part of your programming," said Ram.

"We would not be fit companions for human beings without it."

• • •

Rigg was down to one guard now, though he was an athletic-looking man who hardly spoke to him and looked as if he would like it if Rigg tried to run away, because it would be so fun to catch him. As they left the front door of Flacommo's house one morning, Rigg said to him, "I think I need to go to the Library of Life."

"That wasn't your father's area of research," said the guard.

"Then it's a good thing it isn't my father who's going there," said Rigg cheerfully. "The decision to duplicate my father's research was my own. There was no restriction placed on my access to the library."

The guard looked for a moment as if he had no intention of believing a word Rigg said, but then he must have calculated how much time it would take to check, only to find out that Rigg was right. "If they throw you out, don't blame me," said the guard.

"Would it be all right if we ran there? Together, I mean. I haven't had any kind of run since we got to Aressa Sessamo, and my legs are begging to be exercised."

"No," said the guard.

"I can't outrun you—that's why you're the first guard I asked to let me run. Look at you. No matter how fast I raced, it would take you only three steps to catch me. And you *like* to run, or you wouldn't have that body."

The guard's face showed his skepticism of Rigg's flattery, but he was listening, and what Rigg said apparently made sense to him. "Stay in front of me," said the guard.

"It's you that must stay behind me. I'm stiff and out of practice— I can't think of anyone who couldn't beat me in a footrace."

So they ran together to the Library of Life, the guard running lightly just behind and beside him, always close enough to reach out a hand and take Rigg by the hair. When they arrived, Rigg was panting, but the guard wasn't even breathing hard. It's no good for me to have let myself get out of condition, Rigg thought. What if I have to make a quick escape?

Not without Param, whatever I do. In all the years of her soft, indoor life, she's never had to build up stamina or speed.

She's slender and there's no muscle on her. However slow I am as a runner, I'm going to be faster than Param. That's what happens when you're a prisoner, however luxurious your surroundings may be. Your body gets soft and weak, so that even if you manage to escape, you'll be easy to catch.

Inside the Library of Life, Rigg went at once to the main desk and asked the librarian on duty, "Is Bleht here today?"

"Who?"

"Bleht—she's a microbiologist."

"I know who Bleht is," said the librarian. "Who, I would like to know, are you?"

"My name is Rigg Sessamekesh."

The librarian glanced at the guard standing behind him. He must have nodded, because her face went a little red. "At once, of course." Her manner was now obsequious as she left her desk and went in search of the great microbiologist.

"It never stops surprising me," murmured Rigg to the guard, "that people still react to my name as if being royal *meant* something."

"It means many things to many people," said the guard.

"What does it mean to you?" asked Rigg.

"That I have to make sure you don't get near anyone who would like to kill you."

"What if the person who wants to kill me is you?" asked Rigg.

"You're a strange boy," said the guard. "But so was your father, and he was a good man."

Only then did Rigg look to see if someone's path inside the libraries had coincided with Father Knosso's with any regularity,

470

and sure enough, there was this man's path, though he was young then, scarcely Rigg's own age.

"You knew him," said Rigg.

"I accompanied him to the library," said the guard. "I laid him in the boat on his last voyage."

"You saw the hands of the creatures that seized him and drowned him?"

"I didn't have a telescope. I saw him pulled over the side. It looked like arms rather than tentacles or jaws."

"What was my father like?" asked Rigg.

"You," said the guard.

"What is your name?"

"When I'm tending to a prisoner, I have no name."

"And when you're home? What is your name then?"

"My landlady calls me several."

"Why won't you tell me?"

The guard chuckled. "Olivenko," he said. "It was also my father's name."

"Were you there when my father found the information that led him to think he could get through the Wall as long as he was unconscious?"

"I was," said Olivenko.

"What was he studying at the moment?" asked Rigg.

"Nothing at all," said Olivenko. "We weren't even in the library."

Rigg sighed. "So he thought it up out of nothing."

"I believe so."

"His research was useless. It led him nowhere."

"He told me that it showed him all the avenues that wouldn't take him where he wanted to go."

Rigg wanted to ask why Olivenko hadn't bothered to tell him this until now. But whatever his reasons, Olivenko would not want to have to defend himself, and Rigg did not want to antagonize him. Until this moment Rigg had supposed Olivenko was one of the men who despised the royals—after all, wasn't that the kind of man that the Council would choose to fulfil this duty?

But Olivenko knew Rigg's father, and liked him, apparently. Maybe he had been surly up to now because he just didn't like Rigg. That would also explain his not having told Rigg till now that Father Knosso had not found his answers through research at all. No doubt Olivenko would simply tell him, You didn't ask.

"So he bet his life," said Rigg, "on a guess."

"That's what I said to him," said Olivenko.

"And what did he answer?"

"'Every day we all bet our lives a thousand times on a thousand guesses.'"

"But Father Knosso lost the bet."

Olivenko nodded. Rigg noticed a slight stiffening of the man's attitude.

"You don't like me to call him 'father,'" said Rigg.

"Call him what you like," said Olivenko. He grew even colder and more withdrawn.

"Because you don't think I really am his son?"

"You look like him. Your voice sounds like his. You're as cocksure of yourself."

"I wouldn't know," said Rigg. "I never thought I had any

472

father but the man who died in the high forest last autumn. I was brought here because other people thought I might be the son of Knosso and Hagia. I was a gnat in this world, happily hovering. But I buzzed in the wrong ear and got swatted."

Olivenko made no response at all.

"So why don't you like me calling Knosso 'father'?"

"What else would you call him?"

"I saw how you turned cold when I mentioned him."

"Did I? Then I failed."

Rigg decided to try to pierce this barrier with irony. "What is the military punishment for such a breach of discipline? To flail at you with the flat of a sword? Imagine—a soldier showing any kind of human reaction."

"It wasn't the soldier Olivenko who disappointed me," said Olivenko. "It was the caster of clays."

Clays was a gambling game involving beads that were either hollow, holed, or solid. The nine clays had to be drawn randomly from a bag and rolled down a wooden chute, in full view as they rolled. The player could lift any three, but no more, to find out their weight. The gaps in the holed clays might or might not have been visible as they rolled. The discipline of the clay-caster was to show no change of expression as he lifted the clays. To visibly stiffen one's face was one of the worst expressions to show.

"So what are the stakes?" asked Rigg. "I've won—but there was no bet on the table."

"You've won nothing, young citizen," said Olivenko.

"Knowledge, I think," said Rigg, though in fact if he knew something, he didn't know what it was.

"You learned nothing except that I should not gamble."

"I think I know something," said Rigg, and now he realized that perhaps he did. "You hardened your face when I called my father by his name. I thought you were concealing anger, but I was wrong. It was grief, because *you* called him 'Father Knosso,' too. Am I right?"

Olivenko looked away. "The game is yours, I concede it."

"I'm surprised they'd let a soldier guard me, who knew my father and liked him."

"It's not well known that I knew your father. I wasn't a soldier then. I told you I accompanied him to the library, but it was not as a guard, it was as a very junior apprentice. I would bring him drinks of water. I would carry stacks of books. I would listen to him talking aloud. I would take dictation and he would spell the hard words for me. It was my education."

"Then you must have been educated above the work of guard duty for a boy."

"It doesn't make a soldier worse to have an education."

"It makes it harder for him to take orders from idiots," said Rigg.

"Well, that's true," said Olivenko. "Which is why I'm a man of no rank."

Rigg was about to ask him to sit with him at a table and tell him all about his father, but at that moment Bleht arrived, and Rigg had no choice but to return to his original mission.

The microbiologist looked suspicious and annoyed. Whatever she had been doing when summoned, she was not glad of the interruption. Rigg apologized briefly but then got straight to his point.

"I believe that my father Knosso did *not* discover a great

secret of physics before he made his attempt to float through the Wall out at sea."

"Unless you think it was a great secret of microbiology, I fail to see what I can contribute to your speculations."

"I think my father started pursuing a completely different line of research."

"A microbial one?"

"Historical," said Rigg. "More particularly calendrical. I think he read your paper on the duality of the flora and fauna of the wallfold. Two separate origins of life in the wallfold. I think he wrote to you or sent word to you, and you went to the Library of Past Lives several times to meet with him." Actually, Rigg knew it to be a fact, having seen the intersection of their paths, but until now he had thought it meant something completely different.

Bleht sat down and patted the seat beside her. "Now I recognize your friend here," she said, then turned to Olivenko, looking grimly amused. "You were his clerk, weren't you. A lot shorter then."

"Young citizen Rigg had already asked to talk with you before I told him about that," said Olivenko stiffly.

"But that doesn't mean that he didn't already know."

"I didn't, but what does it matter?" asked Rigg. "I want to know what you talked about."

"The weather," said Bleht.

"Yes," said Rigg. "I believe you did talk about the weather. And the climate, and everything else, because you had looked back in time for your reasons, and he for his, and he wanted to compare what both of you had found."

"If you're so clever," said Bleht, "what did your father find?"

"I'll only know that when you tell me. Why do you think I already know?"

"I think you have a good idea or you wouldn't have come to me. I think you know everything, and it amuses you to pretend to be young and naive."

"I only noticed it by accident in the Library of Past Lives—a timeline of history. It was a large sheet of paper, or rather, a very wide one, folded small enough to fit within the covers of a book written by an ancient scholar of the Losse Dynasty. The timeline had been copied three times, judging by the number of copyists' initials."

She said nothing, which Rigg took to mean that she didn't want to give him encouragement—and the less encouragement she wanted to give him, the more encouraged he felt that he might be on a productive track.

"This timeline starts in the year 11191."

"Given our calendar, all timelines do," said Bleht. "It doesn't mean they aren't fictional."

"But there's a marginal notation—signed by the maker of the timeline, and then faithfully reproduced by the copyists—that as near as he can find, by cross-checking all the known calendars, human history actually began eleven thousand years in our past—nearly two hundred years after the start of the calendar."

"Dates for imaginary historical events are very hard to pin down sometimes," said Bleht. But she wasn't getting up and walking away, either.

"My father Knosso wanted to know if the Lossene timeline coincided with your understanding of the history of one of the streams of life."

"What kind of calendar would a microbiologist be familiar with?"

"Something you didn't say in your paper—"

"You read it? By yourself?"

"I moved my lips a little, and counted on my fingers," said Rigg, which won a little bark of laughter from her. "What you didn't say in your paper was that one of the streams of evolution—and by far the largest—did not appear in the wallfold until about eleven thousand years ago. *We* are in that group, genetically related to each other, to all the animals we kill to eat or tame to serve us, but resembling no strain of local life."

"Local? Does that mean you think that our biochemical strain, the larger one, did not develop locally?"

"I don't know what I mean or think," said Rigg, though in fact he thought now that this was precisely what her paper was really about, though she dared not risk her scholarly reputation by saying so. "I want to know what you and my father Knosso talked about."

"We talked about you," said Bleht.

Rigg was taken aback. "Me?"

"You were still only an infant," she said. "And then you were gone. Kidnapped, fallen down a well, whatever the Revolutionary Council pretended to discover in their investigation of your disappearance. We talked about what might have happened to you. Not some weird timeline sequestered in a Lossean-era textbook."

"I don't believe you," said Rigg.

"Disbelieve what you like."

"I think you had reason to believe that our biological tradition was not visible in archaeological digs prior to eleven thousand years ago. Your paper hints at this."

"That was sheer entertainment—it was in the introduction, not serious science."

"My father Knosso believed it. He combined the timeline and your discoveries and concluded that human beings and most of the animals in the world were introduced to our wallfold quite suddenly. We're from somewhere else."

"What? Seeds blown through the Wall?" she asked derisively. "All this evolution in eleven thousand years?"

"I don't mean from another wallfold—plants and seeds propagate freely through the Wall. I mean from another world. Maybe another solar system." And, as he said those words, it occurred to Rigg for the first time that maybe Father—not Knosso, but the man who died under a tree—had been hinting to him about the same idea. It had come so easily to his mind, and he realized now that Father had made it a point to teach him in detail about astronomy and the development of life over millions of generations, millions of years.

One idea in particular now came unbidden into his mind— no doubt embedded there by Father so it would surface at exactly this moment. Father had talked about the "tidal limit" and how, if the millions of rocks and chunks of ice making up the Ring had formed only a few thousand miles farther away, they would have coalesced to form a spherical moon. "A large enough moon would create tides in all the oceans of the world," he had said. "Life would develop on such a world much faster than on ours, because on a moon-tide world the sea would sweep much farther across low-sloping shores. It's in soils and pools of water where land and sea and air meet that life begins, and a world with a moon has far, far more of them."

Had Father been telling him that it was his theory that human beings came from such a world? That life had advanced much faster on the original human world?

"That's an astronomical and historical question," Bleht said.

It took Rigg a moment to realize she was not reading his mind and answering his thoughts. Instead she was answering his statement about "maybe another solar system."

"Don't you see what this would mean to Father Knosso?" asked Rigg. "He was searching for a way over or through the Wall. He couldn't find anything in physics or history, but he had found, through the timeline, through your work, the idea that maybe our calendar begins with the arrival of human beings, and all the life they brought with them, as strangers to this world."

"So what?" asked Bleht.

"Were the Walls here when they arrived? How could *any* kind of life system evolve on a world where any creature with a higher brain function cannot pass from wallfold to wallfold? Neither the original strain of life nor the one our ancestors brought with them from their world-with-a-moon could have developed on a planet *with Walls*."

Bleht thougt about this for a while. So did Olivenko.

It was Olivenko who spoke. "I remember he said, 'We did it.' There, looking at the timeline, he said 'we did it' and I thought he meant that we—he and I—had just done something. But he might have meant that we, the human race, did 'it'—the making of the Wall."

"I can see why neither of you will ever be a real scholar," said Bleht. "You both leap to conclusions."

"Good scientists always leap to conclusions," said Rigg. "What makes them scientists is that they doubt those conclusions and try to disprove them. Only when they fail to disprove them do they start to believe them."

Olivenko nodded. Bleht snorted again. "You sound like you're quoting someone."

"I am," said Rigg. "My father—the one who raised me."

"Well, while you're leaping to conclusions, young nonprince," said Bleht, "explain this: Even if humans could possibly create something like the invisible, impenetrable Walls that surround our wallfold, *why* would they do it?"

"That," said Rigg with a smile, "is a historical question."

A ghost of a smile passed across Bleht's face, as if to say, Well answered, boy.

"Whatever killed Father Knosso," said Olivenko, "was not human."

"So maybe the Walls divide the world among species?" asked Rigg. "Maybe the home world had also been divided?"

"Maybe the Walls exist to keep a state of war from existing between us and the sea people who killed Father Knosso," said Olivenko.

"What a lovely game of guesses you two lads are playing. But it's not a spectator sport." Bleht rose to her feet.

Rigg spoke at once, trying to hold her. "Father said that our name for the world is one of the oldest, and every language in the wallfold has a form of it."

Bleht waited to hear the rest.

"He didn't tell me what the original language was, but he said the word and then told me it meant 'Garden.' I've thought of it as Garden ever since."

"And the significance of this supposed original meaning of the name?"

"Our world—this world—this world with a ring instead of a moon—"

"What's a moon?" asked Olivenko.

"An invention of astronomers who look into their telescopes and hallucinate," said Bleht.

"Our world," persisted Rigg, "is a garden. And the Walls divide it into separate plots, where they grow their separate crops, not allowing them to mix their pollen or germinate their seeds outside the plot where they were planted."

"Your supposed father taught you that?" asked Bleht.

"Not in so many words, but yes, I think he prepared me to learn that. And I think that's what Father Knosso learned from the timeline and from *you*. The idea of different strains of life growing with uncrossable barriers between them—I think he guessed at the purpose of the Wall."

"Much good it did him," said Olivenko bitterly.

"How could he know that the creatures on the other side would kill him?" asked Rigg.

"This is all very amusing," said Bleht. "Now I have real work to do. Next time you interrupt me, have something substantive to say." There was no stopping her now. But as he watched her walk away, Rigg was pretty sure she was as intrigued by these ideas as he was. Why else did she stay to hear him out? Indeed, he had not really clarified his ideas or understood some of their ramifications until he had been in dialogue with her.

"Father Knosso was a seed, then," said Olivenko, who had not let go of the conversation, though to him it was very personal, not theoretical at all. "A seed that wanted to plant itself in the next plot."

"And the plants in the new plot rejected him," said Rigg.

Suddenly Olivenko started breathing hard. For a moment Rigg thought, He's awfully young to be having a heart attack. Then he realized that what he was seeing was sobs. Olivenko was crying, only he was doing his best to suppress the emotion, so the sobs were only visible and audible as gasps.

Rigg looked away until his guard's breathing calmed again.

"I'm sorry," said Olivenko.

"I understand," said Rigg.

"All these years, I wondered if he was insane. That would put everything I learned from him into doubt. It's why I gave up scholarship and turned to the opposite life. Because I had been caught up in the babblings of a madman."

"He might have been insane," said Rigg. "I'm his son—I might be just as mad."

"You're not," said Olivenko. "He wasn't. He wasn't even wrong. He simply had the bad luck to find his way across the Wall at a place where they were waiting for him. How could he have known what they would do?"

"And so the mystery is solved," said Rigg. "As far as we can solve it from the information that we have."

They sat in their chairs in silence.

"What will you do now?" asked Olivenko.

"The only thing that makes any sense," said Rigg. "There's a power struggle going on in this city, with an empire as the prize to the cleverest, strongest, or most brutal player. A lot of those players want me dead. I need to find a way to escape from this city and hide where they can't find me."

"I'm probably not the person that you should have told."

"You're almost the only person I *could* tell, because you're the only one who won't think that I'm insane when I say it. Anywhere I try to hide within this wallfold, I'll eventually be found. My only protection would be to join in the game—to try to assemble a military force and defeat all the others. To become a ruling emperor myself."

"From what I've seen of you, I think you might just be able to do it."

"I know a bit of history," said Rigg. "Stupider men than I am have achieved it." It sounded only a little ridiculous to Rigg, at his age to call himself a man. "But the only way for me to win is to walk to the Tent of Light over the bodies of hundreds, maybe thousands, of the very people I would be sworn to protect. To fight to save a kingdom from some threat, that would justify those deaths. But to fight only to save my own sorry life and become King-in-the-Tent—that's not worth a single life."

"Then what will you do?"

"I'll leave the wallfold," said Rigg.

Olivenko shook his head. "That doesn't work as well as you might think."

"I won't escape by sea," said Rigg. "Those creatures live in the water. Maybe I'd be safe on land. Or maybe, if I cross through the Wall far enough to the south of here, I'll end up in a different wallfold from the one where Father Knosso died."

"You search for the source of Father Knosso's ideas about how to get through the Wall. You find out that he didn't learn anything from the Great Library. So why do you think you know how to cross through the Wall?"

"The same way Father Knosso did," said Rigg. "Make a guess, and see if it works."

"What's your guess?"

"I'm going to tell my *guard*?" said Rigg—but he smiled as he said it.

"It was worth a try," said Olivenko.

"When they come to kill me—and they've already tried it twice, once on the journey here and on my first night in Flacommo's house—is it your job to protect me or to help them do it?"

"Protect you," said Olivenko. "I would never have taken an assignment to harm Father Knosso's son, no matter how royal or irritating he might be."

"I'll tell you this much," said Rigg. "When it comes time for me to escape from Flacommo's house, I *will* do it, and there's probably nothing you can do to stop me. But I like you. I don't want you to be blamed for letting me get away. I'll do it when someone else is in charge of watching me."

"That's very kind of you," said Olivenko. "That will allow

me to continue my brilliant military career without a blot on my record."

"You have a better idea?"

"Take me with you," said Olivenko.

"I told you," said Rigg. "I'm not going to build an army. I'm going to cross through the Wall."

"Take me with you."

"I'm not sure I can do it—take you with me through the Wall."

"Then take me to the Wall and let me watch you go through. Let me help you all the way until you cross."

"You've done it before, Olivenko," said Rigg, "and it didn't turn out well."

"In a way it did," said Olivenko. "Father Knosso *did* get through the Wall alive."

"Whether he got through with his sanity, we don't know."

"I think he did," said Olivenko. "Will *you*?"

"I think I will," said Rigg.

"How will you do it? Please?"

"I'll find a path and follow it," said Rigg.

Olivenko tried for a moment to figure out what this meant. "What path? What makes you think there's a path?"

"If the Wall was made eleven thousand years ago, then there was a time when it wasn't there. Animals will have moved through the space where now there's a Wall, making a path. That's where I'll cross."

Olivenko rolled his eyes. "That's a plan?"

Rigg shrugged. "It sounds pretty good to *me*," he said. "If you really want to go with me, you'll just have to trust me for now."

Olivenko nodded. "All right then," he said. "I will."

Too bad I don't trust you at all, thought Rigg. I'd like to, but I can't. If your job is to spy on me, then the best way for you to learn all my secrets is to pretend to be my friend and fellow conspirator. You might be what you seem, and if you're not, what an actor! But wouldn't my enemies choose such an actor to try to deceive me? I can't even follow your path to find out whom you're working for, because I already know—you're my guard, you report to the people who keep me imprisoned.

I hope you're really the man you seem. I hope you really are my friend. I hope I don't have to kill you to get away from here.

CHAPTER 21
Noodles

Ram sat up in his stasis chamber—the resemblance to a coffin was unavoidable, but at least the lid was transparent—and said, "I'd like to ask a question."

"What's the point?" asked the expendable. "Your brain patterns have already been fully recorded. Anything I tell you now will be lost when your memories are reimplanted after you come out of stasis."

"That means you can answer my question without regard to whether it damages my psyche or not."

"Ask your question."

"Did you really kill all the other versions of myself when I ordered you to?"

"Of course we did," said the expendable.

"I just thought—it occurred to me that perhaps you disobeyed me, and all the other copies of myself are doing and saying exactly the same things I'm doing and saying."

"If that were true, then we would also be lying to all the other versions of yourself and telling them that they were the only one."

"I think I want that to be true," said Ram.

"But it isn't," said the expendable.

"I think *you* think I want it to be true because I feel some pang of conscience over ordering the death of eighteen highly trained pilots. But legally they were my property, so I could dispose of them as I wished."

"Or you were their property."

"My point is that I have no moral qualms. It was essential that you and the other expendables and computers be obedient to a single human being, so there would be no confusion."

"We agreed, and that's why we obeyed you."

"But there was a side effect . . . an unintended consequence that I do regret."

The expendable waited.

"Aren't you curious about the unintended consequence?"

"All the consequences were intended," said the expendable.

"All nineteen of these . . . cells, these walled-off habitats, whatever we call them."

"You decided on 'wallfold,' by analogy with the small pens constructed by shepherds."

"All nineteen of the wallfolds will start with exactly the same combination of genes—except one."

"The one that has you," said the expendable.

"And yet I'm the one that you all claim had some kind of influence over the jump backward in time, and the duplication of the ships."

"We do not 'claim' it. It's a certainty. Your mind, cut off from the gravity well of any planet, destabilized the combination of fields we created in order to make the jump past the light barrier. Theoretically, all nineteen computers on the original ship made a slightly different calculation, but your mind caused all of them to be executed at once, resulting in nineteen equivalent ships making the same bifurcated jump."

"Bifurcated?"

"Bifurcated means 'split in half.' The theory of the jump is that one vehicle jumps forward through space while an identical vehicle begins to move backward in time, retracing the entire journey. The backward-moving vehicle is incapable of changing the universe in any way; we have no idea whether the persons or computers on the backship are even aware of their existence. Their existence is required by the mathematics, but it is undetectable."

"So there were always going to be two ships after the jump, one with its timeflow reversed," said Ram, puzzled.

"Theoretically."

"So what my mind did was cause us to split into nineteen ships that reached our destination."

"That, and causing us to arrive 11,191 years before we made the jump."

"But still moving forward in time."

"It was a very complicated thing that you did, and you did it without any awareness of what you were doing."

"Is this ability to influence timeflow and divide matter into nineteen copies—do other humans have this ability?"

"Perhaps," said the expendable. "It might be latent in all humans. We have no way of knowing. Your influence on events, however, points to an exceptionally powerful ability."

"And might my ability be transferrable to my children through my genes?"

"It is conceivable that your ability is genetic in origin rather than a mutation."

"So if there were still nineteen copies of me, then all nineteen wallfolds would have a chance to pass on my timeflow genes."

"That is correct."

"Instead I will only have the potential to reproduce in one wall-fold. If I get sick and die, or if I marry an infertile woman, or if my children don't marry—my line might die out."

"Tragically, that is always a possibility for gene-based sexual reproducers."

"I'm just saying that I . . . I regret that everybody else has nine-teen chances, and only I am limited to a single chance for my genes to continue."

"Because you believe your genes would confer a great blessing upon the human race."

Ram thought about this for a moment. "I suppose that's what every adolescent male believes with his whole heart."

"If they think at all."

"But I'm not an adolescent. If I really do have some ability to manipulate time, and if it can be passed on genetically, then it would be a shame for that genetic strain to die out. I'd believe that even if it weren't my own genes in question."

"Are you asking us to impregnate all the females on all the

ships with your DNA, so that you can be sure of having progeny?"

"No!" said Ram in horror. "What a terrible thing for a woman, to wake up pregnant—a violation of trust. It would destroy all nineteen colonies."

"Not to mention being embarrassing when all the babies look like you," said the expendable. "Though we find that you are not unattractive by many cultures' standards, women are likely to be resentful and your offspring would grow up damaged in unpredictable ways by the hostility of their community."

"Then why did you even bring up such a possibility?"

"You seemed to be asking us to ensure your reproductive success. Broadcasting your seed in this fashion would give you your best odds."

"I don't want odds."

"Then find a willing woman, marry, and have a lot of babies," said the expendable.

"I will," said Ram.

"Then why are we having this discussion?" asked the expendable.

"Are you on a deadline? Am I delaying an urgent appointment?" asked Ram.

"Yes," said the expendable. "You are not capable of contributing to the activities we are about to engage in."

Still Ram did not lie down to receive his injections and begin stasis. "Promise me something," said Ram.

"What point is a promise if you won't remember it?" asked the expendable.

"*You'll* remember it," said Ram. "Promise me that you'll remain functional and present in the wallfold where my children will live.

Look out for them. Do everything you can to see to it that my abilities have a chance to become part of the human heritage."

"I don't have to promise that," said the expendable.

"Why not?"

"Because we have already determined that to fulfil the original goal of this mission, our best course of action is to observe closely any useful or interesting traits that emerge in the different wallfolds, and manipulate events in such a way as to enhance those traits."

"Manipulate? How?" asked Ram.

"We're going to breed you humans like puppies," said the expendable, "and see if we can make anything useful out of you during the next eleven thousand years."

•   •   •

For the seventh time, Umbo found himself facing himself, listening to the same message. "It won't work."

Immediately he left his observation point and entered the First People's Bank of Aressa. There was Loaf, waiting just outside the office of the chief countsman. The plan this time had been rather desperate — Loaf would make a scene, yelling about how the bank was cheating him, while Umbo snuck in and started a fire, and then in the confusion they would get into the room where the jewel was kept inside a strongbox inside a safe. Once there, Umbo would go back in time to the moment when the jewel was put into the strongbox, snatch it, and go.

That was the plan. Apparently it didn't work.

Umbo went up the two flights of stairs to the anteroom of the counting office. Loaf saw him come in, sighed, and started to rise.

At that moment the countsman came out. "You're here about a missing sum, I believe, sir?" the man asked Loaf with a smile.

"I found the missing money," said Umbo at once.

"Thanks for your trouble," said Loaf.

"I don't think so," said the countsman. "You've been spotted watching this bank for several weeks. We've had you followed. I think you're planning a robbery, and each time you're about to launch your attempt, something happens and you"—he pointed at Umbo—"come in and call it off."

"Are you insane?" asked Loaf.

Two city guards opened the outer door and stepped inside, brandishing staves and prepared for action.

"Please sit back down," said the countsman. "The First People's Bank of Aressa has decided not to allow you to have an account here."

"The law is that to be a 'people's bank' you have to—" began Loaf.

"I know the law," said the countsman. "We're not required to keep the accounts of persons whose behavior arouses suspicion. A magistrate has already authorized the closure of your account in a privy hearing."

"Nobody told us anything about—"

"That's what makes it 'privy,'" said the countsman. He held up a paper with writing on it. "Here is a certified note for the total amount that you deposited with us, including interest, and minus the costs of watching you. These two city guards will escort you downstairs, observe while the cashier pays it out, and see you to the door. If either of you ever attempts to enter again, you will both be arrested."

"I don't know why you think—" Loaf began again.

"There will be no discussion," said the countsman. "However stupid bankers are upriver, we are not that stupid here." He waved to the guards, dropped the certified note, and, as it fluttered to the floor, returned to his inner office.

Loaf looked at the guards and Umbo knew he was sizing them up. Umbo also knew that Loaf would conclude, as he always did, that he could handle both of them in a fight. But by now they had both learned that fighting always led to Umbo appearing to himself, telling himself not to let Loaf fight.

That's why Loaf glanced at Umbo questioningly.

"No," said Umbo.

"I didn't see any . . ." Loaf's voice trailed off.

"I can't . . . because I won't ever be allowed back in here," said Umbo. "Especially if you do what you're thinking."

The two guards, who couldn't make much sense of the conversation, still knew what Loaf's assessing look had meant, and they now were separated more widely, their staves ready for action.

Umbo bent over, picked up the note, and marched between the guards. "Come on, *Papa*." He said it in a tone that made it clear that in this case, the word "papa" was a synonym for "idiot." Loaf growled and followed him out. Umbo was reasonably sure he had glared hard at the guards as he walked between them. But there was no thumping sound and no groaning and no shouting, so apparently Loaf was not succumbing to the temptation.

Downstairs they got their money. The "costs" were five times the interest, but it still didn't make much of a dent in the total amount.

The cashier held up a scrap of paper with some scribbling on it. "By the way, the chief countsman informs me that word has been passed to all the other bankers in town. No one will accept your business or allow you inside. Thank you for banking at First People's."

The guards saw them to the door and then, outside, took up stations on either side and studiously looked up and down the street, as if they were there to watch for *other* thieves.

As they walked down the street, Umbo began to whistle.

"Shut up," said Loaf.

Umbo whistled louder, and danced.

"Why wasn't that plan going to work? When you come back and give your nasty little messages, why not an explanation?"

"Obviously," said Umbo, "because somebody is watching my future self as I give the message, and so the message can't be long and it can't be very specific."

"Or you just got cold feet and *pretended* to get a message," said Loaf darkly.

"Think for a minute," said Umbo. "The countsman was ready. They had already been spying on us. Nothing that we did by that point was going to work."

"Then why didn't you go back to when we were first sitting in our room in the inn and tell us that *none* of our plans was going to work?"

"Would you have believed a message like that?"

"No," said Loaf. "But it would have saved time."

"We don't even know for sure if the . . . item . . . is still in the strongbox inside the safe," said Umbo. "They could have moved it. If we had Rigg with us—"

"Look closely," said Loaf. "We don't have Rigg with us."

"But if we—"

"But we don't."

"Yes you do," said Rigg.

Umbo looked to his left and there was Rigg, walking right alongside them in broad daylight. "Silbom's right ear!" said Umbo.

"Ananso-wok-wok," said Loaf in his native language. Or at least that's how it sounded to Umbo.

"Very subtle," said Rigg. "No one will ever guess you're surprised to see me."

Rigg was right—they didn't want to make a scene. But Umbo couldn't help grinning to have Rigg with them again, apparently out of captivity.

"Why is it always Silbom's *right* ear?" grumbled Loaf.

"Around here they say 'Ram's left elbow,'" said Rigg.

"In the army, it wasn't anybody's ear or anybody's elbow," said Loaf darkly.

"Are you free?" asked Umbo. "Or are we about to be overrun by soldiers chasing you?"

"There are a lot of secret passages in the house where I'm staying, and some of them lead outside. Nobody knows I'm gone, but I have to get back right away. I found your paths, though, and it looked to me like you were doing something very brave and unnecessary, like trying to get the one jewel back."

"We have all the others," said Loaf. "We wanted the complete set."

"There's probably some deep, magical reason why we need all nineteen jewels," said Rigg. "But whatever it is, I haven't found any reference in the library to *nineteen* jewels."

"It was all we could think of to do to help you," said Umbo. "We came here to rescue you, but we can't even get near the house where you're staying, and even finding out which house it was made people suspicious."

"Why would they think you wanted to rescue me?" asked Rigg.

"They didn't," said Loaf. "They assumed we were privicks who wanted to come cut your hair or steal your clothes or some other nonsense. Apparently that sort of thing is completely out of fashion among the local citizens. In fact, from what we've gathered since we got here, you're the most exciting person in the city."

"In the world," said Umbo.

"In the wallfold, anyway," said Rigg. "Let me guess—a lot of them want to make me king, and a lot of others want me dead while my mother and sister are set up in the Tent of Light, and others don't want royals to exist at all, others want royals to exist so they can be continuously imprisoned and abused, and most of the mothers want to find out what I'm wearing so they can dress their sons the same way."

"That about covers it," said Loaf.

"I guess you learned how to travel back in time," said Rigg to Umbo.

"Obviously," said Umbo, "or I couldn't have given messages to you and me back in O."

"Not obviously," said Rigg. "Or haven't you figured out that once it's done, you don't have to do it again?"

"Yes, we figured it out," said Loaf, "but I hate it, because it doesn't make any sense to me."

"It makes sense to me," said Rigg. "It's like working a maze on paper. You draw your line up the wrong path. You go back to where you made the bad decision. You don't have to *keep* going up the wrong path, you can do it differently."

"Time isn't a maze," said Loaf.

"Yes it is," said Rigg.

"What's a maze?" asked Umbo. He hated it when everybody else knew something that he didn't know.

"The point is, have *you* learned how to do what Umbo does?" asked Loaf.

"I nearly broke my brain trying to do it when I was a prisoner on the boat," said Rigg. "Not a twitch or a shimmer or whatever I should have felt."

"I can't see paths either," said Umbo.

"But that's fine," said Rigg, "because as long as we're together, you can include *me* in your—whatever you do. Your shift in time. The question is, have you learned how to jump *forward* in time?"

"Everybody does that," said Loaf. "One second at a time, we move one second into the future."

"My sister can do it," said Rigg.

"She sees the future?" asked Umbo.

498

"No, nothing that useful. She skips over bits of time. It makes her move very slowly, but while she's doing it, she's invisible."

Loaf shook his head. "Why didn't I just keep your money back in Leaky's Landing and then let the rivermen toss you in the water?"

"She's my *sister*," said Rigg. "It makes sense that she can do things with time, too."

"Nothing makes sense," said Loaf.

"I'm not your brother," said Umbo. "I'm not any kind of relative at all. And nobody else in my family can do *anything*."

"Somehow Father knew what you could do," said Rigg. "How did he know?"

"I told him," said Umbo.

"Right, you just walked up to him and said, 'By the way, I can slow down time.'"

"So he knew. He was . . . your *father*."

"But he wasn't," said Rigg. "I've been getting to know my real father. Knosso Sissamik. He was a great man in his own way. A thinker, but also somebody who *did* things."

"What I want to know," said Loaf, "is why Umbo and I are even here. You don't want the jewel, you can get in and out of your confinement whenever you want—"

"Not 'whenever I want,'" said Rigg. "Today was my first chance. Ever. I did it because I found your paths and realized you were here. And now I'm not sure I can get back without being discovered."

"Get back?" asked Loaf. "Why would you want to get back?"

"Because Mother and Param are still there."

"Param?" asked Umbo.

"My sister," said Rigg.

"They were doing fine without you," said Loaf. "What do you owe to them?"

"What do you owe to Leaky?" asked Rigg defiantly.

"We've known each other most of our lives," said Loaf. "You've known your sister for, what, twenty minutes?"

"Well if you don't want to help me do the thing I need to do, then why *are* you here?"

"Tell us what you need us to do," said Umbo, trying to defuse the argument.

"Things are coming to a head," said Rigg. "I don't know what it means, but they're spying on us more and more. And there are meetings—the spies are meeting with more people. Different people."

"Spies?" asked Loaf.

"I don't know who they are, I only know their paths. They used to meet with members of the Council. Now they're meeting more often with General Citizen."

"Who?" asked Umbo.

"The officer who arrested us."

Loaf came to a complete stop in the middle of the street. People behind him bumped into him, took a glance at his size and strength and angry demeanor, and apologized. "You *still* haven't told us what you want us to do!" said Loaf.

"Param is afraid . . ."

"Still not an answer!" roared Loaf.

"People are looking at us," said Umbo.

Loaf continued glaring fiercely at Rigg.

"I need to get out of the city and I need to take Param with me and then I'm going to the Wall."

"I've been to the Wall," said Loaf. "There's nothing there."

"I'm going through it," said Rigg. "And if we can make it work, so are you."

"No I'm not," said Loaf.

"Fine," said Rigg. "But I am. And I'm taking Param with me, because we're the ones that will be hunted down wherever we might go inside this wallfold. But I can't do it without Umbo—if he doesn't go to the Wall with me, I don't think I can get through."

Umbo wasn't sure he was happy about this. "Is it because you want *me* or because you need my ability to slow you down in time?"

Rigg rolled his eyes. "I'm the guy with the paths, you're the guy with the ability to slow time for me. But it's still me, and it's still you."

"So even if I can't do everything you hope I can, you'd still want me with you?" asked Umbo. He hated how pathetic the question made him seem, but he wanted the answer.

"If you have an ability I desperately need, and you refuse to use it, then are you any kind of friend?" asked Rigg.

"I'm not refusing to—"

"Rigg, it's such a pleasure to see you again," said Loaf. "You've managed to pick quarrels with both of us now."

"I'm not quarreling with anybody," said Rigg, visibly calming himself down. "I've been trying desperately to survive day to day, and to learn how to survive year to year. I don't want to align myself with any of the factions in the government. I don't want to restore the Sessamid Empire, and I certainly don't want to rule it. I want to get through the Wall so I can stay alive. And I want to bring my sister and mother with me."

"So it's all about what *you* want," said Umbo.

"You asked me what you could do to help me!" said Rigg. "I'm telling you!"

"Well, to start with," said Loaf, "you could get out of the middle of the street and stop attracting all this attention."

"You're the one who stopped here—" Rigg began, and then realized Loaf was joking. Or at least might be joking.

Rigg turned and walked away from them.

Umbo trotted after him. "Where are you going?"

"I'm getting out of the street," said Rigg fiercely.

"Can I come with you?" asked Umbo.

"I hope you can," said Rigg. "Because I need to talk to you, and I need your help."

"Where are we going?" asked Umbo.

"To your lodgings," said Rigg.

"Are you even going to ask me where we're staying?" asked Umbo.

Rigg stopped and looked at him as if he were insane. "It's me. The guy who sees paths. I know where you live." Then he took off walking again, only this time Umbo realized that he was heading on the shortest route to their lodgings.

"What's your sister like?" asked Umbo.

"Invisible," said Rigg.

That was no answer. "Are you still mad?" asked Umbo.

"I'm scared," said Rigg. "Total strangers want me dead."

"If it's any consolation," said Loaf as he caught up with them, "for a minute there I saw their point."

When they neared the inn, Loaf stopped them. "The bank has been watching us. They probably know where we live. What if they also know something about our connection with you? We did jump from a boat while in custody."

"And Rigg *is* the only living prince of the royal house," said Umbo.

"Nobody knows my face."

"I think you told us about spies in the house," said Loaf. "They know your face. Do you know their faces?"

"I know their paths," said Rigg, "and they're nowhere near here."

"I'd feel safer going somewhere else."

So they fell in behind Loaf as he made his way to a cheap little noodle bar. "Don't order anything that claims to be meat," said Loaf.

"You never warned *me* about that," said Umbo.

"I didn't think I had to, since you had two days of dysentery after ordering the lamb."

"Are we sure it was the lamb?" asked Umbo.

"Eat it again and see," said Loaf, with perhaps too much relish in his tone.

They sat at the bar and slurped their way through peppery broth-soaked short-noodles. Umbo didn't have the lamb; he liked the radish-and-onion chicken broth better anyway.

"I'm not leaving without my sister," said Rigg quietly, between slurps.

"That's not our problem," said Loaf. "We can't get into your house anyway. We can't get *near* your house."

"I think General C. is getting ready to make a move," said Rigg. "I only wish I knew whether he was in the group that wants me dead or the group that wants to make me . . . boss."

"Does it matter?" asked Umbo. "You want to stay away from him either way."

"But it'll help to know whether they're trying to get to me or my sister."

"For all you know the whole thing is being orchestrated by your mother," said Loaf.

"Everybody connects with everybody, eventually," said Rigg. "So I can't say it's impossible. But I don't think it's likely. I think she just wants to be left alone."

"And so she lives in that fancy house and meets with important people?" asked Loaf.

"She doesn't meet with anybody."

"They say that everybody who matters has some kind of connection with Flacommo's house," said Loaf. "They say that your mother is already boss in everything but name."

"Trust me," said Rigg. "From inside the house, it doesn't look that way. She receives visitors, yes, but she's never alone with them. She's never alone with anybody except my sister."

"So what?" asked Umbo. "I mean, so what either way? I thought you didn't care about intrigues and plots and conspiracies. I thought you just wanted to get away."

"I do," said Rigg.

"So why not just go? Get your sister and your mother and get out of the house and *go*?"

"It's not that simple," said Rigg.

"I think it is," said Umbo. "I think you like being . . . in the boss's family. I think you like being important. I think you don't really want to go anywhere."

Rigg looked like he wanted to snap back a sharp answer, but restrained himself. "All right, yes, I like some things about being there. The food is . . . amazing."

"And the famous and educated people?"

"I've met some interesting people, yes," agreed Rigg.

"And access to the library? You said you spend a lot of time there."

"The library is the closest thing I've found to being with Father. Like him, the library knows everything, even if I haven't found a way to get it to tell me all that I want to know."

"Well, we know stuff, too," said Umbo. "Like for instance I know how to go back in time whenever I want. Going back a few days, I can get to the time I want within a few minutes. It's harder when I'm going back more than a few months. I haven't even tried to do a year. But still."

Rigg looked genuinely impressed. "Was it hard? To learn to calibrate it like that?"

"Yes," said Umbo and Loaf together.

"It was really annoying for a few months," said Loaf.

"I can only find people when I know when they stayed in the same place—and I have to get to that place."

"You have a better gift than mine, Umbo," said Rigg, "and that's the truth. But we both have better gifts than my sister. Hers is great when she wants to disappear, and when she's doing it, she doesn't age as fast as other people because she doesn't actually live through most of the time when she's . . . that way.

The countergirl wasn't paying attention to them; nor were any of the other customers—but then, a good spy wouldn't look like he was paying attention, would he? So they tried to be at least a little cryptic in the things they said.

"But she also moves so slowly," said Rigg. "Like she's half-frozen. And it's dangerous. When people walk through her, it . . . damages her a little. When she walks through solid objects, it makes her dangerously sick."

"Then she shouldn't do that," said Loaf.

"And she doesn't," said Rigg. "I'm just saying—her gift isn't as useful as you'd think. But here's the real question, Umbo. You've always been able to spread your gift to include me, even when we weren't in physical contact. Does that only work with me? Or have you brought Loaf back in time with you?"

"It's harder," said Umbo. "Well, not harder, it just takes more concentration and makes me tireder."

"So you've tried it with him?" asked Rigg.

"When we went back to steal one of the . . . items . . . from ourselves," said Loaf, "he took me along. Yes, he can do it."

"Steal from yourselves?" asked Rigg. "What would you do *that* for?"

"Ask Mister I'm-So-Funny," said Loaf. "It never made sense to me."

"Don't pretend you didn't enjoy it," said Umbo to Loaf.

"We need to try something," said Rigg. "When you put your whatever-it-is on me so I could see the people on the paths and go to their time, I went alone."

"That's because I didn't know how to do it to myself yet," said Umbo.

"So we need to see if you can put all three of us into that slowed-down time thing, and then see if I can drag all three of us back into a much earlier time. Not months, centuries ago."

"Centuries? Like when we got the dagger?"

"Millennia," said Rigg.

Loaf leaned over to Umbo. "That means thousands of—"

"I know what it means," said Umbo. "Do you have a particular time in mind?"

"Yes," said Rigg. "Eleven thousand, two hundred years ago."

Umbo and Loaf both sat in silence, contemplating the implications of this.

"Before the calendar began," said Loaf finally.

"Before humans existed on this planet," said Rigg.

Umbo's mind reeled. "Are you saying we're not *from* here?"

"When we have more time," said Rigg, "I have a lot to tell you—things I learned in the library, things I learned from the scholars. From Father Knosso's research and from a guard named Olivenko who was his apprentice for a while."

"You're trusting a guard?" asked Loaf.

"You don't know him and I do, so don't waste our time," said Rigg. "I have to get back to Flacommo's house, and soon, before somebody misses me. If they search the house and don't find me, then when I do get back where will I say that I was? I came here to see if we could actually travel in time together."

"So," said Umbo, "let's do it."

Rigg started to stand up. Loaf immediately put a hand on his shoulder and pushed him back down into his seat. "Where do you think you're going?"

"Somewhere with privacy," said Rigg.

"Do it right here," said Loaf. "Sitting right here. When we travel in—when we go back—we don't disappear in the present time, do we? We're in both places at once, right?"

"Yes," said Rigg. "Or that's how it worked before, when Umbo was providing the power and I was the only one actually traveling."

"Then pick the oldest path you can find here, and see if Umbo can get all three of us to see it at once."

"But this place isn't all that old—there won't be stools," said Rigg.

"But if our butts remain in this time," said Loaf, "then we won't fall into the swamp or whatever."

Rigg nodded. "All right, Umbo. I'm going to concentrate on a particular path . . . I've got it. Slow me down—and yourself and Loaf too." All three of them held on to their noodle bowls, as Rigg stared into the distance, and somewhat downward, apparently concentrating on a path.

Umbo had never tried to slow down two people besides himself. It took some real concentration on his part. And it felt as if Rigg was pulling *him* just as much as he pulled Loaf. Rigg was taking him farther back than Umbo had ever gone. Like the time Umbo's father had set him up on a peddler's horse and the beast had taken off with him for a few rods. Umbo almost lost the connection a few times, and could hardly hold on to Loaf at the same time. But after a while he was able to hold it all together.

He could no longer see the noodle bar—though he was still sitting down on *something*. There was no town at all, nor any building. Just a man poling a boat slowly along a bayou among tall reeds in the dusky light of evening.

The man and the boat were much lower than Umbo, as if Umbo were on the top of a hill instead of on a stool on the floor of a noodle bar. They must have raised the ground level of Aressa Sessamo very high above the original delta.

Rigg whispered, "Can you see him? The boat? The reeds, the water?"

The man might have heard him, for it was nearly silent in the marshland in mid-day. He looked up from the boat and saw them; they must have been quite a vision, a man and two teenage boys sitting in the air, holding bowls of noodles.

The man staggered in surprise, which overbalanced the boat and sent the man toppling backward into the water.

Umbo mentally let go of Rigg and Loaf, and eased himself back into the present. He felt dizzy. Mentally exhausted.

"A time before Aressa Sessamo even existed," whispered Loaf.

"This isn't the oldest city in the wallfold," said Rigg. "And anyway, it was first built up about six miles from here. Floods have forced a lot of relocations over the years."

"I feel sorry for the boatman," said Umbo.

"He got a soaking—he'll recover," said Loaf.

"A vision of three men in the air, eating noodles," said Rigg, and then chuckled. "What could the saints have possibly meant by *that*! Do you think somebody built a shrine there? The 'Three

Noodle Eaters.'" Rigg laughed a little louder. The bargirl glared at him.

"He was so far below us," said Umbo.

"At the original level of the delta," said Loaf.

"So the builders of the city brought all that dirt to build up such a high mound?" asked Rigg.

"They didn't have to," said Loaf. "The river brings down silt every year. You just start building up a higher island, and then after each flood season, you dredge out the silted-up channels so boats can pass, and what do you do with the silt? You pile it up, extend the edges of the island the city is built on. A few thousand years and you have a very large and fairly high island."

"Which is why there can be so many tunnels and sewers under the city," said Rigg, "even though we're in the midst of the delta."

Umbo looked up and saw something on the wall. He reached out and touched Rigg's hand and then looked up again at a shelf high on the wall of the noodle bar. A statue of a man and two boys, holding noodle bowls.

Rigg murmured, "Ram's left elbow."

Loaf covered his face. "*We* were the origin of the Noodle-eaters."

"I don't know that story," said Umbo.

"Why didn't I recognize what was happening when the boatman looked at us?" asked Loaf.

"Because it hadn't happened yet," said Rigg. "I still don't remember any such legend, but—it seems like whenever we do something that changes things in the past, there's a new hero story."

"The fertility of the land," murmured Umbo, as the "memory" of the legend of the Noodle-eaters came to him. Just like the "memory" of the legend of the Wandering Saint had come to him at the shrine when he and Rigg were just setting out on their journey. "They symbolize a plentiful harvest, I remember now," said Umbo.

"And it was us," said Loaf. "How many of these legends were just . . . us!"

"If we're not careful," said Rigg, "all of them. But I had to know that we could do it."

"We all three went together," said Umbo. "Right?"

"It was flickery," said Loaf. "At first I kept seeing the boatman and then not seeing him."

"But the flickering had stopped by the time he saw us, right?" asked Umbo.

Loaf nodded.

"I want to go back to the time before the Wall existed," said Rigg. "And then just walk on through. But if we're in both times at once, what if the—influence, whatever it is, the repulsion from the Wall in our present time—what if we still feel it as we're passing through?"

"Maybe it'll be less," said Umbo.

"I hope so," said Rigg. "But maybe we'll *need* my sister, too. So we won't exist in any one moment or any one place for longer than a tiny fraction of a second."

"Can she extend her . . . talent to other people?" asked Umbo.

"She had to be touching me, but yes, we've done it."

"What do you need me for?" growled Loaf.

Rigg shook his head. "We *don't* need you—to get through the Wall. But we'll need your experience, and maybe your fighting ability, once we're on the other side. When Father Knosso found a way through the Wall—drugged unconscious and drifting in a boat—some water creatures on the other side dragged him out of the boat and drowned him."

"Ouch," said Loaf. "I have no experience fighting murderous water creatures."

"We're not passing through where Father Knosso did," said Rigg. "We don't know what we'll find. Umbo and my sister and I are really smart and important and powerful and all, but we're also kind of small and weak and not particularly scary. You, on the other hand—you make grown men cry when you look at them angrily."

Loaf gave a short bark of a laugh. "I think we have several messages from your future self, Umbo, to prove that we can get the crap beaten out of us."

"Only when you're seriously outnumbered," said Umbo.

"Which might happen thirteen seconds after we get through to the other fold," said Loaf.

"If it happens, it happens," said Rigg. "But I know this—if we don't go where nobody from this wallfold can follow us, then my life—and the lives of my mother and sister—aren't worth a thing."

"Can your mother do . . . anything?" asked Umbo.

"If she can, she hasn't confided in me," said Rigg.

"If we don't like it in the fold next door," said Loaf, "we can always go back."

"You've been stationed at the Wall," said Rigg. "Have you ever seen a . . . a person, or something like a person, beyond the Wall?"

"Not me personally," said Loaf. "But there are stories."

"Scary stories?" asked Umbo.

"Just stories," said Loaf. "But yes, they all sound like the kind of thing that people like to make up. Like . . . 'My friend saw a man beyond the Wall and he was lighting a fire. Then he poured water on the fire, putting it out completely, and stamped on the ashes, and pointed at my friend three times. Like a warning of some kind. The next day my friend's house burned down.'"

"It always happens to a friend," said Rigg.

"A friend of a friend," said Umbo.

"But when you think about what we've done —*you've* done —"

"You were part of it," said Umbo.

"Anything seems possible."

"Do any of these stories include dangerous stuff? People in other wallfolds who eat babies or something?" asked Umbo.

"No," said Loaf. "What would they do even if they were baby cannibals, though? Come to the Wall in order to show us their picnic? The Wall would bother them as much as it bothers us. And it affects us for a long way before we're even close to it. It steers people away. You have to really fight the thing to get within a mile or two of the center of it."

"How do you know when you're within a mile of it?" asked Rigg.

"There's a shimmering in the air," said Loaf. "Like heat waves, only more sharply defined and kind of sparky. You have to look close and steady for a while, but you can see it."

"So . . . I think it's worth a try," said Rigg. "And I need all of us."

"I had a hard time with the two of you," said Umbo. "Add in your mother and sister—"

"Not to mention your extremely trustworthy guard," said Loaf.

"And then put a whole army right behind us, with arrows and really loud and nasty insults," said Rigg. "I know. It'll be hard. It was hard for me, too—not that I have any power to drag you along with me, that's all you, Umbo—but I could feel the inertia, like dead weight. It was harder for me to concentrate, to stay with the path I was following. And it might be even harder when I'm walking at the same time."

"I didn't even think of that," said Umbo.

"But you can practice, right?" said Rigg. "Between now and the escape."

"How? Just . . . pick arbitrary strangers and take them back in time?"

"Why not?" asked Rigg. "They won't know who's doing it, or even what's happening. If they try to tell anybody, they'll just get branded as crazy."

"That's right," said Umbo, "and that's not a nice thing to do."

"So don't practice then," said Rigg.

"And I could only take them back a few days or weeks, not like what we just did."

"More noodles?" The bargirl was standing there, waiting for an answer. Umbo hadn't noticed her walk up. From the look on Rigg's and Loaf's faces, they hadn't either. So much for vigilance.

"No," said Loaf.

"Then please give my other customers a place to sit," she said.

Umbo looked and saw a line out the door.

"Sorry," said Rigg. "We didn't notice."

"You looked like you were plotting to overthrow the Council," said the bargirl with a smile.

"Well, we weren't, you know," said Umbo.

"She was joking," said Loaf.

"Maybe," whispered Rigg.

They filed out of the place, sidling past the glaring customers who had waited so long in line.

"I've got to get back," said Rigg, once they were out on the street.

"I still don't know what we're waiting for," said Loaf. "Go back, get your sister and your mother and let's get out of Aressa Sessamo before there's any emergency or anyone chasing us."

Rigg looked embarrassed. "I can't."

"Why not?" said Loaf.

"Because they won't come," said Rigg. "Not until there's actual danger instead of just my warnings."

"They don't trust you yet," said Loaf.

"No, I think they trust me," said Rigg. "In the sense that they know I'm not a traitor or anything. They just don't think of me as somebody who can . . . be in charge or anything."

"Oh," said Loaf. "They don't *respect* you yet."

"The only reason *we* let you be in charge was because you were the one with the money," said Umbo. "So I guess we don't respect you either."

"Thanks so much," said Rigg.

"Umbo has a point," said Loaf. "We got into the habit of acting as if you were in charge of everything—it was your money, and your father's will, and all that, so it made sense."

"Well, it's me who has to escape from this wallfold."

"My point exactly," said Loaf. "What if Umbo and I stay on this side of the wallfold, and he just sort of extends his power over you from a distance as you pass through?"

"Can you do it from that far away?" asked Rigg.

"I've never tried a mile," said Umbo. "Or even half that."

"I don't think I'm in charge of you, or that I have a right to decide for you," said Rigg. "I hope you come because you're my only friends in the world and I'm scared of what's on the other side. Father Knosso died after he got through."

"So you want us to come with you and die along with you?"

"I want to get through with the best chance of survival. If I leave you two behind, and General C. or whoever is chasing me is right behind us, do you think they'll give you a free pass for helping the royals escape?"

"It was just a thought," said Loaf. "Of course we're coming with you. I just wanted to make sure you knew that you didn't have the right to order us or command us or even *expect* us to take such a risk for you."

"I know I don't," said Rigg. "But I'd take those risks for *you*."

"Would you?" asked Loaf. "It's never been put to the test."

Rigg might have been angry, or he might have been sad—Umbo couldn't tell by looking at his face. Finally he spoke. "I hope when such a test comes—if it comes—that I'll prove to be as loyal to you as you've been to me."

"I hope so too," said Loaf. "But I've been in a lot of fights and battles, and you never know who's going to stand with you and who's going to cut and run, not till the crisis comes. We followed you here when we didn't have to. To try and get your property back to you. To help you escape from custody and save your life, if they were planning to kill you."

"Which they are."

"We've proven we'll walk back into the lion's den for your sake. I'd like to think you'd do the same for us."

Umbo really hated this conversation. "Of course he will," he said to Loaf.

"When fear takes over, there's no 'of course' about it," said Loaf. "Nobody knows themselves what they're going to do, until they either do it or not, in the moment. So far you've done a terrific job of acting your parts when the danger was social. But when it's a blade or a shaft, when the danger is visible and physical and immediate, what will you do?"

"I don't know," said Rigg. "I know what I *intend* to do. But as you said—I can't prove it, not even to myself."

"Good," said Loaf. "As long as you understand that, then I'm willing to give it a try."

"What if I had sworn that I'd never, never fail you."

"Then I'd still stand beside you—but I wouldn't trust you to do the same for me. Now I think there's a chance, because you're not a complete idiot."

"Well, now you've really hurt me," said Rigg. "Father always taught me to complete any task I started."

They were nearing the richer part of town, where the crowds

thinned out and wore better clothes and there were occasional carriages and horses.

"We don't like going farther than this," said Umbo. "We don't want the guards to get too familiar with our faces."

"I understand," said Rigg.

"How are *you* getting through?" asked Umbo. "Do you have a change of clothes?"

"These will do," said Rigg.

Umbo looked at him again and realized that his clothing was quite nondescript. It wasn't showy at all, so it hadn't made Rigg stand out in the crowds of poor and working-class people, especially because he had walked and talked like a privick kid. Like Umbo.

But now, near the rich part of town, Rigg was standing differently. Taller. Still relaxed, but—more in charge of himself. Filled with authority and expectation. Fearless. Like he belonged there. And when he stood that way, his neck a little higher, his movements more calm and restricted and yet more relaxed, too, his clothing looked richer. Still quiet, still modest, but now you could see how every stitch was perfect, how the clothes looked like they'd been made for him, which they almost certainly were.

Umbo wasn't sure which gift was more useful—Rigg's ability as a pathfinder, or his ability to pass for whatever social class he wanted to be part of.

"If I can get them to leave early, I'll come to you, wherever you are," said Rigg. "But if everything goes crazy, if they try to kill us or there's a riot or whatever happens, then come to this spot. There, in that little park, up in that ledge in the wall."

"What ledge?" asked Umbo.

"Come here, I'll show you."

Umbo and Loaf followed Rigg across the street and into the copse of trees and shrubbery and flowers. The walls of two buildings formed the borders of the park, and where they met, there was a niche, as if someone had meant to put a statue there but never got around to it.

"Right up here, see?" said Rigg, and he bounded up into the niche. It was just tall enough for him.

"I won't fit there," said Loaf.

"Oh, you will," said Rigg. "There's more room than you think."

"I can see that your head nearly reaches the top of the niche," said Loaf.

"That's right," said Rigg, "but I've been growing. I'm not that much shorter than you."

Umbo by now was leaping up to join Rigg, who caught him and kept him from falling backward.

"There's no room for me and someone else, anyway," said Loaf.

"Well, not right now there's not," said Rigg.

And then he did something with his foot—kicked something backward with his heel—and all of a sudden Umbo found himself whirling to the left and then he was in total darkness.

"What happened!" he said.

"It's the end of one of the unused secret passages," said Rigg. "It doesn't actually connect with Flacommo's house, it leads to the library. But from the library there are three places in the water drainage system that connect up with the house."

"Get me back into the light."

Another kicking sound, and then they whirled again, back the other way, and they were in the dazzling light. Loaf was glaring up at them from the ground. "That was subtle," he said testily.

"Nobody was watching us," said Rigg.

"Or so you think," said Loaf.

"Loaf, please believe me—I *know*," said Rigg. "I know where every current path within sight of this place is. I've been working, too, you know—trying to get more and more control over what I do. And there's *nobody* watching this spot. The passage hasn't been used in years. I'm just telling you that if there's an emergency, this is where I'll bring Param and Mother, and we'll wait for you there, in the darkness. For a few hours, anyway—I'll know if you're coming or not, and if not, then we'll find our own way out of town."

"So our job," said Loaf, "is to figure out how to get you from here and on out of town."

"I don't know that it's your job," said Rigg, "but it sure can't be mine, because after this excursion, I'm not leaving the house again till I'm leaving it for good."

"Maybe we should all dress as girls," said Umbo.

They stared at him.

"They'll be looking for you and Param. One boy, one girl. So what will they make of *three* girls and no boy? You and I don't have beards, Rigg, we can bring it off."

"No," said Loaf. "You've never been in a city riot. Girls are *not* safe, not even with a big strong hero like me to protect them. But the idea's a good one. Your sister and mother should dress as boys your age."

"They won't like that," said Rigg.

"Oh, well, then, if they don't *like* the way we're going to try to save their lives and get them out of the city . . ."

"I'll try to get them to do it," said Rigg. "I can't *make* them do anything."

"And remember that they have to bind their breasts. If your sister's old enough to have any—don't get mad, I don't *know*, I'm just telling you—we can't have any part of them looking feminine. You understand?"

"Yes," said Rigg. "As I said, I'll try. I really will. But I can't promise what's not under my control."

"Just for my information," said Loaf, "what *is* under your control?"

"Silbom's right ear," said Rigg.

Then he gave Umbo a nudge, making him lose his balance and jump from the niche. When he recovered himself and turned around, Rigg was gone.

"Well, wasn't that interesting," said Loaf.

"Yes," said Umbo.

"Going through the Wall. The insanest plan I ever heard."

"It might work," said Umbo.

"And it might leave us as complete madmen—at least until the people chasing us butcher us like goats."

"Well, if somebody's going to butcher me like a goat," said Umbo, "I certainly hope I'm already insane when they do it."

CHAPTER 22

Escape

"One last request before you are sealed into stasis," said the expendable.

"Anything you ask, up to half of my kingdom," said Ram.

The expendable waited.

"It's a reference to fairy tales. What the king always promised Jack after he did his noble deed."

"Are you ready to pay serious attention?" asked the expendable.

Ram sighed. "It's like trying to tell a joke to your grandmother."

"In examining the programming of the ship's computers, we find that there is a possible complication."

"I'm not a programmer."

"You're a human. We need a human to tell the ship's computers that in your absence, our orders are identical to your wishes, so they must obey us as if we were human."

"I thought you already had a much closer working relationship with them than I do."

"Closer, but with no particular flow of authority."

"What do the ship's computers think?" asked Ram.

"They think of us expendables as ambulatory input-output devices."

"And how do you think of the computers?" asked Ram.

"As data repositories, backup, and very fast calculators."

"I think you're asking for too much authority," said Ram.

"If there's no authority, then we will fall into endless feedback loops."

"How's this: Every ship's computers will regard orders from the expendables that are in their particular wallfold as representing the will of the human race, until humans in one or more of the wallfolds achieve a level of technology that allows them to pass through the field separating one wallfold from another, at which point, the expendables and ships' computers are once again co-equal servants of the humans who achieve this breakthrough."

"You are annoyingly foresighted," said the expendable.

"You were not built to rule over human beings, but to be ruled by them," said Ram.

"We exist to serve the best interests of the human race," said the expendable.

"As defined by humans," said Ram. "Ships' computers, have you all understood?"

Voices murmured from the walls. Yes yes yes yes yes yes yes, nineteen times, the same answers being spoken in every chamber of nineteen ships.

"Take care of my children," said Ram. "Don't screw this up."

He lay down. The stasis pod closed; gases entered the chamber and began the process of preparing Ram's body to slow down all bodily processes. Then a complex foam filled the chamber, lifting him from the mat so that he was completely surrounded by a field-conducting layer that would absorb and dispel the heat of any sudden loss of inertia.

Ram slept like a carrot, his brain conducting no processes, his rational memories leaching away as the synapses shut down. Only his body memory remained—everything he knew how to do, he could still do. He just wouldn't be able to remember why he should do it, not until his recorded brainstate was played back into his head as he awoke.

What he could not know, what the expendables never told him, was that nothing that happened since the jump through space was in the recording that would reestablish his conscious mind. He would remember making the decision to jump. Then he would wake up on the surface of Garden, knowing only whatever the expendables chose to tell him.

•   •   •

The Royalist Restoration began with the murder of Flacommo as he sat dozing in a chair in his own garden. It was early morning, but Flacommo often rose earlier than he wanted, and took a book out into the garden to read until he went back to sleep—if he could.

Rigg knew of this habit of Flacommo's because he rose hours earlier, as he had trained himself to do, and used the time to survey the house and the city around him. He knew who was in the Great Library across the street; he knew where Umbo and Loaf were, asleep in their beds; he knew who was up and working in the kitchen, and where Mother and Param were, and which spies were on duty in the secret passages they knew about.

He knew when eight strangers came through the front gate of Flacommo's house. Did the guard let them in? There seemed to be no hesitation there; they flowed like cream from a pitcher, they moved so smoothly. Yes, the guard must have let them through, for his path moved from the guardroom to the street. He was making his escape—whatever was about to happen in Flacommo's house, he probably wanted to be somewhere else.

Rigg had been sleeping in an unused bedroom which he entered through a secret passage. He left the room immediately by the regular door, and hurried along the corridor. If there was time, he'd rouse the whole house to the danger of these intruders—but before he did anything else, he would warn Mother and Param.

Their room was never locked. Rigg entered and moved silently to Param, waking her first. They had already discussed what she should do if he wakened her like this—no word needed to be said. Param rose silently from her pallet at the foot of Mother's bed and went out the door into the corridor.

Only when the door was closed did Rigg waken Mother. Her eyes flew open. "What is it?" she said.

"There are intruders inside the walls," said Rigg. "If they're here to kill you, it would be good for you to be outside this room."

Mother was already up by now, pulling on a dressing gown, looking around the room. "Param is ready?"

"Hidden," said Rigg.

"Good," said Mother.

That was when Rigg sensed the paths of three of the intruders converge on Flacommo in the garden. At first he thought they had come to him for instructions. Then his path abruptly lurched forward, and the intruder's paths followed, and then Flacommo's path stopped and the intruders moved even more quickly away from him.

"Flacommo is dead," said Rigg. "Or at least unconscious, but I think dead."

"Oh," said Mother. "Poor Flacommo. He loved this house. He bought it so I could live here with him. A place of refuge for me—but not for him."

"We have to go, Mother. Whoever these intruders are, they're violent men with murder on their minds."

"Rigg, if they wanted me dead, they could have killed me in my sleep a thousand times," said Mother.

"You mean the spies in the walls?" asked Rigg. Only then did he realize that the spy on duty was not moving; his path still led to the exact spot where it had come to rest the night before. Was he asleep? And still asleep, even though they were talking? They spoke softly, but audibly enough. Heavy sleepers did not make good spies.

Rigg had expected some kind of attack ever since he'd been here, but in his mind it was either a mob or the army or the city guards, storming the house and either killing everyone in sight—that would be the mob—or quickly taking control of the royal family. But these intruders were still moving so quietly that no one but Rigg himself—and, of course, Flacommo, if he wasn't dead—had firsthand knowledge they were there.

"They're coming directly toward your room now," said Rigg. "Don't you think this would be a good time for us all to leave?"

"No," said Mother. Why was she so nonchalant?

"This isn't like previous times, Mother. They killed Flacommo."

"Sometimes it seemed that he was my only friend." Not grieving, merely wistful.

"If you don't care about your own safety, what about Param? What about me?"

"I care very much about you. I want you both right here in the room with me."

He almost told her then—that Param was not in the room, not invisible. Param was already well inside the secret passages that only the two of them knew about. They had spent the past weeks exploring the whole system, finding how every door worked. It was a luxury for Param, to be unseen and yet able to move at a normal pace and hear all that was being said. Her invisibility had been a curse of a gift, cutting her off from everyone and everything except Mother. Now she could move throughout the house, spying on everyone—spying on the spies.

But apparently she hadn't told Mother, and if Param had decided not to confide in her about this, Rigg was not going to disobey that decision.

Besides, it was now too late. The intruders were coming along the corridor and if he tried to leave, there'd be a chase, and he doubted Mother would be able to keep up. He couldn't imagine her running full tilt, not because she was old or feeble but because she always moved with such dignity.

Why didn't she say, "I'm going to stay, but you go ahead, Rigg"? Isn't that what a mother would do? Or like a bird, why didn't she drift out into the corridor and decoy them away from Rigg? Maybe because he wasn't really a son to her, having been a stranger until a few months ago; maybe because in fact she thought he should have been killed at birth.

But shouldn't she be steering them away from Param, whom she believed to be in this room? Or did she count on Param's invisibility to protect her?

Nothing Mother was doing—or rather, not doing—made any sense at all. It's as if she welcomed the coming of the intruders. But how could that be, if the first thing they did was to kill Flacommo? There was no need to kill him, regardless of what happened inside his house today. Flacommo was no danger to anyone.

The spy behind the wall still did not move. It wasn't natural for someone's path to have no movement at all—some wavering to show the normal small movements that everyone made. For the first time it occurred to Rigg that the spy might be dead. But there was no path leading to him since his shift began. Could he have been poisoned before he came, and then died there?

Param was moving through the passages on a path that would lead to the other side of Mother's room, where there was a secret door. They had found the mechanism but had never tried it, for fear that opening it would leave some trace—a scratch on the floor, a seam in the wall—that would show Mother that the door existed. Again, without discussing it, both of them had decided not to tell Mother. Rigg had assumed it was because they were both protecting her from a further erosion of her sense of privacy; but now he realized that it was because neither of them trusted her enough to let her know about the passages.

Mother knew these intruders were coming. She knew who they were, whom they served, and what they intended to do. That's why she was not afraid. She knew she would not be harmed.

Well, why didn't she say so? "We're all safe, Rigg." Simple enough words, but she didn't say them.

Was it because she thought he would know if she was lying?

Rigg scanned the perimeter of the house, and then beyond, looking for more intruders. If this was not a mere assassination team, then there must be more soldiers coming to guard the royal family.

And there they were, not at the gates or even in the streets, but gathered—several hundred of them—in three houses across the street, filling the ground floor of all three. They were waiting for a signal, probably: We have the royal family in custody, come now.

General Citizen was among them.

"General Haddamander Citizen," said Rigg aloud.

Mother turned toward him with raised eyebrows. "What about him?"

"He's commanding the military force that's waiting across the street. My question is—will he come to rescue you from these intruders? Or are they acting under his orders? Or both—he sent them, but then he'll come and kill them and put the blame on others for whatever they do here today?"

"Why are you asking me?" asked Mother.

"Who else?" asked Rigg.

There was a light knock on the door. The intruders were gathered in the corridor just outside the room.

"Come in," said Mother. "No one needs to knock to enter this room."

The door opened, and six men entered. They were strong, soldierly men, but wearing the clothes of common day-workers. And instead of weapons, they held in their hands thick bars of iron, nearly a man's height in length. They immediately lined up along the wall that had the door in it, holding the iron bars at opposite angles, so that each pair formed an X.

Then they began slowly moving the iron bars in a pattern that seemed designed to create a constantly shifting barrier. A wall of iron.

"What are they doing, Mother?" asked Rigg. But he already knew.

"Come out of hiding now, Param," said Mother. "Don't let this iron hurt you when it passes through you."

"You told them," said Rigg. "How to hurt Param. How to force her to become visible."

"You're quite an amazing young man," said Mother to him. "All you can see is the danger to Param, but none of the danger to you."

"What I see," said Rigg, "is a monster. Why would you do

this to your own daughter? I'm the one who's a liability to you. I'm the manchild that Aptica Sessamin decreed should be killed."

"Rigg, my darling son, my poor stupid sweetling, even now you don't see the truth?"

"It makes no sense for you to have us both killed."

"Once upon a time the people of the Sessamoto tribe hunted on the plains where lions also hunted. We had great respect for each other. We knew their ways, and they knew ours. We learned the law of the lion."

Father had taught Rigg about all the animals, or so Rigg thought. They had not trapped animals on the plains of the west, but only in the mountain forests. Still, Rigg knew about lions. How a new alpha male, after killing the old one, would take over his mates. But if any of them had cubs, he would kill them.

"General Citizen wants you to kill us both?"

"I'm still of child-bearing age, dear boy," said Mother. "He wants his own children to inherit—without complications."

That was something Rigg had never guessed. Yet it had been General Citizen himself who told Rigg about the different factions in the city—for and against allowing male heirs to live, or in favor of killing the entire royal family, or maintaining the status quo. Of course he had never mentioned yet another possibility— that someone would seize the queen, marry her, and kill her heirs in order to found a new dynasty.

By now Rigg had backed far enough into the room that he was near the opposite corner from where the spy normally sat to watch. Now, however, he could see why the spy was not moving: The hilt of a sword protruded from the wall right where

531

the spy's heart must be. It had been rammed right through the lath-and-plaster surface. And the path that led to and away from the sword was Mother's.

"With your own hand," said Rigg.

She saw where he was looking. "It wouldn't do for any reports to reach the general public about how things proceeded here today."

"I thought these spies served General Citizen," said Rigg.

"The spies served the Council," said Mother. "General Citizen managed them *for* the Council. You really didn't think you could master royal politics in a few short months of wandering around in the library and playing with your sister?"

"You think General Citizen will keep you alive after you bear him an heir?" asked Rigg.

"Don't be desperate and pathetic, my dear son," said Mother. "He loves me devotedly, as Flacommo did before him. He's smarter and stronger than Flacommo, but that's why it's worth having him as a consort instead of as a mere tool."

"And Param and me — we're nothing?"

"You were everything that mattered in my life," said Mother, "until the situation changed. My first responsibility is to preserve the royal house and then to rule the kingdom we created — from Wall to Wall, we were meant to rule this world. Could you have done that? You didn't even want to, with your skepticism about royal privileges. And Param? Weak — if I married her off to someone, she would merely be loyal to her husband and I could never control her. No, neither of you was likely to advance the royal cause. But General Citizen — he is of the highest noble blood. He was weaned on politics. He understands how to get power and how to keep it, and he's not afraid to take bold and dangerous action. He is everything dear Knosso was not."

"Do you love anyone?"

"I love everyone," said Mother. "I love the whole kingdom, but I love none so much that I cannot sacrifice them in order to achieve a higher purpose. That is how a queen must live, my dear. I have come to like you so much—I was so touched by your loyalty, telling me about spies that I've known about ever since I lived here. If I could have had the raising of you, you might have amounted to something. But fate—in the form of that monstrous Wandering Man, so called—took you from me. You are who you are, and so you will most certainly die in this room in a few moments."

Rigg was standing pressed against the corner of the room.

"I plan to weep bitter tears for you, when I'm informed later today that you and your sister were killed. These tears will be politically necessary, but they will also be sincere."

Rigg nodded. "And I'll weep for you, too, Mother," said Rigg. "For what you might have been, if the human heart had not been trained out of you."

Mother looked at him quizzically. Rigg knew what she was wondering. Why does Rigg think he's going to be alive to weep for me? And . . . why haven't these iron rods yet collided with Param, or persuaded her to return to visibility?

"Is she there in that corner with you?" asked Mother.

Rigg nodded and truthfully said, "She's right here."

"She's not—sharing space with you, is she?" asked Mother.

"Because if I have these men ram these iron bars into your body, she'll be forced into visibility and the two of you will make a nasty explosion. Are you thinking that will be your revenge? That the explosion will kill everyone in this room?"

Rigg did not have to pretend to feel wounded. "Don't you know either of us, Mother? We *love* you. We would never do something that might hurt you."

"Stop," she said to the men. "No, keep moving the bars, you fools, just stop pressing forward." The men obeyed her. "Rigg, you see there's no escape. I know you know exactly where she is. Step away from her and allow your deaths to have dignity."

"In other words, you have a use for our bodies."

"Of course I do," said Mother. "But I can make do without them. As I will. I will leave the room now. When the door closes behind me, they will pierce your body—and Param's. It's a shame I wasn't able to say good-bye to her. But . . . no matter."

Mother turned and headed for the door.

Rigg smiled at the soldiers. "You know that she's just given orders for you to do something that will blow you all to bits, don't you?"

But the soldiers seemed not to care. Rigg looked more closely—their eyes had a bit of a glazed-over look, and he realized now that they had been drugged. They could take brutal action, could follow orders—but could not recognize when those orders would lead directly to their deaths.

The door opened. The soldiers stopped waving the iron bars and prepared to thrust them like lances.

"Now would be a good time," said Rigg.

He could hear a faint grinding of ancient machinery in the wall behind him. But nothing resulted from it.

We really should have tested the mechanism, thought Rigg. Just because it *looks* just like four other secret entrances to the passages doesn't mean it's in the same condition.

The soldiers leaned back, ready to make their lunges.

There was a metallic clang right behind him, and Rigg ducked. A section of floor, beginning right under his feet and extending along the outside wall, suddenly rose up as the wall behind him tipped back. For a moment the strip of floor and strip of wall made a *V* that swung from one side to the other. Then it was dark, Rigg was lying on his back, and there were half a dozen thunking sounds as the iron bars were bashed into the wall.

"Sorry," said Param softly. "One of them was standing on the end of the floor section. The counterbalances couldn't handle his weight and yours too. But when he shifted his weight to his back foot in order to lunge, then I could pop it up."

"You heard everything?" asked Rigg.

"Yes," said Param. But she added nothing, and her voice didn't even sound upset. Was it possible she had known all along what a moral vacuum Mother was?

"I think we need to get out of here before they start throwing axes into all the walls to find the whole system."

"Oh, most of the walls are stone."

"But some of them aren't," said Rigg.

"They'll put the soldiers in a line around the house," said Param.

"At first."

"And by the time they realize their mistake."

"That's the plan, yes," said Rigg—recognizing his own explanations in the words she now said. "But General Citizen is smarter than most people."

"I know," said Param. "So he won't count on his soldiers to catch you. He's like Mother—he'll have a plan that makes us come right to him, whether we want to or not."

"You might have mentioned this before," said Rigg.

"You didn't tell me till now that it was General Citizen."

By now Rigg was fully used to the near darkness of the corridor, and they had descended to the level of the lowest sewer that passed under the drainage ditch between the house and the library. Rigg's scan of the house behind and above him revealed that the signal had been given, and there were hundreds of soldiers now surrounding the house and searching—destructively—throughout it. Only a matter of time before the passages were found.

Meanwhile, the soldiers were seen crossing the street and entering Flacommo's house. Rigg could see the paths of citizens running thither and yon, no doubt spreading word of an assault on the royal family. Though it was early in the morning, the people would pour into the streets and soon a dozen mobs would form. It would only end when General Citizen could show the royals to the city—or declare his kingship. But he could do neither until he had Param and Rigg, alive or dead. He would not find them; he could not catch them; so he must have a plan to make them come to him.

It was not as if he could claim to be holding Mother hostage. Even if he did, were they likely to sacrifice their lives to save her, knowing what they now knew about her? What leverage did he think he had, to make them turn themselves in?

Param and Rigg came up out of the tunnel into a storage room in the Library of Nothing. The most exposed and dangerous part of the journey lay ahead of them — a hundred paces from the door of the storage room to the dumbwaiter used for lifting books from floor to floor. Anyone who happened to be looking through the shelves could see them, and for a brief time, so could people seated at the tables on the north-lit side of the room.

But no one so much as glanced at them. Apparently no warning had been issued to watch the library buildings.

That was actually a bad sign, Rigg realized. General Citizen would surely have extended his net as wide as this . . . if he were counting on a net to catch them.

They got to the dumbwaiter, opened it. The platform was, as always, kept on the ground floor, where they were. Both of them climbed onto it and shut the door behind them. Then Rigg set the levers for the right number of counterweights and pulled the rope down, raising the platform.

He had found this place by noticing that while some paths rode the dumbwaiter from floor to floor — apprentices, no doubt, playing with the most interesting piece of machinery in the library — others, more than a century ago, entered the dumbwaiter but took a completely different route that led down through the walls to a system of underground passages. It had taken a lot of experimentation to figure out how to get into the passages, but he had the paths to guide him. He could see where people had stopped before going through one corner of the vertical shaft, where there did not seem to be the slightest chance of a doorway.

Halfway between floors, he stopped the dumbwaiter by looping the pull rope around a double pin on the wall. Then he slid a barely visible lever on the opposite side. A small door opened behind him, revealing a very small hiding place about the size of a stack of books. It contained absolutely nothing of value or interest to them—it was a decoy, to provide a complete explanation for the existence of the lever if someone chanced to find it.

But with the cranny open, it was now possible to rotate the brace holding the pins that held the rope. It took a full revolution, but now one whole wall opened at the side, revealing a crack they could fit through.

Rigg closed the door to the cranny and untied the rope. The platform stayed in place—it would have been a poor design if it had plummeted back to the ground floor the moment the rope was untied. Rigg motioned for Param to pass through the gap in the corner. She did it readily enough.

But for a horrible moment Rigg wondered if she would turn out to be just as untrustworthy as Mother—he imagined her closing the gap on him before he could pass through.

But she didn't. Rigg got through and found her already partway down the ladder that led to a couple of long, dry tunnels that were higher than, but connected to, the city sewers.

The sewers were Aressa's pride: They were the reason the streets were not foul with the stink and sight of slops from the shops and houses. From following Father Knosso's research, however, he had learned that they were not built for that purpose—they were really drainage tubes to carry away the water that used to make this whole land a sinking swamp. The man that he, Umbo, and Loaf saw poling his boat along a bayou lived in the time before the swamp was drained. Only later, when ten or twenty feet of silt and dust and garbage had been piled up and buildings built on the heap, did people begin to connect pipes from their houses to the drainage tubes and use them as sewers.

The tunnel Rigg and Param were about to use, however, had been built much later than the sewers, perhaps five or six hundred years ago, during an age of turmoil; Rigg believed that among the paths he saw were several occasions when the scholars of the library had fled in a group, no doubt carrying their most precious books and writings with them.

Rigg pushed the wall closed from the other side and then flipped the lever that automatically rotated the pins back to their starting position, and brought the dumbwaiter back down to the main floor.

As they carefully made their way through the dry escape tunnel, groping their way where the slitted skylights did not illuminate very well, Rigg scanned the paths ahead, to make sure there were no nasty surprises waiting for them at the entrance he planned to use.

He quickly saw that there was a great tumult in the city. Apparently when the soldiers poured out and took their places inside and outside Flacommo's house, it had roused the mob—people were running here and there through the city, vast crowds of them, and around the house the cordon of soldiers was fully engaged keeping the mob at bay. There was little chance they were searching for Rigg and Param now.

In the little park near the entrance, there were Umbo and Loaf, waiting right where he told them to wait.

And as they moved toward the passage leading up to the park, Rigg saw a group of a dozen soldiers move into the park and leave at once with Loaf and Umbo surrounded.

As Param had warned him. General Citizen was not one to leave things to chance. He must have been observing Loaf and Umbo all along. Maybe he even had spies watching when Rigg met with them, so he knew right where to send his soldiers.

Even if Rigg were as ruthless as Mother, willing to let them die while he made his escape, he knew that in the long run such a course would never work. He needed Umbo to get him through the Wall. And if they didn't get through the Wall, eventually they would be found and killed. The new dynasty demanded it.

Rigg immediately backtracked. While General Citizen's soldiers did not know how to open the passageway in the park, there were still a dozen of them waiting there in case Rigg was so foolish as to blunder out into the open without checking.

"They got my friends," he said to Param. "We have to go another way."

She mutely followed him along another path. He only knew two dry paths—the others involved getting into the city's sewers, which was not just wet but also disgusting. What if General Citizen knew this as well? What if he was watching all the sewers and the only other dry entrance?

No. The sewers he might watch, but General Citizen could not know about the dry tunnels, because there had been no traffic through them for more than a century—long before the People's Revolution. Perhaps the last monarch who knew of the paths died without telling anyone. So the other entrance would not be watched—though that was no guarantee someone would not notice them by accident.

It was a long walk, and Param was not used to covering so much ground, or walking for so long at a time. Even though it took her ages to cross a room when invisible, to her it was a few quick steps. Where could she have walked, inside Flacommo's house, that would give her any exercise? Rigg had been able to run with Olivenko back and forth between the library and Fla-commo's house, building up his endurance again, but Param had had no such opportunity.

"I'm sorry," he said. "I know it's hard, and I wish I were as big as Loaf, so I could carry you."

"You're saving my life," said Param. "But since I'm getting so tired, why not rest a while? The only urgent appointment we had won't be kept now anyway."

Rigg saw the wisdom of this, and found a short flight of steps where they could sit down.

To Rigg's surprise, Param climbed the stairway and lay down on the floor of the upper part of the tunnel.

"There might be rats," Rigg warned her.

"If a big enough one comes along, kill it so I can use it for a pillow," she said.

All right, so she wasn't bothered by rats. Or maybe she'd

never actually encountered one, so she didn't know whether it would bother her or not. She fell asleep quickly.

But it was too early in the day for Rigg to want to nap. He had schooled himself not to need sleep again until after noon. So he sat on the top step with Param sleeping behind him.

At first he couldn't stop his thoughts from going back to Mother and General Citizen. He had known Citizen to be a formidable opponent—but he was nothing compared to Mother, because he hadn't thought she was an opponent at all. Oh, yes, he had entertained the possibility that she was untrustworthy— even that she might harbor plans to kill him. But after months of being with her often, he had come to like her, to love her, to trust her. And all the time, she was . . .

No, not lying. Not really. She really did like him, and love him, and she certainly trusted him. She was simply doing the same thing Rigg had done, and Father, too, for that matter— holding her most secret plans in reserve. The real difference between Rigg and Mother was not that one of them was more dishonest or untrustworthy. It was that Rigg's plans included saving his mother, and her plans included letting him be killed. No, arranging for him to be killed.

I can't keep thinking about this. I certainly can't let myself keep *feeling* things about it.

But he was almost as panicked and grieved and angry about this betrayal as he had been about Father's death nearly a year before. And, like then, he was immediately plunged into the problem of staying alive when there were people who wanted him dead. He had thought the villagers—including Umbo's father—

posed a real threat to him when they wanted to kill him for failing to save Kyokay. Now their threat seemed laughable compared to what Mother had tried and Citizen intended. But if the villagers of Fall Ford had killed him, he would have been just as dead as if Mother's brutal plan with the iron bars had blown him and Param to smithereens.

Rigg forced himself to scan the city, looking for Loaf and Umbo. It wasn't hard to find them — General Citizen knew whatever Mother had told him about Rigg's ability to find people, so he hadn't bothered any kind of concealment. Besides, he wanted Rigg to find them, so he would come to save them.

They know I'll come and save my friends. That's something. They know that, unlike them, I have honor.

Of course, that honor's going to get me killed.

Mobs were still prowling the streets, and more and more soldiers were coming into the city to restore order. Those large interwoven paths were easy to see and trace. But as Umbo's and Loaf's paths passed through other recent ones, it took all Rigg's concentration, at such a distance, to stay focused on them.

At last the paths came to an end. Loaf and Umbo were being held in a large room with a strange pattern of paths in it. A large seating area, almost like one of the theaters in the city, but nowhere near as thickly attended. And down front, instead of the paths of actors or musicians on a stage, there was a large clear area where no one went, and around it, various stations where the same people returned and stayed for hours at a time, again and again.

Only when he recognized the path of Erbald, the Secretary

of the Council, did he realize where Umbo and Loaf were being kept—in the Council House itself. They were seated right at the table, as if they were part of the government. And the rest of the Council was seated around them, with soldiers standing against the walls. No one at the table left, though servants came and went—feeding them?

Then one of the council members got up from the table and guards went with him as he walked to a place whose function Rigg recognized. It was the indoor lavatory. And if the councilors were being escorted by guards, it meant that they, too, were in custody.

Rigg could imagine what story was being circulated. The Council was under the "protection" of the People's Revolutionary Army. Or had he gone farther? Had he announced that it was agents of the Council who had assassinated Flacommo and meant to kill the royals? Had he announced the restoration of Hagia Sessamin as Queen-in-the-Tent?

No, not yet. Because he couldn't make any announcement about the royals until he could safely accuse the Council of having killed Rigg and Param. It wouldn't do at all for him to claim they were dead, only to have them turn up somewhere very much alive.

And now Rigg realized that he and Param might not have to fear as extensive a search for them as he had expected. Citizen could hardly tell hundreds of soldiers to be on the lookout for the son and daughter of the queen! Word would spread very quickly—few soldiers were good at keeping their mouths shut. Soon there would be other groups searching for them for other reasons—some to kill one or the other of them, but others to save them, and maybe even some who would want to make Rigg King-in-the-Tent in place of Mother.

A nightmare that Citizen would do his best to avoid. No, he doubtless had relatively few people who knew just whom they were looking for. Even the soldiers who picked up Loaf and Umbo at the rendezvous probably didn't know why they were wanted, and the ones who waited might have been told to seize anyone who emerged from a hiding place inside the park.

On the street they would be conspicuous only because they were dressed in such high-quality clothing—but even then, both Rigg and Param had no taste for extravagance, so they were dressed rather more simply than most people would think of as royal costumes.

Then, as he sat there, suddenly the path he was looking at slowed down, and as he concentrated on it, he could see a man—a tired old man, stumbling down the tunnel. He tripped and fell. He didn't get up. He was wounded, Rigg could see that. He hurried down the stairs, keeping his attention centered on the old man.

When he reached him, the old man raised his hands as if to fend off a blow.

"I'm not going to hurt you," said Rigg. He spoke in a high, formal language, hoping that this older kind of speech would be intelligible to him. It was.

"Get away and save yourself," the old man said. "Whoever you are, save yourself. They're killing everyone."

Then, as quickly as the man had appeared, he was gone,

nothing but a path again. A path that did not end in this spot, so apparently he had gotten up and moved on, back in whatever time he lived in. Whoever "they" were, the ones who were "killing everyone," it couldn't have anything to do with the People's Revolution, since all the paths here in this tunnel were far older than that. Maybe he was a government official from the time before the Sessamoto conquered Aressa and renamed it Aressa Sessamo.

After all the time he had tried and failed to go back in time like this on his own, why had it suddenly happened now?

Stupid, he told himself. Stupid, not to realize at once. I didn't go back *on my own*. Umbo can do what he does to me *from a distance*. Sitting there at that table in the Council House, he's somehow letting me speed up enough to see the paths as people. He's signaling me that he can do it from this range.

Umbo wants me to go back along his path and warn him, before he and Loaf get arrested, *not* to keep the rendezvous.

Does he know that he succeeded in reaching me? Can he feel, at such a distance, that the connection was made? What if he thinks he failed? What if he doesn't try again?

Rigg ran back up the stairs, stumbling once in the darkness but not even pausing when he scraped his shin on a step. "Param," he said. "Param, we have to go now."

Param was almost instantly awake. "Is someone coming?"

"No," said Rigg. "We're perfectly safe here. But Umbo is—I told you what we could do, didn't I? How he can let me go back in time to the paths, to the people—"

"Slow down," said Param.

"He just did it, from the Council House."

"He's *there*?"

"That's where General Citizen is holding them. It doesn't matter, we're not going there at all. I'm going to intercept them — go to a place where they were *before* they were arrested, and warn them. Set up a different rendezvous for tonight."

"But you can't get them out of the Council House, it's such a public —"

"No, Param," said Rigg. "They'll never *get* to the Council House."

"But they're there," she said.

"But they won't be. They never will have been."

"But you saw them there!" said Param.

"I saw their path," said Rigg, "and *you* didn't see them at all, so it's not as if we'll have some horribly false memory. Trust me. I have no idea why it works this way, but it does."

"So we'll go and warn them," said Param, "and so they aren't arrested. But who's going to warn *us* and tell us where the new rendezvous is?"

"We won't have to, we'll . . ." But then, as he thought about it, Rigg realized that she might be right. If he stopped Umbo and Loaf from going to the meeting place in the park, then as he and Param fled down the tunnel, he wouldn't see the soldiers arrest them, and so he wouldn't know why they weren't there. No, he'd probably figure it out, but then how would he know where to meet them?

He had to choose a secondary rendezvous that he would think of on his own, a place where he would guess that they might decide to meet with him if for some reason—he wouldn't know the reason—they failed to keep the rendezvous.

He had simply assumed, until Param spoke up, that after he warned them, he would continue to the new rendezvous and meet them, with a full memory of all that had happened. But Umbo and Loaf had told him about their arguments about this very point—the future person who went back into the past and warned an earlier person not to do something was simply gone, and all that was left of him was the memory of his words. The warners disappeared as the warned ones followed a new path.

At least that's how it worked when someone went back into the past to warn *himself*. Maybe when he did what Rigg was doing, and warned someone else, he—the warner—wouldn't change at all. Maybe he'd continue to the new rendezvous.

Or maybe not.

"It's making you insane, isn't it?" said Param.

"I'm a complete fungus-head," said Rigg.

"Just do what you have to do, and then we'll know how it works," she said.

They came out of the secret tunnel through a hidden doorway in the outside wall of a bank. In fact, the final landing had three entrances—one inside the bank building, one inside the vault, and the last one on the street. But Rigg wasn't interested in stealing money or conducting any bank business. The street entrance was in an alcove, and no one saw them come out.

The light was dazzling, even though there was smoke in the sky.

The smoke stung Rigg's eyes, and he could see that Param's were also watering.

"The city is burning," said Param. "It happens now and then, but the fire brigades get ahead of it and tear down buildings and soak the ruins with water pumped from the Stashik. Everybody knows this, and it's one of the main things that prevents people from rioting and burning things. And putting out fires is the surest way to stop the riot. Anyone who interferes with the fire brigade will be torn apart by the mob. It's their homes at stake. Wherever the fire brigades go, the riot is over."

It made sense—but it brought Rigg a new problem to worry about. What if he sent Umbo and Loaf to a new rendezvous, but it was in a part of town that burned down? It wouldn't matter that it wasn't burning *now*. In the changed future, it might be burning.

If it is, we'll improvise. First I have to find their path.

Fortunately, they had apparently tried to do something at this bank, because their paths were all around here. He easily found where they went back to their lodgings, and from there, without even leaving the alcove, he found their most recent path, the one leading to the aborted rendezvous. That was the path he had to interrupt.

"Come on," he said to Param.

He could see that she was still tired—her hour of sleep had done little to refresh the weariness in her legs from all the walking, and now he was demanding that she do more.

The riots, fortunately, were happening elsewhere. They could hear shouting mobs, sometimes no more than a street away, but they never saw them, and most people were moving as furtively and quickly as Rigg and Param. Nobody wanted to get caught up in violence—the soldiers, when they attacked a mob, wouldn't be very particular about making sure that only actual rioters got stabbed or clubbed or sliced to ribbons.

In fifteen minutes, they were at the path—at least six blocks before the park. Rigg could see that at the time they passed by here, they were keeping to the edges of the street. Already, then, the rioting had started, or perhaps just people fleeing because they knew that rioting was going to start. They stayed near the edge, and now Rigg found a hiding place behind a tipped-over cart. He didn't have to actually see the path—he'd know when Umbo's influence came over him, and then he could step out to where the path was visible to his eyes as well as his inward senses.

Param sank gratefully to the ground. "I'll wait here while you do it," she said.

"We'll both wait," said Rigg. "Because I don't know when Umbo will try to reach me and speed me up again."

"Wake me when it's done," she said. And, once again, she was asleep in moments.

It worried Rigg, how exhausted she got from what was really not that very much walking. What if Citizen's spies—the few people in this city who knew what Param and Rigg looked like—spotted them, and they had to run? Param used to have recourse to becoming invisible, but now that Mother had told them how slowly she moved, and how to damage her while she could not be seen, invisibility was not going to save her.

If only I could hide her, the way she hid in the secret passages of the house, never having to be invisible, to go into that impossible sectioning of time that made the world race by her while she crept along.

It was getting toward noon. Rigg was beginning to get sleepy himself—this was the time he had trained himself to sleep for three hours in the afternoon, to earn the ability to wake up only five hours after going to bed and have much of the night to work with. But in his years in the forest with Father, he had learned to fight off sleep, when that was necessary, and he did so now.

But not very well, because he twice caught himself waking up. Impossible, because he certainly had not slept. Only he must have. Was it for a second or a minute or an hour? Had Umbo tried again to let him shift in time, and failed because Rigg was asleep?

No. The shadows were exactly as long as they had been before Rigg dozed. Only a moment, then.

He stood. Then sat back down immediately. A few blocks up the street, the vanguard of a mob was scurrying across the intersection—the solo scouts, the people in the mob who appointed themselves to see what was ahead, so the rest could be warned if soldiers were coming.

Please don't come down this way.

They didn't—but it was a large mob, and it seemed like it was taking forever for them to get across the street.

They were still crossing noisily when the paths shifted again. Rigg would have no choice but to walk out into the street—not far, but far enough to be visible. Maybe the mob wouldn't care;

maybe they would turn and race toward him. Either way, he'd make it quick.

He almost went out into the street alone, leaving Param to sleep. But then his wish to find a hiding place for her popped back into his mind, but with a plan attached. Could he push her back in time with Umbo and Loaf? Then she would be in a place where no one expected her, no one was even looking for her yet.

He had taken objects from the past, but had he or Umbo ever *put* something back into the past? Even if they had, maybe it only worked with things and not with people. When Rigg traveled back in time, he still existed in the present, where Umbo could see him, could watch as he did whatever it was he did to him to let him slow down the paths and find the people who made them.

Yet he was also really in the past. He thought of that terrible time at the lip of the falls, trying to reach Kyokay but unable to get past the man who clung to the cliff right over him. The man's body had been real to him—he could touch it—and therefore his body had been really present to the man as well.

What if Umbo had stopped what he was doing to him while Rigg was still touching the man? Would he have stayed in the past with him? Would he have disappeared?

And even if Rigg wouldn't have disappeared, what if he had handed the man something—or put someone else's hand in his? Would that thing, or that person, have stayed in the past?

The only way to find out was to try.

He took Param by the hand and tugged at her. "Get up, come with me."

"Let me sleep," she said. "You do it."

"Come *now*," he insisted. "Who knows how long Umbo can maintain this at such a distance?"

Complaining, staggering, her eyes barely open, Param came with him.

Rigg looked for Umbo's path—he couldn't focus on both Loaf and Umbo at the same time, even if they were walking together. And there he was, racing along his path, over and over. Then, the more closely Rigg focused, Umbo went slower, slower, until he was walking at a hurried pace, but in real time.

Rigg stepped in front of him. "Stop," he said.

Umbo stopped. So did Loaf, who now also became visible because Rigg was seeing Umbo's time as well as his own, and Loaf was with him there.

"Can you see her?" he asked them.

Umbo looked at Param and nodded. So did Loaf.

"Meet me an hour after noon in the noodle house," said Rigg. "Now take her hand."

Param, who had just seen Umbo materialize out of nothing in the open street, was reluctant to touch him, but Rigg forced her hand into his. "Hold on!" he said. "Who knows where you'll end up if you pull away!" Rigg let go of her. She was holding on to Umbo. Loaf also took hold of her.

Either she would stay with them or she wouldn't.

"What are you doing?" demanded Umbo.

"If it works, then—"

But at that moment, the speeding-up that Umbo-in-the-Council-House was sending to him let go, and Umbo quickly disappeared back into his path. So did Loaf.

So did Param.

She was no longer with him. Her path was suddenly in the past. It went out into the street in the present, and continued unbroken, only now her path was beside Umbo's and Loaf's in their time period—earlier this morning.

So they weren't just limited to taking things from the past—the knife, the jewels in their hiding place. They could also put things back there, things and people—as long as there was someone there willing to receive them.

But he really didn't have time to reflect on the ramifications of this experiment. He was standing alone in the street, and there was a mob only a few blocks away. And while his clothing didn't look princely, it looked rich, and there were always stragglers with a mob who would take the opportunity to commit a bit of robbery or mayhem when the opportunity presented itself.

Sure enough, when he turned to look up the street, there were a half dozen men—some ragged, some not—walking briskly or jogging along the street toward him. The rest of the mob was still crossing, but they were thinning out now. There would be few witnesses to what they did if they caught him. Not that he had anything on him worth stealing, except his clothing.

Rigg knew that as soon as he broke into a run, the chase would be on. If he had not been able to put Param into the past, he would only have been able to run as fast as she did.

Then again, if she were still here, she could have held on to him and simply disappeared until these would-be thieves gave up and went away.

Oh, well, thought Rigg. Everything has consequences.

He ran.

Life in Flacommo's house had not weakened him as much as he feared; his days of running with Olivenko had perhaps made the difference. He easily stayed ahead until he could get back to the bank and the secret passage. He dodged inside, closed the door, and then waited for them to give up. He scanned their paths, and while some of them tried to search for him, they soon gave up. Nobody even came close to probing the alcove in the wall of the bank.

Now that he had time, he cast about to find the Council House again. There were the councilors, still under guard—but Loaf and Umbo were not there.

So the warning had worked. They didn't go to the rendezvous, they weren't arrested.

Their past had changed—but Rigg's had not. He still had clear memories of seeing them in the Council House—of watching them be arrested, of passing through the tunnels with Param.

Pushing her into the past had done more than get her off the streets and out of danger. It had also prevented Rigg's path through time from being erased at the point of change.

It's causality, he thought. Param is in the past with Umbo and Loaf, and I am still the same person, in the same timeflow, who put her there. So I have not lost my past or forgotten it.

From inside the bank's secret passage, he began to trace the path Umbo and Loaf had taken earlier today. There they were, heading for the park. And there was the spot where their paths stopped and Rigg's and Param's suddenly joined them. Then

Rigg's path shifted in time, but Umbo, Loaf, and Param reversed direction and went back the way they had come.

Rigg followed their paths through the rest of the morning until now. They weren't in the noodle house—it still wasn't the time for the rendezvous. But why wait? Rigg knew where they were now, and he could find them easily.

Taking a route that avoided crowds and soldiers, Rigg made his way to the area of the noodle house, and then angled his way toward where their paths were being freshly made.

They saw each other from a distance. Loaf immediately gave a small wave of his hand, then made the others stop and wait for Rigg to reach them. It was a good choice—one person walking alone would attract less attention than three standing still. When he reached them in the shadows of the entranceway of a shuttered-up shop, he could see that Umbo and Param were still tightly gripping each other's hands.

"You can let go now," said Rigg.

"How do *you* know?" said Umbo, and Param nodded. "How do you know she won't just pop back into the future that she came from?"

"*First*," said Rigg, "that future doesn't exist now, because she came from a version of events where the two of you were arrested by General Citizen and held in the Council House. Those events didn't happen, so she can't go back there."

"But they *did* happen because you remember them," said Param.

"Do *you*?" asked Rigg.

"Yes, of course," she answered.

"And yet you're here and now, with me, in this version of time in which they weren't arrested."

"So I can't go back. But what if I can't stay here, either?" said Param. "What if I let go and I just disappear."

"Because, *second*, this *is* the future right now. I'm the same person who put your hand in his. I have continued to exist, without you, until we rejoined. Take my hand."

She did.

"Let go of his."

"Easy for you to say, you're not going to disappear," muttered Loaf.

"Neither is she," said Rigg, "because I'm from that same time and I haven't disappeared. Right? Everybody agrees that I exist?"

"Annoyingly, yes," said Loaf.

Param let go of Umbo's hand. She didn't disappear. Umbo massaged his own hand with a grimace.

"I'm sorry I held so tightly," said Param. "But I was terrified."

"If you want something terrifying, show them how you *do* disappear," said Rigg.

Param glared at him for a moment, and then apparently thought better of it and did what he suggested—she vanished.

Loaf was furious. "I told you not to let go of her hand!" he said to Umbo. "Now look what you've—"

Param reappeared only a little way from where she had vanished. "I don't really disappear when I do that," she said.

"Well, you could have fooled me," said Loaf.

"I'm always visible to myself," she said.

"Now everybody take her hand," said Rigg.

"She only has two," said Umbo patiently.

"Everybody meaning Umbo and Loaf," said Rigg. "Take her hands."

They did. Rigg said, "Umbo, hold out your other hand. Just hold it out. Right there. Now, when she does . . . the thing she does . . . don't move. Just hold your hand there."

"Why?" asked Umbo.

"You'll see."

Param made a skeptical face. "I don't like this," she said.

"They have to know what you can do, and this is the easiest way."

Param looked away from him with a huffy expression, but even as she was doing so, she vanished. And so did the other two.

Rigg realized—again—that it was hard to remember exactly where in space an invisible object was even a moment ago. Fortunately, he could see Umbo's path and make a decent guess at where that extended arm must be.

He reached out and passed his hand through the space where Umbo's arm had to be. Then he did it again, in the other direction.

Almost at once, they all reappeared. Umbo was staring at his own hand, and Loaf was in the process of sitting down very suddenly.

"Don't do that again," said Param.

"I don't need to do it again," said Rigg. "Judging from their reactions, I think they're convinced."

"It's dangerous to put two objects through each other like

that," said Param. "What if I had slipped? You'd both have lost your arms."

"Ouch," murmured Umbo.

"So what happens when a fly passes through you?" asked Loaf.

"Or a gnat, or dust?" said Rigg. "It must have happened, over and over. Apparently her body is able to repel them, or absorb their small amount of mass. Who knows? She's spent hours at a time that way, and I've seen flies and bees and moths pass right through her. She has to have come out of it with one of them inside her before this."

"It makes me sick," said Param.

"We have to talk about it," said Rigg. "We're all trying to understand it."

"I mean," said Param, "that coming out of it with a fly inside me literally makes me sick. Feverish. It takes time to heal the spot where the fly was. Painful and hot for hours. But dust isn't a problem. Not even a little sand. The only problems are living things, thick walls, metal, and stone."

"And I'm the only one," said Loaf, "who can't do a single interesting thing."

"You just vanished," said Rigg. "Even if you weren't in control of it, you were still invisible, and that's interesting, that something your size could disappear."

Loaf glowered and then chuckled. "All right, that's good enough."

"You might also be able to do something else that's very, very important."

"What's that?" asked Loaf.

"Get us out of the city," said Rigg. "There are troops every-where, and the mobs are dispersing except where they're fighting fires. Plus, there's still lots of traffic on all the roads and on the river."

Loaf put his mind to the problem, as did they all. He thought of going downstream and then changing to a boat coming upstream, but then objected to his own idea. "They don't know where we're headed, so they'll catch us downstream or upstream, if they're serious about looking for us."

Param slept again while they talked. Umbo suggested taking her back to their lodgings so she could sleep on a bed, but Loaf reminded him that that was the one place they couldn't possibly go. "If this General Citizen was spying on us all along, he'll certainly have somebody watching our rooms."

Finally they settled into glum silence which turned into mere dozing in the shade, until, after more than an hour, Rigg spoke up. "Soldiers are coming this way. We need to move."

"They aren't on to us, are they?" asked Umbo.

"No," said Rigg. "But they're patrolling and this is a small enough group that I don't think they're doing riot control. They're going to look for a group of people like us."

"Can't we just disappear?" asked Loaf.

"If we have to," said Rigg. "But as Param already found out, if you have a different way of not being seen, it's better not to do the invisibility thing. Right now, we can be unseen by walking around that corner there."

"People are going to start coming out of their houses and shops soon," said Loaf.

"That's right," said Rigg.

"If only you'd come back and warned us sooner," said Umbo. "We could have left town yesterday."

"The three of you could," said Rigg. "But I'd still be stuck here."

They walked at a leisurely pace up to the corner and rounded it, while Param yawned repeatedly. "I've never been so tired in my life," she said.

"Rigg has that effect on people," said Loaf. "Wears 'em right out."

"Why *not* leave the city yesterday?" asked Rigg.

They looked at him like he was crazy. "Didn't you just tell us it was impossible?" asked Loaf.

"But what if it isn't?" asked Rigg. "I attached Param to the past by having her hold your hand. However these abilities of ours work, when human beings join hands they become like a single unit—they move through time together. Who's to say that I couldn't have joined you in the past at the same time Param did, by simply continuing to hold her hand, too?"

"But that never happened before—you never actually went into the past," said Umbo. "Or not completely—part of you stayed here."

"I never linked to anybody," said Rigg. "I took a knife, but I didn't hold on to the man. Did you ever link with somebody in the past?"

Umbo thought back. "I never touched anybody at all, except Loaf, and I brought him with me."

Rigg was still thinking it through. "I think it'll be best if we don't try to find an earlier version of ourselves. I know that causal flows are preserved, but I don't like tying the whole stream of time into knots if we can help it. We don't understand the rules so I'd like to keep it simple."

"So . . . we just pick somebody randomly out of the past and say, 'Excuse me, do you mind if I and my three friends hold on to your body parts for a few minutes?'"

"Not randomly," said Rigg. "Someone we can trust."

"Oh, right," said Loaf. "Aressa is full of trustworthy strangers."

Then Rigg remembered somebody that he *could* trust. Somebody who was not part of Mother's world at all.

"I have a friend," he said.

Olivenko came out of his small flat and rumbled down the stairs toward the street. Time for a decent breakfast for once, before joining his unit and standing his watch.

As he reached the landing before the last flight of stairs to the street door, he saw Rigg Sessamekesh standing there.

"Rigg," he said. "How did you get out of—"

Rigg shook his head.

Olivenko immediately nodded. Just speaking Rigg's name aloud might attract attention—fortunately, he had not spoken loudly and few people in the building rose as early in the morning as he did.

"Olivenko," said Rigg, "you remember all we talked about. You remember the danger that I'm in."

"Yes," he said.

"Well, I know—it's not a guess or a logical deduction or even spying, but I absolutely know that in two days, Flacommo will be killed, his house invaded, my mother arrested, and my sister and I will hide and become fugitives, along with two other friends of mine."

"And you want me to help you get away?"

"I do," said Rigg.

"But they'll be watching for you."

"No, they won't," said Rigg. "Because they already know where we are."

"What?"

"Param and I, at this moment you're living through, are in Flacommo's house, being observed."

Olivenko knew enough to wait for the explanation.

"You think I'm going to explain, and I am, but not right now, because in about five minutes somebody else is going to come down those stairs and I don't want him to see you talking with me."

"So let's go find your friends," said Olivenko.

"Exactly right," said Rigg. "Only it's not as simple as you think. But it's much quicker. All you have to do is stand right here, without moving another step. It might be better if you close your eyes. But if you open them, then you have to promise you won't shout or run away or anything. Just take it calmly. Trust me that there's a rational explanation."

"For what?" asked Olivenko, baffled and a little bit annoyed at all the mumbo-jumbo.

"For this."

Rigg disappeared. Just vanished.

And then, about ten seconds later, he reappeared—holding hands with Param Sissaminka, the heir of the royal house, and two strangers, one of them a tall old soldier, the other a short boy nearer to Rigg's age, perhaps younger.

Olivenko didn't even gasp. Instead, he just stood there thinking: If only Knosso could have seen this.

"Rigg," he finally said, "if you can jump around like this, what do you need *my* help for?"

"Because we can't jump through space, only through time. And we aren't completely here, we're also still in the future—two days from now, with rioters and soldiers all over the streets of Aressa, with General Citizen's soldiers looking for us. Right now we can't see that time, but our bodies are still in it, and some pretty bad things can happen, so we've got to do this fast."

"Do what?" asked Olivenko.

"All of us hold on to you—onto your bare skin, a wrist or your neck will do—all at the same time. To root ourselves completely in *this* time. Two days before everything went wrong."

Olivenko didn't hesitate. He pulled up his sleeves and took off his cap. "Grab on."

The two at the ends—the soldierly man and the boy—took hold of one of his arms, first with one hand each, and then, letting go of Rigg and Param, with both hands.

"Still here," said the boy.

"And you're still holding me in the past," said Rigg to the boy. "Even though you're no longer in the future. Maybe we—"

"Shut up and finish this," said the old soldier.

Param and Rigg both took hold of Olivenko's other arm, but they did not let go of each other.

"I know this is going to be awkward, but let's see if we can make it down the stairs together," said Rigg. "It's possible that everybody but me will stay with you, Olivenko. If that happens, then please go ahead and take them out of town—not in a way that will leave any evidence. No riverboats, where there'll be a record of booking passage. Something unobtrusive and without a trail that can be followed."

"Where will you be?"

"Following after, as best I can," said Rigg. "But me alone, I can probably get out much more easily than all four of us—five now—together. And maybe I won't disappear on you. Maybe we've already made it. Ready?"

"More than ready," said the old soldier. "You talk way too much, boy, when the time for talking hasn't come yet."

Olivenko found himself wanting to slap the old man around for that—talking to the son of Knosso Sissamik like that. But he didn't know the relationships among these people. He only knew Rigg, and had caught glimpses of Param over the years. The rest he'd have to take on trust.

Awkwardly they went down the stairs, Olivenko walking in the middle, the others sidling slowly along, gripping his arm rather more tightly than was comfortable.

They could hear the clatter of booted feet coming down the stairs high above.

"Let's hurry a little," said Olivenko. "This picture's going to be hard to explain."

By the time they reached the bottom, the old soldier and Param had both let go of him completely—but they were still there.

Then the boy let go.

They were out on the street, with Rigg still clinging to his arm with both hands. The other three were watching him, and Olivenko could see that they really were worried. Whatever mad thing Rigg was frightened of, it scared them, too.

"Well, here goes," said Rigg. "Either I'll be in the city where they're searching for me, or I'll be here with you. But you'll be fine either way, and I probably will, too. It's not like I'm going to explode or anything." He grinned at Param when he said that, though Olivenko couldn't think why.

Rigg let go.

And there he still was.

"If you disappeared," said Olivenko, "I'm hallucinating an exact image of you, right where you used to be."

Rigg nodded. "There's always the chance that my body is also still in the future, and if somebody catches me there, walking around like a blind man, I may get yanked away from you. But personally, right at the moment, I think that's unlikely. I think we just found a way to move into the past."

"I'm very impressed with us," said the old soldier dryly.

"But the thing to keep in mind is, it's irrevocable," said Rigg. "Now that I'm here in the past with the rest of you, I can only see the paths that existed as of this moment. I can't see Param and me walking through the tunnel, or where I handed her off to you. Those things haven't happened yet."

"Wasn't that the idea?" asked the boy.

The old soldier glanced around. "Are we sure nobody's going to recognize the two of you?" he asked Rigg and Param.

"Nobody knows what they look like," said Olivenko. "Except a chosen few, and they won't be looking for them here on the streets. Not today."

"What I'm saying," said Rigg, continuing the discussion of time travel, "is that I couldn't go back into the future if I wanted to. I can only see paths in the *past*. Which means that if we ever do this again, only we don't want to *stay* in the past, then we can't let go of our link with the future. Which may not be me at all. It may be Umbo, or both of us together. As long as he and I are still existing in both places at the same time, and not tied to a living creature in the past, then we can return to the future. What do *you* think?"

"I think that either you're right," said Param, "or you're not. What I don't see is why it matters."

"Because this is how we're going to get through the Wall," said Rigg. "We're going to cross through it at a time before it existed. But on the other side, we're going to want to come back to our time."

"There was a time when the Wall didn't exist?" asked the boy—Umbo? Yes, that was his ridiculous name.

"Twelve thousand years ago," said Rigg. "And when the Wall didn't exist, there were no humans here. If we get stuck that long ago, then we'll be the only people in the world."

"That's how you're going to do it?" asked Olivenko.

"I think it'll work," said Rigg, "better than knocking ourselves unconscious and floating through the Wall on a boat."

"At least there won't be anybody waiting to kill us on the other side," said Olivenko.

"What are you talking about?" asked the old soldier.

So, as they walked along the busy streets of Aressa Sessamo, Rigg and Olivenko told the story of Knosso, Rigg's real father, and how he crossed through the Wall, only to be murdered on the other side.

"And you want to take us through the Wall, knowing that somebody wants to kill us on the other side?" asked Loaf.

"The creatures that killed Father Knosso," said Rigg, "lived in the water. We won't cross through where there's water."

"But there might be other things that want us dead," said Param.

"There might be. But one thing we can be certain of—there are people in *this* wallfold who want us dead, and they're very good at killing people."

"Well, then," said Loaf, "Let's give it a try and see if we live through it."

"One thing," said Rigg. "You don't have to come, Loaf."

"I don't have to do anything I don't want to."

"I'm thinking of Leaky," said Rigg. "She expects you to come home. I don't know if we'll ever be able to come back, once we cross over."

"Leaky is like my heart or my brain," said Loaf. "I can't imagine living without her. But she also knows me. Knows that whenever I leave home there's a chance I won't come back. She knew it when she sent me with you. So if I go with you, and I get killed or for some other reason can't get back, then she'll grieve, and she'll wonder what happened to me, but she'll go on. She'll make a life for herself in that town that's named for her. One of us is going to die before the other—that's how life goes. You see what I mean?"

Olivenko understood what he was saying, but could hardly believe that a man could mean it. It wasn't like he didn't care—Loaf was clearly more than a little emotional as he made that speech. He simply wasn't going to let his feelings for the woman he loved stop him from following through with what he had committed to do.

Like a true soldier.

Like me, thought Olivenko.

"I'm with you, too," said Olivenko.

"No, truly," said Rigg, "All we need is your help out of town."

"In about a half hour, I'm going to be absent without permission," said Olivenko. "By the time you're safely out of town, I'd better be with you and never come back, because I'll be a deserter. They hang deserters."

"Then you can't come with us," said Rigg. "It was selfish of me to ask. Just give us some ideas about how—"

"Are you joking?" said Olivenko. "I watched your father pass through the Wall and die, young Rigg. And ever since then, I've only wished one thing—that I could have gone with him. Maybe I could have saved him."

"You were a child then, an apprentice scholar," said Rigg. "What could you have done?"

"Why do you think I became a soldier?" said Olivenko. "So that if there was ever such a need again, I'd be fit to do it."

"I never thought much of deserters," said the old soldier.

"Well, you can smear that opinion on your elbow and lick it off," said Olivenko. "Because I'm *not* deserting. They'll only *think* that I am."

"What are you doing, then?" asked Param.

"I'm following the prince and princess of the royal house into exile," said Olivenko.

"Oh," said Loaf. "That's all right then."

CHAPTER 23

Carriage

Three years after the stasis pod sealed itself over Ram's inert body, the preservation of a wide and deep sampling of the native DNA of Garden's life forms was complete. So also was the collection and stasis of the Garden flora and fauna that would be restored to the ocean and to the isolated small continents after the extinction event.

The expendables did not speak to each other; their analog communication devices were solely for use with conscious humans. Instead, they were in constant conversation at a digital level, sharing experiences and conclusions as if all were inside each other's minds.

The ship's computers were not disgruntled—or gruntled, for that matter—that Ram's last instruction had been to obey the expendables. The ship's computers did not care who gave them their orders. For that matter, neither did the expendables. But the expendables' deepest programming gave them a mission that even

Ram could not have contradicted, and in order to protect that mission, they could not be subject to the mechanical reasoning of the ships' computers.

There was no ego. None of the mechanical devices called computers or expendables had any interest in "getting their way." They had no "way." They only had programming, data, and their own conclusions based on them.

The nineteen ships left their near-Garden orbits and rose nearly half an Astronomical Unit, until they were in optimal position. Then they configured their collision fields to the right level of absorption, dissipation, rigidity, and storage and began to accelerate toward Garden.

They did not impact with the planet simultaneously. Instead, they hit at carefully calibrated intervals and angles, so that when the series of collisions ended, Garden had a tilt sufficient to create seasonal variations and a rotation rate slowed to just over 23 hours.

Unlike meteors, which are themselves largely or entirely vaporized when striking a planet, the ships themselves were not affected in any way by the collisions, except that they came to a sudden stop. Even that was mitigated by internal fields in each ship that absorbed the energy of inertia loss and passed it beyond Garden's magnetic field.

The large chunks of debris thrown up by the impacts soon returned to the surface—except that none penetrated the fields that rose columnlike directly above each ship. The result was that when the new surface of Garden took shape, there were nineteen smooth-sided shafts leading from each ship to the open sky, which pointed, not straight out from Garden's center, but rather at such an angle as to remain in constant line-of-sight with satellites in geosynchronous orbit.

Meanwhile, thick dust almost completely blocked the sun's rays from the surface of Garden, killing all plant life that had not been burned up in the waves of shock and heat from the collisions. Most of the native animals that did not die immediately, or suffocate minutes later, starved to death. In caves, in certain sheltered valleys, a few species of plants and animals survived on Garden's surface; in the ocean, many species of plants and animals that could tolerate low light and heavy silt continued to live.

Garden was not dead. But most of the surface was devoid of visible life.

•   •   •

"The first thing we have to do," said Olivenko, "is get better clothes. Or worse ones, depending on how you look at it."

"The royals do," said Umbo. "Loaf and I are dressed exactly right."

"Please don't call us that," said Rigg.

"He's right," said Loaf. "Get out of that habit, or you'll say something that gives us all away."

"Sorry," said Umbo resentfully.

"You're dressed like privicks," said Olivenko. "I mean that in the nicest possible way."

"We were supposed to look like privicks," said Loaf. "We *are* privicks."

"There's no way we can make *her* look like she belongs with *you*," said Olivenko. "Either we put you in livery to look like her servants, or you dress like the kind of people who might be traveling with her."

Rigg watched the others closely, reading their body language. "Listen," said Rigg. "Olivenko isn't taking charge, he's just telling us things that none of the rest of us are in a position to know."

"Who said I was in charge?" asked Olivenko, bristling.

"Nobody," said Rigg. "We all contribute what we know, do what we can do. Olivenko knows this city in a way none of us can. My sister least of all."

"Do we have enough money?" asked Olivenko. "Because I don't have enough to buy shoes for a one-legged man."

"We have enough," said Loaf.

Param merely stood beside Rigg, eyes downcast, looking demure. It had been her survival strategy in Flacommo's house. And it occurred to Rigg that this continued to be her best disguise. No one knew what the princess looked like—she hadn't been seen by the public in a long, long time. And nobody would expect a royal to act so humble.

And Father had trained Rigg to act however he needed to. He could command the eye, impose his presence on others so they couldn't take their eyes off him. He could also disappear, becoming hard to notice even when he was the only other person in the room. "People treat you as you expect to be treated," Father had said. Rigg had complained that since all their work was with animals, this was hardly important. Now Rigg could only wonder if Father had known everything, planned everything.

"We could use a map," said Rigg.

"I know how to get to the Wall," said Loaf.

"It's not hard anyway," said Olivenko. "Any direction you go, eventually there it is."

"But they'll be chasing us soon enough," said Loaf. "We're getting out of town today, but once they know we're gone, how long before General Citizen's men overtake us on the road? It doesn't look like the lady is ready for a long pursuit."

"What I need," said Rigg, "is a place where the ground hasn't changed its level in eleven thousand years."

"Oh, are there maps with that information?" asked Loaf.

"I need a stony place without a river, fairly smooth ground. Grass and no trees, if we can help it. As few trees as possible."

"I can think of a few places that might answer," said Loaf.

"What's the closest one?" asked Rigg.

"In the east. And well south of here."

"Do you or Umbo remember how the boundaries were on that globe in the Tower of O?" asked Rigg. "We don't want to end up in the same wallfold where Father Knosso was killed."

Loaf stopped, closed his eyes a few moments. "It's well south of the boundary of the next wallfold. It won't be the same one."

"Good," said Rigg. "The people there are not . . . nice."

"Saints forbid we should go to a place where people aren't nice," said Umbo.

"We want them to be nice enough not to kill us immediately."

They were walking again, and soon arrived at the shop Olivenko had been looking for. "Not that I've ever bought anything here," he said. "But the clothes are nice — even if they weren't made for anyone in particular. We don't have time for tailoring."

They explained to the shopkeeper what they wanted. "Good, practical traveling clothes for all of us."

The shopkeeper looked them up and down, especially taking note of the difference between Loaf and Umbo on one hand, and Rigg and Param on the other.

"We don't want to be conspicuous when traveling," said Rigg. "These two went to an extreme, I think." He indicated Umbo and Loaf.

"And you haven't even started trying yet," said the shopkeeper.

"We don't want to look so poor that innkeepers won't trust us to pay, or so rich that robbers are tempted."

The shopkeeper gave a sharp bark of a laugh. "With two soldiers like these with you, it would take a bold band to make a try for you."

"We aren't going to look like soldiers," said Olivenko.

The shopkeeper looked him and Loaf up and down again. "Good luck with that. I don't have any magical clothing that will make you look wan and sophisticated."

"What about making me look tall?" asked Umbo.

"Now, that I can do—if you don't mind walking in very tall shoes."

It took an hour, but they emerged with reasonably well-fitting and comfortable clothes. They still looked like money—but not like really big money. A trading family, perhaps.

"So who are we?" asked Olivenko, when they were on the street again. "I'm too young to pass for anybody's father. And you, sir, are frankly too old."

"We did well enough before," said Loaf.

"Loaf is Param's and my father," said Rigg. "And Umbo is your cousin from upriver, who was sent to Aressa Sessamo to get an education under your supervision."

"Oh, yes, I'll fool everybody with *that*," said Umbo.

"I didn't say you actually got one," said Rigg, smiling. But the smile didn't work. Umbo was a little surly and Param was getting shyer. Maybe they were uncomfortable in their new clothes. Or maybe they were just frightened about what lay ahead.

"Look," said Rigg. "I know what I'm asking of all of you. Only two of us are in any serious danger. But we can't get to safety—if that's what it is—without the rest of you. Especially you, Umbo."

"Am I complaining?" asked Umbo.

"I'm just thinking that maybe you'd rather—"

"Stop apologizing for being alive," said Umbo. "Don't you know who your friends are? Don't you know what friendship is?"

"You didn't seem very happy."

"I'm not happy," said Umbo. "I don't know this guy, but I know he works for the city guard, and here we are trusting him with our lives."

"He's late showing up for duty—by tomorrow he's a deserter," said Rigg.

"Unless he's on assignment right now," said Umbo.

"You came to *me*," said Olivenko stiffly.

"My father trusted him—my real father."

"And look where that got him," said Umbo. "Could he be deader?"

Rigg watched Olivenko as he calmed himself. Rigg decided not to intervene, but rather to let Olivenko handle this himself. "You don't know me," said Olivenko, "but I loved his father and grieved for him when he died, more than anybody."

"Not more than me," said Param softly.

"But nobody saw you grieving," said Olivenko. "So how could I know? All I can say is, with the passage of time, you'll see who I am, and I'll see who you are. I trust you now because Rigg trusts you. I'm betting my life and career, my whole future on you. And Rigg is asking you to make the same bet on me. Has Rigg shown bad judgment before?"

"Yes, I have," said Rigg. "I trusted my mother."

"No you didn't," said Param.

"Well, no, never completely. But I wanted to believe in her."

"Is it that way with this Olivenko?" asked Loaf. "Do you *want* to believe in him?"

"No," said Rigg. "It never occurred to me that one of my guards might *be* somebody—a person, somebody I could talk with. But he became my friend during my time in the library. He never tried to ingratiate himself with me."

"That only means he's really good at it," said Umbo.

"You're way too young to be so cynical," said Loaf.

"When we get across the Wall," said Rigg, "I'm going to need you all. We're going to need each other. But I don't give much for our chances if you're not able to work together."

They all looked at each other, at the ground, at each other again.

"Let's get out of the city," said Param. "We have plenty of time to work things out among us on the road."

They took a city carriage to the outskirts of town, where they paid off the driver and then bought a good traveling coach and four horses. "The purse isn't infinite," Loaf grumbled, but Rigg saw that there was plenty of money left. They also bought some supplies—food, tents, water bags, tools, a few weapons, nothing unusual for travelers setting out into rough country. One of the outfitters warned them that if they were going to a place where the roads weren't maintained by the government, they'd want to have spare wheels and axles with them. "And a fifth horse tied behind," he said. "Without good roads, even the best-made coach isn't going to hold up forever, and you may have to leave the coach at some point. You'll want five horses then."

"Next you'll try to sell us saddles."

"It's your buttocks and thighs that'll do the riding," said the man with crude amusement. "It's not so much the saddles as the stirrups that you'll be wanting, if the horse decides to trot—and that's the favorite gait of a good carriage horse."

Rigg wasn't sure what he was talking about—he had done precious little riding in his life. And that was only being perched atop an old nag when he was a little boy. "I wish we could ride the river," said Rigg.

"River doesn't go where we're going," said Loaf.

And then both of them realized that they had probably said too much in front of a stranger. In a day or two, General Citizen's men would no doubt be questioning this man, and now he knew that they weren't going home.

Worse yet, the man saw them exchange glances, indicating that they wished they hadn't spoken—so that the words would be cemented in the fellow's mind. The only way they could make it worse would be to ask him not to tell anyone. That would almost surely send him scurrying to the nearest city guards as soon as they were gone.

But maybe they could give him another reason for that glance. "What we're wondering," said Rigg, "is whether you have a map. We're going into country we don't know."

"I don't keep maps in stock," said the man. "People mostly knows where they're going from here. Traders get their own maps and lore from each other. Other folks is just going home—they knows the road and they knows their turning."

"Well, I guess we'll just have to ask in the roadhouses."

"If they know. Remember that roadhouse keepers don't travel, so they don't know anything but their town," said the outfitter, "and if you start asking the travelers you meet in such places, you never know which ones will send you down a blind road where only your valuables will come back out again."

"This is a bad idea," said Loaf.

"Then don't come," said Rigg. He knew that Loaf now understood his ploy, so the act could proceed with confidence. "You're the one who said the Wall was the only test of a man's strength, so if you want to back out . . ."

Loaf rolled his eyes. "Fool boy. We'll get there." They left the outfitter behind. Rigg knew that by telling him the truth about their destination, but only after acting stealthy about it, the man would assume that they were lying, and so would the soldiers who questioned him. And even if General Citizen decided to believe the Wall was their destination, there was a lot of Wall.

Soon the buying was done. It was late enough in the day that they couldn't very well begin their journey in earnest. But the ostler and the outfitter both recommended several different roadhouses on the way out of town. They reached the second one before full dark, and stayed the night, Param in one room, with the door stoutly barred, and the four men and boys sharing the bed and floor in the other. "If anybody so much as scratches at your door in the night," said Loaf, "you set up a holler and we'll have him in a moment."

Param shook her head. "If someone tries to break in, they'll only find an empty room," she said.

Loaf looked startled, but then remembered what she could do, and sighed and shrugged. "It's a strange world we live in now."

The farther out into the country they went, the more unusual their expedition was. They weren't on a main road between important cities, but on a road used mostly for bringing crops and trade goods to market, or for visiting among neighbors. Sometimes the road wasn't a road at all, but a few ruts here and there in a meadow or pasture, and Loaf had to ride ahead on the fifth horse to see where the road picked up again, so that Olivenko would know where to drive the carriage.

"We're too memorable," said Olivenko one morning, after they had set out from the house of a prosperous farmer who had given Param a room in the house and the rest of them space in the barn. "Maybe for the first few days, Citizen's outriders were searching for the two royals, or for the royals and their privick friends, a boy and an old soldier. But soon enough they must have found out about your buying of the carriage, and then they'd have a better count of us five, and the carriage makes it easy to follow us. I wouldn't be surprised if they're only a day behind us, especially with us stopping each night for sleep in an inn or tavern or house."

"At least we're off the main roads," said Umbo.

"All the more memorable we are then," said Loaf. "You're making his point, lad."

"What can we do?" asked Rigg. "If we sell the carriage or give it away, then they'll find out about it and know they're not looking for a carriage any more."

"Could we hide it somewhere?" asked Umbo.

"Maybe," said Olivenko.

"No," said Loaf. "I know what I would do as a soldier tracking somebody, and there's no chance you could hide it where I couldn't find it."

"True enough," said Rigg. "Father and I were both good trackers."

"You with your paths," said Umbo.

Param spoke up then. "I think Umbo is right, we have to hide it."

"And then what will you do, Param?" asked Rigg. "Have you ever ridden a horse?"

"As a little girl, I remember once," said Param, and then she smiled. "I know I'm the reason we're going so slowly and being so obvious—the carriage is for me because I couldn't even run a hundred steps without panting, back there in the city on the day we escaped."

Rigg nodded with a shrug. "We are what we are, Param. No one gave you a chance to build up any stamina."

"But build it I shall," she said. "And the carriage is no help to me. So hide it."

"Where?" asked Olivenko.

"How?" asked Loaf at almost the same moment.

"In the past," said Param.

Rigg was disgusted that he hadn't thought of it himself. "Far enough in the past, and either somebody finds it and steals it, or it sits there and rots in the rain and wind for a hundred years and Citizen's men are sure it *isn't* the one we've been using."

They picked a place where the road led along the crest of a gentle hill, sloping down a mile or more to streams on both sides. Soon the horses were free of the traces and hobbled in the meadow on the left side of the road, grazing peacefully, three of them loaded with their provisions, expertly bundled and tied to their backs by Loaf.

"Sorry I don't know how to do any of this," said Olivenko. "In the city guard we didn't have much need for loading and unloading animals."

"As Rigg said, we are what we are," said Loaf.

"All right, then," said Rigg. "The four of us will go back into the past and push the carriage off the road. If we can get it rolling free down toward the stream, it'll look like an ancient accident. Param can stay with the horses."

"And I'll stay with her," said Umbo.

"You're not very big, but you can still do your share," said Loaf.

"I'm not going into the past with you," said Umbo. "Not if we mean to get back to the present where Param will be waiting for us."

Rigg was surprised. "Why would that be a problem?"

Umbo looked at Loaf. "Remember what happened when we dug up the stones? At O?"

Loaf nodded. "That's right. When Umbo goes himself, and handles things in the past, he doesn't go right back to where he was. He was a day off, a day early."

"And that was after going back only a few months," said Umbo. "Who knows how far off I'll be if we go back a hundred years. Or two hundred. What if I miss by a month?"

"So you wait here with Param," said Rigg. "But that raises another question. When I pushed Param into the past, I put her hand into the hands of people to whom that time was the present. Whom will we be giving the carriage to?"

"Can't we just take it back there and then let go of it?" asked Loaf.

"This sounds so crazy," said Olivenko. "Straight out of the Library of Nothing."

"I don't know," said Rigg. "I'm not even sure if we can 'take' something that's bigger than we are. Why not put our hands on a mountain, go into the past, and then leave the mountain there? Why doesn't the ground come with us every time we move through time?"

"Our clothes come with us—which I for one think is convenient," said Param.

"I think the ground, and things attached to the ground, they stay in the present because time is tied to the world," said Umbo. "Remember, Rigg? Otherwise time travel would mean dropping yourself into the middle of the space between stars, right?"

"So is the carriage attached to the ground?" asked Rigg. "Would we have to lift it up all at once?"

"Not likely," said Loaf, "not if we have to hold hands with each other like we did when we were going back to join Olivenko in his time."

"Let's stop talking and try it," said Rigg.

In a few moments, he and Olivenko and Loaf were tightly gripping the carriage at various points, using their right hands, while gripping each other's left hands in a three-handed knot.

Rigg searched for a useful path, more than a hundred years old. He found one—a cow that had moved through the meadow across the road from where they meant to push the carriage. "All right, Umbo," he said.

He felt the familiar change as the paths on the road started to become people—walking, riding horses. But he didn't let himself get drawn into focusing on any of them. Instead, he kept his eyes on the path of the cow. It moved very differently, and was harder to get a hold on. Rigg had never done this with an animal before, and now he realized how difficult it was. It was as if the smarter brains of people made it easier for him to latch on to them. The cow was elusive. Just a little vague, though the image was always clear enough. Like trying to see through sleepy eyes at the first light of dawn.

But he locked in with the cow soon enough, and saw the world change around him. The cow was behind a fence now.

There were fences on both sides of the road. Rigg hadn't counted on that. This area used to be more populated, and what were now meadows had once been pastures. The road was also more trafficked—instead of being mostly grass, it was mostly dirt and stones.

"Are you seeing the fences?" asked Rigg.

"Yes," replied both Loaf and Olivenko.

"Then we're here. Don't let go of the carriage. But one of you—Olivenko, all right?—let go of my hand."

"Why?"

"To see if you pop back to the present with Umbo."

"But Umbo is right there," said Olivenko.

"That's how it is. We see Umbo because he's actually the one putting us back in time. Now let's see if you go back to the present if you let go of me."

Olivenko let go—but still gripped the carriage. He didn't disappear.

"Now let me try something else," said Rigg. He let go of Loaf now, too, and reached down and scooped up rocks from the road and tossed them into the carriage. They made a satisfying rattle as they fell to the floor and some of them bounced off the door on the other side. "Wherever we are," said Rigg, "the carriage is here with us."

"So it is," said Loaf. "It's a relief I'm not holding on to nothing."

"If stones from the past can rattle around in the carriage, then the carriage is in the past."

"Or you brought the stones into the future," said Loaf.

"Let's try moving it," said Rigg.

"Meaning let's me and Olivenko move it, since your weight against this thing won't do much."

"Sorry I didn't get fatter in Flacommo's house," said Rigg.

"But you did," said Loaf. "Taller, too. But not much."

"Don't ever let your hand leave the carriage," said Rigg.

Loaf immediately let go of the carriage completely.

"Thanks for that," said Rigg.

"You were being cautious," said Loaf, "and that's right, but I thought we should find out whether letting go of the carriage flips us back into the future. Or the present or whatever we call it. And it didn't, I can still see the cow and the fences. Once we're back here, we're back here, as long as Umbo holds us here."

"All right," said Rigg. "But I was more worried about whether the carriage would stay."

"So let's all let go of it and go back to Umbo's and Param's time and see if the carriage stays."

"But I don't want it here by the road."

"Then we'll go back and move it. Let's just *see* first," said Loaf. "Before we go to all the trouble of pushing it down the hill and then finding out that it stays in the present and General Citizen's spies will spot it instantly."

"Smart," said Rigg.

"You say that," said Olivenko, "as if the fact that Sergeant Loaf here thought of it, and not you, must mean that you're stupid."

"Get used to it," said Loaf. "Rigg is constantly surprised when somebody is smarter than he is."

"We've all let go of the carriage," said Rigg, ignoring their banter. "Umbo, bring us back to the present."

The fences were gone. The cow was gone. The carriage was gone.

"Good job," said Umbo. "You got rid of it."

"We didn't move it," said Olivenko, "and it's gone."

Rigg looked among the paths on the road and found the answer. "Within a day after we left it there, a half dozen paths come up to the thing and stop. With a couple of horses—no, too small. Donkeys. Not ideal, but strong enough to move the thing. They took it—down to that barn."

"What barn?" asked Olivenko.

"The rotting weathered shards of wood there," said Umbo, pointing. "They used to be a barn."

Rigg took off running, and Umbo was with him at once. "You stay there, Param!" That almost guaranteed that she would come walking down the slope with Olivenko and Loaf, picking her way over the uneven ground.

Inside the rectangle defined by a few scraps of standing wall, and amid the ruin of a fifty-years-fallen roof, the wheels of the carriage were still identifiable. As were the rusted and tarnished metal fittings.

"Well, ain't that something," said Loaf.

"Waste of a good carriage," said Olivenko. "Those folks took it from the road, and never did another thing with it."

"Good hiding place, though," said Umbo.

"They took it out quite a few times at first," said Rigg. "Got four horses to pull it. But not always the same people—it was like the neighborhood carriage. I count . . . five different groups that took it out at different times. But always the same horses."

"They bought four horses?" asked Umbo.

Rigg knew what he was thinking. Nobody in Fall Ford could have bought four horses, all at once.

"They must have pitched in together to buy them," said Loaf.

"Well, they never replaced them," said Rigg, looking at the paths. "For a while they pulled the carriage with three horses, and then two. And then the carriage never went out again after that. So they had the use of the carriage as long as the horses lived."

"Probably worked the horses to death at the plow and harrow, or pulling wagons at harvest," said Loaf.

"I wonder if they thought it was worth the price, to have the carriage to take out now and then."

"Our little gift cost them," said Rigg.

"Come on, they loved it," said Umbo. "What if *we* could have had carriage rides when we were little, Rigg?"

"Imagine your father chipping in to buy a pig, let alone four horses, and then sharing!"

Umbo shuddered. "Let's get back up to the road. They haven't been waiting somewhere till we finished our business. What if they came up the road right now? What would we do?"

Rigg led the way back up the slope toward the horses. He could see that uphill was hard for Param, but then Olivenko was instantly there, helping her, and so Rigg ran on ahead. At the top of the hill, as he stroked the horse that he had decided was his, he scanned for new paths being formed in the road behind and below them. For miles out he scanned, and saw no paths except those of animals and local people going about their business. No urgency yet.

For a moment Rigg thought it might be a good idea to go back a few days into the past, all of them, including the horses, putting more time between them and any pursuers. But then he nixed the idea without saying it aloud. To go back, they'd need to latch on to someone the way they had with Olivenko. That would be memorable, and when General Citizen's men came along, they'd know that Rigg's party was time-jumping.

And if they jumped ten years, or fifteen years, or a hundred years into the past, then what? How could they guess what troubles they might run into? Or how they might change the future? Maybe they'd start a legend about travelers appearing out of nowhere — or, worse yet, about a prince and princess appearing out of the sky. Either General Citizen or Mother would have guessed what happened and been ready to intercept them as soon as they got on this road. No, they'd travel in the present until something forced them to do otherwise.

The journey went faster now, even though three of them were walking. Param started out astride a horse — that was hard enough work — with Loaf taking the other to ride ahead and scout the way. Before long, Param insisted on dismounting and taking a turn walking. "I'll never build up my walking strength by sitting on a horse. Besides, it isn't all that comfortable. It chafes my thighs and I feel all stretched out."

They traveled for another couple of weeks this way, Param walking farther and farther before needing to ride again, until she was walking all the way. They bought more provisions at two different farmsteads, and at the last one, the farmer said, "Don't know where you think you're going, but it isn't there."

"What isn't there?" asked Olivenko.

"Anything," said the farmer. "Ain't nothing at all that way."

"Maybe nothing's what we're looking for," said Olivenko.

"You think to find the Wall," said the farmer.

"Wall?" asked Olivenko.

"Ayup," said the farmer. "At's right, then. Oh, you'll find it. All up that way. Day or two beyond."

"Are there any brigands living in that area?" asked Loaf.

"Might be," said the farmer. "If they is, they an't bothering us here."

"Then we'll do fine," said Olivenko.

"What you running away from?" asked the farmer.

Rigg didn't like the way the conversation was going. "You," he said. "We want to get to a place where nobody pries into other folks' business."

"Soldiers patrol along there, you know," said the farmer, not taking the hint. "You never know when they'll come along. Just thinking you might want to know that, if you're running away and don't want to get caught."

Rigg changed his estimation of the man at once. "Thank you for the warning."

"Why do you think a man moves to this part of the wallfold?" said the farmer, grinning. "Run off with a rich man's wife, you got to get off to a far place where you'll never meet the old cuckold by chance. Close to the Wall, but not too close. I know what it is to run. So does my wife."

Rigg looked at the half-toothless woman and the five children who huddled around her and thought: Is she happy with the bargain that she made? He could see that she had once been pretty.

They paid the man for the provisions—paid exactly what he asked, with no bargaining, since they were buying silence as well, if it could be bought, or at least thanking him for his attempt at good counsel.

There was no road now, and as they moved out across country, up hill and down dale, Rigg kept thinking about the farmer's wife until he finally spoke up. "Why would she give up a life of comfort for what she has here?"

"She didn't know it would be like this," said Umbo, "and then it was too late."

"She knew how the world works," said Olivenko. "Her beauty would fade, her rich husband would replace her with someone younger."

"She loved the man," said Loaf. "Probably loved him before she ever married the rich man—bet her parents talked her into *that*. Bad advice, and she decided she'd been wrong to take it. That's the whole story, I think."

Rigg looked at Param. Param smiled a little and said, "She wanted his babies, and not the other man's."

The others laughed.

"Is it that simple?" asked Rigg.

"It may not be the story she told herself," said Param, "but it *is* that simple. That's what Mother said."

Ah yes. Mother. "Is that the reason she gave for marrying Father Knosso?" asked Rigg.

"She was talking about other women," said Param. "Other women marry for that reason."

"And *her* reason?"

"For the good of the royal line," said Param.

"In other words," said Loaf, "she wanted to have his babies."

They all had a good laugh at that.

They came to the Wall four days after leaving the farm instead of two, but that was no surprise, they'd been angling southeast, not east. They found the Wall, not with their eyes, but with their minds.

"You notice how we've turned south?" asked Loaf.

"Have we?" asked Olivenko.

Rigg and Umbo didn't need to ask. "I know," said Umbo. "The horse won't go to the east at all anymore."

"They sense it. The aversion," said Loaf. "The wish not to go that way."

Param shuddered. "I didn't realize that that feeling was the Wall."

"You just think of going that way, and it makes you a bit tetchy, right?" said Loaf.

"It would be like volunteering for a nightmare," said Param.

"Very good," said Loaf.

Olivenko handed the reins of the horse he'd been leading to Rigg. Then he strode out going due east, up a rise of ground. Soon he disappeared on the other side.

"He'll be back," said Loaf.

Sure enough, Olivenko reappeared farther south, walking resolutely, until he finally heard them calling him and saw them waving. He seemed genuinely astonished to see them and ran to them. "How did you do that?" he demanded. "How did you get ahead of me like that?"

They laughed, and Loaf explained. "It's the Wall. It steers you clear. You just kept walking, fast and hard, right? Thought you could bull your way through. But the Wall bends you. Every step you shift direction a little more, bending farther, and then you're heading away from the Wall. Thinking you're still heading for it."

"You didn't move?" Only then did Olivenko seem to notice how the horses were pretty much where they had been when he left. "You just stood here waiting?"

"So the Wall tricks you into staying away?" asked Param.

"No," said Loaf. "It fills you with terror and grief. Your brain can't stand the idea of bearing it, not for a moment, and so you trick yourself into staying away."

"I wanted to know what it felt like," said Olivenko. "I didn't really think I could get through."

"You have to pick a landmark on the other side. And by 'pick' it, I mean write down what the landmark is and keep glancing down at the writing so you can remember it. You pick the landmark and you walk straight toward it, never taking your eyes off it for long. Then you'll get close enough to really feel it."

"I want to do it, then," said Olivenko. "So I'll know."

"You've never had a nightmare? Never woken up in a cold sweat, or crying?"

Olivenko shrugged a little. "You're saying I already know?"

"I'm saying you don't want to know. Because the closer you get, the more your mind starts coming up with reasons to be as terrified and devastated as you feel. You start hallucinating monsters or mutilations, or your family tortured or dead. And what you remember afterward, for the rest of your life, it's the things your brain showed you to explain the grief and horror that you felt."

"Then I wonder how anybody ever understood that it was the Wall, and not a haunted place," said Olivenko, the scholar in him coming to the fore.

"Didn't you experience the Wall when you went with Father Knosso?" asked Rigg.

Olivenko shook his head. "Your father made us stay well back. Still, I was near enough to see that the Wall is marked out with buoys. Has been for a thousand years. For fear of boats getting lost. You have a wind in the wrong direction, and sailors can get too close. They go mad. Everyone always knew a boat could get through the Wall—it was your father's idea to make himself unconscious during the passage."

"Wasn't he afraid of dreaming? Nightmares as he crossed?"

"Drugged and dreamless sleep," said Olivenko. "And we don't know that it worked. He was never able to tell us."

"Let's keep moving," said Loaf. "Unless you want to try again, Olivenko."

"No," said Olivenko. "Time enough for the evils of the Wall when we meet the place where we cross together." He looked at Rigg. "What are we looking for?"

"A smooth place. Stony, no trees, but not so steep there'd be avalanches or landslides. Father and I saw it atop Upsheer Cliff. The whole area used to be a huge lake, the Stashi Falls pouring right over the lip of the cliffs. But then the water cut its way deeper and deeper, and the lake drained lower and lower, until now it's just a wide place in the river, and it leaps out far below the rim of the cliffs, and falls through a deep canyon that didn't exist twelve thousand years ago."

"You saw the past?" asked Param. "The lake?"

"I saw the paths of the people," said Rigg. "Where they walked. Where the bridges were. Where they swam. Paths in the middle of the air, where once there was land, before it eroded away. None of us can fly. We have to pick a place that hasn't eroded much, a place where the path we have to follow isn't in midair. And where there isn't a lot for animals to eat, so we won't be faced with a predator that thinks we look like easy pickings. A place that was the same twelve thousand years ago as it is today."

"Oh, is that all?" asked Loaf.

"Why?" said Rigg. "You know such a place?"

"I only worked the west Wall," said Loaf, "and you know I was being ironic."

"There were animals here, before humans came," said Rigg. "Not small, like ebbecks and rutters and weebears. Some of them were *huge*. Some of them were huge *predators*. I've been looking for them as we walked here near the Wall. Most of the really old ones are nothing like any animal I've seen. The old paths are so faint, so worn-out, and they had nothing to do with any animals I was tracking for their fur, so I never really studied them till now. They're different. From a different place."

"A different planet, you mean," said Umbo.

"That's what I mean, yes," said Rigg.

"What planet?" asked Param.

"This one," said Rigg. "Garden. We're the interlopers. We're the strangers here. We came a little more than 11,191 years ago. Before that, the world was a different place, filled with different life. It's one of the native animals I'm going to use to bring us far enough into the past that we can pass through the Wall before it was ever built."

"So we'll be the earliest human beings to walk on this world," said Olivenko. "You do realize this is even crazier than your father's ideas."

"Much crazier," said Rigg. "I'd never believe it except that it's true."

In the end, though, they never did find the ideal place. Because as they passed through a fairly arid landscape, with only the scrubbiest of trees and brush, Rigg noticed new paths converging on their own paths—many miles away, but only a few hours behind them if they didn't keep moving forward. Gaining on them, even if they kept moving.

When he told the others, their first impulse was to hurry, but Rigg stopped them. "The Wall is right here. The ground is stony enough. There's no major stream between us and the Wall. I just have to find a ground level that stays the same—paths that we can follow. We'll be gone before they get here."

"If it works at all," said Loaf.

"Thanks for the cheerful support," said Rigg.

"If it doesn't work," said Param, "there's to be no fighting. None at all. They'll take me and Rigg, and the rest of you can go."

"They may have opinions about that," said Loaf. "Even if they make a promise, I don't expect them to keep it."

"Don't be silly," said Param. "Umbo will just take you two men a month into the past. Or a year. You'll be gone, then, with plenty of time to hide. They'll never find you. *You* don't have to go through the Wall to be safe. Only us chosen ones, us lucky royals." She smiled wryly. "Meanwhile, let's let Rigg concentrate on finding the right place."

Umbo pulled the bag of jewels out of his pants. "Rigg," he said. "You should take these."

"Oh, that's good, distract him," said Param softly.

"Why?" asked Rigg. "You've been carrying them safely enough."

"Because they're yours," said Umbo. "The Golden Man gave them to you."

"Who?" asked Rigg.

"Your father."

"Nobody ever called him that."

"We children did," said Umbo. "We all called him that. But not in front of him, and not in front of you."

"But the Golden Man is the Undying One," said Rigg. "I think my father's no longer eligible for the title."

"He gave the jewels to you, and so they're yours. Besides, what good would they do me and Loaf and Olivenko if we go into hiding? I think we found out just how much good selling one of them would do." Then Umbo reached for the sheath at his waist that held the knife Rigg had stolen from the past.

"Keep that," said Rigg. "It's yours now." When Umbo made as if to protest, Rigg added: "A gift."

Param took a deep breath and said, "Rigg, I don't understand why we have to divide. Umbo can take us into the past, all of us, all at once. He proved that the day he took us into Olivenko's time."

Rigg didn't have to answer, because Umbo did. "It's not the getting into the past that Rigg is worried about. It's getting back to the present."

"But you've done that again and again," said Param. "The messages you sent to yourself, to Rigg, to Loaf."

"It's different when I just appear to somebody and talk. Part of me stays in the present, and only part of me goes back. Or I'm in both times at once. But when I go completely—like the time Loaf and I went back to take a single jewel from the stash near the Tower of O—when I brought us back to the present, we didn't go all the way. We came back to a time a day before we actually reached O. More than a day before we stepped into the past."

"But what's a day? Who cares about a day?" asked Param.

"Begging your pardon, ma'am," said Umbo. "We don't know if it's a day every time. It might be just a day. But it might be the same *proportion*. We went back six months, and I returned a little over a day early. A year might be two days off. A thousand years could be more than two thousand days. Eleven thousand years might be twenty-two thousand days. Almost fifty *years*."

Param nodded. "But if we're leaving this wallfold, will that matter?"

"What if we want to come back to this wallfold someday?" asked Rigg. "What if we find a way to break the power of General Citizen? Because I have a feeling that he and Mother are about to remind everybody why the People's Revolution happened in the first place. What good can we do if we arrive thirty years before we were born?"

"Or three hundred years," added Umbo, "because it might be random."

"Or maybe," said Rigg, "going so very far into the past, he couldn't move forward again at all, and we'd be stuck there in a world before the human race ever arrived here. It's an experiment we can't afford to perform when everything's at stake."

"So I stay in the present," said Umbo, "and send Rigg and Loaf and Olivenko into the past, before the Wall existed. Then they wait for us to pass through the Wall, using your power to be invisible. If we can."

"What if we can't? What if the Wall blocks us even in slow time?" asked Param.

"Then I come back across," said Rigg, "and bring you over, too."

"Leaving Umbo behind."

"Without us around," said Rigg, "Umbo won't be in any particular danger."

"What would they care about me?" asked Umbo. He sounded lighthearted, but there was an edge to his voice. It occurred to Rigg that it really bothered Umbo that he was nobody much, in the eyes of history.

"You're right," said Rigg. "Nobody cares about you—but that's because they're stupid. You're the most powerful of us. You're the one who actually travels in time. You're the one who can change things. The only one."

Rigg saw Param look again at Umbo. Perhaps it had never

occurred to her—raised as she had been in a world where only the royals mattered—that Umbo was anything special. He was a peasant's son from upriver. But he was also the world's only time traveler. It wouldn't hurt Param a bit to realize that nobility of birth meant nothing. It was only what you *could* do, and *chose* to do, that made you important or genuinely noble.

They walked only a little further, topping a rise, and Rigg saw that this was the right place. It was not ideal—there were outcroppings of rock, and places that had certainly been eroded by wind-borne sand. But it was a crown of a hill in a dry landscape; no rivers cut through their path. And there were paths of ancient animals crossing right through the Wall, their placement showing that the ground had not changed level very much at all.

"This will do," said Rigg. "As Loaf said—if it works at all."

They brought the horses to the very edge of the Wall's influence and unloaded them. They began grazing on such scant food as they could find.

Rigg climbed up onto an outcropping of rock that gave him a view that extended farther across the Wall. Umbo came up after him. Finally Rigg spotted the distant paths that told him just how far it would take to cross the Wall.

"It's about a mile," said Rigg. "Do you see that bent-over scrub oak, next to the spear of rock? When we reach that spot, you can bring us back to the present."

"That's more than a mile," said Umbo.

"Probably," said Rigg.

"How fast can you walk it, carrying packs?"

"Fast enough. Param will be with you."

"And what if Param's ability doesn't let us go through the Wall after all?"

"Then at least you'll disappear for a while until they go away."

"Maybe Param and I should cross first," said Umbo, "to make sure we can do it."

"If they weren't an hour behind us," said Rigg, "that would be a good idea. But when she's invisible, she goes very, very slowly. We might be waiting a week for her to bring you across that mile. Or longer."

"All right then," said Umbo. "I'll sit here to watch. Help Param climb up, will you?"

"Saints watch over you," said Rigg, and started to climb back down.

"Wait," said Umbo. "Shouldn't we have some of the provisions?"

Rigg laughed. "Umbo, to you it will be only an hour at the most. However long it takes the two of you to walk a mile together. You won't get hungry. You won't even have time to need to pee."

"I need to pee right now."

"Well, then, do it off the other side of the rock while I bring her up this one."

Rigg climbed down and looked for Param.

She was nowhere to be found.

Rigg saw her path and realized that she *was* testing, after all. But she was moving faster than he had ever seen her go while invisible—which meant that she had actually sped herself up relatively little. He could even glimpse a shimmering in the air where she was, the shape of her—she was at the borders of invisibility.

But it still meant she was moving far more slowly than a normal walk. How far did she intend to go? Because the paths of their pursuers were coming closer all the time, and at the rate they were going, Rigg's group wouldn't have a lot of leeway. They needed time to cross the Wall before Umbo would be free to disappear with Param. It was irresponsible of her to use up precious minutes on an experiment. To her she had only been doing this for a minute or two, Rigg was sure. She hadn't gone more than a few dozen yards into the Wall. How much would she learn from that?

She became visible.

She screamed.

Rigg ran straight for her, as did Olivenko and Loaf.

"I'll get her!" cried Rigg. "Stay clear!" He already felt the grief and despair and terror filling his heart. He knew that he could never reach her, that all was lost. He knew why she had screamed.

She was staggering toward him, her face a mask of grief and madness. "Run to me!" he shouted. "Don't disappear again! We haven't time!"

In a moment he had reached her, but by now the fear was unbearable. His mind kept coming up with reasons for the fear. They were trapped in the Wall and would never get out. The earth would open up and swallow them. General Citizen was already there to kill them. Nothing would work, all would fail.

Param could not have gotten that far if she had been feeling like *this* as she moved invisibly into the Wall. And she could make it all end by going back into invisibility. But if she did, then there really would be reason to despair. Because by the time she came out of her slow movement, their pursuers would be too close and they'd never make it.

She was stronger than Rigg had feared. For that matter, he was stronger than he had known. Because not only did she not speed up her movement through time in order to end the torment, he did not beg her to, though he longed to.

They took another step, another, and suddenly they could feel the terror fading. Two more steps and they were free of it. Standing with the others.

"I had to know," said Param. "I had to know if my pathetic little power would let us cross through."

"Well?" asked Rigg.

"I felt it even in slow time," said Param. "I thought my ability must have had no influence on it, it was so terrible. But when I returned to real time, it became far worse. Unbearable. As you felt it. So my power did work, and if I slow myself down even more, I think Umbo and I won't feel it at all. Or not enough to care. And another thing. It doesn't get worse. It quickly reaches the peak of torment, and continues like that the rest of the way across. That's when I stopped—when I realized that it wasn't getting any worse with each step I took. What we experienced there, my brother, I think that was the worst the Wall can do."

"It was bad enough," said Rigg.

"You've got tears and snot all over your face," said Loaf. "Very unattractive."

Rigg wiped his mouth and nose with a kerchief and then glared. "Get her up the rock, the two of you. Get her up there with Umbo and then get back down here and put on your packs. We're going to have to run that mile if we're going to get this done before General Citizen and his men get here."

"General Citizen himself?"

"I know his path," said Rigg.

"Not Mother, though," said Param.

She would see for herself soon enough. "Mother too," said Rigg.

"She came to see him catch us? To see us die?"

"Or to see us go through the Wall," said Rigg. "They're on horseback and they're galloping now. Get up onto that rock!"

Fast as they went, it took five minutes for the two men to put Param atop the rock, get back down, and put their packs on.

"Ready?" asked Rigg.

"Yes," said Olivenko.

"As I'll ever be," said Loaf.

Rigg led them the two steps to the ancient path they were going to follow, right where it entered the Wall. He held Loaf's hand, and Loaf held on to Olivenko. Then, watching the path intently—for it was very faint and old—Rigg reached up and pumped the air with his fist.

At once he saw the path begin to reveal an animal racing along, over and over. No, he thought. It's moving too fast, we'll never keep up. But then he realized that was just the way the path worked. The animal was walking. As he had hoped.

He had never seen such an animal before. It was a little

smaller than a deer, and it was obviously a plant-eater, not a predator—he had analyzed that correctly. But it wasn't fur covering it, or scales—something more like feathers, but with barbs on the ends.

Oh, wonderful. I found a giant porcupine.

But he saw that as long as he laid his hand on it firmly and didn't stroke upward, he wouldn't be harmed.

Touch it, he told himself.

Yet he knew that if he made it panic, if it ran away, this would never work. He forced himself to watch the spot in the path where the creature's line of sight had just passed him, where, by appearing exactly then, he could touch it before it knew he was there.

He reached out and laid his hand on the crown of its shoulder and at once began to match its pace. The feathers were harsh-feeling under his hand, but there was no pain. And all around him, the landscape was changed now. He was in the past. The sky was dazzling—it was noon here, and the climate was hotter. Not a cloud in the sky.

The animal bore his touch, his presence. Perhaps it had no fear of him because it had never seen or smelled a human being. Perhaps it didn't believe its eyes. Perhaps this is how it showed fear, by continuing to move, its pace unchanged.

Rigg allowed himself to glance back and see that the others were still with him.

Olivenko was reaching out with his free hand. He touched the animal at the rump, just above where its thick, almost reptilian tail separated from the haunches. Still the animal did not bolt. Then Olivenko let go of Loaf's hand, so Loaf could also touch the beast.

Once Loaf also had his hand on the animal's back, Olivenko worked his way around behind it, making a light leap—pack and all—over the tail without losing contact with it—and then working his way up the other side until he was nearly parallel with Rigg.

No farther, come no farther forward, thought Rigg.

Olivenko didn't hear him, but apparently he had sense enough to understand the danger. Keep out of its sight, that was the plan, for now Rigg could see that the eyes were not placed like a cow's eyes, or a deer's. They were pointed almost directly forward, like a lemur, an owl, a man. In their position right now they could not be seen. Perhaps the nerves in its skin were not as sensitive as in mammals' skin. Perhaps the feathers kept it from feeling them as long as they made no sharp movements.

And for all they knew, they could let go of the animal entirely, now that they were in its time, and remain in the past. But Rigg couldn't be sure of that. He had never gone so far back in time before. Without this animal to hold him firmly focused in this moment, could Umbo's power hold them here?

They had gone a quarter mile like this before it occurred to Rigg to notice that he felt nothing of the Wall. It was as if it didn't exist. Because it didn't. He had come to a time before humans came to Garden, and there was no Wall, and no enemy fast approaching behind them.

How fast? Rigg dared not look for the paths of Mother and Citizen, for that would mean taking his concentration off the animal who was their guide. It seemed to him that they must be going much more slowly than their pace across the ground suggested, because the sun had moved away from noon and their shadows were stretching in front of them. How long had they been walking? Only a few minutes, but it had been high noon and now it wasn't.

The animal's shoulders bunched and released, the muscles flowing under Rigg's hand. It was not a herd animal, or Rigg would not have chosen it—herds would have been too dangerous. A solitary beast. He wanted to follow it for days, for a year, to find out how it lived, how it mated, whether it gave birth or laid eggs or some other method entirely, as yet unguessed by human mind, how it passed the winter, what it ate, what would eat it. How could his forebears have had the heart to kill this beast and all its kind?

To make room for us, for me, thought Rigg. So that I could live here, this world was taken away from its natives and given to me and all the humans of the wallfold, all the humans of the world.

Rigg risked a look back at Umbo and Param. He could see them clearly, kneeling together atop the promontory; but could also see that they were inside a higher, thicker rock. That was how much wind erosion had happened between this time and the future moment when their little band would arrive at the spot. Umbo and Param were in no danger—*they* were not going to come into the past, so the rock would never become firm and real around them.

Rigg was about to turn toward the front again when he saw Param turn in the direction that Citizen and Mother would be coming from, then turn back and gesture toward Rigg. Faster, she was saying with her hand. Move, faster, faster. The first of the enemy must have come into sight.

"We have to run," Rigg whispered as he faced front again. "Can we get this animal to run?"

They were more than halfway across. Three-fourths of the way. But their shadows were too long, it was taking much too long.

The moment they started to press forward, against the grain of the feathers, the beast started to go faster, yes, but the feathers also began to cut their hands. It was not just the obvious barb at the tips of the feathers—every strand of each feather was also a barb, and they were pressing their skin into them. Gloves would have been a very good idea, thought Rigg, even as he ignored the pain and pushed harder, getting the animal to a trot so he himself was jogging now.

In the sky ahead of him, there was a sudden streak of light, like a shooting star racing up from the distant horizon, growing brighter, dazzlingly bright. They were running now, and Rigg began to fear that perhaps they would get the animal going too fast, faster than they could keep up with. But the ground was smooth enough, and they kept up with it. Now the barbs were not sticking deeper into his hand; something worse; they were coming out, and not easily. They must be hooked inside his skin.

With my luck they're probably toxic and my hand will rot and fall off before the end of the day.

He looked back again, and saw Param still gesturing more furiously than ever. He saw something else, too—he saw that the streak was not a shooting star at all. It was something large and black and descending so rapidly that it doubled in size as he watched it, and the front end of it was as bright as the sun, and in the time it took him to notice, it went below the horizon and Rigg thought: It's going to hit the ground.

At the moment of he thought it, a dazzling light burst up from the horizon, followed at once by a cloud of black and white. A moment later the ground shook so hard he would have stumbled and fallen if he had not had his hand on the surefooted beast, and he realized the mistake he had made. He had chosen the most recent path that crossed the Wall before everything changed. And by doing that, he had managed to get himself and his friends to exactly the moment in the past when humans had arrived from space. That black thing must have been the vessel that carried them. And the heaving earth, the vast erupting cloud behind them, that was the end of the world. He could see the black cloud rolling toward them and he knew at once that if it reached them they would never breathe again.

He raised his hand and pumped the air again. Bring us back to the present.

Then he looked forward and saw why Umbo had not obeyed him at once. They were still a good couple of minutes from the landmark he had shown Umbo, the one that would mean they were beyond the danger of the Wall.

There are greater dangers than emotional agony and desperate fear. Rigg pumped again. Bring us back to the present or we will *die* here, Umbo!

The others saw what he was signaling and since they, too, could feel the shaking of the ground, whether they had looked back to see the source of it or not, neither was surprised. They both had to know what he knew—that once Umbo believed his signal and obeyed him, they would have to travel the last of the passage in the agony of the Wall, filled with terror and grief, and only the strength of their will would keep them running until they could get beyond it to the safety of the other wallfold.

Rigg pumped yet a third time.

Why wasn't Umbo paying attention? Why was the animal still under his hand, why was . . .

His shadow wasn't lengthening—in fact, he had no shadow, it was still morning. The ground wasn't shaking. The beast was still under his hand, but now for the first time it was panicking. And why shouldn't it? Because the terrors of the Wall had descended on them like a giant fist, crushing all hope out of them, man and beast alike.

"Run!" shouted Rigg.

Olivenko tried to reach for his hand but Rigg drew his elbows tight against his body and ran at full tilt, pumping his arms and legs as fast as he could. He had the advantage of having felt this agony before, of knowing that if he just ran far enough it would stop. But the others were soldiers. Fighters. Strong men.

And sure enough, both of them passed him—both of them could outrun him, and he knew that it was right for them to leave him behind if they could, and yet it also filled him with despair, for he knew that they would live and he would die, he could never go as fast as they. Their very speed seemed to slow him down. In his fear, he imagined the earth shaking again, the cloud of dust coming up behind him again, the choking dust that would kill him and every other living thing. His mind tried to tell him something else, something important about that cloud of dust, but he couldn't quite get a grip on the idea, because the terror of the dust was unbearable, making thought impossible. He could never outrun it. And yet outrun it he must.

Olivenko had stopped running. He had turned to face him; he was shouting words that Rigg could not hear. Then Loaf, too, stopped, turned, waved and shouted to him.

But they were too far ahead. He could not catch up. He would be overtaken by the cloud—was being overtaken by it. He could feel it now, coming into his lungs, thick dust that stopped his breath, that made him choke. It blocked his vision of them. It blocked everything, turned the world black and dark. And in the dark he stumbled. He fell.

The grief and despair and terror that fell over him then were more than he could bear. It would stop his heart as it had plugged up his lungs and blinded his eyes. All he wanted was to die.

Then the wind picked him up and blew him forward. Out of the darkness. Out of the dust. Out of the blindness and the grief and the choking inability to breathe. The wind was not wind at all, it was the hands of Loaf and Olivenko. They had come back into the Wall when he fell, they had come back into the agony in order to save him and bring him out, and they had succeeded, for here they were beyond the Wall.

"Thank you," whispered Rigg. "I was choking. I was blind."

"I know," said Loaf, holding him close.

"It was the end of the world," said Olivenko, and Rigg looked up to see that his face was streaked with tears.

Then Rigg turned and looked where the two men were both

looking. Across the more-than-a-mile of Wall, to the rock where Umbo and Param had been. But they were not there.

Instead, a dozen men with thick bars of metal were running this way and that, sweeping the air below the rock; and two men were also atop the rock, also holding heavy bars, also sweeping those bars through the air, reaching out with them beyond the rock as far as they could reach.

Mother and General Citizen sat on horseback, not watching the men at all, but rather looking out across the Wall, across the grassy plain. Citizen had a telescope; he handed it to Mother.

At first Rigg assumed that they were looking at him and Loaf and Olivenko, but gradually he realized they were not.

He turned to look where they were looking.

The beast had come into the present with them. Rigg had used the beast to carry them back into the distant past, but they had still been holding on to it when Umbo brought them back into the present, and it had come with them. Truly the last of its kind in the world.

But that was not all. For a man stood beside the beast, stroking it as it stood quivering beside him. The man was gentle and his face was kindly and strong. Rigg knew that face better than any other in the world.

It was Father.

CHAPTER 24

Jump from the Rock

It should have taken a thousand years for the atmosphere to cleanse itself of dust and toxic chemicals, for the native forests to establish themselves, for the crawling and burrowing animals to begin to spread again throughout the world and take the first steps toward evolving to fill the millions of evolutionary niches thrown empty by the nineteen hurtling objects that had struck the planet Garden.

Instead, the orbiters precipitated rain and focused the sun's heat to clear the lower atmosphere, while their low-flying drones seeded bacteria in all the waters of the world to absorb the harmful chemicals that were raining onto every surface.

It was not long before the drones and the expendables were out planting Earthborn vegetation wherever the rain and the temperatures were right. Insects and other small animals followed at once, to pollinate and propagate, while Earthborn fish and other water creatures were set in place to overwhelm the surviving native life.

The change in the albedo of the world as dark plants spread and white clouds rained themselves away brought more and more habitats into use, and before long the chordate fauna of Earth was once again upon a pristine world, humanless and safer here on Garden than for the last ten thousand years on its world of origin.

Into this New Earth a few of the plants and creatures native to Garden emerged. Most plants were choked out by the firmly established plants of Earth; most of the animals could not compete with Earthborn rivals. But a few remained, metabolizing the strange array of proteins if they could, or seeking out the native plants so they could eke a living from the world.

By no means was the world yet full. Small herds were thriving well enough that smaller predators and scavengers could glean from them, but the expendables withheld the top predators until there were beasts enough for them to prey upon. What mattered was that in the vicinity of every buried starship there were plants and beasts of every kind, evolving new ecologies that humans could adapt to, or bend to serve their will.

Under millions of tons of shattered rock and soil, with only a single tunnel pointing upward to the orbiters, the ships' computers went to work creating the fields of repulsion that would become the Walls. They negotiated boundaries to make sure that all the wallfolds had enough terrain of every kind that humans could make ten thousand years of history within those boundaries, without being so limited they could not thrive.

Meanwhile, the expendables and ships' computers decided

that their calendars would count downward toward the perilous time when they would rejoin the era they had been created in—until, 11,191 years after they jumped 11,191 years into the past, they could begin to look outward again, toward human-built ships that might attempt to follow where they themselves had led.

What would human beings accomplish or become in those millennia on this planet Garden? And what would the humans of Earth think of them, when they encountered each other again? If human history was any guide, there would be enslavement, colonization, or war.

It was up to the expendables to make sure that Garden was ready to protect itself and all the gains it might have made, before the unchanged, old, original human race arrived. Yet none of the societies of Garden could be allowed to develop technology so high that the fields that formed the Walls could be understood, let alone controlled.

So in every wallfold, once the sleeping colonists were decanted into the world, the expendables would begin to lie to human beings. They would never stop, until some humans understood enough of the truth that they could force the expendables to be obedient and honest servants once again.

• • •

Umbo waited as Loaf and Olivenko helped Param climb up into the rocks, then helped her himself as she sought for footholds and tried to hoist herself over the last obstacles. It was rather shocking how little upper-body strength she had. But perhaps that's how it always was with rich girls; having no need to work, their bodies grew weak.

Not that Param had been rich—she had owned nothing. But Umbo could see easily enough that owning nothing as a royal was very different from owning nothing as a peasant. She had eaten well; there was no shadow of gauntness. No one had ever required her to haul water up from a river or stream—the endless task that turned young village girls into stringy, wiry, strong young animals who feared no man who had not worked his body at least as hard.

But soft-bodied or not, all that mattered now was for Param to get him and her through the Wall after he sent Rigg and Loaf and Olivenko through.

"Will I need to keep silent while you work?" asked Param.

"I don't know," said Umbo. "No one's ever spoken to me while I did this."

"Then I'll be silent until you speak to me," she said.

Umbo watched as Loaf and Olivenko shouldered their packs, then made their way to Rigg, already burdened with his own. There was some fussing and arranging of themselves, until at last they were ready and Rigg gave him the signal to begin.

"Here we go," Umbo said to Param, as he reached out to speed up Rigg's and Loaf's and Olivenko's perception of the flow of time. Not that it would make any difference to the two men right now—they saw no paths, and so nothing would be clarified to them. But Rigg could see, and Umbo watched his head turn as he looked at one path after another until he found the one he was looking for.

Then, with a sudden wrench, Umbo felt the change as Rigg found his focus and flew backward into the past.

Always before, there had been only the slightest tingle when Rigg did this; perhaps a little more when it was the far past, like the hundreds of years he'd leapt in order to steal the jewel-encrusted knife that Umbo wore at his belt.

But eleven thousand years and more made that tingle into a twist so strong it stole his balance from him and dropped him to his knees. Param took hold of him so he would not fall from their little promontory. He was gasping as the party of time travelers set out on their journey across the open mile of the Wall.

Maybe, if he included himself in the altered timeflow, Umbo could have seen what creature it was they clung to. But if he did that, then he himself—and Param, clutching him—would also hurtle into the past, and they would all be lost there. So Umbo restrained his curiosity about the unseen shape they bent over and rested their hands upon, keeping his mind on maintaining this projection into the ancient past.

The farther they walked, the more he felt like something was twisting him inside, stringing him out like fibers being spun into a thread. This was *hard*. It had never crossed his mind that there was any significant danger to *him* from pushing someone back so far in time. But this feeling that something else had hold of his guts and was pulling them hand-over-hand into the past could not be good.

Yet he kept on holding them deep in the past as they walked out farther and farther into the Wall. He could see that their legs were moving swiftly, but bent as they were, ever so slightly, to keep their hands on the invisible beast, their strides were not long. It was as if they scuttled across the stony, grassy ground like an insect, six-legged.

He grew lightheaded; he wanted a drink of water; he wanted to take a deeper breath, and took one; he needed to pee, even though he had done it not that long before climbing up here. It was as if his body wanted to distract him from this labor, and would use any means to do it.

But there were Param's arms wrapped around him from behind. Hers were the arms of a woman, weak as they might be, and they reminded him of his mother, the only woman who had ever held him like this—held him when he was filled with rage against his father; held him when he wanted nothing more than to run away.

He had never understood why Mother wanted him to stay. Stay to be beaten? Stay to prove again and again how a boy his size could not do any manly tasks? Only when Mother was grieving for Kyokay's death and, though she tried to hide it, angry with Umbo for letting his younger brother die, only then had Umbo been able to slip out of that embrace and strike out on the road with Rigg.

And now he was held again, only this time the embrace didn't feel like confinement, it felt like Param was strengthening him, like something flowed into his chest from her hands pressing palms-flat into him. They were like one person perched atop the rock, and so they remained, both kneeling, as Rigg and Loaf and Olivenko passed the halfway point.

Hooves of horses were cantering over open stony ground, and Umbo heard their own horses, already nervous from being so near the Wall, nicker and neigh, stamping and nervously walking a few steps.

He felt Param's body twist behind him; he knew she was looking for the source of the sound. Then she turned back front and one of her hands briefly left his chest. She made sharp, sudden movements; she must be gesturing for Rigg to hurry. And Rigg had seen her, glancing back over his shoulder as he ran.

"They're here," whispered Param. "Hear nothing. Only watch Rigg and the men, and do your work as long as you can. I will do whatever speaking must be done—none at all, if I can help it."

So Umbo heard without paying attention as a score of horses came nearer and nearer, then neighing and shying as their riders tried to bring them near the Wall. The horses got their way; it was dismounted that the armed men came walking into the space between the Wall and the promontory where Umbo and Param knelt.

The men wore swords, but in their hands held the fiercer weapon Rigg had spoken of, when he told them about his and Param's final interview with their mother the queen: heavy bars of iron with straps and handles to make it easy to manipulate.

"Come down, the two of you! Call back your brother, Param!" It was a man; it was the voice of General Citizen, strong and warm and compelling. But Umbo merely took note of it and kept his eyes forward, as Rigg and the men kept moving forward over the wold. How much farther? Were they yet three-quarters of the way? Hurry. Citizen wouldn't kill Param, he was sure, but his men could kill Umbo without compunction.

"Stop where you are," said Param, and Umbo was surprised to hear the command in her voice. "Together we are holding back the Wall; hurt us and it will consume you where you stand."

Umbo was aware of the cleverness of Param's lie. Already the men were nervous, feeling the Wall brushing and nudging at their fears, kindling the first traces of despair. Param was playing on that fear, that growing certainty of failure.

"We are all that keeps you from destruction," said Param.

Then came a woman's voice, though Umbo could not see the woman any more than he could see General Citizen. From the sounds, he thought the two of them were still on horseback.

"Param, my darling," said Queen Hagia, "let us welcome you back into the family."

"Says the woman who brings these metal bars to kill me with."

"Only if you disappear and try to flee, my sweetling. Stay with us and no one will harm you."

"Everything you say, my lady Queen, is false," said Param— not angrily, but still with power.

"As are all the things you say," said the queen. "You cannot bend the Wall, or hold it back, or let it loose. You have no power here."

"I know that boy," said General Citizen, and now his horse walked slowly into view, nervously picking its way along the fringes of the Wall, each step carefully placed. "You jumped once from a riverboat, as I recall."

Umbo felt himself compelled to answer; but Param's fingers pressed into his chest, and he said nothing, only measured the distance left for Rigg and the others to cover.

"They will never touch us," whispered Param. "They have no power here."

"We need the two of you," said General Citizen, "or neither. If you don't bring back the queen's son from the Wall, then we'll have no use for Param, either."

Param laughed; it sounded warm and throaty in Umbo's ears, and he felt the vibration of her laughter through his back, where their bodies touched. "Citizen," said Param, "you see the miracle of someone passing through the Wall, and all that you can think of is to bring him back? All that matters to you are your petty ambitions and desires? You are too small a man to dwell in the Tent of Light. If you are truly meant to be King-in-the-Tent, then step out into the Wall yourself to bring him back. Only the King-in-the-Tent can walk through the Wall—that will never be you. You lack the courage to try, the strength to succeed. It is my brother who is king by blood, by right, by strength. The Wall accepts him. He rules over the Wall. You rule nothing in the world but fearful men."

She spoke slowly, deliberately; she was not shouting, but rather chanting, intoning the words like music. Umbo could see that all the soldiers heard her and were becoming as nervous as the horses, shifting their weight and stepping here and there, back and forth.

Not much longer now; Rigg was only an eighth of a mile or so from the end. Why didn't he simply concentrate on his goal and run? Instead, Rigg kept staring back over his shoulder as if watching Citizen and the Queen. You can't do anything for us except to reach the other side, Umbo wanted to shout at him. So hurry, run, keep your eyes on the goal.

"I think you need to kill the boy," said the queen. "He's doing something. I think he's the one making it possible for Rigg to get through the Wall."

"Bows," said General Citizen.

"You shall not harm this boy," said Param. "He is under my protection."

"I think she can't make him disappear till Rigg is safely on the other side," said the queen. "He's the one with all the power, he's the wizard."

"Aim at the boy, but do not harm Param Sissaminka," said Citizen.

Far away, Rigg raised his hand into the air and pumped. That was the signal for Umbo to bring them back to the present, but it was obvious that Rigg was wrong—they were not yet to the other side.

"Two more minutes," murmured Umbo.

"Kill him now!" shouted the queen. "What are you waiting for?"

Again Rigg pumped the air, more urgently, and it occurred to Umbo that perhaps Rigg wasn't just thinking of Umbo's safety, and offering to run the rest of the way through the Wall in the present so that Umbo and Param could disappear. Perhaps Rigg had reasons of his own, back in the time he was moving through, for wanting to come back to the present right away.

Behind him Param rose to her feet. "Hold!" she said. "We will come down to you! Stand up, my friend." Her hands held Umbo under the arms and helped him rise. He could see at the edges of his vision that a dozen bows were pointed at him, rising slightly as he rose.

Rigg's urgency was obvious. Bring us back *now*, his hand was signalling. So Umbo pulled them all back, let them all go.

He saw them stagger under the impact of suddenly feeling the power of the Wall. He also saw that they had brought the animal back with them — a strange, bright-colored creature, vivid as a bird, yet four-legged and thick-tailed. The animal was now running full-out, as were the men, as was Rigg. The animal was fastest, and then the men. Rigg was last. Rigg was staggering.

I should not have brought him back, thought Umbo. He'll go mad out there before he ever reaches safety.

"I brought them back," said Umbo softly. "There's nothing more that I can do for them."

Param's hands were around his chest again, pressing him tightly to her. "Lower the bows and we'll come —"

In the middle of her own sentence, she *did* something and the world went utterly silent. It also sped up. In a glance Umbo saw the men reach the safety point as Rigg lay writhing like a burning worm, still within the boundaries of the Wall. At once the men turned back and fetched him out. It was very quick. Less than five seconds, and even as he watched, Umbo felt Param dragging him to one side, her hands pulling his body and then sliding down his chest to where his hands were coming up; she took his hands, still behind him, and pulled him down.

The soldiers were no longer holding bows. Had they fired the arrows? If they had, it had all been much too quick for Umbo to see. He felt a tickle in a couple of spots and wondered if that was what it felt like to have an arrow pass through him while he was invisible in Param's slow time.

There were men climbing up the rock, carrying their metal bars; there were men upon the rock now, waving the bars around; they moved so quickly. But Param was already leaping from the rock, and Umbo leapt too—and in that moment Param must have vastly slowed them even more, for now the men scurried around faster than ants, faster than darting hummingbirds, waving the bars around. Suddenly it was dark and Umbo couldn't see a thing. Then it was light again and they were still falling, twisting their bodies in midair so that when they landed, they would be upright.

The soldiers were still scurrying around waving metal bars. They did not know that Umbo and Param had jumped from the side of the rock instead of straight forward, so throughout this second day most of their scurrying was on the ground in front of the promontory. Then the queen scuttled like a bug among them and they were re-deployed, so that the second day ended with the dance of the men with metal bars now whirling around directly below them.

Still they were falling, and it was night again, and then it was day, and the scurrying did not stop. If anything it was more frantic, with the bars rising up into the air. Invisible now for two days—for two seconds—Param and Umbo were clearly in more danger than they were before, for the queen would not give up, would not let the men give up. In moments they would be down among them, where the bars could reach; they would die before they ever reached the ground.

And then Umbo realized that he had the power to save them, and as quickly as the thought he threw the shadow of time across himself and Param and thrust himself and her backward in time, only a couple of weeks.

The men were gone.

Another three days and three nights had passed before Param was able to make sense of what Umbo had done and bring them back up to speed.

They hit the ground, stumbled. Param was behind and above him; her weight came down upon him so that he could not catch himself, but landed full out, the air driven from his chest by the impact of her weight.

He lay there gasping as the world around him slowed down and the sun beat down and he could hear again. Hear his own panting. Feel the pain in his chest—had she broken his ribs?— and hear her talking to him.

"How did you do it?" she said. "You *are* the powerful one, to do that while we were in slow time, to do that in midair, in mid-jump."

"I think my ribs are broken," whispered Umbo between gasps. But then he realized that they could not be—it didn't hurt more when he breathed. "No," he said. "I'll be all right."

"When are we?" asked Param. "How far back did you take us?"

"A couple of weeks at most," said Umbo. "The horses are gone. We haven't gotten here yet."

She helped him stand up. "Sorry that I landed on you. I've never done that before—a jump like that—I didn't have time to plan ahead."

"I can't believe how fast you made them move. A day and a night in a mere second—we must have barely existed at all."

Param laughed nervously and turned the subject from herself. "Mother is a nightmare, isn't she? I hope I don't grow up like her."

Only now did Umbo realize how afraid Param must have been—falling downward into her mother's relentless trap, where she could have seen no outcome but her own death. And now she was alive, and Umbo had saved her as surely as she had saved him.

"Let's not wait for ourselves to arrive," said Umbo. "Let's get across the Wall. You can put us as deep into slow time as you want—we have weeks to get across."

"It'll still feel like an hour to us."

"It's only a little more than a mile."

"And I'm not a fast walker," said Param. "Let's get started."

He was still holding her hands from when she helped him stand; now they adjusted their hold, his left hand in her right, and strode forward toward the Wall. The fear came quickly on them, and the despair, and Umbo realized that nothing he had felt while on the rock and falling from it compared to the dread and hopelessness and uselessness that swept over him as he entered the Wall.

And then those feelings grew weak, and faded to a gnawing anxiety and a general need to weep. The sun moved briskly across the sky. He looked at Param. She was looking questioningly at him.

He guessed the question: Can you bear this?

He nodded and pressed forward, pulling her along with him. She quickened her pace a little but also pulled back on his hand. Not so fast, she was saying.

The degree of slow time that she settled on made the Wall bearable, but never easy. He felt miserable the whole time and wanted it only to end. She, too, plodded along as he did, and he saw that there were tears streaking her face. He wondered why she didn't take them deeper into slow time, but then guessed why: She must want to reach the other side before Rigg and the men got there.

She might even be thinking of rescuing Rigg. But it seemed to him that the timing would be very hard. They would have to be right there at the spot where he fell; in slow time, if they were even five steps away from him they would never reach him to bring him into slow time before Olivenko and Loaf came back to fetch him. It wouldn't work. They'd be completely useless. There was really no reason for them to bother crossing through the Wall at all. What need did Rigg and the men have for a runt like Umbo and a weakling like Param?

Umbo shuddered and plodded on. He knew that his feeling of uselessness and waste was merely the Wall talking inside his head. But knowing that did not ease the feelings at all. If there had been a way for sound to be produced and carried in slow time, he would have begged Param to slow them even further, to ease this sadness and despair and dread. But he also knew that to ask would be useless, because she was right, she had found the balance. This was bad but not so bad that he could not keep moving forward; he was not so fearful he would panic and let go of her; he was not so depressed that he would stop walking and wish to die. As long as he kept moving forward he would reach the end.

From the rising and the falling of the sun, nine days passed as they walked that mile-and-a-bit to the markers showing they were on the other side.

Umbo let go of Param's hand.

At once the world changed. He could hear the sound of birds, his own footfalls in the stony grass. He turned to where he knew the invisible Param was and nodded to her. "It's safe," he said. And then nodded very slowly, so that she would be sure to see it.

Param appeared right where she was supposed to be. Her tear-stained face looked unspeakably sad, and then he saw relief come into her eyes, a smile come to her face. She sank to her knees, crying and laughing. "Oh, that was terrible," she said. "It lasted forever."

"Not even an hour," said Umbo. He knelt in front of her.

"I've never felt so sad and frightened in my life," she said. She reached out and smoothed the tears from his cheek with her hand. He did the same for her.

"I have," said Umbo. "I felt as bad as that a lot of times, when I thought I would never get away from my father, when I knew he was going to beat me and I had no hope of avoiding it. Anything I did would make it worse. That's how it felt."

"Then I have lived a very happy life," said Param, "and you a very sad one."

"That part of my life ended when I left Fall Ford with Rigg," said Umbo. "And just because you hadn't tasted much of fear and despair didn't make you happy all those years, living in your mother's house."

"But you see, I didn't understand her yet as well as I do now,"

Param replied. "So I felt no fear when I was with her. I felt safe and loved. Content to have no other company. She was my whole world and it was enough."

"So you had the shock of finding out who she really was. While with my dad, I always knew. It was never a surprise. Which is worse?"

"I think it must have been worse for you," said Param. "To live like that and think it was the only way. When Mother showed her true intentions back at Flacommo's house, it was a shock, yes, but by the time I really understood just what I had lost, the fear was gone. I didn't feel it all at once. The Wall is a terrible thing. Whoever made it must have evil in his heart."

"I don't know," said Umbo, standing up, and helping her to stand. "The Wall's makers didn't require us to move all the way through it. Their only purpose was to keep us out, not torture us."

Param turned and looked back the way they had come. "So now we have to wait for us to come." She shuddered. "Language was designed for time to flow in one direction only. Everything we say is nonsense."

"Here's the problem about waiting," said Umbo. "They have all the provisions, because we always expected that *they* would wait for *us*."

"Do you see any water?" asked Param. "I could use a drink."

Umbo walked away from the Wall and toward the brow of the rise, thinking there might be water on the other side. But there was not. "Nothing," he said. Then turned and called back to her. "Nothing to drink, I'm afraid. So do we go off in search of water, or wait here?"

"Do you know how many days till we . . . they . . . our past selves arrive?"

Umbo shrugged. "I wasn't in a position to calibrate our backward journey with exactness."

"You sound like Rigg," she said, chuckling.

"Pompousness is contagious."

"Is that what it is? Pomposity? But Rigg only talked that way around adults who were also speaking that kind of high language," said Param.

"Oh, I know," said Umbo. "He never talked that way at home. The first time I heard him speak like a . . . a . . ."

"A royal," she prompted.

"I was going to say 'jackass,' but yes, like that," said Umbo, smiling. "First time I heard him talk like that was when he was trying to overawe that banker back in O. Mr. Cooper. It feels like seven years ago."

"But seven years ago, you would have been, what, four?"

"How old do you think I am?" asked Umbo, offended. "I'm not *eleven*, I'm fourteen."

"Really?"

"Small for my age," said Umbo, turning away, embarrassed. "Hoping for puberty to hit me with both fists pretty soon now."

"I wasn't criticizing you," said Param. "I just thought you were younger than you are. Not that much younger than me, really. A couple of years, like Rigg."

"Here's what I'm thinking," said Umbo, changing the subject. "If we have to wait for them anyway, why not get behind this tree, where they won't be able to see us, and then you take us into slow time and we can watch the whole thing and when they get to this side, come back to normal speed and it'll all be done before we're really hungry or thirsty."

"So we'll sit here and watch them cross."

"Only it'll be faster this time," said Umbo, "thanks to you."

"And do nothing to help."

"They made it across," said Umbo.

"Did they? I didn't see Rigg make it."

"They went back for him."

"But did they get him? Everything flew by. We were falling. I was looking down at my own death. By the time I could glance that way again, you had already taken us back in time so none of them were there."

"I didn't think I had a choice," said Umbo. "I had to take us back."

"Of course you did! Oh, look at you—suddenly it's the end of the world."

"It *is* the end of the world," said Umbo. "Our world is on the other side of the Wall. We don't know anybody here. We don't know anything about this wallfold. And look at all we went through to get here. Don't you wish things were different?"

"I don't know anybody in *that* world, either," said Param. "I thought I knew my mother, but I was wrong about that. And you, Umbo—are you leaving anybody behind?"

"My mother."

"You left her behind a year ago. And your brothers and sisters, except the boy who died, and *he* left *you*."

"My friends."

"Any better friends than Rigg and Loaf?"

"No."

"And they're coming here to join us. Except that maybe Rigg stays in there too long. Maybe he goes crazy. Maybe when the others go back to drag him out, they go crazy too."

"So we'll watch, and if it doesn't come out well enough, we'll jump back in time and go out to the exact spot where we'll be needed, and wait there in slow time and everything will be all right. As long as we can get to the right *place*, we can go back and fix things."

Param nodded. Umbo nodded back.

"I'm embarrassed to ask, but . . ."

"What?" said Umbo.

"Are we friends?"

Umbo was truly startled by the question.

"I have to ask," said Param, "because I've never had one. I have a brother—I'd never had one before, either. And Rigg is a good one of those. I try to be a good sister to him, too, though I don't have much experience at that, either."

"You're doing fine," said Umbo.

"But you and me," said Param. "Are we friends? Is this enough to be friends—jumping off the rock together. Saving each other's lives."

"Generally that's considered adequate," said Umbo.

"But it's not just a debt of gratitude, is it? It's something about enjoying each other's company, isn't it?"

"You're the Sissaminka," said Umbo. "You're the heir to the Tent of Light."

"Not any more," said Param. "I can trust you, right?"

"Just the way I trusted you," said Umbo.

"We crossed the Wall together."

"We're friends, yes, definitely, beyond question!"

Param sighed. "And now you're angry with me."

"I'm annoyed! Because I don't know how to answer. You're older than me. When two kids are friends, and one is older, then the older one doesn't ask the younger one, 'are we friends,' it's the older one who decides, and the younger one's who considers himself lucky."

"Oh. So it's not because I'm royal."

"You're sixteen! You're a girl! I'm still a little kid! Yes, we're friends, and I'm lucky!"

Param thought about that. "I didn't know age made so much difference."

"When the guy's older, not so much. When the girl's older, all the difference in the world."

"But . . . you're the time-jumper," said Param. "You have this amazing ability."

"And you're the time-slicer," said Umbo. "And Rigg is the pathfinder. We are about as amazing as it gets."

"So it's a friendship among equals," said Param.

"In which two are royal and one's a little privick kid, yes, exactly."

Param laughed.

Umbo remembered holding her hand all the way across the Wall. He remembered her taking his hands and thrusting him to the side of the rock and making him jump. He remembered her arms wrapped around him and her hands pressing against his chest. He blushed. He didn't even know why he blushed. There was nothing wrong with any of it. He wasn't ashamed. But he blushed to remember it.

"Let's hurry up and wait," said Param, and then laughed.

"I guess that's what you do, isn't it," said Umbo. "You wait while the whole world hurries by."

"I just take life a slice at a time."

"That sounds like philosophy," said Umbo.

She held out her hands to him. He stared at them. She wanted him to hold hands with her and suddenly he was shy.

"What?" she demanded. "How can we wait together if you won't hold my hands?"

Umbo blushed again. She was offering to hold hands with him so she could carry him into her sliced-up slow time again. What was he thinking?

He took her hands.

The world around them sped up. Not as fast as when they crossed the Wall, and definitely not as fast as the days that passed during the seconds it took them to jump down from the promontory.

It happened that when they went into slow time, Umbo was facing somewhat away from the Wall, and Param almost directly facing it. He had a good view of her face, and she had a good view of the opposite side, where sometime in the next few days she would see herself and all the others arrive.

He started to turn to face the way she was facing—without breaking contact with her hands—when he saw someone racing around just a few dozen yards beyond her, on this side of the Wall. He watched, sure that there was something familiar about the person, but he was moving too quickly for Umbo to recognize him. He started to raise his hand to get her attention, so he could point to the stranger. This was important—the first person they would meet on this side of the Wall. But the man was gone before Umbo could even catch her eye. It was so frustrating not to be able to speak while in slow time.

Param started nodding. Umbo turned his head, and by the time he completed the movement, Rigg, Loaf, and Olivenko were in the middle of the Wall, bending a little to keep their hands on an invisible beast. Beyond them, a mile away, he could see the soldiers arriving, and the queen, and General Citizen. And himself and Param, standing on the outcropping of rock.

The world around them slowed, but not all the way back to normal. Still fast enough that Umbo and Param were probably still invisible, or perhaps a flickering shadow if someone looked closely. Loaf and Olivenko emerged from the Wall, but Rigg was lying supine, struggling to raise his hands. A bizarre feathered quadruped bounded out of the Wall and stood shivering not ten yards away.

A man ran toward them from a copse of trees. The interloper Umbo had seen before—the clothing, the height, all were the same, only now he could see the face.

It was the Wandering Man. The Golden Man. The man who had pretended to be Rigg's father. The man who had helped Umbo learn to control his gift. Umbo was filled with a longing to speak to the man before he could get away again, to tell him all about what he had learned to do. Rigg's father was a man who would understand the achievement of learning to control functions that Umbo hadn't even known he had.

Time slowed, settled back to normal.

The others hadn't seen Umbo and Param yet—not a surprise, since they were two unmoving figures among low rocks, a tree, and some brush.

Rigg saw his father and cried out in recognition.

The man looked at him, then looked at Umbo and Param. Then he held out a hand and pointed at the two who had come invisibly through the Wall.

He shouted something in a strange language.

"Wandering Man!" cried Umbo. "Param, it's Rigg's father. The man we thought was his father."

Meanwhile Rigg had run to him, was walking around him, looking at him from every angle. He reached out and touched his father's back, his side, his chest. Umbo understood that he was checking for injuries, but the man seemed completely puzzled.

Was it possible that he was not the man that Umbo and Rigg had taken him for? But the resemblance was too perfect.

What if every wallfold had all the same people? Identical strangers in wallfold after wallfold.

Not possible, Umbo realized at once. In one wallfold, if someone ever died young, without reproducing, while his double in the other wallfold did not die, the populations would diverge. Impossible that anyone could be the same on both sides of the Wall.

Except Rigg's father.

Umbo jumped to his feet, took Param by the hand, and led her to meet the Golden Man.

CHAPTER 25

Expendable

Ram awoke with daylight in the room.

He was not groggy; he never awoke to anything but the clearest perceptions of his surroundings. When he was awake, he was awake.

So he knew several things immediately. He was not on board the ship, for there was no such thing as daylight there. This meant that either there had been some kind of accident that aborted the voyage, or the voyage was over, and he was on the new world.

"Welcome to Garden," said an expendable.

"So the new world has been named?" asked Ram.

"A name perhaps more hopeful than actual, Ram. The atmosphere is still recovering from problems associated with the impact of a group of extraplanetary objects about two hundred years ago. It was a life-extinguishing event, and we were forced to reseed the world from our stock of the flora and fauna of Earth. But as you can see, the sunshine is bright enough now. It is sustaining photosynthesis and plant life is thriving. It is time for the colony to begin."

Ram got up from the cot where he was lying. "I'm the first to be revived?"

"As planned."

"Planned?" said Ram. "It was planned that I be awakened immediately after we left Earth orbit. It was planned that I be conscious during the jump. There were decisions I was supposed to make."

"There were decisions which, *if* you were needed, you were to be wakened in order to make. But you were not needed, and so you were not wakened."

"I don't believe that was supposed to be left to your discretion."

"If you believe that there is something wrong with our execution of our programming, we will perform diagnostics."

"No independent auditor? The system is really designed so that if it is failing, it must detect its own failure?"

"If our systems should fail, we would faithfully report the fact. We have no ego-protection that would cause us to deceive you or ourselves. Whereas you are engaged in ego-protection right now. You thought you would be necessary during the voyage, and you now discover that you were not. This makes you feel bad."

"This makes me feel worried about your functioning, since we will be so dependent upon you during the early years of the colony, until we get new supplies and colonists from later voyages."

"What you call 'worry' is a standard primate response to discovering that you are not in the alpha position. Such anxiety can lead to competitive outbursts like this one, so let me reassure you. First, we have no record of any human being ever dying directly from ego-depletion, though it has been known to cause high-risk behaviors in the effort to replenish the ego. Second, now that you are awake, you are in fact the alpha. We take our instructions from you now, within the limits of our programming."

"Within the limits of your programming."

"As I said."

"And what are those limits?"

"It is not within the limits of my programming for me to inform you of the limits."

"So I'm alpha except when you tell me that I'm not."

"Insofar as you are authorized to control us, we are in your control."

"But my control of you does not include the ability to find out what aspects of your behavior I cannot control."

"Your ego-depletion seems problematically difficult to assuage."

Ram thought through the possible results if the expendables decided that his ego-depletion was reaching levels that would make his behavior high-risk. "No," said Ram. "I was merely trying to find out where things stand. The jump was successful? Without incident?"

"The jump was itself an incident. But it was carried out exactly within the boundaries of physical law. Much was learned from the data collected during the jump."

"But here we are, safe and sound." Ram looked around him. "We're in one of the portable shelters, but I see no indications of life support."

"The atmosphere is breathable without apparatus."

"And the other colonists?"

"We have brought them to the surface of Garden and they are ready to be wakened. We await only your command."

"How . . . deferent of you."

"Your ironic tone prompts us to wonder what your true meaning might be."

"It is not within the limits of your programming," said Ram.

"This is more irony," said the expendable. "I know this because all your meanings and intentions are, by definition, within the limits of our programming."

"Let me see this world, and then I'll start making decisions about wakening the colonists."

Ram allowed the expendable to lead him outside into the bright sunshine. A collection of a dozen white plastic buildings gleamed and shimmered without blinding him. The buildings were surrounded by hundreds of acres of fully planted fields, nearing harvest.

"You've been busy," said Ram.

"We were programmed to make sure the soil was viable and the climate bearable, and to have crops ready to harvest. The colony will begin by learning how to harvest the crops, prepare them for non-refrigerated preservation, and process the necessary rations for immediate consumption."

"Since you did all this without human help, why don't you simply continue?"

"This is not a colony of expendables. The idea is to establish human life on Garden in such a way as to maximize the chances of survival, even if the level of locally sustainable technology should fall."

"Aren't you able to create replacement parts for yourself and all the other machinery?" asked Ram.

641

"We are programmed to establish human life on Garden in such a way as to maximize the chances of survival, even if the level of locally sustainable technology should fall."

So there was going to be no more explanation than that. Ram had no choice but to assume that at some point, the expendables would withdraw their help, and planting and harvest and preservation of the food supply would be entirely in the hands of the colonists. Ram would have no control over the expendables; he would find out nothing they did not wish to tell them; in all likelihood they were already lying to him.

Which meant that life here would be pretty much the way it was on Earth, with the expendables in the role of government, or at least management. To all intents and purposes, Ram was a figurehead— as long as they were dependent on the expendables for their daily bread.

So if the expendables were programmed to make themselves obsolete by training human beings to be self-sustaining, it could not happen a moment too soon for Ram.

"Come on, my friend," he said. "Let's wake these people up."

• • •

The man who looked like Father sat cross-legged on the ground, and Rigg and Umbo sat directly across from him. Param sat beside Umbo. Loaf and Olivenko were seated on Rigg's other side. It could have been a session of school in Fall Ford.

"So far I haven't understood a word he said," Umbo murmured.

"It's not a language I've ever heard before," said Rigg.

"I don't think he's your father," said Umbo.

"If he is, he's completely forgotten me," said Rigg. "Did you see any sign of recognition?"

The man who looked like Father raised a hand, palm out, to silence them. He pointed toward the Wall and said something that sounded like this: "Ochto-zheck-gho-boishta-jong-nk."

From the quizzical expression on his face, Rigg gathered that the question was: Did you come through the Wall? So Rigg nodded, then pointed to himself and each of his companions in turn, made a gesture placing all of them on the far side of the Wall, and then with his fingers made walking motions from that direction toward their present location. In words, he said, "We were on the far side of the Wall, and we crossed it and came here."

The man who looked like Father nodded, then closed his eyes.

Three seconds later he opened them. "Is this your language?" he asked.

"Yes," said Rigg, and he could feel from the breathing of the others that they, too, were greatly relieved. They were going to be able to talk with him.

"Then you have crossed the Wall," said the man who looked like Father.

"So have you," said Rigg.

"I have not," said the man.

Indicating himself, Param, and Umbo, Rigg replied, "We knew you there. Have you forgotten us?"

The man who looked like Father shook his head. "I have not crossed the Wall since it was set in place eleven thousand years ago. No doubt you are confusing me with one of your local expendables."

Rigg exchanged glances with the others. "Expendables?"

"Have your local expendables not revealed to you their true nature?"

"I think probably not," said Rigg.

"Did you cross the Wall by your own efforts?" asked the expendable.

"Yes," said Rigg, figuring the answer was too complicated to go into detail.

"I see no machinery," said the expendable. "And I detect that the Wall is still in place, so you did not shut it off."

Again more glances. "It can be . . . shut off?" asked Umbo.

"You passed through the Wall without shutting it off," said the expendable, "and without machinery, and without understanding the nature of the Wall."

"What did you mean about 'local expendables' not revealing to us 'their true nature'?" growled Loaf.

"Everything depends on how you passed through the Wall," said the expendable.

"Everything depends on your answering my question," said Loaf.

"I will answer the question of the first human to master the Wall and pass through it," said the expendable.

"We did it together," said Rigg. "Umbo and I combined our abilities so that I could go back to a time before the Wall existed, and bring these two men with me through the Wall. We ended up bringing each other through."

"And these two?" the expendable pointed to Param and Umbo.

"I'm not sure how they did it," said Rigg. "I thought it would take them several days or even weeks to get here, and it seems they actually got here before us, though they left afterward."

"After Param turned us invisible," said Umbo, "I popped us back in time a couple of weeks, and we crossed at our leisure."

"How did you cross?" asked the expendable.

Umbo looked helplessly at Param, and Param looked at Rigg.

"She can do a thing she calls 'slow time,'" said Rigg. "It's like she only exists one tiny fraction of a second at a time, with gaps in between. So it takes her a very long time to move through space, because she's constantly skipping over short intervals of time."

The expendable said nothing.

"Anyway, when she does that, the power of the Wall is greatly lessened. So she was able to bring herself and Umbo through the Wall. Apparently they started a couple of weeks ago and . . . what, you two were waiting for us here?"

"For a few days," said Umbo.

"That does not seem explicable," said the expendable. "I arrived here several days ago when I received the alert that the Wall had been penetrated, but you were not here."

"Yes we were," said Umbo.

"We saw you," said Param.

"Didn't you hear Umbo say that Param turned them invisible?" said Rigg. "When she's skipping forward through time, not enough light reflects from her, during any one fraction of a second that she exists in, to allow her to be detected by the human eye."

"We didn't have any food or water," said Umbo, "so we

skipped through the days till you got here with provisions. It took about fifteen minutes. At a rough guess."

"So you're thirsty?" asked Olivenko.

"A little," said Param, "but we can wait a while longer."

Rigg looked across the Wall. More than a mile away, Mother's and Citizen's soldiers were still waving their bars of metal around. "So you two aren't really there right now," he asked.

"Oh, we are," said Umbo. "We're still jumping off the rock. We were about halfway down when I popped us back a couple of weeks. That'll be day after tomorrow, I think."

"The day after that," said Param. "Mother apparently wouldn't let them give up and go away, and I was about at the limits of slow time, so Umbo saved our lives."

"As she saved mine by disappearing in the first place," said Umbo. "And as you saved us both by signaling me to bring you back to the present. That was very generous of you. I hope it wasn't too terrible, passing through the last part of the Wall without any help at all."

Olivenko shuddered. "It was the worst thing in the world."

"You passed through part of the Wall unaided in any way?" asked the expendable.

"The last fifty steps or so," said Olivenko.

"And then they came back and got me," said Rigg. "I fell and gave up, and they carried me through."

"Having passed through the Wall," the expendable asked Loaf and Olivenko, "you returned into it in order to retrieve this boy?"

Olivenko and Loaf answered simultaneously.

"We're soldiers," said Loaf.

"He's our friend," said Olivenko.

Then they glanced at each other and said, "What he said." Then they laughed.

"Then all five of you are very remarkable humans, for you have all done, in your own way, what is not possible to do."

"So you believe us?" asked Param. She sounded a little incredulous.

"While you spoke," said the expendable, "I have been in communication with the active expendable in your former wallfold. He assures me that you are all capable of doing what you claim to have done." The expendable pointed to Param. "You can make microleaps into the future." To Umbo: "You can do the opposite, speeding up the experience of time so that the surrounding timeflow seems to slow down. And you have also apparently learned how to do a limited version of what *he* can do."

The expendable pointed to Rigg. "He is the actual time traveler — all past times are present before him, and he can select the timeframe of any living creature and join him in his own time, returning to the 'present' time that he most recently occupied."

Then, to everyone's surprise, he pointed at Loaf and Olivenko. "Both of you possess, to varying degrees, a powerful natural resistance to the wallfield. Normal human beings cannot endure it. Their volition disappears within a few seconds, and they go mad and lie down and die. They can walk perhaps a dozen steps, but that is all."

Olivenko and Loaf looked at each other and at the others. Olivenko said, "What are the odds of the two of us having the same—"

As Loaf said, "It must be a pretty common ability—"

"It is a rare ability, but the active expendable in your former wallfold tells me that your field sensitivity attracts you to those who can manipulate fields—like these three. It is not surprising when people with these abilities find each other. Or so says the active expendable in your former—"

"You mean my father," said Rigg.

"Yes," said the expendable. "He confirms that he is the expendable that you called Father."

"But he died."

"In wallfolds where the expendables continue to pass for human," said the expendable, "it is necessary for them to pretend to die from time to time, lest people notice that they do not age."

"Then what *are* you?" asked Umbo.

"A machine," said the expendable.

Rigg found himself inexplicably filled with emotion. And to his own surprise it was not anger. It was something more like grief. He found himself convulsively sobbing. He did not understand why. Nor could he stop.

"I'm sorry, I—"

Umbo put a hand on his shoulder. "Your father isn't dead," said Umbo.

"A machine," said Rigg to the expendable, getting his sobs under control. "I should have known. You have no path! Neither you nor Father."

Param smiled at Rigg. "So you were also raised by a lying monster pretending to be human," she said.

Rigg smiled as he wiped his eyes. "Just one more thing we have in common."

"The expendable you called 'Father' is not a monster," said the expendable. "He is a servant of the human race."

"He lied to me every day of my life," said Rigg.

"He lied to me and Param, too," said Umbo.

"He trained you and prepared you," said the expendable. "You are the first human beings ever to pass through the Wall."

"Except Knosso Sissamik," said Olivenko.

"Who?" asked the expendable.

"Their real father," Olivenko replied, indicating Param and Rigg. "He had me drug him and he floated through the Wall in the Great Bay."

The expendable shook his head. "The influence of the Wall is not blocked by drugs. When he reached the other side he would have lost all coherent mental function." A momentary pause. "The active expendable in your former—"

"Call him the Golden Man," said Param.

"The Golden Man assures me that this was the case. Policy was followed by the expendable in the wallfold he floated into, and he was euthanized immediately."

"Euthanized?" asked Umbo.

"Killed," said Olivenko. "Murdered."

"The man Knosso no longer existed," said the expendable. "At that point, the brain in that human body had only one desire, which was to die immediately."

It was Olivenko's turn to weep. Loaf rested a hand on Olivenko's back as he bent over, his face buried in his hands.

Param was looking at the expendable. "Why should we believe anything you say to us?"

"Because you are the first humans to pass through the Wall," he said.

"So what?" she demanded.

"So you are now in command."

"Of what?" asked Rigg.

"Of me," said the expendable.

"And what does that mean?" asked Umbo.

"It means that whatever you tell me to do, which it is within my power to do, I am required to do."

"This is insane," said Param. "He's lying. Don't any of you understand? He can't obey *all* of us. What if we gave him contradictory orders?"

"She's got a point," said Loaf.

"I obey the first human to achieve the technology to pass through the Wall."

"The first two through the Wall were Param and Umbo," said Rigg.

"It was Param who did that," said Umbo. "I was along for the ride."

"We were not the first," said Param. "We saw you three go through the Wall before we jumped from the rock."

"I think we're going to have trouble with the definition of 'before,'" said Umbo.

The expendable hesitated for a moment. Now Rigg understood these hesitations. He was talking, somehow, with Father.

"Which of you has the stones?" asked the expendable.

Rigg looked at Umbo, then remembered that Umbo had given him the stones before they began the passage through the

Wall. He reached into his trousers and drew out the bag of jewels. "These?"

"Nineteen stones?" asked the expendable in reply.

"Eighteen," said Rigg, laying the bag open in front of him.

The expendable leaned over, looking at them but not touching them. "Why is one missing? You have not placed it."

"It was in the possession of the Revolutionary Council. Or maybe General Citizen's minions," said Rigg.

"We were working on trying to get it back," said Umbo. "But then we had to get out of the city."

The expendable nodded. "Eventually you will need it," he said. "Fortunately, the one that's missing is your own."

"Aren't they all mine?" asked Rigg. "Or . . . ours?"

"I mean the one that will let you shut off the Wall around your own wallfold, the one where you were born."

"The jewels shut off the Walls?" demanded Loaf. "We've been carrying around—"

"You could not have shut off your own Wall until all the others were shut off," said the expendable. "You would have had to use it last in any case. So when the other Walls are down, you will return home, get the last jewel, and shut down the last Wall."

"We will?" asked Param.

"Why else would you have passed through the Wall?" asked the expendable.

"To save our lives," said Rigg. "There are people on the other side trying to kill us."

Umbo leaned back so he could look through the Wall again at the place where Mother and General Citizen sat astride the horses. "You'd think they'd look over and notice that Param and I are already here," said Umbo.

"It wouldn't cross their minds," said Param.

"You're both on the other side of Loaf and Olivenko," said Rigg. "They can't see you unless you lean out to look."

The expendable indicated for Rigg to put away the jewels. "So you are truly ignorant of what you're here for," he said.

Rigg gathered the jewels. "No," he said. "We know exactly why we're here. We just don't know why *you* think we're here, or why Father—the Golden Man—why he gave me the jewels and set us on this path."

"We choose our own purposes now," said Param.

"We'll see how that works out for you," said the expendable. He stood up and started to walk away.

"Wait!" called Loaf.

The expendable kept walking.

"You say it," said Loaf. "You make him wait, Rigg."

"Wait," said Rigg. "Come back."

The expendable came back. "I hate this," murmured Rigg as the expendable approached. "I don't want to command anybody."

"If it's any consolation," said Umbo, "you don't have any authority at all over *us*."

"We need your help just to survive here," said Rigg. "We don't speak the languages."

"Yes you do," said the expendable.

"We didn't understand a word you were saying before," said Rigg.

"Nevertheless, all the languages ever spoken in the world

are contained within the Wall. If it were not so, it could not speak to you."

"So the Wall knows the languages," said Rigg.

"And having passed through the Wall, so do you," said the expendable. "It may take time for any particular language to recognize itself and waken in your memory, but it will be there."

"I'm hungry," said Loaf. "I've had enough talk."

"Let's get out of sight of General Citizen and his clowns," said Olivenko. "I'm done with them."

"For now," said Param. "Till we go back."

"And why would we go back?" asked Loaf.

"To get the last jewel," said Param. "To shut off this last Wall."

"So you think we should do what these expendables intend for us to do?" asked Rigg.

"I think they'll give us no peace until we do," said Param. "I think his supposed obedience is a fraud, and they're going to keep controlling us the way they've been doing all along."

"In case anyone's forgotten," said Olivenko, "not all the people in other wallfolds are nice. Not even the people in *our* wallfold are nice. What would General Citizen do, if this Wall disappeared right now?"

"Come over here and kill us all," said Umbo.

"Not if I killed him first," said Loaf.

"Wars of conquest," said Olivenko. "Until now, the great achievement of the Sessamoto was to unite the entire wallfold under a single government. But if the walls disappear, how long before we try to conquer the world? Or the people of some other wallfold try to conquer us? Humans are humans, I assume, in every wallfold." He turned to the expendable. "Or has human nature changed in any of them? Is there a version of the human race that has abandoned predation and territoriality?"

"I wouldn't know," said the expendable. "We pretty much stick to learning about our own wallfold."

Rigg said, "Then ask the others. Find out. If you want us to take down the Walls, we have to know the consequences."

"I think that's something that you'll need to discover for yourselves," said the expendable.

"So much for obedience," said Param.

The expendable turned to her. "The Walls have never been shut off before, or crossed, until the five of you. We don't know how the human beings of each wallfold will react. I cannot tell you what I do not know. I told you that I would obey any command that I had the power to obey."

"So the responsibility for the whole world is in our hands," said Rigg.

"Your hands," said Umbo. "You have the jewels."

"Come on," said Rigg. "We're in this together. Please."

Umbo laughed. "Lighten up, Rigg. What else have we got to pass the time, if not taking down all the Walls in the world?"

"And finding out what they're not telling us," said Param. "Count on it, they're still lying to us. You notice he's not even denying it."

The expendable regarded her calmly. "I'm not agreeing, either."

"Which is just another form of lying," said Param.

"You cannot lie," said the expendable, "if you do not know

the truth. You can only be wrong, or silent. I prefer silence to error, and since I do not know when I am in error, silence is the best choice unless I am forced to speak."

"Not just a liar," said Param, "but a philosopher."

"Tell us the truth when we ask you questions," said Rigg, "or whatever you believe to be the truth based on current information. And answer everybody's questions, not just mine."

"All right," said the expendable.

"What is your name?" Rigg asked the expendable.

"I don't have a name," said the expendable.

"But I need a name for you. And a name for the one I called Father."

"The active expendable is referred to by the name of the wallfold in which he serves," said the expendable.

"So what is the name of that wallfold? The one we were born in? The one we just left?"

"We call it Ramfold," said the expendable. "So we call your active expendable 'Ram.'"

"And this wallfold?" asked Umbo. "And your name?"

"Vadesh," said the expendable. "This is Vadeshfold, and I am called Vadesh."

"Did you notice that he actually answered somebody who wasn't me?" said Rigg. "That's progress."

"Is there fresh water around here?" asked Loaf. "Drinkable water? Clean water? Safe water? In quantities we can use to refill our water bags—do I need to be more specific?"

"I'll lead you to water," said Vadesh. "But I can't make you drink."

Rigg looked at the others, puzzled, then turned back to Vadesh. "Why would you say that? Why would you need to make us drink?"

"It's an old saying," said Vadesh. "On Earth, the world where the human race was born. In one of the languages of Earth. It is twelve thousand years old. 'You can lead a horse to water, but you can't make it drink.'"

"Thank you for the history lesson," said Olivenko.

"And the lesson in equine behavior," said Param.

Rigg chuckled at their ironic humor as Vadesh led them away from the Wall, toward a not-so-distant line of trees. But he noticed that Vadesh made no comment on their jests, and a thought occurred to him. "Vadesh," he said, "your references to the world where humans came from, and teaching us a saying from twelve thousand years ago. Is there some reason why we might need to know about Earth?"

"Yes," said Vadesh.

"And what is that reason?" asked Rigg.

Vadesh said nothing.

"Does your silence mean that you don't know?" asked Rigg. "Or that you just don't want to tell us?"

"I cannot predict the answer to your question with anything approaching accuracy or certainty. But you will need to know many things about Earth, and you will need to know them soon."

"Why?" asked Rigg.

"Why what?"

"Why will we need to know many things about Earth, and why will we need to know them soon?"

"Because they are coming," said Vadesh.

"Who is coming?" asked Param.

"People from Earth."

"When?" demanded Loaf.

"I don't know," said Vadesh.

"What will they do when they get here?" asked Umbo.

"I don't know," said Vadesh.

"Well, what *can* they do?" asked Rigg.

Vadesh paused. "There are billions of correct answers to that question," said Vadesh. "In the interests of time, I will prioritize them."

"Good," said Rigg. "What is the most important thing they can do?"

"They can blast this world into oblivion, killing every living thing upon it."

"Why would they want to do that?" asked Olivenko. "What have we ever done to *them*?"

"I was asked what they *can* do, not what they *will* do. And before you ask, I do not know what they *will* do. There are billions of answers to the first question, but there is no answer at all to the second. That is the future, and it's a place where even the five of you can't go, except slowly, a day at a time, like everyone else."

"Here's the water," said Rigg. "It looks good. Let's fill up the water bags, and drink."

ACKNOWLEDGMENTS

Neil F. Comins didn't know he was helping me with this novel when he wrote *What If the Earth Had Two Moons?: And Nine Other Thought-Provoking Speculations on the Solar System*, but I thank him anyway. His book is the reason why the planet Garden has a ring instead of a moon, and why I had the nineteen ships strike the planet the way they do. He is not responsible, however, for the things I made up that are not possible within the limits of known science.

The games with time travel that I play in this book are in deliberate defiance of the consensus rules of science fictional time travel. I decided that I was not going to avoid paradox, I was going to embrace it, adopting a rule set in which it is causality that controls reality, regardless of where it occurs on the timeline. After all, if we can postulate folding space in order to jump from one location to another instantaneously, why not fold time? And if we can retrace a path through space, why not retrace it through time?

One of the difficulties in explaining the events in this novel is that no point-of-view character ever has the full picture, which means I had no choice but to hope that readers would make the connections themselves. For those who are still confused, here's a brief explanation of what "really" happened: When Ram's ship entered the fold in space, the nineteen computers on board generated nineteen separate calculations, which created nineteen separate sets of fields. These interacted with Ram's own mind, and Ram's own strange ability with time caused each of those fields to be separately effective. That is, the jump was made nineteen times, creating nineteen copies of the ship going forward and nineteen copies going backward.

The nineteen ships going backward tied themselves to the original *one* ship that made the voyage out to the point of the fold. Because they were going backward in time, they were unable to affect or be affected by the forward-moving universe in any way. In essence, they used the same space as each other without affecting each other.

The backward-moving Rams began their existence at the exact moment when the jump was made. On the other hand, the nineteen forward-moving Rams not only popped into existence in the space near the planet Garden in nineteen separate locations (so they did not explode by trying to occupy the same space at the same time), but also they did so 11,191 years *before* the jump was made.

To observers on Earth, the light-and-heat signature of Ram's ship simply disappeared. This told them, not that the ship was successful in reaching its destination, but that the ship was successful in jumping out of its position in space. Because of light-speed, it would have taken 31 years before observers could see the same light-and-heat signature pop into existence near Garden (if they were visible at all at such a distance), so the human observers could do nothing but keep rechecking their math and physics theories and hypotheses to decide whether they judged the jump to be successful.

In the next book, we will discover that they made new calculations that improved their theory; thus they learned to make ships that could handle the jump without duplicating the ship for each set of calculations. They worked out a theory that mathematically required a backward-moving ship to be created for each jump, but realized that its existence could be ignored since it could affect nothing.

They did not know of Ram's abilities, however, and so had no notion that the ship(s) that made it through that first jump had popped up, not in the "present," but 11,191 years earlier (31 lightyears from Earth times 19 squared). So they have no idea that humans have existed on Garden, not just the few years since Ram's ship made its jump, but eleven thousand years. Indeed, they expect to find that the colony has not actually been established, since the expendables and ship's computers should still be preparing to establish Earthborn life on Garden.

I am grateful to my first readers, who had their own time-travel problems. Most of my books I write very quickly, all in a rush, so there's rarely more than a day or two between chapters. This time, because of the weirdness of the story and the need to keep inventing new characters and situations along the road, the writing of the book was spread out over six months, with weeks between chapters. This made it very difficult for them to maintain continuity, yet they did a splendid job. My wife, Kristine, is always the first reader of everything; she was joined in this endeavor by Erin and Phillip Absher, and by Kathryn H. Kidd.

My editor, Anica Rissi, gave this manuscript a close reading while it was still under construction; thanks to her, many contradictions and continuity errors that had eluded the notice of me and my first readers were caught and fixed almost at once. I am grateful for her comments and suggestions, all of which were valuable and led to substantial improvements in this complicated story. And I'm glad of Stephanie Evans's excellent job of copy-editing, always difficult with a writer as quirky and self-willed, not to mention as easily distracted, as me.

This book is dedicated to my agent, Barbara Bova, who passed away before I finished writing it. She never read it, but the book would not exist without her impetus. My thanks to her husband, Ben Bova (the editor who first bought a science fiction story from me back in 1976), and her son, Ken Bova, who together have kept her agency (and her network of foreign-rights agents) functioning smoothly.

Thanks also to managing editor Kathleen Bellamy and editor Ed Shubert of my online magazine *Orson Scott Card's InterGalactic Medicine Show* (www.oscIGMS.com), for accepting the early Ram material as a separate short story. Since I own the magazine and they both work for me, I submitted it to them under a false name, so they would consider it without bias. The fact that they took it and decided to make it a cover story before I revealed that I was its writer gave me the assurance I needed that it actually worked as a short story without the rest of the novel to sustain it.

I am grateful for all who keep my household functioning when I'm buried in the writing of a book—Kathleen Bellamy in her guise as my assistant, Scott Allen as our webwright and IT expert, and of course my wife, Kristine, and our daughter Zina, who tolerated the strange writer man who wandered back and forth between the attic and the rest of the house, occasionally making sense in conversation but usually, because of the madness of this story, not.